RED LINED

For Stan, Shel and Saul.

REDLINED

A novel of Boston

by
Richard W. Wise

BRUNSWICK
HOUSE PRESS
P. O. Box 465, Ivy, Virginia 22945

REDLINED
A novel of Boston
By Richard W. Wise

Copyright ©2020 by Richard W. Wise

Copy editor
Rebekah Tressel Wise

Published by Brunswick House Press, P. O. Box 465, Ivy Virginia 22945
First Paperback Edition (2020)

BRUNSWICK
HOUSE PRESS
P. O. Box 465, Ivy, Virginia 22945

ISBN-13: 978-0-9728223-3-6

Printed in the United States of America

Contents

Chapter 1

The Vigil

Born in the northern Arctic, the icy wind swept due south past a freighter steaming east out of Argentia, Newfoundland, veered west, curled round the rockbound Maine coast, hummed a tune through the rigging of the Boston Lightship, crossed Boston harbor, swept up the corridor between Columbus Avenue and the Jamaicaway, ruffled the steel-gray surface of Jamaica Pond, funneled through the narrow canyon of double-deckers packed along Jamaica Plain's Green Street, then cut like a sharpened blade through a down jacket and several layers of wool and sent a shiver tap-dancing up the spine of the young neighborhood organizer who stood lonely vigil on a cold winter's night.

It was half past midnight and Sandy Morgan was still alive.

She rocked up onto her toes then stamped her feet. The night was black and as bitter as the dregs at the bottom of her cardboard coffee cup. The young woman gazed up at stars shining like icy pinpricks in a coal black shroud. She crumpled the cup in her hand and started to toss it into the trash-strewn alleyway, then hesitated, "No, no, mustn't litter," she whispered to herself, grinned and stuffed the crushed cardboard deep into the side pocket in her down parka.

"Very sexy, Sandy! You look like a corndog wrapped in a blue bun." That was her roommate Sara's verdict the day she wore the new parka back to the dorm.

"Didn't Ali McGraw wear something like this in Love Story?" Sandy asked, twisting side to side, admiring her new purchase in the full-length mirror.

Sara was an Ivy League wannabe and Ali McGraw was Sara's role model—she had seen Love Story like a gazillion times, and Sandy had bought the parka partially as a protest against her roommate's stultifyingly conservative style of dress. "Yeah, well," she thought, wrapping her arms around her chest and hugging herself close, "I'd rather be a warm corn dog than a frozen French fry on a night like this."

She leaned back against the door, her eyes closed, her lips curled into a smile as her mind drifted back to a golden August afternoon. For the moment she forgot the cold, forgot that she stood shivering in the cramped shadow of a cellar doorway guarding one of a serried row of hulking tenements, their darkened windows gazing with sightless eyes over Green Street. Instead she stood engrossed in the gurgling melody that played against the smooth hull of her catboat, her mind recalling only the warmth of her family's carefree Nantucket summers.

She felt herself falling and instinctively reached out and steadied herself against the pealing doorframe. "Whoa there, Suze, let's try to stay awake!" She stretched her back, then pushed back her sleeve, exposed the glowing watch dial and sighed—12:50am, just ten minutes since the last check.

She glimpsed something out of the corner of her eye. Her breath caught: was that a light in the first-floor window? She narrowed her eyes and studied the window. "Must be seeing things!" She stamped her feet, checked her watch again. "Shit!" She had been standing in the doorway now for an hour and a half. "Easy, Sandy girl," she admonished herself, "Don't go getting all squirrelly on me!"

Sandy had stopped by the old stone church that served as the project's office just after 10pm to pick up a file. Her meeting with a couple of block-club leaders had run late. The ladies had won a commitment from the city to have a neighborhood firetrap boarded up in record time and the buzz of power was as heady as it was unfamiliar to a pair of working-class Boston-Irish housewives.

She and her boss, Jedediah Flynt, had discussed the surveillance and the wisdom of her getting an early start. "Does the guy ever sleep or take nourishment, she wondered?"

Flynt sat alone in the project's office, lounging in his swivel chair – feet up on his desk with the phone cradled in the crook of his hunched left shoulder. A white porcelain coffee mug stood by his right hand. The office was an open-plan cube farm. Moveable dividers separated it into a crossword puzzle of workstations, one for each of the staff organizers. The eight-foot fluorescent tubes mounted in the ceiling lit up the interior like a fish market. Flynt nodded in recognition, spat a few quick words into the black mouthpiece, dropped it into its cradle and swung his feet onto the floor.

"You're up late," he said.

"Yeah, the block club victory meeting just ended," she said.

Flynt looked up and rubbed his chin. "How'd it go?" he asked.

"Really well. The city has scheduled a board-up early next week."

Armed with Sandy's research and tactical advice, the two ladies had led the charge to secure the abandoned property. It had been a short, tough fight between the neighborhood group and the Boston Building Commissioner.

"You should have seen the commissioner's face. It was a thing of beauty. He asked to speak with two representatives, then opened the door and like you suggested, the whole group filed in kids and all. Pretty big office, but they filled it up like an overstuffed sandwich. Told him they had been complaining for a year and refused to budge."

Flynt grinned. "Then what happened?"

"Well, he got real nervous, tried the usual bureaucratic shuffle, 'state regulations, blah, blah, blah'!" He's running around trying to keep the kids from snatching up the little ornaments he had all over his desk."

"So, after a year of BS over that firetrap, the people weren't buying it. The man was really shocked when Molly corrected him and quoted the relevant passage of the State Sanitary Code from memory. They left with a date."

"Keep your adversary off balance! Congratulations—how is the leadership feeling?"

"Oh, the ladies, they're on a power high! There's a group of neighborhood kids want the city to build a street hockey rink and the block club is already making plans to help them get it."

Sandy stood with her feet apart and her hands on her hips and looked down at Flynt. "You think anybody's going to try and torch that building before midnight, boss?" she asked.

He shrugged. "Hard to say."

"Supposed to be a cold snap all this week?" she said.

He shrugged. "Yeah, it'll be cold. Your call," he said.

"Yeah, right!" she said. She saw right through the feigned indifference. He was being cute, manipulating her, and she resented it. But then, what did she expect? Keeping the place from being burned down before the city had a chance to board it up was her problem, and she knew that she had to deal with it. She was scared of being out there late at night but wasn't ready to admit it to herself, and she was never going to admit it to him.

She and Flynt had an odd sort of relationship. "He's definitely a sexist," she decided, though at one point she had fantasized about a night in bed with him.

"What makes you so sure, Jedediah, about the burning, I mean?"

His dark eyes rounded briefly at her use of his full first name. He had a lopsided smile that played off against the sharp angles of his face. He usually called his employees by their last names and most just called him Jed.

He raised his elbows and stretched his long rangy body. "Come on, Morgan, you've done the math! Except those properly boarded up, every vacant building within two or three blocks of the corridor has been torched. The question is who is doing it and why. The one your club has scheduled for a board-up fits the pattern—and if memory serves, you were the first one to notice that pattern."

Sandy shrugged her heavy bag onto an unoccupied desk and slumped down into the chair.

"Yeah, even a couple bordering the corridor that were well boarded were torched, but is there really a pattern? Me and my big mouth, huh?" she said. "Too many games of Monopoly when I was a kid, I guess."

Flynt smiled at her. "Yeah, well nobody else noticed—shows you've been paying attention."

Her eyes looked boldly back at him. The color was arresting, disconcerting. China blue, one of the other young organizers had called them.

"Really? That sounds almost like a compliment, boss."

Flynt smiled. "Well, don't let it go to your head, Morgan. There are a lot of homeless types looking for a place to crash. They break in, make fires to keep warm, piss all over the floor, strip out the copper to buy booze or drugs, and the fire just gets away from them. Like you said in the staff meeting, lately it's been happening too damn quick, and nobody even bothers with the copper."

"Any word from the district fire chief's office?"

"So far can't get anyone from the district to return my calls," he said with a thin smile. "Better make up a Freedom of Information request, get one of your leaders to sign it. They know they have to respond to that. Talked to one of the flak-catchers over at Little City Hall. She claims all fires are 'thoroughly investigated, Mr. Flynt.'"

He raised his hands and dropped them in a gesture of helplessness.

She made a face. "Guess I better write a letter. So, what's the point? Insurance?"

"Doesn't seem to be a reason. Fire insurance on Green Street? Good luck getting any insurance company to write a new policy in your neighborhood or anywhere else in central J. P. The whole area is redlined."

"Redlined? You've mentioned that before, but I really can't say that I understand it all that well?"

Flynt hesitated and gazed at her for a moment to make sure that she wasn't pulling his chain. Sandy, he knew, typically came on like she knew it all even when she didn't.

"It's complicated. The Northwest Community Organization in Chicago was the first people's organization to get a handle on it. Got an organizer from N.P.A. —that's National People's Action—fellow by the name of Trapp coming in to run a staff training session. Basically, redlining happens when the banks or the insurance companies or all of the above get together and draw a big red circle on a map around parts of the city that they consider too risky to do business with."

"So they write off the whole neighborhood?"

"You got it and once that happens, kiss the central neighborhood goodbye. Ninety-five percent of all residential housing sales are sold subject to a mortgage, and to get a mortgage you must have insurance. So, Catch 22, you can't get one, you don't get the other. If mortgage or the insurance money is choked off, the housing market collapses—which sets the stage for slumlords buying cheap for cash, racial steering and housing abandonment."

"Redlining is the underlying economic cause of most of the shit we have been organizing around. So, basically all the properties in central J.P. are worthless?"

"Yeah, well there it is," he said rocking back in his chair. She noted the stubble on his cheeks and the dark smudges under his smoke-gray eyes.

"You ever read the novel Gone with the Wind"? he asked.

"Yeah, when I was like about twelve, why?"

"Well, there is this scene where Melanie is questioning Rhett Butler about how he made all his money. You recall he was a smuggler, dodging the Yankee blockade to bring supplies into southern ports during the Civil War?"

"Uh, huh."

"Okay, so, Melanie finally overcomes her proper Southern manners and asks the question, and he says, 'There is more money to be made out of the wreckage of a civilization than from the building of one.'"

Sandy rolled her eyes, "Yeah right, okay. I get it."

"Exactly."

"Okay, but what's with the corridor anyhow? I mean whose bright idea was that?"

"Happened before my time. Bunch of community groups got together to stop I-95 running right through the middle of the neighborhood. Finally got the governor to stop it but not until the whole thing was demo'd in from Route 128 to Roxbury. What you see is what's left, a partially demolished six-lane cancer eating out the guts of the neighborhood," Flynt said.

She stood up. "Yeah, looks like Berlin after the blitz and only a couple of blocks down from my abandoned house. Okay, I'll get set up as soon as I leave here. But what do I do if I see anybody?"

"Stay out of sight! Hide in an alley between the buildings. Or just stay in the shadows. If you see anyone or anything suspicious, try for a description or a license plate. Then get the fuck outa there, call the cops, the fire department and then call me."

"And if it's late and you're home asleep?"

"I'm serious, Morgan. Don't take any chances. People who torch houses are not the kind of fuckers you want to screw around with. Call me if you see anything suspicious, no matter what time, day or night, just call me, okay?"

"Aye, aye, sir!" she said, and she tossed off a mock salute.

"Sandy!"

"Okay, okay. I get it. I'll call!"

He had just used her first name, and she felt absurdly pleased.

He picked up his cup and cradled it between his hands. "Chances are, these guys are professionals. They are going to

16

show up in some kind of vehicle and be in and out quick. Try for a description of the car, and above all a license plate—look, can't you get any help? What about your leadership?"

"The whole neighborhood is watching the house, but Cathy and Mrs. Sheehan both work third shift. People have to sleep!"

"Nobody else?"

"Molly Reagan. She lives just up the street. She loves this kind of shit, keeps a lookout on the street all day long, writes down the license numbers of the cars that stop, but she's an old lady and she turns in early. Looks like it's down to me. I can hang out in the cellar doorway along the side of her house, though—it's almost right across the street."

"Right, okay, good. You need some help? I can assign one of the guys to spell you."

"Not one of those assholes," she thought. She liked her three male colleagues well enough, but, like most guys, they were a bunch of chauvinists. She'd be damned if she showed anything that could be interpreted as female weakness. She'd never live it down. She propped her hands on her hips.

"It's only a few days. You think I can't handle it? You say one thing to any of those guys, and I walk right now."

Flynt stood up and held up both hands palms forward.

"I never said you couldn't handle it. But it's spooky late at night. If there are guys out there systematically torching houses it could get seriously dangerous if they catch on to you."

"I'm a grown woman and I can handle anything any of the guys can. So, Green Street is my territory and that makes it my problem, right?"

"Right."

"Okay, that means I'll deal with it."

"Yes, ma'am."

"Okay!" Sandy grabbed the strap of her bag and hiked it up onto her shoulder, turned and strode straight though the vestibule and out the door without another word.

Jedediah Flynt watched her exit, admiring the slim retreating figure in tight jeans. He stood still until he heard the outside door slam shut, and then shook his head slowly side to side and sighed. "My, my, my," he thought, "Keep your eyes on the prize, my son, because there surely lies the road to perdition."

Flynt sat down at his desk, propped his feet up, picked up the phone and dialed.

Sandy was cold, tired and bored. She had been on watch for going on three hours, and aside from the roar of the occasional car passing two blocks up on Centre Street, nothing was happening.

She let her eyes pass along the string of houses that lined the far side of the street like a picket line. Some were broader, hunch-shouldered, and some thicker waisted, but in the end, they were just rectangular boxes that gradually merged into the shadows as they worked their way down the hill towards Lamartine Street.

She looked up toward Centre Street and noticed the dark profile of a church steeple thrusting into the sky like a fat stalk of asparagus above the squat, commercial buildings at the head of the street. What, she idly wondered, are church steeples supposed to represent? A spear or maybe something else, like one of those lingams that they have in India? But then, she giggled, they wouldn't end in a point.

Shifting from foot to foot to keep her toes from freezing, Sandy Morgan began to regret her own stubbornness. Had

Flynt played her? Maybe it was her own pride that baited her into a knee-jerk, macho-feminist response. She looked up and batted her eyes. "Oh, Mr. Man, big strong Mr. Man," she said half-aloud. "It's so cold and dark out here, I just don't know what ever I'm going to do—could you please come over here and rescue poor little helpless me?" She giggled. That was mom all over. How many times had she stood by and watched her mother go into that helpless routine? Her dumb schmuck of a father bought it every time— until, that is, he had run off with his twenty-something secretary. She was the helpless type, too, but with big blue eyes and even bigger tits. Sandy winced. The breakup had really hurt—she'd been daddy's little girl.

The sound of a car engine broke into her reverie. She pressed herself back into the doorway just as a dark sedan with its lights out cruised past her and glided to a stop at the right-hand curb beyond the light pole in front of the vacant house.

"What happened to the streetlight? Shit, that's funny. It was on last night, wasn't it? Damn!"

The street-side car door opened slightly, and the courtesy light lit up the car's interior.

"Hey, Joey, douse that fucking light." The deep growl of a male voice carried clearly through the chill night air.

The light outlined the heads and shoulders of four men, two in the front and two in the back. Sandy made a mental note: all four appeared to be white.

The door was pulled closed, and the car interior went black. Then the back doors opened. This time there was no light. Two men, dark shadows, emerged from either side of the vehicle and quietly pressed the doors shut.

Sandy felt the adrenalin surge. She was now fully alert. She could barely see the man on the street side. He bent down and picked something up—she couldn't make out what it was—then circled around the back of the car, stepped over the snow bank and joined the other guy on the sidewalk. The car eased away from the curb and dropped down the hill towards Lamartine Street. The two men merged into the spidery shadows cast by the tall bare-limbed tree on the opposite side of the street.

She squinted, but the men had been swallowed up by the night. She waited a few minutes. All seemed quiet. Then, out of the corner of her eye she caught a glint of light off metal, and a car—had to be the same one—emerged like a black beetle out of the gloom. It rolled to a stop beneath the tree less than thirty feet from where Sandy stood hugging herself in the darkness.

Sandy's eyes flicked back to where she had last seen the two men. Gone! The hair prickled along the back of her neck. Something sure as hell is going on, she thought. She felt exposed, vulnerable. The faint purr of the car's engine tickled her ear.

Then the sharp sound of splintering wood ripped through the stillness.

"The back door—has to be!" she thought.

Despite the hiking boots and the double ski socks, her feet were going numb. Maybe it was the excitement. She flexed her toes and rubbed her gloved hands together.

"Was that a light in the front window?" she whispered out loud.

She checked her watch. The dial glowed.

1:30am and Sandy Morgan was still alive.

Chapter 2

Home Alone

Flynt pulled up to the curb, yanked on the emergency brake, yawned and checked his watch. Just after 1:00am, an early night!

He unfolded his long frame out of the seat of his VW bug and glanced up at the façade of the fading Victorian. The darkened apartment windows stared sullenly back at him. Nobody's home, as usual! He bit down on one finger of his glove, tugged it off and fumbled in his pocket for his keys.

He mounted the stairs and pushed open the door, stepped into the hallway and breathed in the cool musty odor of emptiness. He supposed that it was just the smell of plaster and old wallpaper, but he hated that smell. It made him aware of the dull ache of loneliness deep in his gut. Well, what the hell. It was late, he had skipped dinner and he was hungry. He turned right and walked across the darkened kitchen to the refrigerator. The sterile light from the white interior lit up the room. Nothing much here—open can of Coca Cola and a pizza box. He flipped up the box top with a tentative finger and eyed two dried-up slices. Pepperoni and extra cheese. You could tell how old they were by the angle of the curve at the edges. "Better not," he thought. He let the box cover drop, sighed and pressed the door closed.

In the hall, the answering-machine light blinked on and off with the rhythm of a beating heart. Hope rising, Flynt pushed the button, then grimaced. His ex-wife's tone of habitual exasperation echoed off the plaster walls as she reminded him yet again that she had still not received her monthly support check. Didn't he care what became of his son, she asked? Had he no sense of responsibility to his family, she wondered? Did he really want to be like his father? Flynt stabbed the delete button. Had he really once thought that voice sexy? His wife's call did nothing to decrease the ache in his stomach. Flynt missed having a woman around—but Linda could take away any man's appetite.

Linda's aim was good. The bit about his father hit a nerve. The old man had left home when Flynt was five, and his mother had raised him by herself, and, as she was fond of reminding him, had worked at two jobs to keep him clothed and fed. Flynt had whispered his feelings to Linda during that phase of a relationship when lovers share their most intimate secrets. He had missed having a father around and had sworn that he would be there for his own kids; in the end, he had followed in the paternal footsteps and the guilt gnawed at him.

On the rare occasions when Jed and his father got together for one of those uncomfortable parental visits, they inevitably ended up in some bar. Give the old man a new tavern and a few hours, and he owned the joint. His father would buy him something with a cherry in it, maybe give him a few nickels to play the bowling machine, then expect him to amuse himself for the rest of the afternoon while he drank beer after beer and socialized with the other bar-flies. Jed had no idea why they had broken up, though his mother had hinted that the old man had been unfaithful.

Jed had listened uneasily to male friends talk about the great upwelling of love they felt with the arrival of their first born, particularly if that child was a boy. Linda got pregnant. When Stephen, his boy, came along, the feelings that his friends described just never arrived.

Flynt went through the motions. He changed diapers and made the right noises when he and Linda socialized with other young couples—but he felt like a total fraud. He was trapped in a marriage with a kid he was indifferent to and a woman he did not love—he had broken off their engagement a couple of months before she called to let him know that she was pregnant. Flynt had done the right thing out of some old-fashioned sense of—obligation? —he could no longer call it honor. Vietnam had taken care of that—but it turned out to have been exactly the wrong thing. And that was clear even before his son was born.

Now Flynt asked himself, at this late hour, with his stomach empty, and an ache somewhere else—should he call up his current girl, Erica?

Sex eased the ache for a few hours, but after the first flush of freedom from the restraints of marriage and kids, Flynt had eventually concluded—practically an insight—that casual sex, like Chinese food, tasted great, but two hours later you were hungry again. But then, he loved Chinese food.

"To hell with it, not tonight!" He was just too tired to make even the pro forma conversation required before he and Erica undressed each other. Erica was a great girl. Never asked those difficult questions that women always ask. Sometimes he wondered why but dwelling on good luck often brought on the bad, and, well, maybe she just doesn't give a fuck!

Flynt padded down the hall, turned right into his bedroom and pulled the door closed. His bed, a plain king-sized mattress bequeathed by a previous roommate, was an unmade tangle. The room smelled like old socks. "Whoa! Gotta spend some time cleaning up this place and wash these sheets!" He hung his jacket on a brass hook on the back of the door, stripped off his flannel shirt and jeans and hung them over the single chair in the corner next to his closet.

Flynt loved a good book. Ever since he was a kid, whatever the problem, he could immerse himself in a book, and for a brief time his troubles were washed away. After he got back from Nam, books had filled in the nights of lost sleep. That wasn't so much a problem these days. The nightmares and the uncontrollable fits of rage that seemed to well up out of nowhere had gradually diminished after he had begun organizing. He felt that he was giving back and that helped, and here, for a change, he was in charge. Not like in the jungle where he had no control over the stupid orders that accomplished nothing except getting his buddies killed. No, the organizing held him together—just—and lately he had more good nights than bad.

Sandy's question niggled at him. "What was the motive behind all the arson? Has to be one! It's too systematic, like on a timetable. Homeless people aren't that predictable, and no one ever seems to see a thing. Redlining and arson. She's right about another thing, too. Redlining is the underlying cause of all the shit we've been organizing around. Cut off mortgage money and the speculators and slumlords take over. Gotta stop that or the neighborhood will just go down the tubes piece by piece. Well, can't think about that now. Got to get some sleep."

He turned on the reading lamp and picked up the paperback off the white plastic bed table. It was a hefty one— The Winds of War by Herman Wouk. Minutes later it was

December 7, 1941; the tropical sun had just breasted the green clad hills above Pearl Harbor. Palm trees nodded in the cool scented morning breeze just as a swarm of Japanese G3M torpedo bombers swooped down out of the rising sun.

A half hour later he turned down a page, put the book down, listened briefly to the bare branches of a tree clawing at the window pane, thought for a moment of Sandy Morgan standing her lonely watch, turned out the bed lamp and rolled over.

In combat you learned to snatch what you needed wherever and whenever you could. He hoped that this would be a good night. That had never been a problem back in the jungle. This night he fell instantly asleep.

Chapter 3

The Wages Of Innocence

Sandy Morgan hugged herself to keep warm and waited for the two men to return. She had been fighting a cold all week and could feel the beginnings of a headache. Ten minutes passed. Finally they reappeared and sauntered out onto the sidewalk. One was carrying what looked like some sort of container, but the thick shadows made it impossible to make a definite identification. They came from the back of the house all right! She stared at the front windows expecting at any moment to see the bright, licking tongues of flame, but all remained dark.

The men crossed the street, walked up to the car and got in. Doors slammed. The car accelerated, and as it passed Sandy's hiding place, the headlights flicked on.

"Gotcha!" she said out loud. She pulled a pencil and notebook out of her pocket and scribbled down the license number. The brake lights flashed briefly as the car made a right onto Centre Street, and all was quiet. Nothing stirred—it was as if the night itself held its breath.

"Ok, half an hour," she whispered checking her watch, "I'll wait. If nothing happens, I'm outa here!"

Her teeth chattered, the wind cut through the stretched material of her jean-clad legs as she waited.

"Am I really cold or just chicken?" she asked herself.

Fifteen minutes later, she stepped out to the sidewalk, looked both ways, then darted across the street, jogged down the sidewalk, ducked into the dark corridor alongside the house and made her way to the back door.

The steady pumping of her heart was audible in her ears. The plywood planking that had been nailed across the door-frame had been torn off and lay on the ground. The door was ajar. The snowy area around the stoop was a jumble of footprints. She could just make out the dull gleam of the metal fence that separated the backyard from the adjacent property.

She took off one glove, reached into her pocket, grasped a handful of keys and with her fingers picked out the small metal penlight attached to her key ring and pushed the tiny button. A weak, yellow beam flickered, barely penetrating the darkness.

"Oh shit, not now," she swore. She shook the penlight and the beam brightened.

"Yes, God," she said and, solemnly promising herself to replace the batteries first thing, pushed open the door and stepped up into a narrow entryway.

It was damp, dank and smelled of mold. She swung the beam. To her left she could see the door to the first-floor apartment; to the right a narrow oak wainscoted stairway disappeared upwards into the murky darkness leading to the second floor.

Sandy twisted the knob on the apartment door and pushed. The door swung inward with a raspy creak. "Shit, the fucking House of Usher." Her voice sounded hollow but reassuring. The raw cobwebby cellar-smell assaulted her nostrils. She shivered.

She was out of the wind, but the dank air cut through her jeans, and she could feel it penetrate down to the bone.

The room she had entered was obviously the kitchen. She caught a glimpse of a patterned linoleum floor. She played the feeble beam of her penlight over the wall. The original wood grain wainscoting had been painted over. Battered-metal cabinets were bolted to the wall. The cabinet doors gaped open like dark mouths. It looked as if someone had cleaned out the contents and left in a big hurry. Above the cabinets, she saw large scabs of peeling paint and spatters of what looked like mold.

"God, it's cold!" she whispered.

"Technically," she thought, "I'm trespassing. Technically, hell, what do I say if the cops show up? What do I tell them I'm doing in here?" she asked, but got no answer.

Ahead, left and right, the dark rectangles of two doorways. The penlight was fading. Best check them both out. Her nose twitched like a nervous rabbit. She sneezed.

"Gesundheit—oh, well, if anyone is looking for the intruder, here I am."

She wiped her nose across the back of her sleeve. "Yuck." Her head throbbed, the headache had gotten worse.

She paused, quivering like a frightened rabbit, ready to bolt, to get the hell out of that house, but she pictured the staff meeting, the smug looks and condescending smiles, and she knew she had to walk through that door.

She took a deep breath.

"Okay, one quick look-see then I'm gone."

Placing one foot carefully in front of the other, she moved toward the half-open, right hand door. She felt something under her foot but didn't look down. She thought she heard the crunch of breaking glass.

She stepped over the threshold and played the thin beam of light over the walls. The room was small, rectangular and empty. In the middle of the ceiling, a fly speckled light bulb dangled at the end of a frayed cord like the victim of a lynching. She shook her head as her light played over a garish pattern of large cabbage roses. "Whoa, somebody had seriously poor taste in their decorator." She stepped forward, and her foot squished down on something soft and yielding.

"Yuck."

Sandy took a breath and directed her light downward. It was a white mound of gunk that crumbled under her foot.

She played the light up at the ceiling. There was a large ragged section of exposed lathe. She heard a sharp cracking sound and froze in mid stride.

"What was that? —oh shit."

She stood perfectly still, strained her ears and waited. Nothing!

"Probably just a rat."

She shuddered, but this time not from the cold.

Sandy Morgan hated rats—dreadful, greasy, nasty things, those sharp little gnawing teeth. She had had occasional nightmares about rats ever since she was a little girl, and her brother had chased her with a dead rat. They had found it one afternoon in the attic of their summer home. The rat had not been dead long. It had oily fur and black, beady little eyes. Her brother had pushed up its lips and showed her its needle-like teeth—then he began chanting. "Kiss the rat, kiss the rat! Sandy wants to kiss the rat."

He shoved it into her face and she bolted. She had outrun her brother, but she was so disgusted she barely spoke to him for the rest of the summer.

Sandy tiptoed to the end of the room, flattened her back against the wall next to the paired windows that overlooked the street. She held her breath and peered out. Empty!

She exhaled gratefully, turned, and tiptoed back the way she had come, turned right and pushed.

It was one of those old-fashioned solid swinging doors that were sometimes used in big houses to divide the dining room from the butler's pantry. It seemed odd to find one in this small apartment. Maybe the house had once been a single family, and this was the door between the kitchen and the dining room. "Yes, that would explain it," she thought.

This room was considerably larger, and it was not empty; a stack of geometric shapes that might have been furniture had been assembled in the center of the room and covered over with some kind of tarp.

At the far end of the room, a bay of three tall windows the shape of a half hexagon, jutted out over the street. She stepped gingerly, skirting the pile, her feet crunching broken glass, and made her way to the window and looked out.

"Silent as the grave," she whispered. "Oh, shut up, Sandy??

She sniffed the air. The same dank, wet moldy newspaper smell but different this time, overlaid with a sharper odor.

She sniffed again. The acrid smell was very familiar, but she couldn't quite identify it.

The penlight flickered, and the room went black.

"Damn! Not now! Just what I don't need," she whined.

She shook the penlight, and the light flickered on. She was breathing heavily.

"Thank you, God! Better get a move on. This light is not going to last much longer," she said out loud.

The stink of the place had made her headache worse.

"Time to get the fuck out of here, take a couple of aspirins and get some sleep. I'll call Jed Flynt tomorrow. He will, no doubt, have a few bright ideas."

She turned to retrace her steps, and out of the corner of her eye she caught a tiny glint of something coming from the center of the pile.

A little flicker that made her catch her breath.

Sandy tiptoed to the edge of the pile. She put her hand on the canvas. Whatever it covered felt solid. She stood up on her toes and leaned forward to look over the top.

The sharp smell was much stronger. The canvas was wet, and so was her hand.

She sniffed at it and this time, even with a stuffed-up nose, the odor was unmistakable. "Nail polish remover?" She asked herself out loud.

Her eye caught a flicker of light. Suddenly it was all too clear. She understood why men had come to this vacant building in the small hours of a cold winter night.

"Oh, my Jesus, God!"

The adrenalin rush hit her like a sledgehammer. She pushed herself upright, sidestepped around the pile and launched herself towards the dark rectangle of the doorway. She was a terrified, a panicked animal with only one narrow focus, escape.

Just for a millisecond, a flicker of regret, "I should have snuffed it out!" But for Sandy Morgan that thought arrived just a bit too late.

From behind her, a sound erupted like the wind rushing through the mouth of a narrow canyon.

Sandy felt herself being lifted off her feet and propelled forward like an errant leaf in the wind. Her face smashed into something hard, and her world exploded in blinding light and searing pain.

The arsonists had been sloppy—every room had been thoroughly doused. The hot, rapidly expanding gasses pressed the walls of the old house outward. Like a pair of puffed out cheeks, the explosion ripped out the tinder-dry walls and shattered the windows into a million shards, like glittering diamonds, shot gunned out into the night.

The time was 2:15am, and Sandy Morgan was no longer alive.

Chapter 4

The Morning After

The thin ringing sound nagged at his sleeping mind. Something tugged at him. He was holding his breath ready to burst. His eyes turned upward, he kicked and felt himself ascending, following a chain of silver bubbles as they fled upward from the murky ocean depths toward the light. The ringing grew more insistent, drawing him up to the surface of consciousness. He woke up drenched in sweat. "What the—," he growled.

He flipped on the bed lamp and reached for the phone.

"Hello, yes—what? Yes, this is Flynt. " He squinted at the clock radio—the hands read 3:38 am.

"Yes, of course I remember you, Mrs. Reagan. Fire? When? Where? No, Sandy—yes, don't worry. She went home hours ago. Yes, I'm sure she's fine. Yes, I know. I'll have her call you right away."

He glared angrily at the telephone receiver for a moment, then slammed it into its cradle and rubbed his face with both hands. His mouth tasted sour. The Green Street house had been torched—but where the hell was Sandy goddamn Morgan?

Why hadn't she called?

"Well, wake up, little Suzy, I mean Sandy!" he said mouthing the title of an Everly Brothers tune. He reached for his pocket secretary. It was right where he always put it on the night table next to the phone.

He let her number ring. No answer!

Flynt dropped the receiver into the cradle, threw his legs over the side of the bed and sat up.

Not at her apartment. "Where is she? Dammit, girl!"

He pulled a pair of worn corduroys from under the pile and plucked yesterday's flannel shirt off the chair-back. If she's not at home, where the hell is she? He walked into the bathroom and pulled the chain turning on the ceiling light. He turned on the cold water and splashed his face with a double handful, grabbed a grubby towel, patted his face dry and raked back his dark hair with splayed fingers.

Flynt was worried. She should have answered her damn phone. He shrugged on his faded foul-weather jacket, pulled a black wool watch-cap over his ears, slammed the door and gazed out at the parked cars that lined both sides of the empty street. The battered red VW Beetle started right up. "Unsafe at every speed," he thought. He backed out of his space and wound through the gears.

A pumper, its emergency light rotating lazily, splashed patches of red diamond off the windows of the houses along the street. The big truck had its searchlights aimed directly at the abandoned house—or what remained of it. Half the first floor on the right side was gone, and the whole upper level was scorched. The cockeyed hulk of an old enameled stove stood out in high relief in the midst of the blackened rubble. Smoke still curled up into the beam of the searchlight, and the air was filled with the acrid smell of smoldering timbers and wet wood.

Flynt made his way over to a small knot of people who stood hunched together talking on the sidewalk, just at the edge of the property line.

"Anybody know what happened?"

One of the group, a short, scrawny old man, knobby knees pushed halfway through threadbare wool work pants and a narrow unshaven chin just visible beneath his battered fedora, squinted up at him. He was using one hand to shield his eyes from the broad beam of the truck's searchlight. His knuckles were overlarge. He had come out without his teeth.

"What's it look like, cock?"

"I'd guess a fire," Flynt said, trying to soothe the man's hostility with a friendly smile.

"Then you'd have the right of it," the old man said, his eyes narrowing.

Portrait of a disappointment, but whose? He had a drinker's nose, doughy and vein-lined. It looked like it had been broken once or twice. His accent still carried with it the burr of County Cork. The two others, women, plump, middle-aged and frumpy, stared curiously but remained mute.

"It's cold as the devil's hind tit," Flynt said, putting the slight musical lilt of southern Ireland into his voice.

The old man's demeanor altered slightly.

"Right as rain," he said. He looked up at the black sky and pulled up the collar of his coarse tweed coat up around his ears. "Where ya from?"

"Name's Jedediah, Jedediah Flynt. I live a couple of streets over. I work with Father Gale," he said, naming the assistant pastor at Our Lady of Lourdes Catholic Church. Naming a local priest was always a good, quick way to buy some credibility. "I was on my way home, and the flashing lights caught me eye."

"From across the water, by the sound of ya," the old man said.

Flynt shook his head.

"I was born in Brighton, my people are from Skibbereen," Flynt said, lying smoothly. His features were not distinctive, so he could pass for a lot of ethnics. He had been baptized Catholic but never confirmed. He was good at accents, and most people in the neighborhood took him for black Irish, an impression he did nothing to discourage. Truth be told he was a mutt, small-boned and intense, with the dark eyes, sharp features and coal black hair that were more typical of the Picts, a tribe that ranged the British Isles long before the coming of the Celts, who were in turn overrun by the Angles. He looked not at all like that of the typical big, bluff-faced Irishman.

"Do you work with that nice, young girl from over at the church?" the woman standing next to the old man asked. She had a babushka tied under her chin, a flannel nightgown peeked out from beneath the hem of her long wool coat. Her feet were covered with huge fuzzy, pink slippers.

"Yes, Sandy. Do you know her?"

"Sandy, is it? I'd forgotten her name. Nice girl. She's trying to do something about the abandoned buildings in the neighborhood." She turned to the man. "You remember, Billy, the girl I was tellin' ya about?"

The old man answered with a truculent shrug. "Aye," he said.

Just then Flynt noticed an ambulance parked ahead, its low silhouette screened by the boxy bulk of the pumper.

He felt a strong hand clamp down on his guts.

Two attendants dressed in whites with dark hooded coats emerged from behind the smoking building and were carrying a stretcher.

"Oh, God," he groaned.

Flynt ran toward where the attendants, watched by a pair of firemen in hats and hip boots, were hunched over the gurney.

One of the firemen angrily motioned him back.

Flynt paused. "Is it a woman?" he asked.

All four turned and stared at him.

He moved forward a few steps and cleared his throat.

"I think I might know her," he said, his voice cracking.

One of the firemen, the tallest in the group, beckoned him forward. The gurney was set on the ground between the men—there was a zippered plastic bag.

After eighteen months in Vietnam, Flynt knew a body bag when he saw one.

Flynt focused on the tall fireman. A pair of questioning, pale blue eyes beneath the rim of the traditional, metal fireman's helmet, and above the rim, a shield and the number fourteen in stainless steel letters, reflected in the pulsing light of the truck's emergency flasher.

"Can I have a look?" Flynt asked.

"What? Are ye daft?" the short fireman cut in. He glared at Flynt with open suspicion. "Course not! This ain't no place for rubberneckers—And how do you know it's a girl we got here, anyways?" He was shorter and thinner than the other firemen, with a thick nose and a pockmarked face.

The taller man placed a restraining hand on the man's forearm and turned to Flynt.

"She's not a pretty sight, lad. Tell me your name, and what business you have here?" he asked, his voice soothing.

"My name is Flynt. I'm the project director over at J.P.S.A.C. —you know, the Social Action Committee. One of my neighborhood organizers, Sandy Morgan, has been working with the neighborhood group that got this place boarded up. We've been concerned about the fires in the neighborhood. She's been standing watch on this building."

Number Fourteen looked questioningly into Flynt's eyes. "Standing watch? Why, were you expecting something?"

Flynt nodded. "Like I said, there have been a lot of fires in the neighborhood."

"I see. Well, it's a young girl, all right. The body is in pretty bad shape. You ever see a burn victim before, Mr. Flynt?"

Flynt edged closer. He didn't want to look, but he knew he had to. "No, but I saw a lot worse in Nam," he said and swallowed hard. "If it's her, I gotta know. I sent her. It's my responsibility she was here."

"Ok, it's your funeral. Open her up, Conley," he said.

"If you say so, chief." The short fireman cast a none-too-friendly glance at Flynt, kneeled and worked the zipper down, exposing the head and upper torso.

Flynt was familiar with sudden death. He had lost buddies in the war. You never get over it completely. It leaves its own after image forever imprinted, and here, in this quiet Boston neighborhood, it seemed so out of place.

What had been Sandy Morgan's face looked like a marshmallow burnt crisp over an open fire. A bit of blond hair. Her lips were burned away exposing white teeth clenched together in the macabre parody of a smile—her arms raised as if to protect her face—her blackened hands curled and soldered into claws. Of her lovely young face, only the eyes and forehead remained untouched, and the eyes stared wide open with terror. The color was distinctive... a lovely China-blue.

"Oh my God!" Flynt managed a couple of steps before bending over and spewing the contents of his stomach into the crusty black snow. His head spun, he dropped to all fours like a dog, gagged and heaved and gagged and threw up some more until there was nothing left. He felt spent and hollow. His lank hair framed his sweating face. Thin cords of mucus dripped from his mouth.

He took several deep shuttering breaths and looked up; the gurney was gone. The attendants were loading it into the back of the ambulance.

Number Fourteen stood looking down at him. "You alright?" he said extending a hand.

Flynt grasped it and pulled himself unsteadily to his feet.

"You understand, I'll need answers to a few questions," the chief said.

Flynt nodded, "She worked for me. I sent her here. To this."

"Yeah, that's tough! Come along, I'll take you down to the station." The chief took Flynt gently by the elbow and steered him toward the small truck. "Got some hot coffee there. We'll set you up. Leave your car. You're in no shape to drive. I'll have someone bring you back to get it later."

Flynt nodded. He felt disconnected from his body, a marionette hanging slack from its strings.

"What about the cops?"

"Don't worry, they'll get to you in their own good time. But I wanna talk to you first, while everything's still fresh in your mind."

Flynt remembered nothing of the ride to the station. The picture of Sandy's beautiful sightless eyes kept replaying before him like a broken record. He was sunk in a deepening pool of guilt. He had sent this lovely young woman out on a cold night to her death—the most horrible, inconceivable, excruciating kind of death—alone, all alone.

"So what do you know about all this?"

The chief poured two cups of coffee from an urn set on a table at one side of the room, slid the cup in front of the organizer and took a chair opposite.

Flynt was staring down at a pair of grimy hands, his hands, wrapped around the porcelain mug. Suddenly he remembered where he was. He raised his head and met the man's eyes. "Sorry?" he said.

"No problem. Take your time," the fireman said, his voice soft.

Then after a while, he asked, "First time you've seen a burn victim?"

"She didn't deserve that," Flynt said.

"You're right, but then, no one deserves a death like that. I believe you said that you had been watching the building," the chief continued. "What made you think something was going to happen to that house?"

Flynt raised the cup to his lips, took a slug, his eyed widened, and he grimaced.

"Sorry about the coffee," the chief smiled. "We're between shifts. Somebody will get around to making a new pot in an hour or so."

Without the helmet he looked older. His name was Murphy, and he had no hair on top of his head, and what was there, on the sides, was gray and buzzed short. His face was full and round. His title, Deputy Chief, was engraved on a black plastic tag that was pinned above his right breast pocket. "Tell me how you figured out about the arson?"

Flynt's head jerked up, his eyes narrowed, looked straight at Murphy. "So you know that it was arson," he said.

Murphy nodded. "Yes, unofficially. Officially, the investigation is ongoing. The fire marshal's office handles that. But, yes, evidence—seems to point to—I'd say, these guys are pros. There's been a lot of suspicious fires in that neighborhood lately."

"So why all the secrecy? Why hasn't it been made public?"

"Like I said, we've sent what we had to the fire marshal, but his office has made no official announcement. That means that the investigation is ongoing," Murphy shrugged.

"I don't understand the problem. Either it's arson or it isn't."

Murphy looked cautiously to his left and right, leaned across the table and lowered his voice. "Look, Mr. Flynt, the guys that are doing this aren't all that sophisticated. Any idiot can see it. That building on Green Street reeks of accelerant. We know that a lot of it is arson, but the mayor's office has been very sensitive lately. We are told that a public announcement might cause panic. Next year is an election year, and hizzhonor is girding his loins for a tough race. Joe Timilty, the state senator, is running against him. Two sons of the auld sod, both native Bostonians. Timilty is popular; he's from Mattapan, so Mayor White's office is being very careful about saying anything about anything—or that's how my boss put it."

"Bullshit! Maybe the fact that someone is systematically torching properties in J. P. just makes the mayor's office look incompetent."

"Yeah, maybe so, ya got me. Maybe they are planning to hold a press conference and make a big thing out of it once we catch these bastards. I stopped trying to figure out the politics of this town ten years ago. It's safer that way."

"Got any leads?" Flynt asked.

Murphy shook his head slowly side to side. "Not a single one. I mean we know that somebody's burning them, but that's about it."

"Sandy spotted the pattern," Flynt said.

Murphy grunted. "Sandy? Was that her name?"

"Yeah, Sandy Morgan."

He nodded and wrote the name down on the yellow pad in front of him

Flynt stared down into his cup. The ceiling light, reflected in the tarry black liquid, stared back at him like an accusing eye. "Yeah, Sandy Morgan. Green Street was part of her territory. She was the one who organized the group that got the place boarded up."

"Poor thing. Damn shame, pretty young girl like that. We'll need her complete name and address for the official report. Do you know what she was doing inside the building?"

Flynt stared down at the cup between his hands. "That's what I keep asking myself. Wait and watch! That was her job. She was never supposed to go near those people, never mind go inside the house. She was supposed to be standing hidden about three doors up on the other side of the street. I told her, someone comes, just watch, see what you can, then hide until they leave and call the cops—and call me."

"Maybe she saw something, waited until whoever it was left and went inside to investigate. Most arsonists use some kind of a timing device, so's they can get away from the scene."

"Maybe. Dumb little shit!" Flynt stood up. "Thanks for the coffee," he said. "I've got her personnel file back at the office. I'll give you a call." He looked down at his stained fingers. "I need to wash my hands."

Murphy sat back and stared up at him. His eyes showed concern. "Bathroom's through that door," he said, pointing. "Hey, you sure you're okay? If you give me a minute, I'll run you back to your car." He pronounced it *kah*. The accent denoted South Boston.

"Not necessary. I gotta walk, need to clear my head. But thanks, thanks for—you know." He gestured vaguely. "One question, she had her hands up, you know, like she was defending herself. Do you think she was...!"

Murphy shook his head, "No, you see it all the time with burn victims. The body tries to protect itself by curling up into the fetal position, and the heat forces the arm muscles to contract."

"Like roasted chicken wings."

Murphy winced, "Yeah, something like that. So what are you going to do now?"

"First, I'm going to the office and call Sandy's mother and try to explain why her daughter died. Then I'm gonna find the fuckers who killed her!"

The chief shook his head, then stood, and extended a big, right hand.

"Okay, but keep in touch, will ya? And listen, Flynt, I'll help if I can, unofficially, of course. I don't like people who set fires and kill little girls."

"Thanks," Flynt said. "By the way, the name's Jed, and I'll remember that."

The two men shook hands, and Flynt walked out into the frigid gray dawn.

It was 6am, the beginning of the morning commute, and the traffic was heavy on Blue Hill Avenue. Flynt walked, took a left onto Washington Street and another up McBride. He pulled his hat down and his collar up and hunched his shoulders against the head-wind and trudged up the hill toward Centre Street. Just as he reached the intersection, one of the battered old Green Line trolleys passed in front of him on its way to Haymarket Square. Its steel wheels drummed a clattering rhythm against the steel tracks. He crossed Centre, mounted the curb and pushed open the door to Lenny's Diner.

On any other day, he would have welcomed the steamy heat and the soft buzz of talk that welled up and enfolded him like a warm blanket. Flynt squatted down on a stool at the end of the crowded counter just inside the door.

Flynt was a regular, and Lenny Klausmeyer, the owner, was working the grill. Lenny spotted Flynt as soon as he was through the door.

"Hey, look what the cat dragged in! Waddya say, Troop, the usual?"

Lenny stood in front of the grill and peered down the long counter at the organizer over a pair of thick half-spectacles that perched scholar-like at the end of his nose giving him a disapproving mien, as if the world and all its contents was a perpetual source of disappointment. He wore a sweaty tee shirt. Like Flynt, Lenny Klausmeyer was an ex-Marine, and his thick forearms were decorated with tattoos, faded souvenirs of a lifetime of overseas' deployments. He wore a stained white apron, the strings tied in a bow over his hard paunch. He poured coffee into a heavy mug and put it down in front of the organizer. "Hey, Troop, something wrong down at that commie-pinko outfit you head up? You look like shit."

"Thanks."

"Don't mention it. Breakfast?"

Flynt felt a hollow ache in the pit of his stomach. The sense of disconnect was still there. A wave of dizziness washed over him as he was sitting, and he broke out in a cold sweat. He remembered he hadn't eaten much, and he had lost that in the gritty snow on Green Street. Combat duty had taught him to never refuse a meal. He unzipped his foul weather jacket and drew the back of his hand across his brow. "Yeah, two over easy, home fries, bacon and rye toast."

"Comin' right up."

Flynt raised his cup and took a swallow. The hot liquid burned his tongue going down. He tried to focus, but his mind just kept replaying the horror.

Lenny's Diner was a classic Art-Deco style eatery, straight out of a magazine advertisement. The interior was a prefab made by an outfit in Georgia, shipped north, and assembled on site. The counter faced a wall sheathed in quilted stainless steel. A hood of the same material descended like a potentate's umbrella from the tin ceiling about center stage. The floor tiles were black and white checkerboard.

Lenny Klausmeyer had landed with the 5th Marines at Inchon, served a tour in Vietnam and retired a gunnery sergeant. Flynt had met him in Khe Sanh when he reported fresh out of boot camp for duty with the 3rd Marines. Lenny had been his platoon leader. Sixteen months later, Flynt was a squad leader, and Lenny had rotated back to the states and taken his retirement. He used his savings to come home to Boston and realize his dream of opening his own diner. Lenny, or his short order cook, a skinny black Jamaican named Rodney, presided over a wide, polished iron grill. Today it was Lenny.

Moving like a jazz drummer improvising a riff, Lenny dipped and swiped a four-inch sash-brush, dripping with oil, lightly across the hot grill, then hefted an egg in each hand, tapped both firmly against the grill's sharp edge, pried open the shells and let the contents ooze gently into the sizzling puddle of oil, yokes round, cartoon-yellow and intact.

Responding to a customer's bellow, Lenny turned, grinned a sarcastic reply, then pirouetting like an overweight ballerina and wielding spatula and tongs, he plucked up two slices of bacon and placed them beside the sputtering eggs while his spatula flipped a couple over easy.

He dropped the tongs, lifted a pitcher, poured a short-stack of pancake batter onto the sizzling steel, then shoveled Flynt's eggs onto a white china plate, added two strips of bacon, and a spatula blade of home fries, hit the toaster button, snagged the two slices in mid- air, dropped them on his cutting board, and with a single motion of his knife, sliced them into neat triangles. He brushed on butter, steered the plate with one finger along the chipped Formica counter and parked it in front of the organizer. Flynt looked up.

"Voila, mon-sewer. Breakfast, as we say in gay Parie, is soived. Did I mention that you look like shit-on-a- fucking-shingle?" Lenny said.

Flynt made eye contact but did not respond. Lenny shrugged. He had a good nose. He sensed there was a problem and could see that Flynt was in no mood to talk. Lenny was patient. Sooner or later, he figured, he would hear all about it.

They hadn't kept in touch. Six years later Flynt had stumbled into Lenny's, just after he signed on to the organizing project. It was old home week and the two ex- jarheads had re-bonded. Lenny was a guy who had lived all his adult life within a rigid chain of command, and he just shook his head when Flynt tried to explain his current mission, but Flynt was a brother Marine, so they'd have drinks together down at the Roslindale VFW with a couple of other ex-marines who had joined the Boston police. They could talk. These were the only guys who understood.

Lenny became a source of what he called "useful intel." Big shots and small, everybody ate at Lenny's. The local politicians appeared whenever they needed their working-class tickets punched—usually just before election time. Lenny was known for his sympathetic ear and a closed mouth, and that made the big man a font of local gossip.

The organizer stared straight ahead and shoveled and chewed mechanically until the plate was empty—then sat, head down, and nursed his coffee.

He gazed vacantly out through the steamed plate glass at the commuters hurrying along Centre Street on their way to work. The day was beginning to busy itself, the shops and businesses that lined both sides of the street were open, and people were going about their normal business.

In Country, Flynt and his squad had shared a bond. "Under his own steam or in a body bag, whatever the mission, no matter the risk, every man who went out on patrol was brought back home. Last night he had sent Sandy Morgan out on a mission, and it was that mission—his mission—that had killed her. "Sandy was in my squad, she was my responsibility–and now she's dead. It was my duty to protect her, and I failed." This was bloodguilt, and there was only way to wash it away. Flynt knew the code. He would avenge Sandy's death or never know peace. He forced himself to shelve the pain and the whining voice inside his head and began a methodic analysis of the facts and the events of the last few days.

Chief Murphy had said that the arson was a professional job. So the burnings must be part of a systematic plan. Therefore, somebody, somehow stood to benefit. Sandy had researched the guy who owned the Green Street building before they had approached the city. That was standard operating procedure. The guy lived in Taunton, a little town forty miles southeast of Boston. He had inherited the house from an aunt and had no other holdings in Jamaica Plain. So how did he stand to gain? It made no sense, but, logically, the land that he and everyone else saw as worthless had to be of some value to somebody, substantial value given the risks. Remove all other possibilities and what remained, no matter how improbable, had to be true. He remembered that from reading A. Conan Doyle. Whatever it was had to be right in front of him. Why couldn't he see it? The money was the key. Had to be. Follow the money. That would lead him to the men who killed Sandy.

He wracked his brain. Scattered sites! Different owners! It just didn't make any sense.

When Flynt was growing up, his mother used to say he had a one-track mind. Once he got hold of something, he was like a terrier worrying a bone—he kept after it until he got whatever it was he was after. In Jedediah Flynt's mind that morning, guilt began to transform itself into something else—a hardened kernel of resolve, made up of equal parts anger and hate.

He stared through the glass and saw Sandy's face imprinted against the leaden winter sky. Not her face in a body bag burnt beyond reason and pity but the memory of a face, a pair of lovely eyes, a woman with grit, the girl he had known.

Tears filled his eyes. He squeezed them shut, gritted his teeth and made a silent vow.

"Sandy, I hope you can hear me," he whispered. "I swear to you that no matter how long it takes, I will get the bastards who killed you."

"I will find a way."

Jedediah Flynt got up off the stool, placed two dollar bills down onto the counter, shouldered open the diner door, turned left, pulled up his collar against the cold breeze and marched off in the direction of Green Street.

Chapter 5

The Researcher

Flynt normally arrived at the office at 10am. He was usually the first. He liked the short interval of morning quiet before the staff arrived. Time to plan the day. By noon, the five incoming lines would be ringing constantly. Answered democratically by whoever was not currently on the phone, the recipient's name was shouted out over the din.

This morning he was surprised to find his English organizer, Swift, usually a late riser, with his feet propped up on his desk, straw blond hair poking out from all sides of his head, phone at his ear and the smoke from his cigarette hovering above him like a low-hanging cloud. Swift placed his hand over the mouthpiece. He looked up with a brief grin, "Mornin' Guv'nor," he said, then burrowed like a groundhog back into his conversation. Flynt was pleased.

Sandy's death had cast a pall over the office. Morale plummeted. The young staff members seemed in a trance. It took most of two weeks before Flynt realized that he was the one in a funk. The staff was tiptoeing around trying not to upset him.

It was like a cold shower. He braced himself, met with each organizer individually and forced himself to focus on their specific projects. It was just what he needed. Sandy would be missed, but youth is focused on the future, and things slowly returned to normal.

By early afternoon, when Alexis Jordan walked into the office for her appointment with Flynt, the office was buzzing like a bookmaking parlor. Every phone line was lit, and the mimeograph machine at the back of the office was cranking along like a steam train.

Alex Jordan was looking for a job. She had finished her course work and was scheduled to graduate from Harvard in June with a degree in political science. She had been recommended to Flynt by her major professor. Alex had never been in this part of Jamaica Plain. She had borrowed her roommate's car and parked it on the other side of the street—maybe not such a great idea. She hoped it would still be there when she finished her interview.

Alexis Jordan had wide-set brown eyes which glinted with tiny flecks of gold, a generous mouth and full bowed red lips. She wore a blue, goose-down vest over a cable stitched Irish sweater. She carried a green rucksack over one shoulder and a red cardboard folder under her arm.

The office was warm, inefficiently over-heated by several old-fashioned steam radiators. She pulled off her knitted wool cap and shook out her mahogany brown hair, which drew every pair of male eyes. As her hair fell to her shoulders in silky abundance the noise level fell, as if someone had pushed the mute button.

Flynt noted her arrival from where he was standing reviewing a fact sheet, by Sigel's desk in the back of the office. He waited until she put down her baggage, shrugged off the down vest and unbuttoned the first few buttons of her cardigan. As he walked forward to greet her, he got a glimpse of a pair of taut nipples outlined against the tight fabric of her mauve, turtleneck pullover.

He felt a twinge of longing and averted his eyes. "Lord protect me," he begged silently.

Flynt had been three years out of the Marines and in his junior year in college when the woman's movement swept across American campuses like a prairie fire. Bull Connor's fire hoses seen up close on the television news convinced Flynt that black people were an oppressed minority. Martin Luther King and the March on Washington had inspired him. It made him want to do something. But the idea that women were oppressed was a new and not particularly welcome concept in the macho world of campus politics.

To Flynt it seemed that most female college graduates in Boston in the mid-seventies—at least those who applied for jobs with his project—were pretty militant. It was hard to know how to treat them or what to say. Most, as he saw it, were a mass of contradictions: they didn't want to be seen as trading on their looks, though the more attractive ones did little to hide their charms. They affected scorn for the most obvious feminine prerogatives: they believed that if a man opened a door for them, it implied that they lacked the strength to open it themselves. On the other hand, some, again usually the more attractive ones, got very prickly if their femininity was not acknowledged in other, less obvious ways.

Women were demanding equality and rejecting traditional feminine behavior models and, unfortunately, often imitated the worst aspects of masculine behavior. Difficult enough to deal with in a man—particularly unfortunate, in Flynt's eyes, in an attractive young woman.

"Alexis Jordan?" Flynt extended his hand. The etiquette was unclear. Some young women made a point of looking you in the eye and shaking hands. Others didn't. He was curious to see how this woman, who had a name that sounded like something out of a movie magazine, would respond.

"Mr. Flynt, I presume?" She looked him in the eyes, smiled, gripped his hand firmly, and pumped it stiffly up and down three times, and let go.

"Okay, great," Flynt thought, flexing his fingers.

"Please, this way," he said as he stepped back and held open the conference room door.

Alexis Jordan hesitated for just an instant, then preceded him into the empty room. He pulled the door closed behind him, and the thick walls of the former church completely blotted out the office noise.

"Please," he said, "take a seat."

Flynt watched as the young woman slid the scarred straight-backed chair out from beneath the desk and sat primly down on it as if it were a rare antique. He pulled out the one next to it, turned it back to front, mounted it like a horse.

"I've seen your resumé, Ms. Jordan," Flynt said nodding toward the folder Alex had placed on the table. "Professor Gardner sent it over with a note. He also called—he is obviously impressed. He says you're a girl who wants to learn to organize."

Was this man baiting her? Alex wasn't sure. Her male classmates often used the term girl to needle her, but they wielded it like an epée with a certain glee in their eyes. Flynt displayed none of that. Dr. Gardner had given Alex a rundown on Flynt and his accomplishments and some of his well-known foibles. She was petrified but determined not to be intimidated. She lifted her chin and looked him in the eye. "We read Rules for Radicals last semester in Dr. Gardner's Contemporary Urban

Issues class, and what Saul Alinsky says makes a lot of sense to me, sir. I did my final paper on Alinsky's concept of strategy and tactics."

Flynt swallowed a smile. "Really! Please, tell me more!"

She looked thoughtful for a moment. "Well, to begin with, he recognizes that human beings are neither good nor evil but are motivated by what they perceive to be in their own best interests," she said, gazing at him levelly.

"Yes, please go on!"

"Okay. He says that issues must be immediate, specific and realizable and must come right from the people, not be some sort of scheme imposed from above. He seems to have had a lot of faith in the common sense of ordinary citizens."

"You mean he thought ordinary people might be able to solve their own problems without the help of an agenda supplied by a bunch of do-gooders with a degree from an elite college?"

Alexis paused, her face reddened, but she refused to take the bait. "Well, yes, I guess so. Honestly, Mr. Flynt, I think I understand where you are coming from, but it's not like that. I believe in what Alinsky has to say, and I don't think that I'm any better than anybody else."

"Okay, what is it like, then? Let's talk about your self-interest. What's your agenda?"

She thought for a moment. "Well okay, Dr. Gardner told us about your project. I think what you are doing is important, and…relevant… and frankly, I see it as an opportunity for me to learn something."

"Fair enough! What conclusions did you draw about Alinsky's ideas on strategy and tactics?"

"Well, I liked his tactical approach. Avoid flak-catchers. Focus on the decision-makers who can move the issues forward.

That made a lot of sense to me. But I have a problem, ethically, with his stance on ends and means." Alexis Jordan felt on firmer ground. This was just the sort of theoretical discussion she loved and where she felt most at home. "He seems to be a situationist. I mean, if the ends justify the means, then logically any means are acceptable."

"So you would subject organizing tactics to an ethical standard?"

"Well, yes, of course. Don't you?"

"And who would set the standards of acceptability?" Flynt asked.

"Well, uh, I'm not sure. There must be some sort of universal standard. I guess I haven't thought that through."

"Would a given tactic have to be acceptable to say a cocktail party audience of Harvard graduates?"

"Well, no, of course not. I see your point, but…"

"I doubt it," he said, cutting her off. "Look, in the final analysis, it is only the ends that can justify the means. What else is there? Alinsky refused to get hung up on abstractions. The reduction of all things to one thing, the attempt to reduce all particulars to a universal rule, inevitably leads to a reductio ad absurdum—and that is pretty much what Western ethical philosophy keeps banging its head against.

Jed continued. "Alinsky's point was that the particular ends must justify the particular means. The more extreme the problem, the more extreme the allowable means. Right? For example, the idea of cannibalism is repugnant to most of us, but to a lifeboat full of starving people, lost at sea, the idea becomes less and less repugnant as time goes on. There have been any number of recorded instances of people in similar situations eating their dead. In extreme situations, Alex, the repugnant becomes reasonable. Who should be allowed to judge, the starving people in the lifeboat or a well-fed jury of their peers?

"What do people call you, by the way?"

"I prefer Alexis. Do I call you Mr. Flynt?"

"Jed or just Flynt will do. Alexis sounds a little hoity-toity. Let's try Alex. It might work better in a working-class Irish neighborhood. What does your father do for a living?"

"My father?" She was taken aback by this abrupt change of subject. "He's a, a corporate lawyer in New York."

"A rich corporate lawyer in New York?"

"Rich? I don't know. Well, yes, I suppose so, but pardon me, Mr. Flynt, I mean Jed—what does my father's income have to do with my suitability for this position?"

"You are asking me what role money and social class play in American society. Surely you are not that naive. I see you went to a private high school. Where was that exactly?

"It's– it's on the upper east side of Manhattan," she said.

"It's a private girl's prep school, am I right?"

"Yes, but–"

"Pardon me, Miss—or is it Ms. Jordan? But how do you figure that a girl like you, a society girl, who attended all the best schools and has wanted for nothing her entire life is going to relate to some poor Irish house-frau, a generation removed from the bog, who got knocked up by her boyfriend in the eighth grade, dropped out of school at sixteen, who has three kids, no money, no education and no prospects?"

Alexis Jordan stared down at the table for a few moments. No one had spoken to her that way before, and she was angry. She took a deep breath and looked up. "It's Ms., and I am not a society girl, and my family may be comfortable financially, but I was not spoiled, sir!"

"Really!"

"Yes, really! We were required to work, my brother and I. I spent every summer since my last year in high school doing corporate research for one of my father's associates." Her face felt hot. Dr. Gardner had warned her that Flynt would try to get a rise out of her. She had sworn to herself that she wouldn't take the bait, but she had. Did she see a look of satisfaction in those cold dark eyes?

"Research?"

Rile them up and you find out how they really feel. Flynt had gotten the reaction he was hoping for and was beginning to be interested. He had an idea. He kept his voice matter of fact. "What sort of stuff did you research?"

"All sorts of things." Alexis said, picking her words like a tightrope walker, gingerly placing each foot down precisely just in front of the other. "My father's practice involves corporate malfeasance. Last summer I researched one company that was illegally parking assets in an offshore tax haven, using all sorts of sophisticated accounting tricks to hide what they were doing. I followed the money trail, and even my father was impressed."

Alexis's father was set on her going on to law school. She supposed that she would become a lawyer, eventually, but the idea did not excite her and, much to her father's disappointment, she had decided she needed to spend a year or two in the real world before making her decision.

"Okay, Alex, point taken. You weren't spoiled, but you do come from a privileged background. You see the problem, right?"

She nodded.

"Do you know why I have a job opening?"

"Yes, Dr. Gardner told me. A woman, one of your organizers, died?"

"Not died, she was murdered, Ms. Jordan, burned to death in an abandoned house in the middle of the night. A young woman very much like you–smart, well spoken—a B.U. graduate, the whole world in front of her. Her body was burned almost beyond recognition. I, I had to identify her body." As he talked the image of Sandy Morgan's lovely blue eyes erupted from his subconscious, staring, just staring.

Alexis watched Flynt's expression change, saw him blink hard and swallow. She could see that he was in pain and wanted to reach out, perhaps to comfort, but she hardly knew this man and instinct told her that he would not welcome her pity. She lowered her eyes and waited.

"What do you know about this project?" he asked as soon as he could trust himself to speak.

"Dr. Gardner said that you were building a classic Alinsky-style organization, organizing block by block, covering the central neighborhoods of Jamaica Plain. He said that you were the best, and that if I really wanted to learn about community organizing, I should work for you. "

Flynt nodded. He had made a decision. She was bright and apparently had done some pretty sophisticated research. He saw an opportunity. Alex Jordan might just be the person he was looking for.

"What I need right now, Alex, what I really need, is a researcher. The pay is eighty a week, no benefits. I expect you in the office by eleven every morning. At the same time, you will be training to be a street organizer, which means three to four nights a week you will be either at meetings, or out door-knocking with one of the more experienced guys. So you can figure a ten to twelve hour day, probably six days a week. What do you say?" he asked watching her closely.

"May I ask what it is that I will be researching?"

"Whatever is needed! Look, Ms. Jordan, let me draw you a picture. You talked earlier about immediate, specific and realizable goals. You go pick out a block and knock on doors, talk to all the people. Right in the middle of the block there's this ten-unit apartment building. You talk to the tenants. They are mostly poor and elderly. The landlord hasn't fixed anything in years. The place stinks. It's infested with rats, cockroaches. There are holes in the walls and sewerage backed up in the basement, and it's a firetrap with an electrical system that looks like a rat's nest. That's immediate, yes?"

"Yes, absolutely."

"The people are angry, but mostly they're scared. So you find this one little old lady who is angry enough, and you talk her into sponsoring a meeting in her apartment and you start to organize. You have the meeting, help make up a list, a list of specific demands. You write up a letter demanding a meeting with the landlord, and you're on your way, right?"

Alexis nodded eagerly, "Yes, I guess..."

"Wrong! Two days after the meeting, all the tenants who attended get eviction notices. Next time you knock on the door, nobody answers. You get a whole bunch of old ladies thrown out on the street, and poof, your tenant organization evaporates."

"A landlord can't do that! It's, it's unconstitutional," she said.

"Yeah, right, except that in the Commonwealth of Massachusetts a month to month tenant can be evicted at the landlord's pleasure with thirty days written notice, and there is no law that protects unionizing tenants.

"Is that really true?" she asked.

"You're damn right it's true. Landlord-tenant law is based on English Common Law, hence the term land lord—and it favors the landlord except in very specific instances."

Flynt shifted into high gear.

"We talked about immediate, specific, realizable issues, right? Immediate means gut-level and is often sparked by fear.

In declining neighborhoods there is much to inspire fear, and fear is a great motivator because fear can be turned into anger, and anger into action. You understand specific. It's the list of demands that can be met, but the difference between realizable and total disaster is…research. If you had done the research you would know that the law says a tenant who has filed a health code complaint cannot be evicted—so you make up a form letter, get every tenant to sign it, and then you take the whole group personally down to the Boston Health Department, file the complaints, and make sure they get receipts."

"Did that really happen? The evictions, I mean?" she asked in a quiet voice.

"Yeah," Flynt sighed. "It happened to a smart-ass young organizer named Flynt about three years ago. Want the job?"

"Yes, yes. I think so," she said.

"Good!"

"Can you give me some idea about what you want me to look into first, so I can think about it over the weekend?" she asked.

Flynt paused and gazed at her intensely for a moment then smiled. "Do you know what a ratter is, Ms. Jordan?" he asked.

"A ratter?" She shook her head. "No sir, I don't think I have ever heard that term."

"A ratter is a dog specially bred to kill rats, and we have a rat, Ms. Jordan, a very smart rat, a totally unscrupulous and very dangerous rat, that is after something. We don't know what, but we do know that this rat won't stop, even at the murder of an innocent young woman. I think we are going to find that this particular rat is burrowed very deep, but you are going to be my ratter, Alexis. You are going to burrow down into the muck and find that rat, and when you do, we are going to trap it, cut it off so it can't escape, and then we are going to kill it," he said his eyes ablaze. "Still want the job?"

Alexis Jordan looked across the table and felt a jolt of energy crackle across the space that separated them. Well, she had wanted to get out of the classroom and into the real world and this, she sensed, was as real as it got. This was her very first interview, and she really wanted this job. She took a quick breath and decided.

"Yes," she said. "Yes, I do, very much."

"Great, see you on Monday. We work late so be in in the morning by 10:30 so I can get you started. And Jordan!"

"Yes, sir?"

"When you come to work, you don't have to dress up— jeans or a modest skirt will do, but make sure you wear a bra!"

Alex blushed deeply and started to protest.

Flynt raised his hand. "Look, at Harvard going bra-less is a political statement, and I am sure much appreciated by the male students and faculty, but in a working-class Irish neighborhood, it's considered indecent."

"Bras are a symbol of male oppression. What about raising people's consciousness?" she protested.

"Really, whose consciousness are we talking about here, yours or the people's? You'll certainly raise the men's consciousness, and the women will think you're a slut. Lesson number one: people trust people who look and act like themselves. An effective organizer is a chameleon. She blends in, takes on the colors of her environment. You want to organize, right?

"Look Alex," Flynt lowered his voice and continued, "I'm not asking you to pretend to be something you're not. I'm asking you to respect the customs and mores of the people you are going to be working with. The women's issue has no immediacy to people who are scratching just to get by. You're here to work on people's agendas, not yours. Don't talk down to people and don't advertise your education. Like Alinsky said; you won't get far in a Jewish neighborhood munching on a ham sandwich."

Chapter 6

Door Knocking

Descending the scarred steel walkway of the Orange Line, Alex spotted Swift's hooded figure standing in front of a Spanish bodega at the corner of Washington and Atherton. Swift wore a woodsman's plaid wool jacket over a blue hooded sweatshirt and a pair of jeans. He had a clipboard tucked under his arm and was holding a cup of coffee in both hands, sipping and jigging nervously from one foot to the other, trying to keep warm. The sidewalk was littered with trash, and behind him the bodega's two filthy plate glass windows were covered by scabby dark-green iron mesh.

It was Saturday afternoon, the end of her first week with the project. Alex had attended her first staff meeting the night before. It had lasted four grueling hours. Each of the neighborhood organizers reported on the previous week and laid out his plans day by day for the following week. Tactics, strategy, meetings, actions! The meetings were of two types, planning and action, and each organizer was expected to put together three to four a week. It was all gone over in minute detail.

Everyone was expected to participate, and Flynt's critiques were sometimes brutal. Swift had been with the project the longest and was planning to start organizing a new block club on Atherton Street. It was virgin territory, and Swift seemed pleased when Flynt assigned her to work with him.

The El, the elevated track that supports the Orange Line, runs right down the middle of Washington Street, blocking out what little comfort might have been gained from the weak afternoon sun and cloaking the sidewalk in shadow. A frigid wind gust whipped Alex's skirt up around her thighs as she stepped off the bottom of the steel staircase. She had spent a half hour in front of the mirror trying to decide what to wear. In the end she had dressed conservatively in a knee-length wool skirt, a sweater and her ski parka. Her teeth chattered, and she thanked God that she had pulled on a pair of thick woolen tights at the last minute.

Swift spotted her as the light changed, and she made a dash across the street.

"Right, about time you showed up!" To make himself heard over the loud rumble of the downtown train clattering overhead, he had to half-shout it. "God, this shit is awful," he said, ostentatiously emptying the steaming liquid onto the pavement and tossing the cup.

Jordan decided to ignore Swift's littering. "I thought you Englishmen drank tea," she said just to make conversation.

"Yeah, too right. If you could find anyone in this friggin' colony who could make a decent cuppa," Swift said, with a grimace. "I been standin' here for fifteen bleedin' minutes."

"I believe you said 1:00 o'clock." She pointed at her watch. "It's just one now," she said, smiling sweetly.

A car went by with loud mufflers. Swift shook his head. "Can't 'ear a word you're saying, luv!" he shouted into her ear.

She cupped her hands around her mouth and repeated what she had said, six inches from his right ear. There was a roughness about Swift that put her off. She had heard him speak at staff meetings and figured the heavy cockney was a put on. She was also determined to make a good impression. She wanted him to like her.

"Yeah, right, whatever. Listen luv, it's cold as a witch's bleedin' a-hole, and we have got a lot of bleedin' ground to cover…"

"What part of England are you from?" she shouted.

"Liverpool, ever been there?"

"No, but I've been to London twice, and Liverpool—that's where the Beatles are from. Did you ever meet them—before they became famous, I mean?"

"Oh, yeah, a course. luv. Paul was one of me mates. We used to hang together all the time down at the Casbah," he said with a smirk.

"Really?"

Swift laughed.

"Yeah, really, and I was almost a Beatle me-self except that I can't carry a bleedin' tune." Swift pulled up his collar. "Come on, luv. We'd best get going. Sundown's about four, and nobody in this neighborhood is going to open his door to strangers after dark. So we ain't got all bloody day."

Paper and bits of trash played about their feet like a parody of autumn leaves as they dashed under the El and across Washington. They turned onto Atherton and walked about fifty feet up the street to where the noise diminished enough to carry on a normal conversation. "Listen, luv," Swift said, "the guv'nor wants to get you up to speed, so you come with me to the first couple of houses, then I'll let you talk at the next couple. Then we divide up and do the rest of the street, right"?

"Right," she said, "if you think I'll be able to figure it out that quickly."

"No worries, luv. You graduated from bleedin' Harvard, yeah? Went to B.U. myself. Believe me it don't take a bleedin' genius. You have just got to keep listening for the real issues. You remember the mantra, yeah? On this here street there will be plenty of potential issues to pick from, believe me. You studied the cheat sheet, yeah?"

She nodded and pulled a plastic covered clipboard out of her bag.

"Right, like the guv'nor says, 'immediate, specific, realizable.' You just watch and listen. Then, monkey see, monkey do. Right?"

Alexis nodded.

They approached the first house. It was a single family with natural cedar shakes that had weathered over the years to a chocolate brown. A chain-link fence divided the street from the front yard. Swift took hold, rattled the gate and paused with one ear cocked. "Some of these folks have dogs. Bloody dangerous! Hate the bloody things," he said.

He looked left and right through narrowed eyes then pushed the gate gently inward, strode up the cement walk and knocked at the white, aluminum combination door, leaving Alexis to bring up the rear. The inside door swung open immediately, and a tall well-built black man in his late thirties stood staring down at them through the glass outer door. He had obviously seen them coming. "May I help you?" he asked, in a deep baritone voice.

"Good afternoon, sir. My name is Swift, and this here is my colleague, Alex Jordan. We are neighborhood organizers, working with a coalition of Jamaica Plain churches. We're canvassing the street and talking to people about problems in the neighborhood."

The big man looked them over skeptically and pushed open the door a crack. "You mean like the drunks buying liquor at that bodega," he said, nodding toward the head of the street. "Then crossing over here and hanging out in front of my house, drinking liquor out of brown paper bags and relieving themselves into my wife's flower garden. That the kind of problem you are interested in hearing about?" he asked, eyeing Swift.

"Yes sir!" Swift looked sidelong at Alexis. "Pay dirt!" his eyes exclaimed.

"What can you do about that, Mr. Swift? Can you make it so my wife is not afraid to open the door to her own home? You've got some sort of an accent. Where are you from?"

Alexis Jordan almost laughed; she noted the dramatic change in Swift's manner. A slight accent remained, but now he sounded upper class and the profanity was gone.

"I'm from England, graduated from Boston University, and well, sir, I think we can help you with that problem. I don't know if you read about it in the papers, but about a month ago people were complaining about a similar problem. You know Cully's Tavern, up on the corner of Dumaine and Roland Street, yeah?"

"Yes," Rogers answered cautiously, "I do recall reading something about that in The Globe."

"Right, same sort a thing, sir, blokes yellin' and screamin' all hours of the night. We helped organize a group of neighbors. They formed the McBride Street Block Club, went to the Boston ABC. That's alcohol and beverage control, sir, and got Cully's late-night liquor license revoked."

The tall black man's eyes narrowed. He stared at Swift for a long moment. "That was your group?" he asked.

"Yes sir," Swift replied. "We organized them, helped with the research, and the block club dealt with the issue."

"My name is Rogers. John Rogers." He stood aside and pushed open the aluminum door. "I think you had better come in. It's cold out here, and I want to hear more about this block-club idea of yours."

"And you say that you've tried calling the police?" Swift asked after Rogers had told his story. He jotted a note on his clipboard. The room was beautifully appointed. Quite a contrast to the exterior, Alexis thought, looking about her. They were seated on a cream colored sofa. Rogers had introduced his wife who sat across the room watching quietly in a matching chair. The wall-to-wall carpet was a dove-gray. The venetian blinds that covered the windows were closed, and the room was dim.

Rogers sat hunched forward in a leather armchair gesturing with both hands. "Yes, of course, we called. The neighbors called. The police came right away at first, and as soon as they saw the police car, the men scattered."

"So, what did the coppers do?" Swift asked.

Rogers lifted both arms, his hands open, fingers spread trying hard to suppress a grin at Swift's colorful language. "Nothing—what could they do? No laws had been broken. Urinating on private property and making lewd propositions is apparently some sort of misdemeanor," he said, glancing across the room at his wife who sat primly upright in her chair.

"You see the problem is, Mr. Swift, we live under siege. We are prisoners in our own homes. My wife is afraid even to go outside in the middle of the day and tend her garden. Do you have any suggestions, Mr. Swift?"

Swift scratched his head. "Yeah, well, right. There is a law against loitering and drinking in public, and that bodega has a city license to sell liquor. If they are seen as running a public nuisance, like, they could lose their license, and police patrols could be increased. That might drive those derelicts off the corner."

"We mentioned some of those same things, and the police officers just shrugged. We asked for increased patrols, which seemed to work for a week or so, but as soon as the patrols stopped, the whole thing started all over again and the next morning, you know, after the cops had come by, there was a big red swastika spray-painted on our front door. We called the police again, but they said that they didn't have the funds or the manpower to keep up the patrols."

Swift shook his head sadly back and forth. "Well, you see that is the problem. You are a citizen, a taxpayer; you have a right to be safe here in your own home."

"It's outrageous," Rogers said. Look, I'm no shrinking violet. I grew up in the Mission Hill Projects, then got a scholarship to Northeastern, but I'm about to go out and get myself a gun to protect myself and my home.

"Would you say most of your neighbors feel the same way?"

"Oh yes. We've talked to quite a few of them. There's Johnson, he lives three doors down on this side of the street, and there's Mrs. Edwards and Tim O'Brien and Don Rodrigues. They all live on the other side of the street. Don's wife was followed home and threatened by a couple of thugs one night, and Tim's place has been vandalized. They're decent people, and they're as scared as we are."

"We'll go and maybe have a little chin wag with some of those folks. Mind if I tell them that we have spoken to you? And would you be willing to, like, chair a meeting here at your house, say, some night next week?" Swift asked.

"Damn right, I would! If you think that it will do any good," Rogers said.

"'Absobloodylootely! I mean course it will," Swift said, looking earnestly at Rogers. "The more people you have to back you up, the better. In unity there is strength. Yeah, I think you got that on your dollar bill. Otherwise the lot of you would still be drinkin' tea and singin' God Save the Queen," Swift said, with a disarming smile.

Everyone laughed, including Mrs. Rogers, who put her hand to her mouth and tittered primly. The humor seemed to break through the remaining tension.

"Alex and I will look into it, find out how many complaints have been filed down at city hall about that bodega. You know, build a case, like, and if you will give me your phone number, I'll ring you and let you know what we find out before the meeting. I'll review the paperwork on the Cully's issue and see what the law says. We'll have a fact sheet ready for you folks to review at the meeting."

Alexis was impressed. She watched the interplay closely, saw Rogers' wife's encouraging nod when Swift asked him to chair a meeting and saw that Swift was already recruiting leadership for a block club meeting.

Alexis and Swift spent another half hour with the Rogers couple. When they finally left, Swift was pumped up. He figured that Rogers was a real live wire, and he was full of plans to build a block-club around him.

At the second house they were not quite so fortunate.

It was a small white clapboard house with no fence. A cement walk led between the brown, broken and tangled remains of flowerbeds that flanked either side of the walk. The beds were neatly lined with bricks, which only emphasized the look of seasonal devastation.

A thin, older-looking woman opened the door. She wore a neatly ironed house dress and had large luminous brown eyes.

"Good afternoon," she said in a chirpy voice, "how nice of you to call. Come right in."

She stepped aside and pushed open the aluminum storm door.

Swift gave Alexis a significant look and walked through the door, leaving her to follow.

The woman ushered them into her living room and sat them on the couch. "Isn't it cold out today. I'll just make tea. It won't take a minute."

Alexis began to object, but Swift touched her forearm. "Tea would be lovely, er, Missus…?"

"It's Miss, Miss Partridge. What a lovely accent you have! Please, it's ever so nice to have visitors on such a cold gray afternoon. Please, make yourselves comfortable. The tea will be ready in just a few minutes."

Miss Partridge left the room.

Swift and Alex looked at each other. "Isn't she being awfully friendly?" Alexis whispered. "She acts as if she were expecting us."

Swift shrugged. "Some of these older birds are just lonely. It's better than standing out in the cold, yeah! Just follow my lead, luv."

"Okay," Alex said and sank back into the couch.

She looked around the room. The furniture was conventional. The couch they sat on was upholstered in that scratchy textured fabric that was popular in the forties. This one was maroon. A dark brown gas space heater sat in front of a fireplace that had been boarded up and painted over but served as the room's centerpiece. A collection of gaily-painted ceramic figurines graced the mantelpiece above the heater. A glass-fronted bookcase sporting a pristine set of the Encyclopedia Britannica sat in the far-left corner. There was a braided rug beneath their feet and a Formica-topped walnut coffee table in front of the couch.

Miss Partridge returned a few minutes later with a tray she set down on a table in front of the two organizers. It contained a blue china teapot, matching cups and saucers, and a dish piled high with cookies stamped Lorna Doone in raised letters.

"There we are," said Miss Partridge, as she poured the tea. "I do enjoy a hot cup of tea on a cold afternoon, don't you?" she chirped, smiling brightly. Alex noticed that her heavily-permed brown hair was gray at the roots. "There" she said, balancing her cup and saucer and carefully lowering herself into the matching stuffed maroon chair that faced the couch. "That's better. Enjoy your tea, and please, help yourselves to a cookie."

Swift leaned forward, took a sip of his tea and put the cup on the plate in his lap. "Miss Partridge, we are here representing the Social Action Committee. We are a church-funded group—"

"Church, yes," Ms. Partridge said cutting in. "I thought you might be from the church. Which church did you say?"

"Ah, well, it's not a church as such. It's more a coalition of churches, like," Swift said.

"I see, yes" she said, sitting up primly in the chair. "You two make such a lovely couple. May I ask, are you married?"

The question caught Swift in mid-sip. "No," he sputtered, "I mean, we aren't . I mean we kinda work together, like, on this project, see."

"Oh yes, I see," she said with a prim smile. "May I ask you both a personal question?"

"Well, a course luv, fire away," said Swift, placing the cup gingerly on the saucer in his lap.

She paused, then asked, "Have you accepted Jesus as your personal savior?"

Swift's face reddened. He looked sideways at Alexis who was sitting quite straight at the edge of the couch admiring her hands which were folded neatly in her lap. "Uh, sorry, I don't know about the personal savior bit, madam, but I am definitely down with Jesus, if you know what I mean."

"I'm sorry, down with Jesus? I don't think I have ever heard that term. Is it English?"

"Well, in a manner of speaking, yes, indeed it is, Miss Partridge. Now, you see, the reason we are here is to talk about problems here on Atherton Street."

"Do you believe that Jesus died for our sins, sir?"

"You mean like it says in the Good Book?"

She nodded, "Yes, that is exactly what I mean, young man."

"Well, yes, I guess so, I mean that's what the priest taught us in Sunday school, but..."

"Priests? Are you a Roman Catholic, sir?" she asked, her smile becoming strained.

"Well, no, Church of England mostly," Swift said and jumped to his feet. "Lovely tea, Miss Partridge, but we've got to be off. Alexis here and I have to talk to everyone on the street this afternoon, so we must be going. Right Alex?"

Miss Partridge stood up. "Really, must you go so soon? We were having such a nice chat!"

"I am sorry, but Mr. Swift is right. We really do have to be going," Alexis added, as she stood up. "Thank you very much for the tea and cookies, Miss Partridge."

Swift tossed Alex a grateful look, took her by the arm and steered her towards the door, then reached in front of her and yanked it open.

"Well, if you must go," Miss Partridge said, fluttering behind them. "What did you say your name was again?"

"Swift—yes, that's right, Teddy Swift." He called back over his shoulder as he hustled Alex down the concrete steps.

"Thanks again for the tea, Miss Partridge. It was lovely!"

Finally they reached the safety of the sidewalk.

"Blimey, I thought we'd never get out of there—that one's not batting on a full wicket, and a Bible basher on top of it. Just what I didn't bloody-well need!" He looked at Alex accusingly. "You could have helped a bit more back there."

"What, me? I'm just an 'umble trainee followin' your lead, guv'nor," she said, suppressing a smile.

Swift regarded her sourly. "Too right," he said.

By the time Alex emerged from the Charles Street MBTA station, just two blocks from the Mt. Vernon Street apartment she shared with her college roommate, it was just past 7:00 pm. After their escape from Miss Partridge, it had taken them another three hours to canvass the rest of the street. By the time they finished, it was fully dark, and they had still missed half a dozen houses. They planned to cover the rest the following afternoon.

She was famished. The air was apple crisp. It seemed more like late October than March. A thousand stars spread across the sky like a jeweled carpet. Her favorite little pizzeria was on the way. Oh well, I might as well enjoy it while I can, she thought. The Back Bay apartment was much too expensive. She had decided to look for a cheaper place in Jamaica Plain. Living right in the neighborhood, getting to know the people. That's important, she had decided. Alex turned right and set off down the narrow, bricked sidewalk beneath the golden glow of antique gas streetlamps, dodging the flow of foot traffic—students hurrying along, gawking window shoppers, well dressed matrons walking tiny dogs, people going in and out of the shops, boutiques and the brick- fronted apartment buildings.

The restaurant was just starting to get busy with the supper trade. She pulled open the door and the tantalizing smells of aged Parmesan and spicy sausage made her stomach groan. The place served Sicilian-style. She ordered a small pie with sausage and mushrooms and a glass of the house red from the dark-haired coed manning the counter. She picked up her glass and sat down at the narrow bar that lined the long display windows facing the street and sipped at her wine while she waited.

Canvassing was hard work. They had spoken to three of the four people on Mr. Roger's list, and they all were as angry as he was and willing to attend a planning meeting. She looked out to the street. Despite all the bustle, it seemed so peaceful here. Quite a contrast! How was it that two such different neighborhoods could co-exist in the same city within just a few miles of each other? The people in Back Bay move freely and go about their business without fear while the people on Atherton Street live—how was it that Mr. Rogers had put it—under siege.

At the staff meeting she had been shocked at the way Swift and Flynt had goaded Sigel, the Jewish organizer, into taking a bunch of tenants and neighborhood people to a slumlord's home on a Jewish religious holiday, but after an afternoon spent listening to the stories of the people on Atherton Street, she was beginning to understand. The house was a firetrap and the slumlord had refused to meet with the people. What else could they do? Politeness was one of the social graces that people in that neighborhood could ill afford. The neighborhood was a combat zone. Look what had happened to Sandy Morgan.

"Door knocking was kind of an art form," Alex mused. "People are naturally suspicious. Most simply wanted to go along and get along. They didn't like to make waves. Still when I mentioned a source of worry, it's was like touching an open sore—in those neighborhoods open sores were everywhere. What Alinsky termed 'rubbing raw the sores of resentment' was really not much more than pointing them out. The resentment—the fear really, was already there, just below the surface."

The waitress slapped the steaming hot pie down in front of her. Alex nodded her thanks.

"Still, can I truly agitate people?" she wondered, as she nibbled delicately around the edge of a hot slice?

Talking to the residents of Atherton Street, Alex had felt their anger and their frustration. She shared that outrage. The trick was to turn that frustration and outrage into effective action, and that meant organization. "Other women had done it. So, why not me?" she asked herself. "Jed Flynt thinks I'm some sort of hothouse flower. Well, I'll just show Mr. Jedediah Flynt! Dad won't understand, that's for sure, but then they hadn't agreed about much of anything in years."

It started with Jacqueline. They had met when Jacqueline transferred into Alex's tony East Side private school mid-semester of her junior year. Alexis had never met anyone like her. She was tall, thin and statuesque with black, almond-shaped eyes and café au lait skin. A couple of inches under six feet, she had long glossy black hair. Alex had just begun to fill out and was uncomfortable with the bold stares and sidewise glances she attracted from the boys in their set. Jacqueline positively reveled in the effect she had on boys.

The new girl was Haitian and the only black girl in the school. The rumor that her mother was the mistress of one of the city's powerful business leaders only added a sense of mystery and increased her allure. The girls in her set disapproved, but in spite, or maybe because of it, Alex had sought her out. Jacqueline lived in a beautiful apartment in a building with a doorman right on Park Avenue.

Jacqueline's mother had an almost regal bearing and was even more beautiful than her daughter, and more distant. Alex felt that she didn't really approve of their friendship. She tried to ignore the rumors. One afternoon during a visit to her new friend's apartment while her mother was out, Alex caught a glimpse of a framed picture on the night table in Jacqueline's mother's bedroom. She recognized the face. He was one of the partners in her father's law firm.

They both loved to ice skate. They often brought their skates to school, took the downtown bus and went skating together at Rockefeller Center.

Like most girls her age, Alex was indifferent to politics. Jacqueline had strong political opinions. She mocked her friend's political naivete and talked a lot about what she called the black struggle.

Alex said how much she admired the work of Martin Luther King.

Jacqueline sneered. "King is an Oreo, black on the outside, white inside, just another step-and-fetchit begging for scraps at the white man's table. Black people aren't interested in scraps," she informed her white classmate. "We want real power. Black Power."

Alexis was shocked. Her mother was secretary of the League of Women Voters, and she and all her friends considered Doctor King a hero.

"Black Power. Like the Black Panthers? Those guys are scary," Alex said.

"Exactly." Jacqueline arched one eyebrow. "Listen, you want the truth about the black struggle?" she challenged. "The Panthers are holding a rally Saturday at a church in the village. Brother Stokely Carmichael is speaking. I'm going. Meet me at the subway station. I'll take you."

"Really, the Black Panthers? Is it safe?" Alex asked.

"Don't worry, you'll be safe. All the brothers know me," Jacqueline said.

They arrived early. Alex told her mother she was going to a movie. They met at the 86th Street Station and took the Number Six train to Bleecker Street and walked to the church. Alex had prepared with care. She wore her oldest jeans and the stonewashed chambray work shirt her mother had bought her at Bergdorf's. She ironed her chestnut hair so it hung straight down to her shoulders.

The seating was in old-fashioned, polished, wooden pews. The girls found seats toward the back of the church. Alex was surprised that the audience was about two-thirds black, but there was bunch of scruffily dressed, white college kids, sprinkled like salt amidst the pepper. Stokely Carmichael took the stage flanked by black men in black leather jackets and berets. He was young and charismatic and delivered a message that challenged everything Alex thought she believed. His tone was emphatic. He didn't ask, he demanded. Carmichael mocked King and all things liberal. The crowd reacted with raised fists and shouts of "right on!"

Alex was profoundly affected by the speech. She sat quietly on the subway ride uptown.

"So, what did you think?" Jacqueline asked.

Alex looked at her friend. "Do you really believe all that stuff about white people committing genocide?" Alex asked.

"Damn straight, I do."

Jacqueline rummaged through her bag and handed Alex Carmichael's book with a sly smile. Alex read it and bought a copy of Malcolm X's autobiography. The more she thought about the concept of Black Power, the more sense it made.

Things came to a head with her parents at one of the elegant, black-tie dinner parties her mother liked to organize. Their apartment had a beautiful dining room overlooking the East River. The guests included several of her parent's friends and business associates. It was just two weeks after Martin Luther King's assassination. Her father was holding forth about King's death and the riots that followed.

"It's all the fault of these Black radicals. Carmichael, Brown, all this talk about Black Power, stirring things up."

There were several nods of agreement around the table. Alex's father was a handsome man with a slightly swarthy complexion and dark hair thinning on top and graying around the edges. He prided himself on his flat stomach and the fact that he still fit into his old college tux.

Alex squirmed in her seat. She could hardly believe what her father was saying.

"King had lost some focus, but he was on the right track. It's the Black Muslims and the Panthers and all that radical talk that got King killed. So, what do they do? Burn down their own neighborhoods. It doesn't make sense," her father said.

"I think people like Rap Brown and Stokely Carmichael are just saying that Dr. King's approach is out of date. White people have power. What's wrong with black people having power?" Alex asked.

Her mother's fork froze in the air above her plate. Her father glared across the table at her as if she had just parachuted in from another planet. Alex surprised herself. She had rarely spoken up before and never disagreed with her father.

After that, family discussions became more heated. Alex' father wanted to know where she had gotten her crazy ideas. Her mother demanded that she stop seeing her friend. Her father was on the school's board, and when she refused,

Jacqueline abruptly disappeared from school. One day after school she went over to Jacqueline's building and spent ten minutes arguing with the intercom, but Jacqueline's mother refused to let her even speak with her friend.

She never saw Jacqueline again. She heard that the girl had been shipped off to boarding school. Alex blamed her father and their relationship worsened. They were always at each other. Her mother tried to referee, but between her clubs and charities, she was hardly ever at home. They were both relieved when Alex graduated and moved to Boston to attend Harvard. She worked at her father's firm in the summers of her junior and senior years, but her parents spent their time at their summer place in the Hamptons. Alex loved the beach, but she stayed at the apartment, and she and her father kept each other at arm's length.

"Oh well," Alex sighed, thinking about their latest quarrel. He had disagreed with her decision to put off law school, stay in Boston and take the job with the organizing project. She loved her father. "Why can't he see that I'm grown up and respect my right to make my own decisions?" she wondered. Chin propped on one hand, the fingers of the other absently entwined itself in her hair and twisted as she gazed at the people walking by outside the restaurant window.

Chapter 7

The Spider & The Fly

Flynt mounted the rusting steel stairway and climbed up to the elevated platform at Egleston Station. The sky was overcast, and the platform was a grubby gray concrete, with a good view northeast toward the high tower of the Prudential Center. Flynt loved riding the T. The station was a mere two blocks down Atherton from his office, and it was a lot easier to hop a downtown train and walk a few blocks over to the restaurant for his meeting with the monsignor than to try to find a parking space in downtown Boston during the middle of the workday.

He emerged from the gloom of State Street Station, blinked up at the sky and watched the wind tear the clouds into ragged scraps. An anemic noon sun was breaking through, but there was a cruel sea breeze blowing in from Boston Harbor. Flynt pulled up the collar of his foul-weather jacket, hunched his shoulders into the wind and headed down Boylston Street towards Newberry.

He was jumpy. The funds that supported the community-organizing project came almost entirely from The Campaign for Human Development, the radical arm of Catholic Charities. The money was a grant from the national campaign, which was very sympathetic to local grass-roots organizing, but the local diocese retained a veto. If the politics became difficult or if the local bishop was hostile, he could deny the grant. All it took to queer things was one or two outraged Catholic bigwigs, whose interests had been stepped on, and the project had stepped on some powerful toes. He had received assurances of support from the national office, but this was his first face-to-face meeting with the archbishop's aide Monsignor Michael Benedetti. When he first hit town, he called the archdiocese in the naive belief he would meet with the archbishop. After several oh so politely worded rebuffs, he was referred to Monsignor Benedetti's office, but those calls too had not been returned. Now,, with Flynt's first- year grant but four months to run before it was scheduled for renewal, the monsignor, the archbishop's point man on campaign affairs, suddenly wished to meet. Flynt wondered what that might portend.

Sandwiched between a boutique and an art gallery, the restaurant was located basement-level five blocks up from Boston Common. It was plainly furnished, not the typical chintzy Chinese restaurant décor. There were no painted lanterns, just black lacquered tables, each with a simple white vase of fresh flowers and a red tablecloth. Scrolls with graceful brush paintings in the black and white Sumi-e style decorated the otherwise plain, white-plaster walls. The lunch hour had passed, and the restaurant was half empty. Flynt had no trouble recognizing the priest, who was already seated.

Men in priestly garb made Flynt feel uncomfortably like a penitent and that, he knew, was precisely the idea. He had been baptized Roman Catholic. His mother, a Congregationalist, had signed the paper agreeing to raise her kids Catholic, and she had dutifully packed Flynt off to a school run by the Sisters of Mercy. But after they split and Flynt's father defaulted on his child-support payments, his mother decided that the contract had been broken. She couldn't afford the tuition anyway on a bookkeeper's salary. Young Jedediah had been promptly enrolled in the local public school.

Monsignor Benedetti rose, and they shook hands. The priest was tall, slim with an olive complexion and a full head of curly, dark hair. A handsome man, Flynt judged him to be about forty. Benedetti had a boyish look. He seemed young for such an exalted position.

"Please, sit down," Benedetti said, playing the host. "I hope you like Szechuan style," he said, smiling affably. "This place is a favorite of mine. I took the liberty of ordering a carafe of hot sake?"

Never much of a drinker, Flynt avoided alcohol in the afternoon. It gave him a headache and brought back to mind unwelcome memories of his father, the all-day, any-day drinker.

"Yes, thank you," he said, smiling. "I spent some time in Okinawa while I was in the Marines. Sake was very popular with the marines stationed on the island."

"I can imagine," Benedetti said. "It is fairly popular amongst my brother priests as well."

The monsignor gingerly filled two delicate china cups from the hot flask, handed one to Flynt and raised his glass, "Kanpai," he said, holding his cup aloft.

Flynt raised his, repeated the toast. They both drank the heated rice wine.

"By the way, may I call you Jed or do you prefer Jedediah?" Benedetti asked, refilling both cups.

"Jed will do fine, Monsignor." Flynt said. "I'm not familiar with this style of Chinese food, but I'm not fussy. I'm sure whatever you order will be fine."

Benedetti nodded. "The chef is Japanese, but he learned his trade in Hong Kong, and Szechuan is all the rage among students these days. By the way, I save the 'Monsignor' for formal occasions, Jed. Please call me Father Michael, or just Michael, if you prefer," he said, gingerly sipping the hot liquid. "I took the liberty of calling ahead and had the chef prepare a few of his special dishes. Szchuan food can be a bit spicy, if that is a problem?"

The organizer shook his head, "Nope, spicy is fine by me, Father," he said. He blew softly on the hot liquid, sipped a bit, felt it slide smoothly down his throat.

"Good. Since this is a semi-official meeting, perhaps you could start off by telling me a bit about yourself, Jed. I have read your file. I understand you have a degree in philosophy?"

"Yes, I guess you could say that I mustered out of the Marine Corps in search of the eternal verities."

"Ah," said Benedetti, smiling, "An intellectual activist. Did you find it? The truth, that is?"

Jed grimaced. "No, not so's you'd notice, monsignor."

"So you became a social activist. I see that you trained in Chicago. What drew you to Alinsky? Most social theory coming out of college campuses these days is pretty hard left."

The organizer smiled and nodded. "Well, you know, Father, what else would a philosophy major do but sign up to save the world? I don't have much faith in these social band-aid programs. They don't seem to work. For emergencies, okay, but what does a handout lead to other than another handout? Alinsky's point of view made sense to me so I went to Chicago and got a job working the streets. Alinsky's method is steeped in what seems to me is man's true, immutable, selfish nature. The Reds believe that a man can be molded, changed, improved. Lenin was a great admirer of Pavlov."

"I see," said Benedetti with a chuckle. "Humanity as a convocation of canines, salivating on cue. I take it that you don't share that view?"

"No, Father, I don't. I believe that man's nature is pretty much hard-wired. You don't scour away instincts forged by a hundred million years of clawing and scratching with a handful of tired slogans or a couple of years in a re-education camp."

"Good point, but how do you square that with our Christian belief that man is made in God's image?" Benedetti asked, gazing at the organizer with a slight smile playing on his lips.

Flynt hesitated. Was this a trap? "I'm an enlisted man, monsignor, I figure questions like that are way above my pay grade."

Flynt looked the monsignor straight in the eyes. He sensed that they were fencing, each wielding a blade, probing for weaknesses, seeking advantage. But it was an unequal match. The priest held the purse strings which meant that Flynt was always playing defense. The man affected an urbane manner and seemed sympathetic to the cause but somewhere, Flynt's instinct told him, there was a false note.

Catholic parishes are turf-based. They grew up in the neighborhood, and the neighborhood grew up around them. So, some of the Church's urban parishes were tied to the fate of decaying city neighborhoods—therefore, the Catholic Church's Campaign for Human Development funded a lot of organizing. Sure, they wanted to save the parishes, but the politics could get complicated.

Flynt recalled a situation that occurred while he was still in training. One of the local parish's more important financial supporters was also a local slumlord. The man complained to the pastor when the leaders of a tenant union Flynt had organized called a rent strike. The pastor's support evaporated overnight.

Lunch arrived, served by a Japanese man in his fifties with a salt and pepper crew cut. Colorful portions in an array of delicate, white porcelain dishes.

The food was tasty and the sake warming. The priest began telling a story about his experiences as an assistant pastor at an urban parish in another diocese. Manipulating his chopsticks with grace, he selected bits and pieces from the tiny plates set between them. His fingers were long and tapered, the nails well-tended, his gestures at times languid, almost feminine and sometimes quick and economical, depending on the point he was making.

Flynt self-consciously removed his left hand from the table and placed it in his lap, like a schoolboy, to hide his own ragged fingertips.

"Isn't it fair to say Alinsky had an almost mystical faith in democracy?" Benedetti asked, abruptly returning to business.

Flynt paused and thought a moment. "Roman Catholic doctrine holds that man possesses free will, and so has the ability to choose between good and evil, correct?"

The monsignor paused, the chopsticks halfway to his mouth and arched one eyebrow. "Indeed, it does," he said.

"And wasn't it St. Paul who reminds us that Adam chose evil—or was it self-knowledge? —and was ejected from the Garden of Eden?" Flynt pressed.

"Yes," Benedetti replied, "if, that is, you take your Old Testament literally."

"Okay, Alinsky's method assumes that man—every man—chooses what he perceives to be good."

Benedetti leaned back and studied Flynt's face closely for a long moment. "Well," he said, breaking out of his apparent reverie with a laugh, "I see that you are a man who likes to cut to the heart of the issue. I am not sure that I agree. Each man chooses not what is good in itself, but that which he perceives to be of maximum benefit to himself. Good and evil are objective truths that exist in the mind of God. Truth is not relative to the needs or desires of the individual man. By the way, you are suggesting that any of man's actions are predictable once you understand where his self-interest lies?" He held up the sake flask. "You'll join me in another, I trust," he said, signaling the waiter. "Philosophizing is thirsty work."

Flynt nodded and laughed, a harsh barking sound. "I wish it were that straight forward, monsignor. A man may define self-interest in many ways and unless you are aware of all the factors…!" He shrugged. "And of course, the theory fails to account for outright stupidity."

The monsignor chuckled. "Stupidity, yes. How often have we judged a man's conduct to be irrational when he has either been convinced by a clever politician or is merely lacking in intelligence? I hadn't thought of that. The idea is that communities have common interests, and the organizer harnesses that common interest to build an organization capable of making change. Good is defined by what benefits the majority?"

"Yes, the greatest good for the greatest number," Flynt said.

"Hum, yes, I suppose. Cesar Chavez was Alinsky-trained, I believe, and he has done a good job with the California grape pickers," Benedetti said, switching tacks.

Flynt nodded. "Chavez trained in Chicago, but he is a bit of an apostate. Strictly speaking, an organizer builds indigenous leadership. He stays in the background and pushes the leadership forward. Chavez became the organizer and the leader all in one—which is okay, I guess, if you are part of the community."

The monsignor cocked his head to one side. "That is really the more natural thing after all, isn't it? Leadership arising out of the community? Sooner or later, the organizer makes his exit, yes?"

"Yes, that is why the primary objective is building a stable organization and that presupposes strong leadership," Flynt replied.

"Your plan, I take it, is to stay in the background?" Benedetti asked.

"Yes, absolutely, my job is to build a local organization," Flynt said, raising both hands in an open gesture. "When an organizer gets too far upfront, he becomes the issue."

Benedetti leaned forward.

"Good! Jed, I hoped you would say that. I want you to know that I have done some checking, and I have heard some very good things. I believe in community organizing and its objectives. It's practical, and it has proven to be effective. I realize that certain tactics can seem extreme, viewed from the outside, but I understand the need, and I hope also that you will think of me as a friend at the diocese. I will support the project in any way that I can."

Flynt leaned back in his chair, lifted his cup and sipped.

"I appreciate that, monsignor," he said, with a real sense of relief.

Monsignor Benedetti raised his hand in dismissal. "Please, put that completely out of your mind. Yes, there have been a few complaints here and there that have reached the archbishop's ear, but I believe that I have managed to convince His Excellency that such things are a measure of success. We recognize that some of our own are part of the problem," he said with a shrug. "Now tell me more about this tragic accident. His Excellency expressed concern that it was tied to the organizing project, and I would like to put his mind at rest."

Flynt sighed.

"There is not that much to tell. We have been concerned about a rash of fires in abandoned properties, especially those just adjacent to the Southwest Corridor. It seems that as soon as we get an abandoned building boarded up, it gets torched. Sandy Morgan noticed the pattern and was investigating."

Flynt held the tiny cup between his thumb and index finger, took a sip and watched the Monsignor's face.

"Pattern, what sort of pattern? Fires in abandoned buildings are not unusual in a transitional neighborhood, surely," Benedetti said, his tone casual.

"No, but we, that is Sandy, noticed that they had been torched a little too quickly, and mostly burned right to the ground with no attempt to even scavenge the copper plumbing."

The priest's eyes looked thoughtful. He raised the tiny cup to his lips. "I agree it doesn't seem to make much sense. Properties like that are pretty much worthless."

Monsignor Benedetti sipped his sake and stared past Flynt as if looking deep into some dark and secret place.

"Who could possibly benefit from burning down worthless properties? Perhaps" he said, putting the cup down next to his plate, and smiling into Flynt's eyes, "it is simply a series of tragic coincidences."

"The Boston Fire Department doesn't think so," Flynt responded. "I talked to one of the deputy chiefs, a guy named Murphy, and he says it's definitely arson."

Why had he said that? Murphy was a valuable source. He didn't know this priest, and he regretted mentioning the chief's name as soon as it came out of his mouth. Murphy had spoken to him in confidence. "Damn! Must be the booze," he thought.

He noticed that the timbre of Benedetti's voice had subtly changed, and the left hand had lost its air of controlled nonchalance, had stopped moving, and now firmly gripped the table's edge.

"Really," the Monsignor said, "The papers said that the girl's body—Sandy, was it?—was found inside the building. Why was that?"

Flynt felt his throat tighten.

"Her name was Sandy, Sandy Morgan, and I have no idea what she was doing in there. I gave her strict orders to keep her distance and call me if there was any sign of trouble," he said, his voice cracking. "And not to go into that abandoned house."

"I understand, my son. You were close?"

Flynt raised his head, held the other man's eyes, and slowly shook his head.

"Close? Not personally, monsignor, but she worked for me, and that makes me responsible. She was just a kid! I sent her out to keep watch on that building, and she was killed—murdered—and I intend to find out who. And why."

Benedetti picked up the sake cup and took a sip. "You were saying that the fire department has classified these fires as arson?" he asked. "Have you decided on your next step?"

Flynt lowered his voice. "Officially the fires have been classified "suspicious." The chief was voicing a personal opinion. "There are politics involved," Flynt said, and moved hurriedly on. "To be honest, I'm not sure what to do next. I've got one of my new people doing research, but she's pretty green, and so far, we haven't turned up much of anything."

"Really, such a tragedy, a young girl dying like that, all alone. It seems so senseless, but you are right, of course, to follow it up. Even if, as I fear, your enquiries may lead nowhere," Benedetti said. His voice radiated sympathy.

He reached across the table and gripped Flynt's forearm. "Thank you, Jed, and please, take care of yourself. You have had a terrible shock. People, particularly young people, do foolish things, and sometimes those things result in tragedy. You are,

I fear, putting too much responsibility on yourself. You will be in my prayers Unfortunately, I have other appointments this afternoon, and I must be getting back to the chancery."

Flynt dropped his eyes, nodded and stood up. He reached for his wallet, but Benedetti raised a hand.

"Please, lunch is on me. I shall inform the archbishop of the substance of our conversation. I am satisfied that you acted correctly, and I don't believe you will hear any more about it. Please be sure to let me know right away, Jed, if there are any further developments.

They clasped hands. "And," Benedetti said, grasping Flynt's shoulder and gazing straight into his eyes, "if there is anything, anything at all I can do to help, Jed, or if you feel the need to talk, about anything," he said, tightening his grip, "anything at all, please feel free to call on me at any time."

"Thank you, monsignor."

The priest removed his hand, reached into the top pocket of his suit coat, withdrew his wallet and handed the organizer a card. "If I am not at the diocese, you can usually reach me at this number. Call me anytime," he said smiling, "any time at all."

The organizer flexed his hand thoughtfully and watched as Monsignor Benedetti shrugged on his long black wool coat and paused by the front door to pay the check before looking back over his shoulder. He raised his hand in a parting wave, then walked through the door and mounted the three steps to street level, turned left and set off with a confident stride down Newbury in the direction of the Public Gardens.

Flynt felt the beginning throb of a headache in his left temple. The meeting had gone well. "Okay, so how come I feel like I just got back from a reconnaissance behind enemy lines?" he asked himself, as he reached to lift his jacket off the back of his chair.

Chapter 8

Redlined

The staff meeting began later than usual. A rather unusual-looking figure sat in the chair next to Flynt. He was at the short end of medium height, dressed in a well-worn tweed jacket, open-collared dress shirt and baggy dress slacks. His head was almost perfectly egg-shaped, which in most men would have been mitigated by his hair, but the Reverend Mr. Trapp had no hair, no hair at all, no hair anywhere on his body, a condition known as *alopecia universalis* that he had contracted at age twelve. His skin was fair, smooth and relatively unlined and that, together with his watery blue eyes, made him look like a giant-sized version of the Gerber baby.

The effect was mitigated to some degree by a broad nose, a deep gravelly voice, a porkpie hat, a pair of black, plastic-rimmed glasses and the ever-present thick, black maduro, which he sometimes used as a pointer when speaking, and which at all other times jutted from one corner of his mouth.

Sheldon Trapp was from Chicago, an ordained, non-practicing Methodist minister who was lead organizer for National

People's Action. Trapp had come to town to do a training session for Jed's staff on the effects of redlining in urban neighborhoods. NPA was the vanguard of the national fight to outlaw the practice and was on the lookout for a Boston group to add to his coalition.

Flynt introduced him around the table and then sat back to listen and learn.

Trapp's presentation was short, pithy and to the point. After he finished, Alexis Jordan put up a tentative hand. "Why do the banks do it? Aren't they the ones who lent the owners the money in the first place?"

Trapp bowed formally from the waist. "Thanks, I was hoping somebody would ask that question," Trapp said, waving his cigar in the air. "Saves me from asking it myself," Trapp said, smiling at Alex.

"The banks' argument is that they have a fi-du-ci-ar-y responsibility. You'll hear that a lot. Basically, it means that their stockholders expect them to make money. Often, they define it as meaning to the exclusion of all else. A neighborhood in decline increases their risk. Investing people's money carries with it an obligation to reduce risk, and it's a helluva lot less risky to lend in the suburbs. You've heard of 'white flight'—well, you might call this green flight—because now it's the money that's fleeing to the suburbs! Problem with their argument is this: Once the neighborhood is redlined, it's doomed. Property values crash, blockbusters and slumlords move in with cash offers and buy cheap. The bank's decision becomes a self-fulfilling prophecy. You wanna sell? You take mister slumlord's low-ball cash offer."

"It's hard to argue with that. I mean, it is the bank's money, isn't it?" Alexis asked.

Trapp leaned forward and extracted his cigar. "No, darling, it's not, and that's the supreme irony here. Look, banks have neighborhood branches—why? They do it to get neighborhood deposits. Who are the depositors?

"The people in the neighborhood?" Alex suggested tentatively.

"Exactly! The same homeowners! They are getting screwed, and the banks are using their own money to do the screwing. For most working and middle-class people, the major part of their net worth is the equity in their homes, and, remember, it was a bank that lent them the money to buy that home in the first place! Make sense?"

"Yes, but don't they do some sort of study before deciding that a neighborhood should be redlined?" Sigel asked.

Trapp snorted, "Not that I ever heard of! Remember, according to the bankers, there is no such thing as redlining, which, by the way, was originally invented by the federal government. What I've been told is that they do a drive by. See a couple of dilapidated properties, maybe a black face or two, and wham! Once one bank does it, the others follow, then the insurance companies, and kiss the neighborhood goodbye."

"Really," Alex said, and sat back thinking.

"So what you're saying is that redlining is the underlying cause of bleedin' neighborhood decline," said Teddy Swift.

"Bullseye!," Trapp said, pointing his cigar at Swift. "Give that man a kewpie doll. You guys are like the little Dutch boy. Remember the story? He stuck his finger in the dike and stopped a flood. Well, in this case, no matter how many little fingers you stick in the dam, it will keep springing more leaks because the underlying economic structure has been kicked out from under you.

"My people, the homeowners in the neighborhood, blame the tenants," Sigel said. "Welfare mothers with no man in the house. The kids run wild and wreak havoc—the single mothers can't control their own kids. That's what Molly Reagan said at a planning meeting the other day, and just about everybody agreed with her."

"Yeah," said Trapp "that's what's staring people in the face. So they don't look any further. Remember these neighborhoods were designed for owner-occupancy. Concentrate hundreds of low-income tenants, usually single mothers, in one place and as your leaders pointed out, there are bound to be problems. But that's a symptom not a cause. Once they come together and compare notes the homeowners begin to see tenants as human beings with similar problems, shift their focus to the slumlord, and maybe stop blaming their fellow victims."

Flynt cut in. "There was this one case when the project first got started. You remember, Swift? Twenty-four-unit apartment building right down the street on Amory. The landlord bought the property for twenty-five thousand down at a city tax foreclosure sale. The previous owner hadn't done any maintenance or paid his property taxes. Somehow, he got all the tenants on protected rents, meaning the welfare department paid him directly so no collection hassles. When we traced back the ownership, we found out that the former owner lived at the same address as the present owner, and guess what, the guy is a Boston housing inspector. The guy was doing nothing and netting twenty-five thousand a year. "

"Wow," Alex said, "that's a pretty good return on investment."

"What you are saying is that we are all just shoveling shit against the bleedin' tide," Swift said.

Trapp took his cigar out of his mouth, examined it for a moment then smiled.

"Eloquently stated, my British friend!" He sat back and regarded the group.

"Anybody got any idea about how often the average mortgage turns over?"

Everyone looked at each other.

"No? Well, it's seven and a half years," Trapp said.

"Less than one generation," Sigel said.

"Right, so figure ten to fifteen years. That's about the life expectancy of a healthy neighborhood once it's been redlined. From what your boss tells me," he said, glancing at Flynt, "parts of Jamaica Plain are maybe halfway there."

Trapp placed his cigar firmly in the side of his mouth and folded his arms.

No one said anything. Flynt looked around the table, then gazed at Trapp who raised a non-existent eye-brow. "They're a bright bunch," Trapp's glance said. "They get it!"

Chapter 9

Breakthrough

Alexis Jordan stood next to Jed and watched the organizers file out of the staff meeting. "Jed, can I talk to you a minute, privately?" she asked in a soft voice.

"Shit," he thought, "not even a month and she's ready to quit. Was the staff meeting that scary, or was it the door knocking?" Flynt wondered.

Flynt was dog-tired, but he figured he should at least buy Trapp a beer or two before bed. He motioned Trapp through the door ahead of him. "Shel, why don't you go on down to Doyle's with Swift and Sigel. I'll meet you in a few."

"Right," Trapp said.

"Okay, Jordan," he said, pushing the door closed and lowering himself to a chair. "What's up?"

"It's about those burned out lots. I think I have something interesting."

"Ok," Flynt said, hiding a real sense of relief. "Great, talk to me!"

"Well, the survey is done. It was really pretty simple. A few days walking the streets, and I cataloged fifty-six vacant lots and burned out properties within three blocks of the corridor. I cross-checked the addresses against the tax rolls and got a list of the owners. Then I went down to the district fire station and spoke to Chief Murphy. He's a very nice man, by the way. Said to say, 'hi.' He gave me a list of suspicious house fires during the past eighteen months, and every one of them is on the list."

"That's fast work." Flynt was impressed in spite of himself.

"Thank you, and, Jed, guess what? All but five of the torched properties have been sold within the last year, usually a month or two after a fire. All the ones that changed hands flank the Southwest Corridor, and from what I can make out so far, each of the owners was approached by an attorney and offered a low cash price."

"How the hell did you find all that out?"

"I talked to one guy on the phone and contacted two of the former owners. I used a fake name, pretended that I didn't know they had sold and told them I was interested in buying. The thing is, they all told a similar story. In each case they were approached by one of two lawyers both from the same law firm. One of the men gave me the lawyer's card and several remembered the name of the firm."

"What about the five that didn't sell?" he asked.

"From what I can make out, nobody can locate the owners."

"One of the buyers was an attorney named James McLaughlin; the other, Thomas O'Neill. The thing is, believe it or not, there is no lawyer registered by the bar association of the Commonwealth named James McLaughlin. There are two Michaels and a Robert but no James. There are two Thomas O'Neill's; one's dead, and the other is presently incarcerated at the Bridgewater State Correctional Center serving a ten-year term for fraud. Here's the card," she said, putting it down on the table in front of Flynt. "The law firm doesn't exist. I checked the address. It's a Dunkin' Donuts shop in the South End."

Flynt was alert, his fatigue forgotten. "Interesting—so who was the buyer?"

"Albion Partners, a Massachusetts Realty Trust."

"Thirty-two properties.... and who owns Albion Partners?"

"That's as far as I've gotten so far, but the easy part is over. The rest is going to take time. Trusts can be very difficult to penetrate. Chances are the next step will take me to another lawyer, a real one this time, one who will simply refuse to tell me who the principals are. The next one will probably be off-shore. If they really want to hide, there are several small countries—the Bahamas, Lichtenstein, Mauritius —that derive a substantial part of their revenue by offering a safe haven to people and corporations looking to act anonymously."

Flynt looked skeptical. "Isn't that illegal?"

Alexis shook her head. "No, a corporation is a legal entity just like a person, and, besides that, hiding your identity is not a crime. It's pretty clear that there is some sort of conspiracy here. The question is what kind of conspiracy, and who is behind it?

Flynt studied his new researcher for several moments. She was an unknown quantity, but he was impressed. The information proved that there was something going on.

"Alexis, what we are discussing I want you to keep strictly between us. I don't want you to talk about it, even with the other staff. Understand?"

She smiled quickly, then nodded gravely, her eyes on his face.

"Look, I can't make it out. If the price is low enough, an absentee landlord might buy and rent out a property, but nobody's gonna build. The numbers just don't work and nobody will finance it! So why would anyone buy these seemingly worthless lots? If we can find out the who, maybe we can get to the why."

"Well, I have sort of a theory about that," she said, her tone tentative.

Flynt laughed and threw up his hands. "Harvard University, training tomorrow's leaders. Go ahead!"

Alex made a face. "Look! Here's a map I made, with the derelict properties that have been purchased by Albion marked in red. You see the cluster along the edge of the Southwest Corridor."

"Yeah, great map, looks almost as if someone was trying to widen the corridor. What's your theory?"

"Well, if you think about it, what is the Southwest Corridor?" she asked.

"Well, what it was supposed to be was a six-lane highway running right through Boston which would unite Route 95 north and south and produce a single uninterrupted highway running from Maine to Florida."

"Yes, but forget the history for a minute. How would you describe it, like physically?"

Flynt laughed, "What is this, a Socratic dialogue?"

"No, but this is how I got to my theory, Jed. So please, just bear with me a minute, okay?"

Flynt shrugged, "Okay, right now what we've got is a fifty-plus acre construction site, a no-man's land running right through the center of the neighborhood from downtown all the way out to Route 128.

"Okay, right," she said with a quick nod. "Fifty empty acres of land in the middle of downtown Boston with potentially six lane access to a major highway. That has got to be worth a lot of money, probably millions of dollars!"

Flynt stared at Alexis for a few moments. "Well—yeah, I never thought of it that way—but, yeah, it makes sense. I mean—a sports stadium, a factory, something like that. Right now there is a planning group. It's called the Southwest Corridor Commission. Frank Sargent, our esteemed governor, set it up after the protests stopped the road. It's made up of planners and neighborhood reps. Problem is, the community representatives can't seem to agree on anything.

"So you think my theory makes sense?"

"Yes, Alex, so far it is the only thing that I've heard that makes any sense at all. Politically the city is in flux. Hizzhonor Kevin White is running for a third term, and he's going to have a tough fight against this other Irish democrat, Joe Timilty. Governor Sargent is up for reelection, too, against Michael Dukakis. So, somebody with beaucoup bucks waltzes in, and with a politically popular project, say a hospital, museum, whatever. All that lovely acreage up for grabs, and suddenly the land around it is worth a fortune.

"I was hoping you wouldn't think I was crazy," she said.

"Crazy? No, not at all! Look, forgive the sarcasm, okay. It's been a long day. So, here's the plan, Alex. Comb the papers, find out what big projects have been discussed in the last, say, five years. Start with the Globe and the Herald. If anyone has submitted anything to the Southwest Corridor Commission that will be a matter of public record. Check at the state house. Good work, you're a genius, kid! Now come on, let's go to Doyle's. I owe you a beer."

"Thank you. I wasn't sure I was invited," she said.

Flynt stood up. "Hey, you're part of the staff, right? Of course, you're invited. Come on!"

"Yes. Yes, I guess I am," she said, and followed Jed out the door, very pleased with herself.

Chapter 10

Room Mates

"So how'd it go?" Carol asked without turning around as Alexis padded into the kitchen the next morning and sat down at the old, oak dining table.

Carol was always up early and sometimes entirely too chipper, Alexis decided. The after-staff session at Doyle's had run late, and the last few beers had been a blur. It was Saturday, and Alexis was looking forward to at least a quiet morning before she had to meet Teddy Swift for more doorknocking.

"Good morning, Carol," Alexis said yawning. Like her roommate Alex wore a thick terry cloth bathrobe and slippers. Carol was stationed in front of the kitchen sink, making coffee in the new French press coffee maker her mother had given her as an apartment-warming gift.

"Good morning, yourself," Carol said as she walked over and placed a steaming mug in front of her.

Just then the table began to vibrate, and the whole apartment shook like an old man with the palsy. The coffee from Alex's cup slopped all over the table. The two girls turned to the window above the sink just in time to see a line of bright orange subway cars, interiors awash in bright yellow light, flash by like a film playing on fast-forward, the roar not ten feet from the apartment window. As the downtown train raced by Alex could read the ad posters above the car window and made momentary eye contact with a hard-eyed, buxom black chick decked out in gold chains and a purple leotard with a plunging neckline.

"You're kidding, right?" Carol said when Alex first told her about the apartment. "Washington Street, eight feet from the El?"

It was the best they could afford with Carol still out of a job. Alex had insisted on living in Jamaica Plain. All they had between them was a little money saved from graduation gifts, and Alex's substandard earnings from the organizing project.

The apartment was roomy. It had two bedrooms, a living room and an eat-in kitchen, and the rent would have been way beyond their reach in any of the better neighborhoods. The oak floors had been newly varnished. The cabinets, the stove and refrigerator were new, and the apartment was completely furnished. Washington Street was one of the seediest sections of JP, but Carol had the only car, and Alex liked it because it was within walking distance of the project's office.

"Well, you've done it now Alex. We are really down with the people. You know I'm starting to get used to the trains," Carol said, "I mean its only one every twenty minutes, and the Orange Line shuts down at eleven. It's that first downtown train at six in the morning I can't quite get used to."

"Better than an alarm clock!" Alex took a sip from the half empty cup. "Hey, this is really good coffee," she said.

"Yeah, right, who needs peace and quiet," Carol said, sourly mopping the spilled liquid off the table with a dishrag.

"So, you'd better speak fast. You've got eighteen minutes by my watch before the next train?"

"Right! It went pretty well. I took him aside at the end of the meeting and laid it all out."

"And he said? Come on, Ali!" Carol knew that she hated that name. "Tell!"

Alexis pushed her hair back out of her face and gazed up past her friend and out the kitchen window. Beyond the rusty raised platform of the El, dark clouds hovered above the high tapered brick chimney of the factory across the street. It was shaping up to be a typical gray New England winter day.

"He was impressed. In fact, he said I was a genius. 'You're a genius, kid!' —if you want his exact words. And he called me Alexis."

"Kid, huh? You let him get away with that?"

"Well, I am quite a bit younger than he is," Alex said, yawning.

"Yeah, right, what, five years? Is he married?"

"Six, I think, and no he's not married—divorced, got a couple of kids he doesn't talk much about."

"So when are you going to fuck him?"

Alexis shook her head. "Honestly, Carol, sometimes you can be, so, so vulgar."

"Oh, pardon me, Little Miss Muffet," Carol laughed. "Get off your tuffet, whatever the hell that is. Remember who you're talking to. It's me, Carol, bosom buddy, sharer of all secrets. I seem to recall a certain grad assistant you set your sights on. Remember, second semester, junior year? He held out, what, three weeks before you had him in the sack."

"Two weeks, and that was different."

"Different? Yeah, right, you know you have a thing for this Flynt guy."

"Look, for the record, I'm not interested in him, and, besides, he's my boss."

Carol turned back and smiled at her friend. "According to you, you weren't interested in the graduate assistant either until you fucked his brains out," she said, and turned back to the sink.

Alexis stuck out her tongue at Carol's back. "Look, can we drop it, Carol, really? I was up half the night, I'm tired and what I really need right now is some peace and quiet and a nice hot cup of coffee."

"Peace and quiet? You've still ten minutes before the next train. Hey, maybe we'll meet someone interesting on the uptown leg. Your father called, by the way."

"Oh shit, really, when?"

"Last night. He wanted to know why you were working so late."

Alex sighed. "I forgot. I'm supposed to call in once a week. He treats me like I'm still in high school."

Carol folded her arms and leaned back in the chair. "He's worried about you. Asked why I thought you were wasting your time doing social work."

"Oh great, that again. Community organizing is not social work. What did you tell him?"

"I said I didn't know because I don't. I mean, with your grades you're a shoo-in at Harvard Law or Yale even. He think's you've got a brilliant career ahead of you, and I agree," Carol said.

"Yes, I know. I should be looking for a nice guy from a good family with good prospects and be thinking about settling down, having kids, right?"

"Well!"

"B-o-r-ing! The guys we went to school with? You've got to be kidding, Carol."

"What's so wrong…Take Jim Toliver for instance, what's so wrong with him?"

"Come on Carol, so self-satisfied. All that expensive education, and all they're interested in is climbing that ladder of success. The 18th century colonial, a Mercedes 190SL, the country club! It's like our parents and all our friends are living in a climate-controlled bubble. Down here in the real world, people are in pain. Things have got to change, Carol! Don't you feel an obligation to be a part of that?"

"You mean go on marches, carry signs? Not really. My family never had the kind of money yours has. I'm a scholarship kid, remember? You grew up with everything. My old man started off as an auto mechanic. Hanging out around the country club pool sounds pretty good to me."

"Come on Carol…"

Carol raised her hand. "Stop, okay? Look, I know we used to talk about all that stuff back in college, but that's all over. I want my slice of the American dream. What's wrong with that? Besides, why are you so concerned about what happens to those people? You don't have anything in common with them. Are you really going to spend the rest of your life working on Lamartine Street?"

"Look, you wouldn't understand, so let's not fight about it, okay? Got any plans for the weekend?" Alex asked anxious to change the subject.

Carol flopped down in the chair across from her friend. "It just so happens I have. You haven't been around much, so I haven't been able to tell you, but you remember Billy, the guy from Sigma Nu I went out with sophomore year?"

"Yeah, he was a senior, right? The stuck-up one," Alex shouted, trying to compete against the rising roar of the oncoming train.

"Sorry, what?" Carol shouted.

"I thought you dumped him, or he dumped you," Alex shouted back. Suddenly the train was past and the vibrations rapidly receding. "I don't remember which," she said lowering her voice.

Carol made a face. "Yeah, well, he went on to law school, and now he's an associate in a big Boston law firm. Great prospects. He'll be a partner in a year or two, or so he says. Anyhow, he called last week out of the blue and invited me out to dinner. It was great! We really connected. We're driving down to the Cape this afternoon. He's got a new Healey 3000, and his parents have a house in Hyannis. They're in Europe, so don't wait up," she said arching one eyebrow. "I'll be back late Sunday night."

"You know it would be nice if a person could sleep beyond six thirty in the morning around here." Carol said.

"Well, you remember what Richard Nixon said?"

"Tricky Dick? No, but something tells me I'm about to find out."

"'The American dream does not come to those who fall asleep.' That's a direct quote," Alex said.

"Oh great, that helps a lot. A good night's sleep would help even more."

Alex arched one eyebrow. "Okay, have fun and try to get a little sleep on Cape Cod," Alex said.

Chapter 11

The Leadership

Flynt's eyes watered in the smoke. Willie-Joe liked to hold meetings at his house to head off complaints about his chain-smoking. He shook another Marlboro from the pack and lit it with the stub, then ground out the stub in the big glass ashtray that overflowed by his elbow. He was a tall dark-haired attorney with a receding hairline. His full name was William Joseph Patrizzi, but after a few beers, he usually referred to himself as Willie-Joe. He wore a white dress shirt, sleeves rolled up. The jacket of his blue pinstriped suit was draped over the back of the kitchen chair.

"Don't misunderstand, Mr. Trapp. We all know what you say is true."

Trapp had just given his redlining pitch to a committee of neighborhood leaders Flynt had put together.

Patrizzi waved his hands in the air. "Hell, I went through the exact thing myself when I bought this place four years ago," he said, gesturing around the small brick townhouse. "My banker looked me right in the eye and said, 'forget it, Patrizzi.

We are not giving you a mortgage in that neighborhood.' That was it, word for word. Luckily, an old Coast Guard buddy of mine supervises the loan department over at the Five. He fixed me up. My question is: what chance do we have going up against the banks?"

"We won some concessions in Chicago," Trapp said. "Seems to me the question is, when it comes time to sell this place, what're the chances you'll get back your investment if we don't try?"

Patrizzi sat back and thought about that. Ethnically it was hard to pin the big man down. In his late thirties, with a paunch that overflowed his belt, a broad face and fleshy nose and lips, he looked vaguely Italian, but as he explained to Flynt when they first met, he was, in fact, a mutt. "One of my ancestors jumped the fence. Hell, two of 'em did. My mother's family is WASP," he said in his deep baritone. "Christ, don't misunderstand, I'm an Italo-Yankee-Jew, and damn proud of it."

Sitting across the kitchen table from Patrizzi was Mary Kavanaugh, a middle-class Irish housewife in her early forties. She was slender and stood only a bit over five feet tall. Mary had a wide heart-shaped face, lovely skin, a generous mouth, sparkling blue eyes and a mischievous sense of humor which hid a lively intelligence and an adamantine will. A practical idealist, once she made up her mind that something was wrong, she set out to change it. Mary and Frank, her husband, were urban pioneers, one of a small cadre of well-educated, native Bostonians who had reversed the trend and moved back from the suburbs to the city, partly to take advantage of bargain basement prices on some of the venerable older homes and partly because they loved Boston. She had proven her leadership skills with the Stop I-95 Committee, and Flynt was doing his best to cultivate her.

Flynt had managed to get one of Sandy Morgan's and one of Sigel's block leaders plus two other old-time neighborhood activists to test, to see if regular people would relate to the redlining issue. Don Gaffer was an ordained minister, short, stocky, with a balding head and a graying goatee. Gaffer was the prime mover behind a new non-profit real estate company called City's Hope.

The group's objective was to draw more urban pioneers back into Jamaica Plain. Gaffer had spent months recruiting and massaging bankers who lived mostly in the upscale Jamaica Pond and Jamaica Hills neighborhoods.

"Here's my question, Mr. Trapp," Gaffer said. "Assuming that the banks are redlining, and you are able to stop it using your confrontational tactics, where do you propose to find the families to purchase these properties?"

"You don't believe the neighborhoods are being redlined?" Trapp asked.

"I believe there are more sellers than buyers. People are moving to the suburbs. It's a national trend. They're tired of the crime, the dirt, corrupt city government and poor-quality schools. Correct those conditions, and you create demand. Yes, banks are reluctant to lend, but can you blame them? It's difficult to find qualified buyers. That's the crux of the problem."

Trapp listened respectfully, then responded in a soft voice. "Well, Don, I can only tell you what happened on the North Side of Chicago. Like Jamaica Plain, it was a nice neighborhood, with well-kept houses, tree-lined streets. Then the banks stopped lending. The blockbusters moved in. First, they engineered it so that a black family bought a house on the block. Then, they went door to door suggesting that the white homeowners sell out before the blacks took over.

"They bought houses, good houses which had been lovingly maintained for decades. Bought for pennies on the dollar, they sub-divided and moved in a few welfare tenants on protected rents. From there it accelerated, property values dropped to zero. Ten years later you wouldn't recognize the neighborhood. The old residents had fled, there was trash in the streets, houses were falling apart, crime rates skyrocketed, and the speculators got rich."

"I think Don believes that City's Hope will bring in young families willing to buy the old homes and keep them up," Mary Kavanaugh said.

"With all due respect, Mrs. Kavanaugh," Trapp said gently, "that is like shutting the barn after the horse has gotten loose. Don't get me wrong. I think Don is onto something, but City's Hope can't operate in a zero-financing environment. How many abandoned properties are there in Jamaica Plain right now?"

Eyes turned to Flynt. "We made a count, and counting partly burned-out buildings, there are sixty-eight, all in the central neighborhood. About a third are a total loss. About a third still need to be secured, boarded up. From what we can make out, the life expectancy of a vacant property, especially adjacent to the Southwest Corridor, is about ten days. First, the windows are broken, then the copper piping is stripped out, and then the derelicts move in—or it's torched."

"Sixty-eight? That's a lot of housing stock at risk," Trapp said. "Something is going on, Don. If it's not disinvestment, what is it?"

Gaffer scowled. "Look, no one wanted these properties, or they weren't marketed properly. That's why they ended up abandoned. That's what our non-profit agency is set up to do. We will market these properties before they are abandoned."

"Aren't you making an assumption, Don?" Trapp asked. "What makes you so sure there were no buyers? Maybe there was no financing. Do the banks publish statistics on applicants they turn down, or have you checked with the former owners?"

"Mind if I say something?" Molly Reagan looked anxiously from face to face. Molly had lived in Boston for most of her life, but her voice retained the soft lilt she brought from the old country.

"Please, Mrs. Reagan, go ahead," Patrizzi said.

"Well, since you are asking about loans, I live on Green Street. Just up the street from where, you know, that terrible tragedy, that lovely girl, Sandy, died in that awful fire," she said, pausing to compose herself. "Well, my husband and I tried to get a loan from one of the local banks to winterize our porch, you know put in aluminum windows and such. Well, the bank said the house wasn't worth it, and they wouldn't give us the loan. We got good credit, too. I always see that we pay the mortgage on time. So I said to my husband, Bill, we should go to the Boston Five. So we did, and they turned us down flat."

"Well, that is something," Mary Kavanaugh, said looking around the table, "and it sounds like redlining to me."

"Another thing, my friend Barbara Last, you know her, Mr. Flynt. She lives over in that little house back of that building the block club is trying to get torn down, over near 271 Lamartine Street."

Flynt nodded. "Yes, I do. She's a real fire-cracker, one of the most active people in the group."

Molly Reagan smiled. "That's Barbara for you. So it is— well, she's getting along now, and her daughter Jean, she lives with her. Well, Jean was going to buy the house, you know, so's Barbara could have a little security in her old age? Now I don't know what kind of credit she's got. Jean was kinda wild when she was younger, but she's got a good job, and the bank wouldn't give her a loan to buy the place."

"Does anybody keep statistics on this sort of thing?" Kavanaugh asked.

"I can answer that one," said Trapp. "In a word, no. That's why National People's Action has been sponsoring a disclosure bill in Congress for the past two years. The bill would mandate that the National Home Loan Bank Board require all federally chartered savings and loans to report their lending patterns annually, broken down by U. S. census tract. So far, we have gotten nowhere. Both the industry and the feds and have come out against our bill."

"What's the problem?" Patrizzi asked.

"According to the feds, there is no problem, and no such thing as redlining. The reporting requirements would put an expensive and undue burden on the banks. The chairman also said that community people wouldn't know what to do with the information!"

Kavanaugh's eyes flashed with anger. "Really! Disclosure sounds like a very good idea to me!" Kavanaugh looked over and caught Gaffer's eye. "Don?"

Gaffer looked down at his hands and nodded. "Yep, I guess that would prove the case one way or another."

"Yes, and that is why the banks are fighting it," Flynt said. "The data could be easily correlated with other census data. Problem is a federal law wouldn't do us much good. Apparently, there are no S & L's in Massachusetts. Research tells us that most of the mortgages in the Commonwealth come through state-chartered savings banks," Flynt said.

"Really," Mary said.

"Yes. You've all met Alex Jordan," Flynt said. "She has been doing some research on mortgage lending in the Common-wealth. I brought her along today to share her results. That okay, Mr. Chairman?"

"Whoa, slow down now," Patrizzi said raising his hands. "I'm not in charge here. I only agreed to chair this meeting because it's here at the house. Go ahead, Alex."

"Thanks, Mr. Patrizzi," Alex said shifting forward in her chair. "From what I have been able to determine, ninety-five percent of all mortgages in Massachusetts are granted by state-chartered savings banks. Massachusetts is just about the only state with zero federally chartered savings and loans."

"Well, that's interesting. Who regulates the state savings banks?" Kavanaugh asked.

"They're regulated by the state banking commission, and the state banking commissioner is appointed by the governor. According to the Massachusetts General Laws, at least as I read the statute..." she said, thumbing through her notes. "Here, it is. The banking commissioner has complete authority over state-chartered banks and can require that the banks do just about anything. I've xeroxed the statute," she said, handing the sheets to Mary, "I've brought along plenty of copies if you want to read through it yourself."

"The banking commissioner can order disclosure without legislation?" Don asked.

"That's how I read it," Alex said.

"As far as we know, yes," Jed said. "I sent a copy of the statute to Willie-Joe to take a look at it. What do you think, counselor?"

Willie-Joe nodded, "The statute is pretty straight forward. Based on the language, I believe she has the power," he said.

Trapp put in, "NPA got disclosure in Chicago. Mayor Daley himself came to our annual meeting and said he would write a letter to the banks demanding that any bank that did business in Cook County disclose. He did it, too. The banks fell right into line, and the facts proved that redlining was rampant on the on the South Side."

"In this case, we might demand it statewide," Flynt said.

"Yes, why not? I'm sure the problem isn't restricted to Boston," Mary said.

"I guess that's it," Patrizzi said. "We put together a community meeting, invite the state banking commissioner and ask him politely to require disclosure by census tract. Agreed?" he asked, gazing around the table.

"It's a she, actually," said Flynt. "Her name is Louise Winthrop Gray. My question is, what do we do if she says no? If she won't attend our community meeting?"

"Good question," Patrizzi said.

"One this committee should discuss internally before we invite the commissioner to meet with us," Flynt said.

"Jed is right, but let's not forget, next year is an election year," Mary said. "With Dukakis running, it's going to be a tough race for Sargent, so if we send a copy of our letter to the governor's office, I don't think we will have too much trouble getting the commissioner to meet with us. If we can introduce redlining into the political debate, we should be in a good position to play the two candidates against one another and get what we need."

The table was silent. Everyone gazed at Mary while they absorbed what she had said.

Mary looked around. "What's everybody looking at?" she asked.

"Damn astute analysis, if you ask me!" Patrizzi said.

"Just because I'm short and female, doesn't mean I don't have a brain," Mary said.

"Lots of people make that mistake with Mary," Gaffer said.

"We've got just eight months until the election. If we form a committee and move quickly, I think we can inject the issue into the campaign and get the press," Flynt said.

"Ok, let's do it, and I think our committee just elected a chairman," Patrizzi said nodding toward Mary. All in favor," he said, raising his hand.

Chapter 12

The Agenda

"Whuddya think?" Flynt asked raising his arms in an expansive gesture. "Being as you are from Chicago, I figured I would introduce you to a real Irish pub. Doyle's is one of the oldest in Boston."

Flynt and Trapp sat across from one another in one of the narrow booths with a pair of frosted mugs between them. Doyle's Cafe had been a neighborhood hangout since 1882. It was Boston's answer to a real Irish Pub, nondescript brick on the outside. Its well-worn hardwood floors peeped out from broken linoleum squares. It had a foggy mirror above a mahogany bar, golden oak slats and wainscoting.

"Another Irish bar? What joy—you think we don't have Irish in Chicago? The city is filthy with 'em. You ever hear of Mayor Daley or the Irish Mafia?" Trapp asked, gazing around at the framed faded photos and posters that lined the booth.

"This is one of the few bars in Boston that serves Guinness by the pint," Flynt retorted.

Trapp took a sip of the dark brew and shuddered. "Guinness? Who but a bloody Mick would drink this vile stuff? I'm a Miller man myself."

"Miller, the champagne of bottled piss. My mistake. Allow me to order you one—or maybe we should convert this to a black and tan."

"Now you're talking." Trapp signaled the waitress, a short rosy-cheeked blond named Jesse ambled over to the table.

"What can I get for ya, gents?" Jesse asked, dipping forward just enough to give them an eyeful of the joys struggling to free themselves from the thin elastic material of her low-cut leotard. She listened, turned her head and smiled seductively at Flynt. Then scooped up Trapp's half-filled mug and strode toward the bar.

"Looks like you've got another fan. Don't know what these women see in you," Trapp said, twisting his lips in mock disgust.

"Who, Jesse? Just a friend," Flynt said. "You think we made a good start with the leadership group"?

"Yeah, I guess, but what's with that Gaffer guy?"

"Protecting his turf!"

"He's a local, right?"

"Right, but not a native, more of an urban pioneer type. Lives in The Parkside, like Mary. Bought a big house cheap and moved into the neighborhood six or seven years ago."

"What fucking planet has he been living on? He's in real estate, and he's never heard of redlining?"

"Oh, he knows about it, all right. It's more about the turf. He was against bringing in the organizing project. Figures if he plays nice with the banks they will open the spigot."

"Yeah, right they might throw him a bone while the neighborhood goes down the shit-shute."

Jesse walked up to the table and slid a mug in front of Trapp. He smiled his thanks, picked it up and took a long pull.

"Now that is a tolerable brew," he said, wiping the froth from his lips with the back of his hand.

"Glad you approve."

"Gaffer is going to be trouble."

"Yeah, I know, but I had to invite him. He and Mary Kavanaugh are good friends. They worked together on the road issue."

"I like Kavanaugh. She's sharp," Trapp said.

"Subtle, too. You see how she pushed Gaffer into agreeing about the disclosure issue?"

"Yup, what's her agenda?"

Flynt shrugged.

Trapp scowled, "Come on, everybody's got an agenda."

"Well, she and her husband have probably got every dime they own in that big Victorian they own on Olmsted Road."

"You think that's all?"

"There's a rumor that some of the liberal types want her to run against Craven, the state rep. Guy's a Neanderthal," Flynt said.

"That figures. What about Patrizzi?"

"Lawyer, originally from the North Shore. Bought that townhouse about five years ago. Kind of a showboat, but fast on his feet He'll be good with the press."

Trapp removed the cigar, studied it for a moment and replaced it in the right corner of his mouth. "Using untested leadership is chancy," he said.

Flynt took a sip and held the mug at chin level and smiled inwardly at Trapp's manner. Like many of the older generation of organizers, guys who had actually worked for Alinsky, Trapp had adopted his mannerisms and way of speaking. "Yeah, I hear you, but I think that Mary is reliable She has been active in the neighborhood for years. She's good people, and this is a damn complex issue. It's the best I could do on short notice."

Both organizers knew from experience that the best leaders were forged in the crucible of a good local fight. Organize a block around an immediate need, toss them up against a city bureaucrat, and see if they are tough-minded enough to wade through the bullshit and prevail. Power, even a little power, is a heady drug, particularly to someone unused to it.

On the other hand, the pure pig-headedness sufficient to win a small victory was not enough to deal with an issue as complex as disinvestment. The leadership had to be intelligent, flexible and tough. Trapp's mandate was to build a national coalition, Flynt knew, so he stifled his misgivings.

Trapp lifted his glass in salute: "Issues come from the people," he said with a sly smile.

"Oh, please don't give me that shit, Trapp. We're doing our best here to bring this issue to the people,"

Trapp shrugged. "Right! Problem is, if you wait until the local block-club leaders connect all the dots, Jamaica Plain will be a wasteland. Gale Cincotta, the president of NPA, is from Austin. That's the biggest neighborhood in Chicago. She was active in the PTA when I met her. I was working for Tom Gaudette, building OBA, The Organization for a Better Austin.

"Cincotta sounds like a real firebrand. I'd love to meet her."

"Oh, you will. NPA is building a national movement. Chicago, Detroit, Minneapolis and about a dozen others are on board, and my boss, the archbishop, is willing to pay the freight for me to help other cities to organize by putting together these regional housing conferences to educate neighborhood leaders. So assuming you can deliver the troops...," he said with a shrug.

"A New England housing conference. Sounds like a plan. But how come the Archbishop of Chicago is so involved?" Flynt asked.

"Inner-city neighborhood, inner-city parish—as one goes, so goes the other. Most of your neighborhoods are eighty to ninety percent Catholic, right?"

Flynt nodded and smiled ruefully. "Seems like a good issue to bring the working-class and middle-class neighborhoods together. The middle-class areas are where the project is getting the most resistance."

"Oh yeah! Middle-class types tend to look down on working people and mass power tactics, but once you show them how the banks are screwing them, they catch on real fast. If there's one thing Middle-class people understand, it's equity. They want to believe that the system is working for them, and they get really pissed off when they find out it isn't."

"And that's why Mary is going to be fine. She has a real stake in J. P., and if she wants to run for the state legislature, this should give her some credibility," said Flynt, raising his glass. "A toast, to our meeting with the Commissioner of Banks and may she never know what's about to hit her."

"A woman?" Trapp asked, his eyes thoughtful. "What do we know about her?"

Flynt put his glass down and grinned. "You're gonna love this—Louise Winthrop Gray. Pure Boston Brahmin. Those families have been around so long that her ancestors were probably waiting at Plymouth Rock when the Pilgrims arrived."

"Probably charged them to come ashore," Trapp said with a snort.

"Yeah, and from what I hear this one suffers from terminal lock-jaw, absolutely guaran-fucking-teed to piss-off your average Irish working stiff."

Trapp's eyes danced, and he chuckled in his gravelly voice. "Sounds like fun," he said, lifting his glass again. "Skol!"

Chapter 13

The Commissioner

The commissioner scowled and punched the intercom button. Louise Winthrop Gray was not having a good day.

"Sally, bring me the letter from that community group, will you?"

"The Jamaica Plain Banking group, Commissioner?"

"Yes, that's the one." What in the world was this civic association doing involving itself in things that were absolutely none of its concern? She had a good mind to ignore this impertinent little group, but the governor's office had received a copy of the letter and had called and reminded her that next year was an election year and that these people were likely to get some press. Louise Winthrop Gray was tall, slender, with a short cap of steel-gray hair; she looked every inch the Boston Brahmin, but, in fact, she was nothing of the kind. She had been born Levana Holtzhacker, the only child of Anna and Meyer Holtzhacker, German-Jewish immigrants who had emigrated to the U. S. just after the end of World War I and settled in the Bronx.

When Louise met John Winthrop Gray, he saw a sexual opportunity—she saw a stepping stone from which she would pole vault into the upper class.

Johnny Winthrop Gray was a 4th generation direct descendent of Black Jack Gray, a homeless buccaneer and slave trader who, like many Boston Brahmin families —the Cabots and Fanueils of Beacon Hill —had made his fortune in the triangle trade.

By the time Black Jack Gray's great-, great-, great-grandson was brought, red- bloated and squalling, into the world all memory of the manner in which the Grays had obtained their fortune had been forgotten. John Winthrop Gray was a mediocrity. He attended Groton and matriculated at Yale, his father's alma mater, where he lost large sums in late night card games, chased girls and received the nourishing gift of a gentleman's C.

Gray was a womanizer. He found the young women at the bank's back offices to be easy pickings. Louise was not at all what the young Brahmin was used to. She played him as a matador works a bull, coming close, teasing, then withdrawing out of reach and tossing her skirts until she had him half mad, panting and pawing the ground with frustration and desire.

Johnny was in a fever, and by the time the fever broke, much to his family's chagrin, he had eloped with his secretary, and when, three months later, Louise announced her pregnancy, the family surrendered, and the contract was sealed.

Louise proved herself to be tougher than any of the Grays and more Yankee than the Winthrops. At age fifty her husband succumbed to cirrhosis of the liver and died; her only child, a daughter, had been married off long since, and Louise cast about for something to occupy herself. She became a major donor to the Republican Party and was rewarded with her present post by the Brahmin governor, Francis W. Sargent, who was a family friend.

Louise opened her compact. It was Art Deco, a period piece, 18k gold, with a lovely carved jadeite plaque by Cartier. It had been a wedding present from her late husband. She peered into the mirror. The angles had sharpened, the eyes sunken slightly, and lines of disapproval were etched permanently around the mouth. She shrugged; her looks were going. So what, they had served her well, and men were such fools, she had no intention of going through that again. She quickly glossed her lips and snapped the compact shut just as her secretary entered and placed the folder on the desk in front of her.

"Will there be anything else, Commissioner?" Sally asked brightly.

Commissioner Gray raised her eyes, glanced at her secretary and thought for a moment. In a hurry to get home to that squalid apartment and those two insufferable little brats, are we? "No, that should be all for today, Sally. James will be attending the meeting with me this evening. He will lock up when we leave."

"Oh, thank you so much, Commissioner Gray. It's Robbie's birthday, and I was hoping to get home a little early and bake a cake."

"Humm, yes, well, goodnight," the commissioner said, without looking up, and she flipped open the file folder.

Chapter 14

Confrontation

Flynt would have liked to have positioned the banking commissioner at a small table all alone facing his leadership, but Mary Kavanaugh vetoed that idea.

"Let's put all the tables together into a circle, Jed. We don't want to begin by alienating the good commissioner altogether," she said, with a sweet smile.

"It's not supposed to be a coffee klatch, you know," Flynt replied.

Mary looked up and studied Flynt's face. "True, but it doesn't hurt to be nice," she said.

Mary believed in being nice, and though many of the other Parkside types were suspicious of him, Mary liked Jed Flynt. To most of the people she knew, he was an enigma. His job, his motivation, was something beyond their understanding, but Mary was friends with a couple of the people on Flynt's board, and she had supported the idea of the project. Flynt's enemies, and there were quite a few, were suspicious. Some called him a rabble-rouser, and without the support of the local churches, he would have been branded a communist. Still, she did not plan to allow him to push her around.

Flynt reminded Mary a lot of her brother Timmy. Mary was the eldest of four children. She had been born in Ireland and came over with her parents at the age of six. Her father, a butcher by trade had, after years of savings, been able to open a small meat-market in Dorchester's Savin Hill neighborhood where Mary had spent her first few years in America.

The youngest of six, Timmy was the runt of the litter, and an idealist and a dreamer. Her Timmy had been dead for twenty years, killed at fifteen——still a baby——knifed in a fight between rival neighborhood gangs. Like a heavy stone, the sorrow still pressed down on her breast and left a hole in her heart. Flynt looked a bit like Timmy and was another lost soul—a man seeming to be so much in control, but in so much pain. She couldn't help wanting to nurture him.

"We are likely to get between fifty and sixty people. A seminar arrangement will cut out half of them, and Willie-Joe should be facing her when he reads the demands," Flynt said and unfolded one of the gray metal chairs and lined it up with the others in a neat row.

"Oh, very well. I suppose a single table facing the audience would be best," Mary said.

"It is important that we keep the commissioner's attention focused on our demands," Flynt said.

"Yes, the demands, as if I'd be forgetting the demands, what with you pounding them into my head day and night for the past two weeks. It's simple enough. We want the banking commission to require banks to report their loans by either census track or postal zip code. Isn't that about it?"

Flynt nodded a little sheepishly. "Census tract would work better, and she has the power!" he said.

"Aye, so she does." Mary's Irish came out when she was tired or nervous, and she was always nervous before a big meeting.

Flynt checked his watch, five minutes to seven. People were already beginning to file in. That was a good sign. Everyone was bundled up. Father Gale had turned on the heat at six, but Our Lady of Lourdes church hall was a cavernous room with worn wood floors, whitewashed walls and a vaulted ceiling that could easily seat five hundred people. The long fluorescent lights set in the ceiling lit the hall like a supermarket. He was afraid that the fifty or sixty people he was hoping for would be swallowed up in its drafty expanse. He had looked for a smaller space, but Father Gale had offered, and Mary had accepted, and that was that.

Commissioner Gray was due at 7:45. Flynt quickly checked around. One eight-foot table upfront with six rows of ten chairs facing the audience. Alex had placed one of the mimeographed fact sheets at the head table and on each chair. Your Property Values Are at Risk, the headline shouted in big black block letters. It had been hard to reduce the disinvestment issue to a single typewritten page, but Alex had been succinct and with a bit of editing by Trapp the main points were covered.

Ten minutes later Mary called the meeting to order. There were about forty-five people seated in four neat rows facing the leadership table. Flynt eyed the crowd and recognized a Boston Globe reporter and another from the Citizen. Where were Molly Reagan and Barbara Last? Both had experienced problems getting loans, and they had both promised to come and speak about their experiences. Personal experiences worked best. People might question statistics, but they believed their neighbors.

Trapp made his pitch, and they spent about a half an hour going over the fact sheet.

Mary Kavanaugh stood up.

"Thank you, Reverend Trapp. We are expecting the banking commissioner, Mrs. Gray, to arrive momentarily. "Thanks to the Community Organizing Project," she said, smiling towards Flynt where he stood toward the rear of the hall with his back against an exit doorframe, "we have researched the laws governing the banking commission, and we know that the state has the authority to require a comprehensive disclosure of bank lending patterns in Boston. We know that redlining is happening here in J.P., but before we can convince the powers that be to do anything about it, we need proof. That is why we formed the Banking and Mortgage Committee and organized this meeting."

The sharp, metallic groan of one of the heavy, steel double-doors opening echoed through the hall, and a tall, slender figure in a full-length mink strode in followed by a stooped, balding man in a Harris tweed topcoat carrying an old-fashioned leather satchel briefcase. Flynt straightened up and moved to intercept.

"Commissioner Gray, may I take your coat?" Flynt asked.

Louise Winthrop Gray paused and ran a cold appraising eye over the tall organizer in his wrinkled chambray work shirt and worn corduroy jeans.

"No, thank you. That won't be necessary," she said, waving him off. Her lips were set in a tight line.

Her eyes swept the room. "James, let's get this over with, shall we?" she said. Then, with the clicking of her high heels echoing off the plaster walls, she strode directly toward the head table. Mary Kavanaugh stood, smiling primly, waiting to greet her.

Introductions concluded, Louise Winthrop Gray shrugged off her coat into her assistant's waiting hands, then sat, tugged her short A-line skirt over her knees, folded her hands primly in front of her and gazed about her as if she expected to be offered a menu. James wrestled the slippery garment over the back of a metal folding chair. To his horror, it immediately slid off onto the floor, drawing a raised eyebrow and a fish eye from Commissioner Gray.

"So sorry, Commissioner," James mumbled, his face reddening. Bowing, he scooped the coat up and attempted to hang it on his own chair. It promptly slipped off and puddled onto the floor.

There were a couple of snickers from the audience as James' face turned ever redder.

"If you please, James," the commissioner said, wrenching the coat right out of her assistant's hands. She draped it across her lap.

"Sit down," she ordered.

James sat down, wrestled with his briefcase, and drew out a yellow legal pad from its battered interior.

"Well, if everyone is ready?" WillieJoe asked. He began the presentation by reading the prepared script that he and Flynt had worked out. He did a professional job of hitting the salient points and ended with the punch line:

"Commissioner Gray, we believe that savings banks, chartered by the Commonwealth, are redlining our neighborhoods and destroying property values in Jamaica Plain. Under the law establishing your office, Massachusetts's banks are chartered to serve the public good, and you have the authority to require that these banks disclose their lending-patterns. We are asking that you use that power."

Louise Winthrop Gray cleared her throat.

"Thank you, Mr. Patrizzi, for your presentation. I sympathize with your problem, but you must understand that banks are in business to make money. They have a fiduciary responsibility to their stockholders. They have no obligation whatever to their mortgagees."

The hall went silent with shock.

"What about to their depositors and the areas in which they do business?" Mary Kavanaugh asked.

Commissioner Gray raised one long, elegantly manicured finger. "Mrs. Kavanaugh, my job as Commissioner of Banks is to see that banks adhere to their legal responsibilities as set forth in their charters. They are responsible to their shareholders, and to a lesser extent, their depositors—not to those who borrow from them. We care what the banks do with their money—not where they lend it. I doubt that what you describe is happening, but banks naturally evaluate risk as part of the loan-making decision. If they make high- risk loans, they are breaching their fiduciary obligations."

"I think the commissioner is forgetting," Patrizzi retorted, color rising in his cheeks, "that the banks are chartered by the Commonwealth of Massachusetts for the benefit of the people of Massachusetts. It says exactly that in their charters. The money they lend comes from their depositors, and these are the same people who live in the neighborhoods they are redlining. To give a man four percent interest on his saving, then use that money to destroy his property values! That's a pretty raw deal."

"I don't wish to argue with you, Mr. Patrizzi. I can only reiterate what the scope of my responsibilities are as Commissioner of Banks."

"We have done the research, Commissioner Gray, and as a lawyer I can tell you that you do have the authority under the statute to require the banks to disclose their lending-patterns," Patrizzi snapped back.

Gray's assistant scribbled a note and slid it in front of the commissioner.

Gray read it and nodded.

"I am sorry, Mr. Patrizzi, but what you are asking is quite impossible. First, it would be a complete waste of time. Second, gathering this information would place an onerous burden on our banks and require additional staff in our office, and that would require funding to be approved by the state legislature."

Patrizzi gaped at the commissioner. Flynt looked around in a panic. Barbara Last and Molly Reagan were no-shows. Both said they would come and speak at the meeting, but neither had shown up.

An old woman in the second row stood up. Flynt had never seen her before. She wore a threadbare, calico coat and a gray woolen headscarf.

"Commissioner Gray, my name is Jenny Quinn, and I must say you seem almighty concerned with the well-being of the banks, but what about us? What about the working people? My old man and me, everything we own is tied up in our house. For twenty-five years we worked and scraped to pay off our mortgage, never missed a payment, not in all those years and now we got a chance to go live with my daughter. She and her new husband got a nice little place down in Fort Lauderdale, but we can't sell our house. I live on McBride Street. My nephew was ready to buy it, but he couldn't get the banks to talk to him. You say there's no redlining, but he's a hardworking boy, got a good job, too, working for the city. He's got the money for the down payment, only the banks won't give him a loan. If that ain't redlining, what would you call it?"

Don Gaffer stood up. Flynt grimaced.

"Don Gaffer, City's Hope. Speaking as a realtor, Mrs. Quinn, I can tell you that there are a number of reasons why a bank might deny a mortgage loan. The value of the property, the ability of the borrower to come up with a down payment, even the condition of the property can be a factor."

Jenny Quinn looked at Gaffer, then down at her feet, shrugged, shook her head and sat down.

Commissioner Gray gazed briefly at Gaffer and rewarded him with a thin smile.

"Yes, you see, as the gentleman said, there are many factors that go into the granting of a mortgage. I think, upon investigation, you will find that in most cases that the credit-worthiness of the borrower is the real issue."

Flynt snorted in frustration. He was beginning to sweat. He had expected some sort of a double cross from Gaffer, and here he was sucking up to the commissioner. Come on Mary, somebody, don't let her wiggle away so easily. He caught Mary's eye.

Mary stood up. "I am very sorry, Commissioner, but the committee finds your response unacceptable!"

Gaffer stood up. Mary held up her hand.

"Now, Don, you have had your say, and now I'll be having mine. If you would please sit down."

There was iron in that sweet smile. Gaffer sat.

Flynt gave a silent cheer.

"Many of our neighbors, and some of us in this room, including myself, have experienced problems getting mortgage and home-improvement loans, and we believe this problem is widespread. It is not the credit-worthiness of the borrower that is at issue here. That is why we are asking you, as commissioner of banks, to order disclosure. If you are correct that redlining does not exist, disclosure will prove it.

"We have also researched the cost. According to Mr. David Ronan of Berkshire Data Corporation, much of the information we are requesting exists, and could easily be re-configured. That disclosure of lending patterns, by census tract or postal zip code, would cost less than ten thousand dollars statewide. So, Commissioner," Mary Kavanaugh said, again smiling sweetly, "if, as you contend, there is no such thing as redlining, why not order disclosure and prove us wrong?"

The commissioner was visibly displeased. Mary had cracked Gray's aristocratic veneer. The phone call from the man at Berkshire Data had been a godsend, and Mary had injected it at just the right point. Flynt was elated.

Louise Winthrop Gray was suddenly on the defensive. She had been reasonable. She had listened politely, and she had given her answer. "Why do these people continue to badger me?" she wondered.

"Mrs. Kavanaugh," she said, pausing for a moment to settle herself, "I really do not know how you arrived at your estimate, but I...."

Mary cut in.

"Mr. Ronan's company is in the business of gathering just this kind of data and tells us that his company will supply the data, statewide, at that price," she said.

"I heard what you said, but I have never heard of this Mr. Ronan, or his company, and in my opinion, what you are asking for will be much more expensive and will burden the banks unnecessarily. I will take your request under advisement, Mrs. Kavanaugh, but I must say to you that I see no reason to order the banks to do as you ask."

"Thank you, Commissioner, we are asking that you consider our request with an open mind and perhaps do a little actual research. You don't live in this neighborhood. We do, and we know that redlining exists and is a real problem, and I believe that once you do the research, as we have, you will see that our request is more than reasonable. Now may we set up a meeting for one month from today for you to meet with us and give us your decision?" Mary asked, smiling.

"Good going Mary," Flynt thought. "Hold those delicate patrician feet to the fire."

Mary's request surprised the commissioner. She froze for a moment speechless then turned glared at her assistant, who had his head down and was busily studying his notes.

The commissioner sighed. "Very well, Mrs. Kavanaugh, if you will call my office to confirm the date, I will look into your request and meet with you next month. And now," she said standing, "If you will excuse me, I have another engagement."

"James!"

Her assistant jumped to his feet and took the coat and held it for Gray. She nodded curtly to the head table and strode off, heels clicking against the floor. Her assistant gathered his notes, stuffed his notebook into his case and scurried off almost running to catch up to where his boss stood arms crossed, impatiently waiting for him to open the door.

Flynt smiled to himself. He was elated. Mary had saved the day. Untested leadership indeed! He looked at the two reporters, Rogers from the Globe was interviewing Mary and Willie Joe, and the Citizen reporter was sitting with her head down scribbling away. Had the commissioner really said that the banks had no responsibility to the community? Flynt could almost taste the morning Globe's headline. Gray had even agreed to the follow up meeting though, he knew, that that meeting was never going to happen. She would either be a no show or more likely have a flunky call with some phony excuse and cancel at the very last minute. Either way, he figured, the pot sits on the flame, set to boil.

Chapter 15

Greenlining

A haze of cigarette smoke hung over the barroom like a late morning fog. Doyle's was so crowded you had to shout to make yourself heard. Alex pointed at a big empty table over in one corner. Attorney Patrizzi nodded, slipped and shouldered his way through the crowd like a lineman with the rest of the committee following along in his wake.

Jesse, the barmaid, rushed over and after favoring Flynt with a toothy smile emptied the ashtray, piled the bottles, half-empty glasses and other detritus onto a tray, and tidied up with a bar rag.

"A large pitcher of Bud. No better make it two. This looks like a thirsty crowd," Willie-Joe Patrizzi ordered.

"Well, I don't know about everyone else, but I thought that the meeting went very well," Mary Kavanaugh said loudly and with a giggle after everyone had settled down around the table.

"You did a wonderful job, Mary," Alexis said, nearly shouting to make herself heard over the din of boisterous drinkers.

Mary favored Alex with a smile. "Well, Mrs. Gray's attitude really ticked me off. By the way, what happened to Molly Reagan? I spoke to her just yesterday, and I know that she was planning to come," Mary said, addressing Flynt, who was sandwiched between her and Trapp.

Trapp glanced sideways at Flynt. "The thing with the coat was fucking beautiful," he said in a confidential tone. "I can't believe she wore that mink to a neighborhood meeting."

"I guess she was cold," Flynt said, turning and gazing innocently at Trapp.

Trapp snorted.

"I don't know what happened to Molly, Mary. She told me the same thing. I do agree that for a state official, Commissioner Gray seemed incredibly arrogant and unconcerned with people's needs," Flynt said, addressing the table. "Alex is right, you did a great job, Mary. You, too, counselor," he said smiling at Patrizzi. "You made some great points."

"She just didn't get it, or didn't want to," Willie-Joe said. He was seated next to Alexis Jordan, but he had a big voice, and it carried even in the noisy bar. "If she used that word fiduciary one more time," he said, shaking his fist. "Pow, right in the kisser!"

Laughter greeted his mimicry.

The mood of celebration was enhanced by the arrival of two brimming pitchers of Budweiser. Flynt stood and filled everyone's glass.

"Well, cheers, everybody," Mary said, holding up her glass.

The table followed suit.

"You know, Jed," Mary said, turning her head towards him, "I've been thinking. We have got to overcome this idea that banks have responsibilities only to their shareholders. I think that they have a responsibility to their depositors and mortgagees as well.

"Exactly right, Mary. It's the depositors' money they are playing with, and they are selling the mortgages. Like Willie-Joe said, they are chartered by the Commonwealth to serve the public good. If they pay you four percent on your savings, then redline your street, that is clearly not in the public interest."

Trapp leaned forward to listen.

"Well, I have an idea," Mary said, "which I think might bring the whole thing home. Suppose we started a campaign and get neighborhood residents with savings accounts at the local banks to agree to move their accounts to a bank that will commit to lend the money right here in Jamaica Plain?"

Flynt turned the idea over in his mind quickly. "So, we negotiate a deal with one of the banks, and instead of redlining, they would be greenlining?"

"Exactly," Mary said, clapping her hands. "'Greenlining,' that's good, Jed. That's what we will call it. It will show the banks we're serious."

"Sorry," Alexis Jordan said, shouting across the table, "I heard greenlining, what's greenlining?"

"It's Mary's idea," Flynt said. "I think it has real potential." His brain was already working, figuring out the angles and the difficulties of putting such a program together.

"Listen, it's just an idea so far," Mary said. "The money the banks lend is basically our money, right? The banks get it from neighborhood depositors and use what are really our savings to lend out as mortgages. Suppose we could somehow pool that money and negotiate with the banks to keep that money in our neighborhood?"

"Wow, what a great idea!" Alexis said, with an eye on Flynt.

Everyone was now straining to hear.

"Is anybody doing anything like that?" Flynt asked Trapp.

"Nope," Trapp said.

Trapp was chewing the ever-present unlit cigar. Flynt marveled that he could chew with one side of his mouth and speak out of the other.

"We did some stuff in Chicago and called it greenlining, but what you're suggesting is an entirely new thing."

"Well, what do you think of the idea, Mr. Trapp?" Mary asked.

The table had gone quiet, and everyone was straining to hear over the bar noise.

Trapp reached up and removed the cigar. "I think it's the best damn idea I have heard in the last ten years," he said, in his usual deadpan manner.

Mary blushed.

"I'm not sure how we would go about doing something like that," she said.

"A pledge campaign," Flynt said. "We can really spotlight the redlining issue and its effect on the neighborhood. The press will love it. And it's no risk. Savings deposits are federally insured, yes?" he said looking at Trapp, "and all the banks pay about the same interest rate. So all people would have to do is to sign a form giving the committee permission to negotiate on their behalf and fill in the amount in their savings account."

"Christ, that sounds good. I like it so much it should be illegal," Willie-Joe said.

"Do you really think so?" Alex asked worriedly.

The big lawyer laughed. "No, I don't. Pooling money is as American as apple pie. Mutual funds do it all the time. These stuffed-shirt bankers will hate it, but how can they criticize it? A little humility will do them good. Christ, it's our job to help them."

"Help them? I don't think I understand what you mean, Mr. Patrizzi," Alex said.

"Listen, this is how it is—and call me Willie-Joe, Alex. Winthrop-Gray and her banker friends need help to see the error of their ways, and it is up to us to provide that help," he said, straight-faced.

"I see. Are you certain they are in error?" Alex said.

"Christ, yes! We'll be reeling in the sheaves and introducing these greedy mother's sons to the light of the Lord!"

Willie-Joe held up his mug in salute, "To greenlining!" he said and grinned gazing around the table.

Jedediah Flynt glanced over at Alexis Jordan, raised his eyebrows, then gazed briefly up at the painted murals that lined barroom wall. One, a scene from the American Revolution depicting a Boston crowd haranguing a platoon of redcoats; another depicted colonists, dressed as Indians, throwing boxes of tea into Boston Harbor.

"Yes," he said grinning, "Willie-Joe is right, a community investment pool is 100% American. I have an idea that this greenlining thing is going to work really well."

Chapter 16

Classmates & Conspiritors

"You are the first, Mr. Tate. Your guest has yet to arrive," Victor, the maître d, said as he pulled back the heavy curtain, pushed open the dark paneled door and stepped back to allow his guest to precede him. Tate was a tall man, dressed in a double-breasted, navy blue blazer and gray slacks. He had slightly stooped shoulders, pale blue eyes and thinning blond hair carelessly combed into a shaggy Ivy League cut. He stepped into the room. The door closed behind him with a discreet click snuffing out the noise from the main dining room.

The restaurant's private dining room was simply but richly furnished, containing only a Sheridan period dining table set on an antique rug, a sideboard and two chairs set on a floor of parquet oak. The chamber's dark paneling was in the austere Regency style. Bone china and old silver flatware gleamed in the candlelight. The table had been set for two.

On the sideboard, the bottle had been decanted per his instructions. He had been looking forward to this. He examined the label: Château Ausone '66; according to Victor, the best year in a generation and at its peak.

He placed the bottle on the sideboard with the label facing the wall, picked up the decanter and poured a small portion of the dark liquid into one of a pair of Baccarat crystal balloons. He swirled the dark liquid, held his glass up to the light of one of the candles that burned in one of the paired Georgian sconces and admired its rich almandine hue. He then placed the lip under his nose and inhaled. Ah, just a touch of the cellar. He was about to take a sip when the chamber door opened.

"My dear, Monsignor."

"Andy Tate, here and on time? Remember what we used to say back at school? 'Tate would be late for his own wake'." Benedetti smiled.

Tate grinned, elbowed past Benedetti's extended hand, encircled him in a bear hug, and then grabbed him by the shoulders.

"Guido, it's good to see you, too," the developer said, giving him a gentle shake.

Benedetti's full lips twisted as he disentangled himself. "Andrew, please, is it possible that after all these years we might find a way to give that nickname a decent burial? You know how I detest it."

"Well, of course, Guid—I mean Michael. That offensive appellation shall never pass these lips again."

"Thank you, Andrew," the priest said. He tugged at his crimson sash to straighten it.

"I was just about to sample the wine. Will you join me?"

Without waiting for an answer, Tate lifted the decanter, filled the second balloon precisely a third of the way full, and handed it to the monsignor.

Benedetti studied Tate's face and noted the slight tan. He raised the glass and took a sip. "Marvelous! Excellent choice! I trust that your Asian trip was successful," he said.

Tate raised his glass. "Salut!"

They touched glasses and drank.

"Excellent—right bank, yes? A St. Émilion?" Benedetti asked, with a raised eyebrow.

Tate nodded. "Exactly right, Michael. You were always the connoisseur." Benedetti's snobbishness was well known, and he had suffered for it.

"You've obviously become quite the connoisseur yourself. I seem to recall that rum-coke was your drink of choice back at The Saints."

They had been classmates at Saint Smithen's, an exclusive Swiss boarding school located in the Alps outside Lucerne. The school was normally referred to as The Saints by its students and privileged alumni.

Tate took another sip. "Ausone, '66, best year since '54, or so I'm told," he said, recalling Victor's fulsome description.

"Marvelous! I would have guessed Pavie.

Despite its alpine location, Saint Smithen's was modeled on the English public school. Staffed by Jesuits, it catered to the sons of rich WASCS—white Anglo-Saxon Catholics. Each of the boys in their set had assumed one of the prescribed roles expected of public school boys: the snob, the hale fellow well met, the jock, and, of course, the jester. Benedetti easily adopted the role of a snob, and Tate had played the buffoon to perfection.

Like Tate, most of the boys came from wealthy families. Benedetti, an orphan raised by the Jesuit order, was included by sufferance, and he resented it. He resented even more the breezy self-confidence of rich boys like Tate. He envied them the fine houses that he was allowed to enter only as a weekend guest, and he lusted after the expensive cars, the fine furnishings.

Benedetti affected a connoisseur's eye. Early slights had burned into him an ambition to acquire all that the accident of his birth had denied him. Having literally grown up in the church, the choice of the priesthood as a vocation seemed natural. He found that he had little interest in sex with either men or women, and a career in the church posed no real barrier to his ambitions.

Where else, after all, could a man of humble origins aspire to be a prince? Benedetti decided he would become a prince of the church, a cardinal. His model was Guido Mazarini, another Italian orphan who had risen from poverty to become Cardinal Mazarin—Louis XIV's Finance Minister and the richest man in Europe at that time. Mazarin had amassed a fabulous collection of art, antiques and jewels, and had acquired palaces to hold it all. He had made the mistake of mentioning that admiration and had been immediately dubbed Guido by his school chums.

Following graduation, the two boys had taken widely divergent paths. They had not remained in touch, and Benedetti had been surprised to receive a letter from Tate the previous year informing him that he would be in Boston and suggesting that they meet. Tate had followed Benedetti's career from afar, and he had, he said, a proposition that might interest the monsignor.

Benedetti had dismissed Tate's proposal. It seemed impossibly far-fetched. But the profits he mentioned were enormous, amounting to a temptation which, once it took root in Benedetti's mind, he found difficult to shake. And in a moment of weakness, Tate had secured his promise to present the idea to the archbishop. To his surprise, Archbishop Doherty seemed intrigued, and he was, Benedetti knew, desperately in need of a large sum of money to finance a project, as he put it. Tate's plan seemed his best hope of obtaining the needed financing, and so a partnership had gradually taken form.

Tate went on, "Yes, my Hong Kong trip was most successful. Congratulate me. The investors are on board, Michael, and the cash is in the bank. I believe that the timing is right to move our agenda forward."

Benedetti took a sip of the wine and met Tate's eyes over the top of his glass. "I do hope so, my friend," he thought, "or this is the end of it." He sat quietly and waited for Tate to continue.

"By the way, Michael, you will be pleased to hear that just this morning I transferred one hundred seventy-five thousand dollars to your Swiss account. Consider it a down payment." Tate raised his glass. "I have complete confidence in your ability, Michael, as well as your powers of persuasion."

Benedetti's eyes widened briefly. Thank you," he said.

The two men sat facing each other at opposite ends of the table.

Summoned by a buzzer placed discretely beneath the table to Tate's left, a pair of waiters arrived, and they paused while dinner was quickly and efficiently set out.

Benedetti gazed about himself with admiration.

"Beautifully appointed!"

"Yes, I thought you would like it. This was originally a town house, formerly owned by some insufferably wealthy Boston Brahmin. I believe this was originally the gentleman's office," Tate said as the servers exited. "Perhaps he was one of your parishioners."

"The Wellington is perfect," Benedetti said, ignoring Tate's thrust. His former classmate was, as always, trying to get a rise out of him. "Sorry to cut short the pleasantries, Andrew, but it's time that we moved beyond the small talk and got down to business. You are aware that while you were away, we have had a major problem?"

"Apologies, old boy. Once the deal was sealed I had business in Europe. My man gave me your message. I have not been totally out of touch—tragic situation, tragic," Tate said.

"Tragic, indeed," Benedetti said. "A young woman burned to death. Horrible! The archbishop called me on the carpet, Andrew. We both understood. Well, I think it would be a good idea to lower our profile for a few months. Are you absolutely sure there is no danger that these purchases, these property acquisitions, can be traced back to us?"

"No, nothing to worry about there. I've seen to that." Tate leaned forward and lowered his voice. "I did speak with my man, and he tells me that someone has been sniffing about—a young woman trying to discover who has been buying the empty lots."

Benedetti frowned. "I was afraid of that. I don't recall if I mentioned it, but there is a social action project in Jamaica Plain. It's called the Jamaica Plain Community Organization Project, JPCOP, for short, and a professional community organizer, man by the name of Jedediah Flynt, runs it. The young woman who died was one of his neighborhood organizers."

Tate lifted his glass. "Lord, how I detest acronyms," he said, examining the almandine liquid.

"Andrew, be serious, please. As it happens, the project is sponsored, in part, by the archdiocese. I couldn't reach you—so, cloaking my interest as part of our annual evaluation, I had lunch with Mr. Flynt two weeks ago."

"Really? Excellent vintage, lovely tannins," Tate said swirling the liquid. "Tell me more about this Flynt fellow, Jedediah. Is that his name, some sort of do-gooder? The name sounds positively Biblical," he said and placed the glass back onto the table.

"Yes, the name means 'beloved of the Lord,' but I warn you, Andrew, Flynt is no bleeding heart and more to the point, nobody's fool. He and his people were suspicious before the fire. That's why the girl who died was watching the building. And it seems that your people have been careless. Someone in the city fire department has determined that the fires were set," Benedetti said.

Tate's smile vanished. "That is not good news. What else did he say? He doesn't suspect you, does he?"

"No, of course not. Why should he? There is absolutely nothing unusual about the archdiocese taking an interest, particularly after such a horrific incident. Let me repeat, Andrew, the archbishop hates bad publicity and is very concerned. Nothing like this was supposed to happen, and this man Flynt is angry. He is determined to locate and punish this girl's death. The contact was likely one of his people."

"Yes, a woman. Spoke like a solicitor. Claimed to have principals interested in purchasing one of our properties. Perhaps she mistook him for the original owner. The whole thing sounded odd," Tate said.

"What did your man tell her?"

"Nothing. He said he would ring her back, but she refused to leave a number, and said she would get back to him."

"It has got to be someone working with Flynt!"

"Good, one mystery solved. But we must discourage the Flynt fellow, mustn't we?" Tate picked up his wine glass.

"How do you propose to do that?"

"Not sure, actually, but I will think of something to scare him off," Tate shrugged, then drank.

"The man's an ex-marine. He won't scare easily. Andrew, I need your promise that there will be no further incidents like this past one."

"Don't worry, Michael. You have my word. And whatever action is necessary, it won't be traceable back to you. But we must find out what this fellow Flynt knows and discourage him. Have you established a relationship with the man? Do you think he would confide in you?"

"Yes, to a degree. I've met with him and established a degree of trust. He is naturally wary. You really can't expect me to get directly involved in this business. Good God, Andrew, I have done what I can, more than I should have. This was never part of our arrangement, and I don't dare rouse Flynt's suspicions or directly involve the archdiocese."

"Yes, quite right, my friend. You may put your mind at ease. This is my problem, and I shall attend to it."

Tate's nonchalance was feigned. He was troubled. Secrecy was the key to the project's success. If word got out before he had all the ducks lined up, opposition would have time to form, and the price of land anywhere close to the Southwest Corridor would escalate overnight. Flynt and his snooping must be stopped before anyone caught the scent.

"This brings me to my second point, Andrew. You say you have the financing in place. Fine, but if you expect the archdiocese to put its support seriously behind the project, it is time to show us the money."

"But my dear chap, you and the archbishop are partners with a twenty-five percent interest in the entire project, and I just made that deposit."

"That's all very fine, Andrew, but thus far, all we have to show for our efforts is title to a few dozen worthless properties. We have been waiting patiently, but given this latest incident, what is required is some earnest money, Andrew, a sweetener I believe it's called," Benedetti said.

"How much?"

"An even million should get the archbishop's attention."

"A million dollars?"

"Yes, immediately and in cash. I have spoken to His Excellency at length, and he sees the potential benefit to the church, but the girl's death has put him off. He has an ambitious agenda, but this…ah…incident has unnerved him. The fact is, Andrew, he is tired of talk and promises. We both are. Thus far he has agreed to move forward based upon my word, but you say you have the money. Prove it. Once the cash is in hand, Andrew, the entire project will seem less, shall we say, abstract."

"Damned fine sweetener," Tate said.

"And," Benedetti continued, "an additional one million deposited to my Zurich account. Plus, an additional four million to the archbishop, and the same to me, prior to any gesture of support from the archdiocese," Benedetti said quietly.

"Ten million dollars!" Tate exploded. His mouth dropped open, his eyes bulged. "You can't be serious."

"Oh, but I am completely serious. Plus," he said pausing to make sure that his old classmate was paying attention, "a final payment of ten million to the diocese, once the legislation has passed, and an ongoing donation from the profits to the archdiocese—say, one million a year for the first five years."

Tate's face was red and getting redder. "You're asking for twenty million with an up-front commitment of ten million dollars! Impossible! This is not what we discussed. Get real, old man!"

"I think that it is time for you to 'get real,' as you put it, old man," Benedetti said pointedly. He held up his glass, studied the richly hued liquor for a moment, took a sip and put it down. "Andrew, I have done a bit of homework since we last met. We are talking about a project with the potential to generate not millions but hundreds of millions of dollars. How much do you stand to make with my help? A hundred million, perhaps a hundred fifty. More? What I am asking for is a mere pittance. Think of it as a commission."

"There will also be a great many expenses," said Tate, cutting in. "We stand to make substantial profits from the properties we are acquiring for the trust, in case you have forgotten."

"Fine, keep the properties and the profits. We, the archbishop and I, will take the cash. I admire your élan, Andrew, truly, but this grand scheme of yours would be politically impossible without the active support of the Church, and that support cannot be gained without my help."

Tate sighed audibly. He had hoped to get away with a couple of hundred thousand, but his old friend had him by the short hairs, and he knew it. And he badly needed Benedetti to believe in him. "You are a thief, Michael, but, very well, let us cut to the chase. Will a total initial payment of five million to the archbishop and five million to your Swiss account seal our arrangement?"

"Yes, Andrew, I believe it will. Shall I speak with His Excellency?" Benedetti asked.

"Yes, please do, and I will guarantee one million as an annual donation to the archdiocese for ten years," Tate said.

"Ten years, even better. And the final payment?"

"The day the governor signs the bill into law."

Benedetti thought for a moment. He had expected more resistance. "Very well," he said, feigning reluctance. He did not altogether trust that his old classmate could pull this off, and the prospect of immediate cash had awakened his greed. Win or lose, both he and the church should be five million to the good. He was sure that the prospect of an additional five million plus the annual contribution would cement the archbishop's support. Let Tate and the archbishop hammer out the terms of the final payment between themselves. That should be amusing to watch.

"Very well, assuming that my five million is in addition to the hundred seventy-five thousand, I believe I can sell that to the archbishop, provided the funds are conveyed immediately," Benedetti said.

"What? Oh, very well," Tate sighed, "I will transfer the balance of the one million dollars to your account first thing tomorrow morning, Michael, and I will bring one million in cash with me to the meeting that you will set up for me with the archbishop. Once I am satisfied that he is with us, I shall transfer the additional eight million. In return, I will retain all profits from the land acquisition. I assume that you wish our little side-arrangement to remain confidential," Tate said.

Benedetti smiled. "Agreed, and, yes, confidentiality is key. Andrew, do bear in mind that any whisper of my financial involvement would destroy my credibility with the archbishop and thus my value to you. I will speak with His Excellency tomorrow afternoon and set up your appointment. I will leave it to you to negotiate the final details with Archbishop Doherty," Benedetti said, and raised his glass.

"Good, that's agreed! Now getting back to our, or should I say my, acquisition program," Tate began. "As you know, the corridor is narrow, and we will need to acquire a few additional parcels. I must accelerate the acquisitions. In order to pay your commission, I'll need more parcels put to offset our investor's cash commitment and maintain my percentage of ownership."

"Do what you need to do, Andrew, but proceed carefully, very carefully. The five-million-dollar payment to the archbishop will demonstrate our, that is, your, seriousness, but another incident remotely like this last one would be a disaster. Particularly given your timeline. The archbishop would back off immediately. He is very sensitive politically. Believe me, I've studied the man."

"Yes, of course, Michael, I understand completely. There is too much at stake to fail. I shall proceed very carefully, never fear."

Tate leaned back in his chair feeling very satisfied. Benedetti's demands had not surprised him all that much. Guido was a smart boy! "You were right; twenty million really is a pittance, Guido, old chap. I had budgeted for thirty." He had not mentioned to Benedetti the fact that he had been back in Boston for a week. He was still bathing in the afterglow of the Hong Kong trip. The fifty percent down payment on the one hundred million had been deposited in the offshore account.

"Guido's sign off on the acquired properties is an unexpected bonus," Tate thought, congratulating himself. He had the germ of a plan to offer the Red Sox a new stadium with five thousand additional seats. "Right-o, thanks old boy."

"This fellow Flynt is the one fly in the ointment," he mused, "must be part of the group that had launched that greenlining campaign." Tate had read about it in the Globe. He was confident that his acquisitions were well protected. But Flynt's campaign was placing too bright a spotlight on the housing market in that neighborhood. With his partners onboard the timetable had tightened. He could not wait.

"I'll simply have to contact the remaining owners and make them cash offers. The prices would be higher," he thought, but that can't be helped. He thought about his partner, an Asian gentleman, a very impatient Asian gentleman. This Flynt fellow's continued meddling might bring others sniffing around and make those last acquisitions difficult.

He had the name of a local contact in Boston's Chinatown. The man, he had been assured, would be make himself and the local organization available at need.

"Something," he decided, "must be done, and done now."

Chapter 17

Break & Enter

Flynt drove the battered VW up Amory Street and turned left on Atherton. He had spent the last few hours at a planning meeting and decided to make a quick stop at the office to pick up a file he wanted to study.

He pulled up in front of the old stone church that served as the project's headquarters and stepped out of his car onto the curb. The street was deserted. He gazed down the hill towards the old railroad bridge. The blackened, crumpled hulk of a burned-out automobile, like the desiccated corpse of a giant beetle, crouched beneath the jaundiced glow of the streetlight. The shadowed underpass was a favored spot for joy-riding young vandals to torch their trophies. The average was once a week, sometimes in broad daylight. "Is it still March? Damn!" he muttered and pulled up the zipper of his aging, foul-weather jacket, turning up his collar against the chill wind. He looked up at a sky as crisp as blackened toast, pricked with the needle-bright points of a few prominent stars visible through the haze.

New England-born, Flynt hated the winters and dreamed of moving to a warm climate. "Someday," he thought, as he ascended the stone steps to the church door. "That's odd. The night light's out," he said out loud. He checked his watch, 12:15am. Flynt was a methodical man, and he clearly recalled flipping on the night-light when he left the building several hours before. "Bulb must have blown," he thought, shrugged, and slid the key into the lock.

The church's design resembled a fortress constructed of roughly dressed stone, with long, narrow archer's windows and an arched doorway. The thick wooden door swung silently inward, and he stepped into the dark vestibule, eyed the inner door, leaned back and pushed the outer door firmly closed. He was immediately enveloped in Stygian darkness. He grunted, reached out and using both his hands like a pair of insect antennae quested forward. He had an uneasy feeling as his hands found the latch, and he pushed it open. Inside, the murk was mitigated by the dim glow of a streetlamp shining through the frosted glass of a pair of narrow arched windows set high in the office wall.

Flynt's hand slid along the right wall, groping for the bank of light switches. His nose caught a whiff of something acrid and his ears the faint rustle of cloth. It was barely enough warning. A heavy club whistled in an arc towards his exposed head. Without anything resembling conscious thought, Flynt's arm bent inward at the elbow to an angle of ninety degrees and rose like a crane's wing in a block that met and absorbed the downward force of the blow, stopping it just above his hairline.

In a confrontation, the difference between life and death is measured in micro seconds. A fifth of a second is the minimum time it takes the mind that apprehends a threat to make the decision and respond—provided that it is not paralyzed by panic or fear. During that tiny interval, an automobile traveling at sixty miles per hour covers 17.6 feet and a punch thrown at close range will impact and often destroy its target.

The heavy wooden club struck Flynt's raised left forearm with a force that would have splintered the bone of an arm that had not been hardened by years of constant, methodical conditioning. Still, a numbing shaft of pain drove the organizer to his knees. A vicious kick caught him just above the ear, and his head rebounded off the plaster wall like a basketball off a backboard.

Flynt's vision blurred. The dank heat of a jungle night surrounded him. He heard a shout of warning from the man on point. It was an ambush. The Cong had been waiting for them on either side of the dark trail. He heard the lieutenant's shouted orders, the screams of the wounded. The pop-pop of the automatic weapons, the smell of cordite and the stink of fear. He had warned the lieutenant. His mind screamed! This isn't real!

Adrenalin surged! Flynt shook his head and blinked. He eyes refocused. His mind followed. This was not the jungle. He was under attack. He had no idea who his adversary was, but from the speed of the attack, he knew that the man he faced was no wine-soaked derelict looking for a cozy bolt-hole to pass the night. This was a trained fighter. With desperate speed, Flynt dropped his right shoulder, tucked his arm and somersaulted along the edge of the wall, landing like a cat on both feet. He pivoted. His trained body dropped automatically into the classic Sanshin stance, weight centered, feet a hip's distance apart, right foot forward and turned in to protect the groin.

Flynt's assailant had learned a lesson. He switched the club to his left hand, stepped forward and thrust the blunt end straight at Flynt's midsection, a technique difficult to see and even more difficult to block. Now in a state of hyper-awareness, the organizer sensed the attack and stepped into it. His arm performed an inside-out circular block which shielded his upper body and diverted his attacker's club outward, ending with Flynt's right hand grasping his assailant's forearm. Flynt flowed forward, piercing his attacker's guard.

He thrust his left arm straight forward and upward in an open-handed palm-heel strike.

Flynt did not seek to kill. Even in the dark with his assailant little more than a shadow, his training allowed him to alter the trajectory of his thrust slightly to the left of center toward the *youru*, one of the body's thirty-six vital points. Properly focused, this technique impacts the rib cage just below the heart and induces a temporary paralysis in the left arm and shoulder. Launched from a stance like a firmly rooted tree, the force of the strike lifted his attacker off his feet and sent him sprawling onto his back. The club flew from his hand and spun across the bare, wooden floor.

The young Chinese thug rolled to the side and sprang to his feet. His chest heaved as he fought to catch his breath. A curious numbness radiated out from the left side of his chest. Johnny Lowboy had learned a lesson, a lesson that shattered his confidence. The power of Flynt's counter attack surprised and unnerved him. The man who now faced him had countered his technique and swatted him away like a pesky fly. He had never felt such power.

That man now stood before him like a dark hulking shadow. Johnny had not signed up for this. What was it the boss dragon had told him? A quick in and out? Yeah, right! Shit, why doesn't the fucker make a move? Johnny was a bully, and like bullies everywhere, his bravado masked an underlying cowardice. He was unnerved. His mind chugged away like a runaway steam engine. He was covered in sweat, his fear roiling his guts like a nest of angry vipers. "Time to make a break," he told himself. He turned his head and glanced toward the door.

"Go ahead. Try for it," the shadow's voice broke through the silence. The tone was mocking.

"Try what? What the fuck you talking about, man?" Johnny responded between panting breaths.

"The door. You know you want to make a run for it. Go ahead. Try!" the voice said.

"Who said anything about running, fucker?" Johnny said. He took a step backwards and felt his legs press up against the edge of a desk. He began massaging a numbing pain that was slowly spreading down his left arm.

"Guess you're wondering about that funny itching in your arm and shoulder?" the voice asked mockingly.

Johnny jerked back his right hand and drew his forearm swiftly across his forehead to wipe away the sweat. "Hey, shut the fuck up, asshole. What you got? Some kind of death-touch?" he shouted. "I heard all that bullshit before. You've been lucky so far, but I'm sick of this shit. You get in my way, and I'm about to put you into a world of fucking hurt!"

The shadow remained totally still. It chuckled, "Okay, my friend. I could use a light workout. Let's see what you've got. Come on, boy, make my night."

"Make mine. Shit, man, who do you think you are? Fucking Dirty Harry?" Johnny's fevered mind hit on an idea. He grinned. "Tell you what, man, whuddya say we just call it a draw. You back off, and I'll just walk away, and we can pretend like this never happened, and you won't get hurt, okay?"

"Oh, you can leave all right, after you answer a few questions, if, that is, I'm satisfied with the answers."

"Hey, forget you, man, I ain't answering no fucking questions. You're startin' to piss me off."

The guy wanted answers that Johnny knew he couldn't give. Every member of the Triad knew the rules. Nobody talked, because if you talked, you died. He had an idea. "Ok, you wanna talk, let's talk," he said. He took a step forward then skipped off his back foot which brought him in range of Flynt's body, then launched a vicious right-front snap kick at a spot just above the organizer's groin. Johnny was quick. It was a good move. The skip step covered a lot of ground, and he had surprised a number of opponents with it in and out of the ring. It always worked. But this time, instead of the satisfying impact of hard leather against soft yielding flesh, his foot met a brick wall.

The shadow melted backwards and compressed as Flynt dropped his right foot back into a horse-riding stance. This move dropped his center of gravity and slid his center back just beyond the range of Johnny's kick. Using his left hand, palm forward, as a backstop, he made a scooping motion with his right hand and caught Johnny's foot just behind the heel. Johnny's outstretched leg was trapped just above waist level. It was a simple and economical movement honed by years of repetition.

Flynt now had a choice. He had Johnny's leg, and that meant he owned his body. He could simply hold the foot, leaving Johnny hopping about with his leg at full extension or continue the motion and use his extended leg as a lever. He chose to continue. Using both hands, he tossed Lowboy's leg straight up toward the ceiling. The young tough's crotch became the fulcrum, and his thin body pin-wheeled backwards. The young thug did a backwards somersault and came down hard. He crashed, face first, flat on the floor, and the lights went out.

Sometime later Johnny came to. It was like waking up from a bad dream, but this dream was real. He was still flat on his face. He moaned, blinked and closed his eyes against the pain. He wasn't sure how long he had been out. The room was all lit up, and the bright lights hurt his eyes. He had a blinding pain in his head. He tried to move his arms and legs. Good, nothing broken, but his left arm felt numb. He put his right arm under his shoulder and attempted to lever himself up, but the sharp pressure of Flynt's booted foot in the small of his back pushed him back down hard.

"How do you feel?" It was the same voice, the voice of the shadow. It sounded concerned.

"I hurt, man. How the fuck you think I feel?"

"Good!" Flynt eased up on the pressure. "Ready to answer my questions?"

"Fuck, no! I already told you once, man, I ain't got nothin' to say."

"Too bad. You married, got kids?"

"Married, shit!" Johnny twisted his head, trying to get a look at his tormentor, but all he could see was a single hiking boot and a jean-sheathed leg. The other one, he knew, was pressed down firmly against his spine. "Why you asking me that, man?"

"Just wondered who you might be leaving behind. I hate to see young kids left all alone in the world without their daddy."

"Hey, fuck you, man. You don't scare me. You ain't gonna do nothing to me. You're some kind a fucking do-gooder. Am I right? I mean, what would fucking Jesus say, man?"

Flynt reached down, took hold of a hunk of Johnny Lowboy's hair, lifted his head, stretching his neck upward, held it for a moment, then smashed his face into the oak floor. The bridge of Johnny's nose cracked like a dried wishbone and exploded in a white-hot stab of pain. Blood fountained onto the floor. Johnny cupped his hands over the pulped remains. Flynt removed his foot. Johnny rolled over on his back moaning.

Flynt looked down at the man, and his mind flashed back to the dark interior of a grass hut, blood pooling on a dirt floor, a man writhing in agony, a woman screaming, children sobbing. He could hear the rhythmic whooshing of helicopter rotors. He felt a stab of guilt, but then he saw Sandy's face. Flynt's face was bathed in sweat. He started to pant. His mind was consumed with just one thought: kill this son-of-a-bitch. Flynt gritted his teeth, grabbed the front of Johnny's shirt and, with one hand, hoisted him to his feet. He shook the young punk like a dust mop, slammed him into the wall and let go. Johnny slid down the wall and lay like a rag doll in a heap on the floor. He looked up at Flynt with the eyes of a frightened rabbit. Flynt shook his head, took a deep breath and felt the rage flow out of him like a lanced boil.

He reached down and raised Johnny to his feet, wrapped his hand around Johnny's neck and pressed. "I'm finished playing with you, boy," he croaked, his face just inches from Johnny's, his eyes, twin drill-bits biting into the young punk's brain. "You broke in here. You tried to kill me and burn my office down. The evidence is all over the place. Your fingerprints are on that can of kerosene. Maybe you had something to do with torching that house over on Green Street. You know, the one that killed the young girl! So pay attention. Here's how the story ends. You broke in. I surprised you. You attacked me. We struggled...and you died!"

"My picture will probably be in tomorrow's Boston Globe. I'll be a hero. You want to know what Jesus is going to say about that, you scrawny piece of shit? Well, you can ask him yourself because you've got an appointment with him in just about two minutes from now if you don't start talking. You fucking get me, man?"

Through the tears and the pain Johnny looked into those dark eyes sunk deep into Flynt's face like a twin barreled riot gun. What he saw there turned Johnny Lowboy's bowels to water. His mouth went dry. "Okay, okay, he croaked. He raised his arms in supplication. "Ok, I'll tell you," he said, and he did and by the time he stopped babbling Johnny Lowboy was squeezed as dry as a sponge.

What Flynt learned only left him more confused. It was almost dawn before he finished with his questioning. He was dead-tired. He had wrung out the young Chinese thug like a wet rag, found out what papers the kid was ordered to find. That, unfortunately, was all the young punk really knew.

So it was tied in to the abandoned buildings. Maybe Alexis had not covered her tracks as well as she thought. Who was this boss dragon, and what was this Ghost Dragon Triad? Was this punk really off his nut? It sounded like something made up out of a comic book. Criminal organizations, triads Flynt knew, existed in Asia. Some of the Hong Kong triads had been suspected of selling arms to the North Vietnamese. But this was Boston, Massachusetts. The back of his neck felt suddenly cold and his scalp bristled. Who were these people? What was their interest in a bunch of derelict properties in a rundown Boston neighborhood? What did they think he knew that was important enough to burn him out? He had no documents, no proof of anything at all.

Flynt had been up for over eighteen hours and had a splitting headache. Maybe they were just trying to scare him off. He found himself feeling a little sorry for the kid. He called himself Johnny Lowboy, but Lowboy was the moniker, the name he was known by inside the triad. He believed the punk. No one would pin such a nickname on himself.

His real name was Fong. He was obviously a low-level flunky. His job was to burn Flynt out. Claimed he had nothing to do with torching abandoned properties. Flynt believed him.

He forced the young thug to clean up the mess, then shoved him out the door. Johnny Lowboy tumbled down the stone steps, picked himself up and sidled off down the street like a beaten dog.

Flynt watched him until he disappeared into the gloom, locked up, drove to his apartment and fell into bed. "Maybe it will make more sense after some shut-eye," he thought. He fell across the bed fully clothed. The rhythmic throb of the Huey's rotors haunted his sleep.

Chapter 18

Leakage

"Honestly, Jed, there's no way anyone could have traced me to the project."

Flynt sat on the far side of the conference table. The late winter sun streaming through the tall windows behind him framed his face and flung a long rectangular pattern across the table. Alexis Jordan noted how the pale sun emphasized the tiny spidery web of care-lines at the corners of his eyes. "He looks tired and vulnerable," she thought.

Flynt had managed to snatch four hours sleep before waking in a cold sweat. The alarm clock read 9:30 am. He had seen Sandy's eyes again in a dream. He knew Alexis was usually in by 10:00 am. He threw on a pair of worn brown corduroy jeans, a flannel shirt, his hiking boots and foul weather jacket and stepped out the front door.

"No Jed, it's not possible," she said. "I was very careful. I used a pseudonym, and I only spoke to one guy over the phone who might have been a lawyer."

"What about the sellers, Jordan, the men you talked to?"

"Same deal, I posed as a buyer and gave a false name," Alexis said, sitting down across the conference table. "I'm not exactly new to the research game, Jed. I went straight home, and nobody followed me. I was very careful."

Flynt rocked back in his chair, puffed out his cheeks and exhaled loudly.

"What about you?" Alexis lowered her eyes and spoke softly. "Did you talk to anyone about what we are doing?"

"Nobody, I..." then Flynt thought back to his conversation with Monsignor Benedetti. "I mentioned we were doing research, nothing more, and that was to a priest from the diocese," he said, dismissing the thought with a wave of his hand.

"Yes, obviously, a priest would have had nothing to do with it. That Chinese hoodlum, do you think he had anything to do with Sandy's death? Did he tell you anything else?" she asked.

Flynt shrugged. "A punk! Small potatoes. I wrung him dry. He didn't know anything more than I've told you."

"Well, what about this Chinese gang, the Triad. Was that what he called it? Did you call the police? How do you know he won't come back? How about Chinatown? Maybe I could make some..."

"Don't even think about it," Flynt said cutting in. "Believe me those people are very clannish. You'd stick out like a sore thumb. Nobody's about to talk to a round eye, and walking around down there by yourself could be seriously dangerous. I doubt that he or any of his colleagues will show up again, not without a lot of backup. If I involved the cops, I'd have had to answer a lot of questions, and it would have made the papers. What we don't need right now are reporters crawling all over this, asking questions. The organizer stays in the background and your name might have been brought into it. Alex, this thing is becoming more dangerous by the minute. I'm not about to get another one of my people killed."

Last night he had been awakened by a vision of Sandy's blue eyes. Alive and sparkling, then paralyzed with fear, the life slowly draining from them like a fading candle.

Alexis Jordan ignored the obvious point. "Well, I have some new information that might be of interest?"

"Great, talk to me!"

Flynt shook his head in admiration. "I have traced the ownership of our mysterious trust back to a holding company in the Duchy of Lichtenstein," she said.

"A holding company! Lichtenstein! Where the hell is Lichtenstein?" He leaned back in his chair, and clasped his hands behind his head. "How did you manage all this?"

With a self-satisfied smile, Alex pulled a steno-pad out of her pack and flipped a few pages. "As I told you, Albion Partners is registered as a Massachusetts Realty Trust. As such, it is required to file annually with the Secretary of State. So I went down to the statehouse office and looked it up. The incorporators are the lawyer and two others. One is a secretary in his office. I checked! She is also a licensed notary. The third is another corporation registered in New Jersey, a corporation called A-Z Partners. I have a girlfriend who was a paralegal in my father's office before she got pregnant and decided to become a full-time mommy and move to Trenton.. I called her, and she did some quick leg work. New Jersey has similar filing rules. She checked out A-Z Partners. It's owned by Paladin Properties, S. A., a holding company registered in the Duchy of Lichtenstein."

"Mmm, interesting. Tell me, why Lichtenstein? No, don't tell me. Let me guess — because the law allows the shielding of ownership."

Alex nodded. "Exactly right, Jed, and Lichtenstein is an ideal choice because there are no tax treaties between the U.S. and the duchy. There were a lot of small principalities in Europe into the 19th century, but Lichtenstein and Monaco are the only ones left. It's a tiny place, about the size of Rhode Island, sandwiched between Belgium and France and ruled by a grand duke.

"To set up a holding corporation in Lichtenstein, you hire a local lawyer who files the paperwork, provides an office address and will, for an additional fee, take the position of chairman. It's called a nominee trust. Nominees can also legally be anonymous, though their names must appear in the trust documents, which are held by the lawyer. So the attorney is the only one who knows who the owners are, and he is well paid to keep that information to himself.

"I used to run into a fair amount of this sort of thing at my dad's firm. Lichtenstein is a tax haven, Jed. People have been trying to avoid paying taxes like forever. We can trace it back to the ancient Greeks. Ancient Athens imposed a 2% tax on goods imported into the city. The local merchants leased one of the offshore islands and warehoused their goods to avoid the tax. Voilá, the first tax haven!

"Say the owner of a profitable U. S. company wants to avoid income taxes. He sets up a company in Lichtenstein, hires it to do consulting work, bills his U. S. company, deducts it as a business expense and exports a whole lot of pre-tax money to the duchy. From there, the cash can be transferred to, say, a numbered Swiss bank account. Money in transit is not taxed. The authorities in Lichtenstein won't talk, and Swiss banking laws make it illegal to release the name of account holders. It's simple, neat and very difficult to trace. This is big business, Jed. IRS figures indicate that offshore holding companies currently hold eight point three billion dollars in assets."

Flynt sat back. "Very thorough, Alex. How would a U. S. citizen go about getting hold of the money without being taxed?" Flynt asked.

"Oh, there are a number of ways. A suitcase full of cash is probably the simplest, but that is risky. A million dollars in one hundred-dollar bills weighs twenty-two pounds and will fit into a medium-sized suitcase, but it's illegal to import more than ten thousand dollars without declaring it. Aside from ghost-billing, a loan is probably the safest. The loan is made from the off-shore corporation directly to the U. S. taxpayer. A loan is not income, and it incurs no U. S. income tax. The recipient can even deduct the interest from his other income. Pretty neat, huh?"

"Very neat! So a criminal gang, say a Chinese Triad needing a legitimate front to hide behind, might choose Lichtenstein, right?"

"Sure! Cash can be wired in an out-of-accounts setup in the duchy without incurring any tax liability," Alex said.

"Ok, now what? No, listen, Jordan—you have done a great job—really, I mean it. But you know what happened to Sandy Morgan. I'm sorry to sound so old-fashioned, but I'm taking you off this project. Th is is no job for a woman."

Alexis stood up and put her hands on her hips. "So— you're just going to give up and let the people who murdered Sandy get away with it?"

"No, absolutely not, but-..." Flynt winced. Th e stance, her response to any suggestion of sexism, even the way her slim figure fi lled out those tight jeans, brought back memories of Sandy.

"But what? Where do you plan to find someone with the skills to identify these people, someone willing to work for the starvation wages that you can afford to pay? And, let me tell you another thing, Jedediah Flynt. You think I've done a lot of research—well, what I have done so far is the easy part. A competent paralegal could have done it. Uncovering the men behind Paladin Properties is the hard part, —and I think I know how to get it. And you don't. And, if you are ever going to get justice for Sandy Morgan, you need me."

Flynt gazed at her sourly. Her anger highlighted a fundamental truth. If he was going to identify the people who were responsible for Sandy's death, he needed her, and he knew it. Hell, he would have never gotten this far, and if he was ever going to discover who was behind the burnings, he would need her.

"And you think you can find out who is behind this nominee whatchamacallit?"

"You mean succeed where both the I.R.S. and the U. S. State Department fear to tread?" she asked brightly. "Yes. That is, no. But I know someone who specializes in finding what we need. His name is Jean-Luc, Jean-Luc Farge. He's a lawyer in Paris, a very tough guy, ex-paratrooper, used to work for the SDECE, the French Secret Service. He specializes in this sort of work. I got to know him through my father," she said, her face reddening. "I worked with him for a short time one summer in Paris."

"Sounds expensive."

"Yes, he is, very. I mean he would be, but we…we're good friends."

Flynt noted the beginnings of a blush on Alex's cheeks.

"And I think he might look into this as a favor to me."

"He must be a very good friend!" Flynt said, gazing at Alexis with an amiable smile.

"Well, yes." Her face turned up a shade.

"How will he be able to get hold of the names of the partners?"

"He'll have to get a look at the files."

Flynt leaned back and stared at Alex for a long moment. "Can I ask you a serious question?"

She eyed him uncertainly. "Sure, I guess so."

"You understand that from here on, things could get very nasty. Hell, they already have, and what you are now proposing to ask this guy Farge to do is sure to be illegal. I know you're far from stupid. So why do you want to involve yourself in this?"

Alexis flopped back down into the chair. "I don't know, Jed. I guess I want to do something useful. Look, I know I've had advantages and, as you have pointed out, opportunities most people never have. I think what you and this project are doing is important. I've been out door-knocking a few times. I've met the people on Atherton and on McBride Street. They're good people, and they're getting a very bad deal. This project is giving them hope. I want to be a part of it."

What Alexis Jordan didn't say was that she had never felt so totally alive. The smell of the streets. The organizing and her part in it sent adrenalin pulsing like an electrical current through her system and the buzz was like an aphrodisiac.

"You know what I always tell the staff, beware of do-gooders. If you can't identify a person's self-interest, you've got to ask yourself why are they involved?"

She cocked her head, "Ok, why are you involved?"

"It's what I get paid for."

She looked into his eyes and laughed before she could stop herself. "Right, the hired gun, is that it? Come off it, Jed. That's a bunch of macho bullshit, and you know it. None of the staff on this project has any direct self-interest in what happens in this neighborhood. Sure, you get paid, but if you count the hours, you're probably not even making minimum wage."

Flynt put his head back in the chair and grinned impishly. "Lately I feel more like that guy Quixote, tilting at windmills." He shrugged. "Maybe I do need you, but if you are going to continue, we need to keep you safe, okay?"

She sat up and saluted. "Yes sir!"

Flynt winced as if he had been struck.

"Did I say something wrong?" Alexis asked, alarmed.

"No, —the salute thing—reminded me of Sandy, that's all."

"Sorry."

"Forget it. You've sold me. I need you, but if you are going to continue, we have to establish some ground rules. First, we have a hole in our security somewhere, and until we figure out where, we can't take any chances. So don't come into the office unless you have to. If we need to meet, we can do it early morning before the staff arrives. Do your work from home, and don't leave any of the paperwork here. Work by phone, but no more personal visits to anyone associated with this thing. All right?"

"That makes sense."

"Second, this Triad shit is seriously dangerous," Flynt said, and pointed his finger straight at her. "I want your word you'll stay out of Chinatown. I don't want you playing Lois Lane. No phone calls! No research! Nada! Nothing! Do not allow the word Triad to pass your lips. Especially around here. Understand?"

She nodded vigorously. "I promise."

"Good, and if anyone asks you —staff, anyone —you have hit a dead end and can't go any further. You are frustrated, and I've got you working on a fact sheet on redlining. Get it?"

"You think someone on the staff might be talking?"

"Somebody is. I haven't told them much. I talked to Swift a bit about it. He really liked Sandy. Have you said anything to him?"

"No, probably would have but we've been too busy. Jed, you're not planning to drop this thing are you?"

He turned to her. "Drop it?" His eyes were black and hard as obsidian. "No! You've found the key, Alex, and we're going to follow this thing as far as it goes and wherever it leads."

She nodded and began fumbling and shuffling files into her rucksack. "No, I just wondered. You know, what if the Church found out. And something else has me worried. How did these people get on to us so quickly?" Alexis raised her head. "I don't know, Jed. I'll call Jean-Luc from home tonight."

Flynt's decision was made. He had crossed the line, but that was never really in question. "Let me know what Jean-Luc has to say."

"I'll call and let you know. And in the meantime, I'll keep going on the redlining. There really isn't much more I can do on this anyway, at least until I talk to Jean-Luc. If he won't help, I'm afraid we've reached a dead end."

"Got it! Sounds like this guy Farge can take care of himself. Look, getting back to redlining. If we're going to fire up the leadership on this issue, we've got to have proof that it is really happening in J. P. I'm talking real proof—facts and figures. It's tough to prove a negative. Nobody counts the people the banks have turned down," Flynt said.

"Okay, Jed. I think we can get a pretty good idea of what's going on locally by tracing the lending patterns of state-chartered banks that have branches here in J. P. They are the most visible enemy, right?"

"Yes, very good!" he said.

"And that means The Boston Five and the two local banks. The thing is, it's going to be time-consuming."

"Can you do it?"

"Yes, I think so. There's a weekly publication, Banker and Tradesman. All the realtors subscribe to B & T because it geographically lists every real estate transaction that takes place in the Commonwealth—buyer, seller, the amount of the mortgage, and mortgage-holder. Problem is we'll have to go back at least five years and go through each issue one at a time to comb out all the relevant transactions."

"A couple of hundred magazines—sounds like a piece of cake," Flynt said, rocking backwards, a smile playing about his lips. "That should keep you out of trouble while your boyfriend does…whatever he does. Go home and get to work."

"Right! Just for the record, he's not my boyfriend. And thanks, Jed," she said, with a tight smile. "You're a sweetheart, you really are."

Chapter 19

The Kingmaker

Tate bent his lanky frame and pressed his lips to the archbishop's ring. "Your Excellency, so kind of you to take the time to see me," he said, releasing the prelate's hand.

The archbishop remained seated, smiled and gestured towards the chair in front of his desk. "Please take a seat, my son. Can we offer you anything to drink—tea, coffee?"

"No, thank you, Excellency," Tate said, unwinding the cashmere scarf from around his neck and shrugging off his coat into the hands of the young priest who stood behind him. He rubbed his hands together briskly to restore circulation. Archbishop Doherty nodded to the secretary, who gently pulled the door closed as he exited.

"So good to meet you in person at last," the archbishop said, ostentatiously ignoring the heavy leather case that Tate had set down on the floor beside him. "I understand you have come to make a substantial donation, Mr. Tate. Please accept my thanks. A million dollars is a great deal of money. You are doing the Lord's work, my son. This donation will help a great many people. I have had regular reports from Monsignor Benedetti, as I am sure you know, but I thought, and Michael agreed, that it would be a good idea for us to have a private chat, just the two of us. Before things proceed any further."

"Of course, Your Excellency. May I?" he asked, and noting the archbishop's nod, hefted the case onto the desk, snapped open the twin locks and turned it toward his boss.

"My word," the archbishop said as he contemplated the neat stacks. One hundred-dollar bills wrapped in packages, stamped $10,000, completely filled the case. "Is this truly what a million dollars looks like all together in one place?" He rubbed his hands together and looked up at Tate who stood hovering above the desk. The archbishop picked up one of the neatly bundled stacks of hundred-dollar bills and fanned it. "Why is it, do you suppose, that money is called the root of all evil when, in the right hands, it can accomplish so much good? Now—please sit down and tell me more about the project, Mr. Tate. How far along are your plans?"

Tate watched the archbishop fondle the money with some amusement. He prided himself as something of a psychologist. He was playing the game, enjoying the hypocrisy. "Life," thought Tate, "is a paradox. Men are greedy bastards. Hypocrisy, avarice and selfishness are three fundamental human traits that could always be relied upon. "Men," thought Tate, "who didn't fool themselves, who accepted themselves as they were. These were the only truly honest men. What was it the philosophers said? Know thyself!" Well, Tate accepted himself. He was selfish and greedy. He knew it, and reveled in it. "Men like the archbishop like to believe themselves to be selfless. Such people are both dishonest and deluded. They engage in an elaborate charade of self-deception and the motives of others," he thought, "and are difficult to discern by one unconscious of his own."

"Well," he said, "as I am sure Michael, that is, Monsignor Benedetti, has told you, the financing is in place. For the moment, we will avoid a public announcement. Once I begin approaching key legislators, rumors of our plan are bound to leak out. I thought it best to wait until we were in complete agreement between ourselves before I began the process."

"Very good! Discretion is always advisable, Mr. Tate. In some quarters it's considered the better part of diplomacy. As to the financial arrangements, I am quite satisfied with what I understand you have worked out with Monsignor Benedetti."

Archbishop Doherty rocked slightly back and forth in his leather-upholstered chair, gazing benignly at Andrew Tate.

Tate bowed his head and let out a long breath. "I am pleased to hear that, Your Excellency."

"Good, and now if you would please outline the details of your acquisition plan."

Tate sat up straight. "Yes, we plan to either buy the casino parcel outright or offer the state a one-hundred-year lease, whichever makes the most political sense. Our syndicate will bear one hundred percent of the casino development costs. The state's only financial obligation will be to construct the access road, and we believe that the cost of the road is fully reimbursable from the federal highway trust. So, in the end there should be no real cost to the Commonwealth at all, and the casino will bring in a great many benefits to Massachusetts."

"Yes, yes, of course. And the acquisitions, have you secured all the properties you need?"

"Not all, Excellency, about eighty-five percent, but we have made a provision in the proposed legislation and should be able to secure the rest by eminent domain. But Michael, I mean Monsignor Benedetti, tells me you would prefer not to be involved in that."

"Yes, quite right. I believe this will make things, ahh, simpler. And the money, when might we expect to see the remainder of the agreed-upon sum?"

"My principals have directed me to provide four million dollars in bonds or by wire transfer to an account designated by Your Excellency immediately upon the issuance of the church's letter of support."

"Mmm, I see. You were expecting a letter. I hope that you have not been misled, Mr. Tate, but there can be no letter. If we are to be successful, the archdiocese must be in a position to control events. Timing is of the utmost importance. Both Monsignor Benedetti and I will make the necessary contacts to ensure that the church's position is clear. A public statement of support will be issued once the legislation has passed and before it goes to the governor for signature. I assume that you can supply me with pertinent facts and figures, number of permanent jobs, and so forth."

"But I assumed —Benedetti said—."

"Please, my son," Archbishop Doherty raised his hand and smiled beneficently across the desk. "We must not act prematurely. Were I to issue a letter of support before the bill is submitted, it would appear that the archdiocese is sponsoring Mr. Tate's proposal. That would raise questions and attract unwanted publicity. There are factions, you understand, Mr. Tate, and though as archbishop, I have the final say, we must avoid stirring things up unnecessarily. Monsignor Benedetti will provide you a list of the key people, all good sons of the Church, who will expedite passage of your bill. I have already spoken to two of the most important legislators, and they see no barrier, but it will not be cheap. Both suggest that quick action prior to the beginning of the election season is essential to passage—before opposition has had an opportunity to form."

Tate was thinking furiously. "Damn Guido, the slippery, bloody sod. Work out the details with the archbishop, right! Sure! Son of a bitch!" Could Doherty be trusted to keep his word?" Tate was sweating. "No written statement. How would Yang react?" Well, he had not mentioned anything about a guarantee to Yang, and what the Triad boss did not know would not hurt him. Oh well, damn and blast, in for a penny, in for a pound. He took a deep breath and made his decision.

"What if the church's position becomes an issue in the debate?"

"If we were asked? At that point we would, of course, issue the necessary letter of support. However, I don't believe things will reach that point. It is important that the church be seen as reacting," the archbishop said.

"I see. Very well, Excellency, if I have your word?" Tate said.

"You do, Mr. Tate. We have an arrangement, and, trust me, I know how things work in the Commonwealth."

"Your Excellency's word is guarantee enough." Tate said smoothly. "May I suggest that I deliver the entire down payment personally in bearer bonds? The bonds will be in denominations of one million dollars, each negotiable by the bearer, and completely untraceable."

The archbishop leaned back in his chair, pretended to think for a moment, then nodded and smiled at the developer.

"Yes, excellent idea. And the last payment, the additional five million?"

"Due and payable on the date the governor signs the legislation."

The archbishop pursed his lips and spread his hands. "The Church cannot be expected to guarantee the governor's signature, Mr. Tate."

"True, Your Excellency, but I am sure there are a number of things that the archdiocese can do to influence the governor's decision. I understand that this fall's gubernatorial race will be contentious. We are prepared to make a substantial donation to both campaigns, if necessary, to ease things along and would appreciate any suggestion that you may have as to how that is best handled. We feel, my principals and I, that with this first payment, we are demonstrating our good faith. And we are betting five million dollars on your influence, Archbishop Doherty."

The archbishop leaned back in his chair and stared at Tate.

Tate smiled and met the prelate's eye. "Between the cash payments and the annual grant, this arrangement promises to net the archdiocese more than twenty million dollars," he said.

"Yes, and the Church is very grateful. Monsignor Benedetti was not clear on the terms of the second payment," he said. This was, of course, a lie. Benedetti had completely briefed his superior. It was the archbishop who had insisted that there be no paper trail. If events turned against the legislation, Doherty had decided but had not informed his young protégé, the church had an exit strategy.

"To be completely candid, Your Excellency, Michael made no mention of your terms either. We had discussed a letter. I understand that you must be cautious, and I am sure you understand that we must be equally circumspect. That is why I was so pleased to be able to meet with Your Excellency personally. My principals and I have a great deal at stake. May I tell them that we are in agreement?"

Tate was searching for something in the archbishop's eyes.

The prelate folded his hands on the blotter in front of him, sighed and chuckled. "Well, Mr. Tate," he said, "I suppose if we are to be partners, we must trust each other. We will earn your down payment. But you must understand, Massachusetts's politics would make Machiavelli blush. I am sure you also understand that it would not do, would not do at all, for our financial arrangement to become generally known."

"We are in complete accord, Excellency. As I said, the payment will be in bearer bonds. There need be no public acknowledgement of the gift at all."

"Very good, Mr. Tate."

"I should be able to hand-deliver the bonds early next week. May I have an appointment for, say, Tuesday, at the same time?"

The archbishop smiled, rose and extended his hand.

"Yes, of course, Mr. Tate, we are agreed. It has been a pleasure meeting you, and I look forward to our continuing relationship. If there is anything further that I can do to move our plan forward, I wish to know of it. I believe that Monsignor Benedetti has given you his private number. He is in constant contact with me. Please call him should you need anything. Anything at all."

There was a soft knock and the slender veiled figure gently pushed open the door and entered the paneled bedchamber. As part of her evening ritual, the nun placed a tray on the table next to a comfortable chair upholstered in red silk damask. Positioned diagonally across the room from a king-size, four-poster bed, the table and chair sat in front of a half-wall of built-in bookcases glowing in the soft light filtered through the patterned damask lampshade. The nun turned toward the archbishop, who had just come in from his dressing room clad in a blue, silk dressing-gown.

"Your tea, Excellency," she said with a brief smile and a quick curtsy. "May I pour?"

"Sister Mary Benedict, lovely to have you back with us. I trust your dear mother is on the mend?"

The nun beamed. "Yes, yes, she is. Much better. Thank you for asking and for granting me the time to be with her, Your Excellency."

The archbishop waved his hand in dismissal. "Come, come, Sister, need I recall the words of our savior in Matthew verse 25, to a Biblical scholar of your stature? 'I tell you the truth. Anything you did for any of my people here, you also did for me.' I shall continue to remember her in my prayers and don't worry yourself about the tea, Sister. I'll see to it myself. You may run along, and a very good evening to you."

"Thank you, Your Excellency," Sister Benedict said with a wide smile. "I shall look to Matthew for consolation before I retire. Good night, Your Excellency."

The nun quietly closed the door behind herself.

The archbishop sat down, framed in a narrow pool of light. He ignored the tea implements, picked up the phone and dialed a private number.

The hand that picked up the receiver at the other end was brown-spotted with age and trembled slightly.

"Good evening, Your Eminence."

"Timothy, what a pleasant surprise. How good of you to call."

"I hope I am not disturbing you, Eminence."

"Not at all, it is always pleasant to hear your voice, old friend."

"Thank you, Eminence. I have news that I think will please you. But first, may I ask how things stand in Rome?"

The cardinal sighed. The Holy Father is not well; we fear that he is failing."

"That cannot be too much of a surprise."

"No, I suppose not, but we had prayed for another year at least."

"As serious as that. Events will move quickly, then?"

"Yes, I fear so, Timothy. Tell me your news."

"We are to receive a substantial anonymous gift, four million dollars, and I have complete freedom in its use."

"That is very good news, indeed, Timothy. Praise the Lord! Such an enormous sum! You are to be congratulated. It could not have come at a more crucial time. A quarter of it should be more than enough to secure your elevation to the college. I will begin spreading the word tomorrow. I have a conference call with the Vatican secretary."

"I only hope that it will also be enough to allow me to be present to see Your Eminence as the first American raised to the Chair of St. Peter," Archbishop Doherty said.

The cardinal sighed. "That is in God's hands, Timothy."

"Yes, of course, but with the remainder of this money we will be in a position to address the needs of some of our poorer brothers."

"Four million, did you say? Tell me, how is the sum to be delivered?" the cardinal asked.

"Yes, four million dollars in bearer bonds, in denominations of one million each. I should have them within days. There may be an additional sum, but that is some months, perhaps a year, away."

The cardinal chuckled.

"Excellent! It is unfortunate that we must resort to such measures, but the money will do God's work. Those of us with responsibilities to the living Church must also live in the real world as we prepare the way for our savior."

"True, if his holiness's health is… Perhaps, to facilitate matters, if Your Eminence would provide me with a list, I will direct the funds as you require."

"Thank you, Timothy, that will be a great help. I will prepare a list tomorrow."

"I pray that it is enough!" the archbishop said.

The cardinal sighed. "The Italians will oppose us, as always," he said.

"Do they suspect anything?"

"They dominate the Curia, my friend, and they suspect everyone."

"We must reach out to our African and South American brothers," the archbishop said.

"Yes, and that is where the funds will be of most use. These are poor people, constantly in need of the where-with-all to facilitate our work."

"I believe that God has brought us this gift, Eminence. I shall pray that with His help and guidance we shall overcome."

The cardinal chuckled. "We shall overcome. Indeed, you have always been a most amusing fellow, Timothy. Again, my congratulations! With luck you shall soon wear the red cap. Goodnight, and go with God, my friend."

"Good night, Eminence."

"Sleep well, Timothy."

Chapter 20

Almost Romance

"That went well. I signed up half a dozen volunteers," Alexis said, as she settled herself into the right-hand bucket seat of Flynt's VW. Flynt had just given a talk on community organizing to the students in the Department of Urban Affairs at Boston University. At the end of the Q and A, he directed students interested in volunteering to where Alex sat at a table in the back of the hall.

Flynt raised an eyebrow and shrugged. "The check will help, too. Do I, perhaps, detect a note of criticism here, Ms. Jordan?" Flynt asked as he shifted into gear.

"No, not really! It's just that you basically organized your student audience to help organize the pledge rally," Alexis said, her face turned, gazing at the passing brownstones as they drove down Commonwealth Avenue towards the Common.

"So?"

"Jealousy, maybe! I can't see myself ever pulling something like that off. You are a consummate opportunist, Mr. Flynt."

"Yes, I suppose that proper young ladies see putting oneself forward as indicating a certain lack of breeding."

Alex sighed. "Yeah, something like that, I guess."

"Well, get over it, Jordan! I'm willing to bet your father would not have gotten where he is today if he weren't a consummate opportunist. Let me put it this way; opportunism in the service of good is no sin."

"You're paraphrasing now," Alex said.

"Right you are," Flynt said.

"Not to change the subject, but did you ever wonder who lives in those beautiful houses?" she asked, gesturing out the window.

"Opportunistic folks with a lot more money than I'll ever have," he said.

"Okay, okay, point taken. I just sometimes wonder about the lives of the people who live behind those bright windows. Sometimes I make up stories about the people inside, and sometimes I look in one of the windows and pretend that it's my house, my kids," she said wistfully, then lapsed into silence as they made a right on Columbus Avenue.

"They say we grow up wanting those things that we felt deprived of when we were kids," Flynt said as he turned the steering wheel.

"Well," she said, casting Flynt a sidewise glance and sitting up straight in the bucket seat, "I'll have you know I had a very happy childhood."

"Really?"

"Yes, really. Well, yes, for the most part anyway."

"What about the other part?"

"What other part? You wouldn't be trying to psychoanalyze me, would you?"

"No, just making conversation," he said.

She snorted. "Right! Well, I don't want to talk about it, okay? Where were we anyway?"

"We were talking about needing all the help we can get with the campaign," Flynt said.

"How can I help?" she asked.

"We'll be calling every list we've got. I need someone to train those student volunteers to deliver a pitch. I think you would be good at it."

"I've never done anything remotely like that before."

"Piece of cake. It's just like door knocking. We'll need a fact sheet and a list of answers to the most obvious questions. You've already worked one up. Write it up like dialogue; you know, question and answer. You've been to most of the committee meetings. Think of the questions that people asked. I'll draw up the sales pitch, and you can work from that. Just make sure they understand the issue and then put them through a role play."

"You know, Jed, you're really good at this. I could never do the things you do; my mind just doesn't work that way."

"Why not? You're doing a pretty good job so far."

"With the research?"

"Swift tells me you're a pretty good door-knocker. That's the toughest part of the job," Flynt said.

"Maybe, but, I'm not much of an opportunist. "Teddy says that you're very good at creating a pitch, very convincing. How do you learn to do that? It doesn't seem like it would be part of Marine basic training," Alex said.

"Selling magazines door to door," he said.

Alex's jaw dropped. "You're kidding, right?"

"Absolutely not. I sold magazines all the way through my junior and senior years in high school. Tried encyclopedias too, but that was a summer job, and I lacked the gravitas," Flynt said, smiling into the windshield. "Talk about selling ice cream to the Eskimos! Some of those guys were true artists. We're just selling a different product!"

"I suppose so, but recognizing and knowing how to seize an opportunity, that's a talent, or an instinct maybe. Either you have it, or you don't. Jed, do you ever think about the future? You know, give any thought to what you might be doing say five or ten years from now?"

"Not much, I've got my hands full dealing with the present," he said.

"You can't do this forever, can you?"

"You mean organize? No, I guess not. Organizing is a high burnout profession. Most people only last a year or two. Sooner or later, unless you're a saint or some kind of a nut, you've gotta move on."

"What will you do then?"

"Not sure, but my resume is not likely to land me an executive position in corporate America."

"Somehow I can't quite see you working at I.B.M, but I bet you'd make a great businessman."

"I suppose when the time comes something will turn up."

"Dharma, huh?"

"Yeah—well, no. I don't really believe in fate or luck or whatever you want to call it. Serendipity plays a part, but once you're in a situation, what you do with it is up to you. Fortune favors those who prepare. I have never known what I wanted to do when I grew up. There was this guy I grew up with. Always wanted to be a doctor."

"Mmm, did he? Become a doctor, I mean?" Alex asked, still watching the houses go by.

Flynt kept his eyes fixed on the road. "Yeah, as far as I know, but it doesn't always work out like that. I've kinda lost touch with the old neighborhood. Listen, playing twenty questions is hard work. You hungry?"

"Yes, I missed dinner. Got anyplace in mind?"

"Doyle's? That's just up the street from your place, right?"

"Yes, we can park at my place and walk. Seriously, Jed, do you think you might ever get married again and settle down, you know, have a family?" she asked, her voice seemed far away.

Flynt cast a sideways glance at Alex. She was sitting up, looking straight ahead. He was wondering where this conversation was going.

"Have I mentioned that I'm not much good with kids," he said.

"It probably just wasn't the right time," she said.

"No, I don't think so! How about you?" he asked. "What's next for Alex Jordan?"

"Marriage, kids, at some point, I guess. I'm in no hurry. My father wants me to go to law school. You know, join the firm. That's the next step, I suppose."

"You'll make one hell of a lawyer," Flynt said.

She turned to him and grinned. "Do you think so? Really? Thanks! It's always been my dad's dream. You know—follow him into the firm, and I guess I just sort of pretty much bought into it without thinking too much about it."

"Go for it!" Flynt exhorted..

"I probably will, someday. Meanwhile, I'd like to do something that makes a difference. Any idea what you will do when you finish this project?"

"I don't know. I'd like to travel. Got a taste of it in the Marines. I really like meeting interesting people, but I'd rather not kill them this time around. I've been looking at those cheap round-the-world plane tickets you see advertised in small print in the New York Times."

"Wow, sounds great!"

"Yeah, but it's probably just a pipe dream. I've still got an ex-wife and kids to support. Is this your street?"

"Yes, turn here. The parking area is at the back of the building. Do you see much of your kids?"

Flynt pulled into a vacant parking space and shifted into neutral. They sat for a moment in silence, the motor running.

"Not too often. Your car in the shop?"

"It's really my roommate's car. She went way into hock for it. She's gone home to visit her parents for a few days. Want to come up for a cup of coffee?" she asked, staring straight ahead through the windshield.

"What happened to Doyle's?" Flynt said, looking sideways at her.

She turned her head away. "We could always order out. The Chinese place up the street delivers until 11pm." she said in a soft voice.

Flynt hesitated a moment. "Better not," he said, gazing out the windshield. "It's been a long day, and I've got an early meeting tomorrow morning. Better get home and get some sleep."

"Coffee won't take a minute," she said, staring down at her lap.

He turned and looked at her. "Yeah, but the caffeine will keep me up all night. Look, Alex, you are a very attractive woman, and you have no idea how much I would like to take you up on your invitation, but we work together, and the work that you are doing is very important. What neither of us needs, right now, are complications."

"One of your rules?" she asked.

"Yes," he said.

"Okay, no problem," she said. She popped open the car door. "Alex!"

"No, really, I quite understand." She stepped out of the car, pressed the door closed, and fled toward the back door of the double decker.

"Damn!" he said, watching her receding figure, "Nicely handled, Jed." He sat for a moment drumming his fingers on the shift knob as she disappeared through the back door. She didn't turn around. "Well, what the...? Damn!" he said. The light came on in the second-floor window. He saw a shadow pass in front of the curtains. He pushed down the gearshift, wrestled it into reverse and drove away.

Chapter 21

The Pledge Rally

Mary Kavanaugh tucked Andrea, her youngest, into bed. Mary was dressed in a simple print with a bright silk scarf held in place by an antique cameo she had inherited from her mother. She could hear the TV in the family room blaring. It was turned up much too loud. She tiptoed out of the child's bedroom, shut the door and walked downstairs. Bucky was sprawled out on the couch, his eyes glued to the TV watching Happy Days. He held a king can of Budweiser clutched between his knees. It was his fourth.

"Well, I'm off!" she said.

"Ok, see you later," he replied.

She decided to try one last time. "This is a really, really important meeting, Bucky. I can still have Molly run over from next door. Are you sure you won't come?"

He looked up at her with a tired smile. "You know I'm no good at meetings. But good luck."

Bucky turned his attention back to the TV screen.

The theme repeated: "These Happy Days are yours and mine!"

"Really, yours and mine?" she shrugged, and thought back wistfully. She and Bucky—his real name was Frank—had come from identical backgrounds. They had been high school sweethearts. They had gone off separately to college, saw each other on school vacations, then gotten married after graduation, just as they had promised each other. Their first house was in Newton, but Mary had never been happy in the suburbs—she was a city girl.

When they had first moved back to the city and into the big Victorian, they had become very involved in local community issues, and Bucky had been good at it, at first. But then the drinking started, and he began to withdraw. Now most of his evenings were spent in front of the TV. He rarely went anywhere at night, except maybe to Doyle's or one of the other local watering holes to hang out with his drinking buddies. She glanced at the beer can and tried to think of something else—alcohol, the curse of the Irish . . .

Mary had spent most of her growing-up years in Jamaica Plain. When she was in the fifth grade, her parents had moved from Dorchester into a three-decker on Washington Street, in the shadow of the El, not more than three quarters of a mile from where she now stood. The trains were noisy, but the rent was cheap. In those days the Parkside neighborhood had seemed unobtainable, an enchanted island just down the hill from Franklin Park with its quiet streets and manicured lawns. She had worked as a babysitter for the Carey family right in this very house.

"I might be a little late!"

"I'll be fine," he said.

"Right!" She could be carrying on a torrid love affair, she thought, and Bucky would never notice. There had never been a great passion, not like in the movies, but each knew the other and, well, they were comfortable with each other—like a pair of old dogs, she thought as she stood watching him, his belly straining against his shirt buttons—that paunch hadn't been there a couple of years ago. He was still a handsome boy, but he had put on a lot of weight. He would probably finish the six-pack and fall asleep on the couch. That's where she usually found him when she got back late from a meeting.

She walked out through the kitchen toward the back hall. The Parkside had deteriorated some. The rich Protestants had moved out, but to Mary, moving into their present home had been an adolescent dream come true. She had made it to the Parkside.

I'm lace-curtain Irish now, I suppose. She smiled and thought about how her mother had used that term to describe those jumped-up neighbors who, once they had made a little money, put on airs and looked down on their working-class Irish cousins. "Well, better than living in a shanty and wallowing in the bog," she said, setting her chin.

She pulled on her long, serviceable tweed winter coat. "One thing's sure, I'm here now, and I'll not let some stuffed shirt banker from Beacon Hill destroy what I've built." She smiled at her image in the framed oval of the hall mirror. It had been built into the golden oak wainscoting, and the varnish gleamed under the yellow glow of the entry light. She loved that mirror. She buttoned her coat to her chin, nodded to her image, stepped out into the cold, black night, and pulled the door firmly closed behind her.

6:30pm.

Jedediah Flynt paced back and forth. The auditorium doors of the Mary E. Curley School were still closed. The school had been named after the first wife of Boston's infamous James Michael Curley. Curley had been reelected mayor while serving time for fraud. Flynt stood in the center of the balcony, his elbows resting on the polished oak balustrade and looked down at the empty floor. The janitor had not yet turned up the lights. The red glow of the exit signs barely illuminated the ghostly interior.

The auditorium floor was shaped like a wedge. It flared out from the curtained stage. Three columns of upholstered chairs fanned out from the proscenium in regimental formation to the wall. The balcony would not be needed. The first floor would hold five hundred people. Each chair stood quietly at attention and waited. It was a big hall. If they managed to fill two thirds of those seats it would be enough to establish redlining as a viable issue. He would count that a victory.

Flynt surveyed the hall, analyzing the layout of a battlefield like a general before committing his troops. But the troops were already committed, and the hour before a big meeting was always the worst. He had mobilized the entire staff and neighborhood and student volunteers. The neighborhood had been wallpapered with posters. Reams of flyers had been mailed. Hundreds of phone calls made. But the fear was still there. "What if no one comes?" Flynt whispered to himself.

Flynt rarely slept well the night before a big meeting, and alone in his bed, last night had been particularly rough. He had awakened from a dream, smiled and stretched his hand across the bed in expectation before realizing where he was. Who had he been expecting? He had a good idea but shook off the thought. This must be how a playwright feels, he decided, on opening night. Success or failure. An hour maybe two would tell the tale.

At 7:15 people started climbing the wide stone steps toward the school's high-carved Art Deco façade. The sprawling brick edifice occupied several acres along Centre Street. At 7:25, he walked down the side aisle toward the stage. All the seats were filled and people stood lining the back wall.

Flynt found Mary, Willie-Joe, Don Gaffer, Father Gale and Steve Sigel clustered in a corner backstage. The priest had been added to give the effort the Church's imprimatur. Lourdes, Gale's parish, had been one of those that had originally sponsored the organizing project.

"Looks like a full house," Flynt said.

Mary smiled. "Yes, isn't it great?"

"I've got the volunteers ready to pass out the pledge envelopes. The forms are inside. All they have to do is fill out the form, seal it and write the pledge amount on the outside. We should have a preliminary count before the meeting is over," Flynt said.

"Then we can announce the total tonight," said Willie-Joe.

Flynt rubbed his chin, pretending to consider the idea. "You could—the press is all here. But I suggest you hold back. The campaign is going to get big play on the eleven o'clock news and front page of tomorrow's Globe, regardless. If we wait a couple of news cycles, then hold a press conference to announce the total, that should get us another big splash."

"Jed is right. We covered this at the planning meeting," Mary said.

Willie-Joe, who had missed the planning meeting, shrugged. "The more press the better. Let's go."

"Perhaps Father Gale might be willing to start the meeting off with a benediction," Flynt suggested.

"Great idea," said Mary.

The priest thanked everyone for coming, gave the benediction and introduced the planning committee. Mary outlined the problem—then Willie-Joe took a deep breath and walked up to the podium.

"Can everybody hear me?" he asked, tapping the microphone. He winced at the audio feedback. "Microphones and kids," he said, grinning, "they all love me." People laughed. "We hear you fine," one fellow yelled from the back wall.

. "What have I gotten myself into," he thought. His speech at the press conference had gotten a lot of TV coverage, and a couple of the guys down at the courthouse had made remarks. His career had just begun to get a little traction—he had never thought of himself as either a leader or a radical. He shrugged. "Well, let's hope I don't embarrass myself." He took a deep breath and tapped the microphone one more time.

"There, that's better! Good evening, neighbors. My name is Bill Patrizzi. I live at 133 Blue Hill Avenue. I've lived in Boston all my life. I grew up in the North End on Hanover Street. I love this city. My dream since I was a teenager was to own a house of my own in Boston. Four years ago, I found it, a great house. I made an appointment and went to see my banker. He looked over my financials. 'Best investment you will ever make,' he told me. 'The amount of the mortgage will be no problem, Bill, no problem at all,' he told me, but when I told him where I planned to buy, suddenly there was a problem. Maybe some of you know what I'm talking about." Willie-Joe paused and looked out over the crowd.

"I see several of you nodding. How about a show of hands? How many have had problems getting mortgages or home improvement loans in J. P.?"

About one hundred hands shot up, and a murmur flowed through the audience and spread outward toward the corners of the hall.

"Now I don't know about the rest of you, but I keep a little money in the local branch of the Boston Five Cents Savings Bank. Damned little. I'm not ashamed to admit it, and I suspect, like most of you, most of what I have in this world is tied up in the equity in my home. That is my biggest investment. I believed—hell, my banker assured me—that over time, the value of that investment would increase, and when I got too old to work, I'd have a tidy sum available to ease me into the Odd Fellow's Home. Fact is, that is getting closer every day," he quipped, drawing another laugh.

"But you know what? I think my banker lied. What do you suppose will happen to that equity if bankers start choking off access to mortgage money in Jamaica Plain? You all have read the fact sheet we distributed. The facts are these my friends, over ninety-five percent of all homes are sold subject to a mortgage. How many of you have mortgages?"

Patrizzi gazed with satisfaction out over a forest of raised hands.

"Right, just about everybody. So, what happens if mortgage money dries up? I'll tell you what happens. The housing market crashes, and that 'best investment you will ever make' goes right down the toilet."

Flynt caught Trapp's eye. Trapp had flown in from Chicago for the meeting. They were standing more or less out of sight behind the railing in the darkened area at the back of the hall. Trapp nodded. "He's good," he whispered.

"Last month, we met with the banking commissioner," Patrizzi continued. "Some of you attended that meeting, and some of you probably read about it in the Globe. You know what the commissioner told us? She said that the banks have a fiduciary responsibility to their shareholders to maximize the return on their investment."

"According to Commissioner Gray—remember now, we are talking about banks which are chartered by the Commonwealth to serve the public interest. At least that's what it says in those charters. According to our commissioner, those banks have no responsibility to their depositors—the people in the neighborhoods, you and me, the people who put their hard-earned money into those banks. The banks have no responsibility, even to the people they lend our money to in the form of mortgages. So if they decide to write off a neighborhood, even if it's the same neighborhood that supplies them with the money, well, that's just too damn bad, and that's not the business of the Massachusetts State Banking Commission." An angry murmur rose toward the stage.

"We argued, we pointed out that the money they lend is their depositor's money, that people in the neighborhood are the depositors and are the same people being denied mortgages and home improvement loans."

"None of this made any impression on Louise Winthrop Gray. The commissioner says that that Banking Commission of the Commonwealth of Massachusetts has no interest in where the banks make their loans. But then, Louise Winthrop Gray is a Boston Brahmin, and we all know where she lives."

"Yeah, Beacon Hill," a man shouted from the audience.

Trapp took the cigar out of his mouth and glanced sideways at Flynt. "That bit always gets 'em," he said.

"Right," Patrizzi said, "Beacon Hill. And we all know that Beacon Hill isn't redlined because that is where all the bankers live," he said to general laughter.

People had begun nodding and whispering to each other. Patrizzi had definitely captured their attention.

"When we pointed out to Commissioner Gray the simple fact that the depositors and the mortgagees are the same people, the commissioner had nothing to say. We gave her concrete examples of redlining. She said that it was something else. We asked her to require disclosure of bank lending practices by zip code. She said that it would cost too much and be a burden on the banks. If you ask the banks if they are redlining, they will say it ain't so, Joe, but when you or me or one of your neighbors goes looking for a loan, it's different story. A bank that gives us four percent interest on our savings and at the same time uses that same money to destroy our property values is giving us a pretty raw deal."

"Damn right," somebody shouted, and applause broke out anew.

"What we propose tonight is to do something about it. It is clear that Commissioner Gray will not help, so we must take the burden on ourselves. We have a strategy. We call it greenlining. You know there is a reason why the Boston Five has a branch on Centre Street. They want our money to lend in the suburbs. We are asking you tonight to pledge your savings to greenline Jamaica Plain. We are not asking you to risk your money, and we are certainly not asking you to give it to us. Every bank in the Commonwealth pays the same interest rate, and all deposits are federally insured. All we are asking you to do is to pledge to move your money out of the Boston Five or wherever it is and deposit it in the bank that pledges, in turn, to lend it right here in Jamaica Plain. We call it the Jamaica Plain Community Investment Plan. What do you think? Are you with us?"

The hall erupted in thunderous applause.

"Ok, great. So without further ado, would the volunteers please pass out our pledge forms. Please fill out the form then place it back in the envelope provided. Seal it and put the amount of your pledge in the upper right-hand corner where the stamp goes. The pledges will remain sealed. That way, no one will know your name or the amount of your pledge until we get a bank willing to sign on the dotted line. Then we will open the envelopes and notify everyone."

Flynt cued Steve Sigel who stood peering out from behind the curtains, and Sigel placed the needle on the disk. "Money Makes the World Go 'Round" blasted from the auditorium speakers. Organizers and volunteers swarmed down the aisles and began passing around the blank pledge forms. Two TV stations had set up in the aisles. They turned on their cameras, and the klieg lights lit up the hall, adding to the drama.

Patrizzi stood quietly while the forms were passed around and signaled to turn the music down.

"Please open the envelope and take a look at the form that the volunteers have given you. It has a place for your name, address and phone number. If you believe in protecting your most precious investment, the equity in your home, fill out the form and join us. Fill out the form, place it back in the envelope and write the amount of your pledge on the outside of the envelope. We will add up the amounts on the outside of the envelope and open the envelopes once we get a bank to agree to implement our plan. Your pledge will remain completely confidential. The volunteers will be around to collect it shortly. Make the pledge and join us. Let's all work together to put our money to work for Jamaica Plain. Come on, everybody! Let's show the banks we mean business!"

Flynt sent out Steve Sigel a couple of days before with the assignment to find an upbeat marching song. Somewhere he dug up an old recording of "Happy Days Are Here Again," the unofficial theme song of the Democratic Party. Sigel cranked up the volume again. The song blasted out of the sound system, the volunteers began passing baskets to collect the completed pledge forms, and the klieg lights lit up again.

Alex Jordan walked up to Flynt and held up her basket. "Most people seem to be filling out the pledge forms," she said.

Flynt nodded. "Yeah, only thing missing is the confetti and balloons."

Alex made a face. "You're such a cynic," she said.

Flynt ignored her and scanned the hall, mentally tallying the numbers.

"Damn!" It's working, Jed, my lad!" he said, mentally patting himself on the back. "Greenlining!"

"Gotta hand it to Mary," he shouted back at Alex. "She came up with the perfect tactic."

"Who could possibly object to a pledge drive? Pull em' up by their bootstraps. As American as apple pie," he thought, smiling.

Patrizzi was in his element. He enjoyed the role of the huckster, the sideshow barker. He beamed at the audience. "Hurry, hurry, now everyone," he shouted. "Fill out those forms. Let's show those Beacon Hill bankers we mean business."

Flynt looked over the crowd. A man was just getting up out of his seat. Flynt recognized a familiar profile. "Well, I'll be damned!" The big man turned toward Flynt and made his way up the aisle.

"Whuddya say, Troop?" Lenny Klausmeyer said, holding his hand out with a grin.

"Lenny, what the hell are you doing here?" Flynt said, shaking the hand of his old diner-owner friend and retuning the grin. "You're the last guy I expected to see."

"Well, you know I been threatening to come to one of these Commie rallies of yours. So when I read about this thing in the Citizen, I decided to have a look."

"Well, what do you think?"

Lenny's smile faded. He stepped closer. "Fact is, Troop, this redlining shit hits home. "

"Yeah?"

"Yeah, I found a place right in Sumner Hill, you know? Nice old house. I can walk to the diner. I've been trying to get a loan to buy it, and all I've been getting is the run-around down at the bank. You know I've been here for five years, and I been doing business down at the Boston Five the whole time. Money in the bank, credit's good, so I figured, you know, no problem. And there wasn't, until I found this place, and I gave my banker the address."

"What did he say?"

"Suggested I look at those new condos in the South End or in Newton."

"Actually tried to steer you out of J. P.?"

"There it is," Lenny said, holding out his hand, palm up.

"Damn, I wish you had told me before the meeting. I would've loved to have you tell that story."

"You mean up there on stage?" A look of panic crossed Lenny's face. "Not me, I'd rather face a squad of charging Chicoms! But this greenlining thing sounds like a good idea. Look, I've been taking orders all my life, but this redlining shit ain't right. I like this neighborhood, so sign me up, skipper. I just turned in my pledge. I'm enlisting in this fight."

"Welcome aboard, Gunny," Flynt said with a grin. "Feel like a beer?"

Lenny shrugged, "Sure," he said, looking up at Flynt. "You buyin'?"

Flynt put his hand on Lenny's shoulder. "Maybe you can twist my arm. Give me about twenty minutes to finish up here and meet me at Doyle's. I'll be bringing a group with me. There are a few people I'd like you to meet."

Chapter 22

Organize, Educate, Act.

"The Regional Housing Conference will take maybe six, eight weeks to put together. I think you can use it to push your agenda. It's worked well in other cities. We'll do it under the auspices of National People's Action. The campaign will co-sponsor, and my boss, Cardinal Cody, will call your guy, so the Boston archdiocese will have to go along. I'll do it if you are sure you can deliver the troops," Trapp said.

He removed the half-chewed cigar stub, studied it for a moment, then tucked it back into the right corner of his mouth. He looked expectantly at Flynt.

"We had five hundred at the pledge meeting," Flynt said and gazed across the table.

"Yeah, that went well," Trapp said.

"Went well, hell!" Flynt chuckled softly at the understated turn of phrase.

"Gale Cincotta will come. Best leader I've ever had. She's been head of National People's Action now for a couple of years. She relates well to neighborhood folks, gives a good speech. How about she does the keynote?" Trapp asked, raising a non-existent eyebrow.

Flynt nodded. "Sounds good. Should get us some press attention. I'm looking forward to meeting Gale. Did she really say, "We want it, they've got it—so let's go get it?"

"Yeah, uses that all the time. Great line for getting people up and onto the bus," Trapp said.

"So we put together a few seminars, and that should draw a lot of the liberal bureaucrats from around Boston to show up and help fill the hall," Flynt said.

"You think you can you get both Sargent and Dukakis?"

"With all the press coverage, I don't see a problem. The timing is perfect to play them off against one another before the November elections. Dukakis will come for sure. He's the underdog, and if he agrees, Sargent will have to show or send a high-ranking flunky," Flynt said.

"Yeah, that makes sense."

"One way to find out," Flynt said.

Trapp shrugged.

"One thing I'm not quite clear on," Flynt said.

"Yeah, what's that?"

"Given the fact that redlining in Massachusetts is a state rather than a federal issue, what's in this for NPA?"

"The publicity will help."

"And?"

"And we could use some help with Brook. Your senior senator is on the Banking Committee, and we are having a problem getting the national disclosure bill out of that Committee. The S&L lobby is fighting hard, and we figure that the Republicans will try to bottle it up. Proxmire's the chairman. He and most of the Democrats are for it, so Brook's influence and yes vote could be crucial."

"You want the Banking and Mortgage Committee to invite him to the conference?"

Trapp took the cigar out of his mouth and studied it. "Yeah, that would help. He probably won't come, but..."

"It might give us enough leverage to get him to agree to meet with a delegation in his Boston office?"

"Right."

"Okay. Sounds like a plan. I'll talk to Mary and Willie-Joe. By the way, Shel, you ever pull off an action on a bank?"

Trapp's mouth creased into a slight smile. He sipped from his glass and leaned across the table.

"We did our first one when I was director of The Northwest Community Organization. This Italian guy walks into the office one day, see. He's all ripshit. His son had just mustered out of the army and wanted to buy a house close to the old neighborhood near his granddad, and the Northwest Security Bank refuses him a loan. Tells him it's a bad neighborhood and tries to talk him into buying a house in a new development out in Schaumburg, a little suburb off of Route 90."

"'What's NCO going to do about it?' the guy wants to know. I'm scratching my head. What do I know?" Trapp said with a shrug. "Anyway, the next week, same thing happens. This time a Puerto Rican guy, one of my leaders who owns a small business on Division Street, goes down to Northwest Security looking for a business loan. They turn him down. The bank president tells him 'Division Street is a riot area.' It was a riot area because Hispanics owned businesses on Division Street. In those days NCO was about a third black, maybe a quarter Polish and Italian, and the rest Hispanic."

"So the Puerto Rican guy brings it up at a board meeting, and we send a delegation of leaders down to meet with the bank president. I could of tongue-kissed the guy. At first everyone's making nice. Then the guy says, 'Of course we don't make loans in that neighborhood. It's a slum!' and all hell breaks loose, everybody yelling and screaming. They all lived in that neighborhood. They really wanted to kill the guy."

"What did you do?"

"Look, this was the early sixties. In those days, nobody had ever even thought about redlining. We were focused on block-busting, and it took us a while to figure out that it was part of the same thing. So we call another board meeting and decide to picket the bank. Went down there the next Saturday with about a hundred fifty people. NCO was pretty tough in those days. We picket all day. The following Saturday, seventy-five people. By the third Saturday we were down to about thirty. People are bored, and I could see the issue was dying, so we had another meeting and decided to do a bank-in."

"A bank-in?" Flynt said, "I love it."

"Yeah, nobody had ever done anything like it. We didn't know what to call it. We just made it up as we went along. We put people in the bank. They lined up, put a dollar in their account, ordered a dollar's worth of pennies, then made the teller count them out, stuff like that. Anything to shut the place down. Well, after about an hour this thing is getting old. You know, like Saul said, any tactic that drags on too long becomes a drag. People are milling around, what do we do next? Then Josephine, one of my leaders, she was in her early fifties at the time, takes a roll of pennies that she just bought. She yells 'shit' and throws the pennies on the floor."

Trapp stopped and slowly shook his head side to side. "Throwing money in a bank! It was like a priest in church had just blessed the host then dropped it on the floor. Everything stops, and the guard comes running over. 'What's this?' he yells, kneels down and gathers up the pennies and puts them back in Josephine's hand. Anyway, something tells me we are on to something, so I turn to another woman with a roll of pennies, and I tell her, 'yell shit, and throw them on the floor,' and she does it. Then a couple of other ladies do it, and then the bank president comes running out of his office, all excited, yelling, 'Who's in charge here? What do you want?' 'We want a meeting at 2pm this afternoon with you and your board.' 'Okay!' the guy says—and we leave."

"So we go back to the office and try to figure out some demands. I mean, shit, we had no demands. In the end we decide, four million in first mortgages and four million in business loans, and on the way out somebody suggests a thousand-dollar donation to NCO."

"How did it turn out?"

"They gave us everything, wrote out the donation check right there. We took it back to the office and had a party. Course we didn't set up a monitoring committee, and we had no way to check to see if they actually made the loans." Trapp threw up his hands. "What a bunch of dumb shits—live and learn, right?"

"Well, it was early days. Sounds like you guys did good," Flynt said. Reminiscing had put the light back in Trapp's eyes.

"After that we formed a coalition with this Italian group from Our Lady of The Angels—basically a bunch of racists trying to keep out busing and NCO. Most of our people were blacks from South Austin. Well, one night this guy Al Christi leans over and says, 'My guys really hate these joint meetings, but they told me, hey, we really need them niggers, so they stay with it.'" We had a very tough coalition."

"Amazing!"

"That's what I love about organizing. Half the time you don't know what you're doing, you just do it! It's like life! So tell me your plan."

Flynt smiled. "Well, we've got this follow-up meeting scheduled with the banking commissioner."

Trapp screwed up his mouth, which made him look like a highly disgusted infant. "Like that's ever going to happen," he said.

"Right, we know that. But it may come as a surprise to some of the leadership. So I suggested to Mary Kavanaugh that we invite Robert Sparks as a back-up—he's president of The Boston Five Cents Savings Bank. They're the second largest mortgage-lender in the Commonwealth, and the only big bank with a branch in J. P. Our research shows that they are hardly lending any money in the neighborhood."

"Okay, so?"

"I was thinking of something along the same lines as your bank-in tactic, bring in as many folks as we can during the height of business. Alexis Jordan did a little research on the Boston Five. You know, it's state-chartered—Alex actually read the charter. Back in 1659 when they set up the bank, the deal was you could literally open a savings account for as little as five cents, and that is still enshrined in the bank's charter.

A smile spread over Trapp's hairless baby face like the sun coming out from behind a cloud, and his eyes twinkled. "Holt was right about you," he said. "You are an evil bastard."

"Stan Holt? He helped get me this job. What did he say?"

Trapp smiled. "I asked him about you and he said: 'You and me, Trapp, we both organize out of some sort of religious conviction. Jed Flynt organizes because he's a prick.' That's a direct quote."

Flynt shrugged. "Thing is, after Alex told me, I sent her down to open a savings account and time it. It's fairly complicated. You've got to fill out an application and a signature-card. Then they have this special machine to type up the passbook.

It's handled right at the teller's window and takes at least fifteen minutes. You could probably stretch it out to a half hour if you took your sweet time filling out forms. What do you think?"

"Think? What's to think? It's beautiful. You could close the bank down for a whole afternoon. Think that hoity-toity committee of yours will buy into it?"

As it turned out, Flynt was wrong. It took over half an hour to fill and process the forms and issue a passbook, particularly when every other teller was also busy doing the same thing, and the bank had only one machine that printed the pass books. Flynt passed out copies of the Boston Five's charter at the planning meeting. Willie-Joe Patrizzi read the highlighted portion, and his face lit up. Flynt had casually mentioned the bank-in idea in a phone call just before the meeting.

"Christ, this is great," he said. "We've got them by the…" He glanced at Mary Kavanaugh, and his cheeks reddened. "Well, you know what I mean."

"Oh, yes, I think I do. Does this mean the bank is legally required to open these five-cent accounts?" Mary asked.

"Legally, yes, absolutely. It's right here in the charter!" Willie-Joe said, stabbing the paper with his index finger. "Don't misunderstand. They might refuse, but if they do, it would be a violation of their charter and give us cause to seek a revocation of said charter—and that would be sure to bring even more media focus on redlining," Willie-Joe said smiling and gazing around like a puppy looking for a pat on the head.

Don Gaffer, as Flynt had predicted, hated the idea, but the other members of the planning committee overruled him.

"Look, Don," Mary said reasonably. "The bank action is only a back-up plan. We are simply requesting a meeting. If Mr. Sparks agrees to meet with us, we go forward without the bank action."

"Bob Sparks is an important man, and we should try not to antagonize him," Gaffer said, eyeing Flynt. "I know him, Mary, and I'm sure that he would be more than willing to meet with a small delegation down at the Five's offices. I'll call and arrange it myself, if you like."

"Don't you dare," Mary said. "I'm not about to go along with a meeting in some downtown office and be talked down to by a bunch of stuffed-shirt bankers in pin-striped suits. Let him come down to the church hall. It won't hurt him a bit to get a first-hand look at the neighborhood his bank is helping to destroy."

Flynt smiled.

"And don't you be sitting there looking so smug," Mary said and stamped her foot. "First, we will give the man every opportunity to respond!"

"Yes, ma'am," Flynt said.

Flynt had warned her that Gaffer would probably make just that suggestion. Mary had not believed him and was not pleased at being proven wrong.

Flyers were mailed out. The meeting was advertised with Sparks and Louise Winthrop Gray as the invited guests. Flynt and his staff, along with a couple of volunteers from Flynt's class, made hundreds of phone calls. Would Sparks be there? Yes, people were told, he had been invited, and they expected him to attend. "If someone presses you," Flynt instructed the volunteers, "tell them the truth. He's been invited but has yet to respond." About one hundred fifty people showed up.

As Flynt had predicted Louise Winthrop Gray, backed out, due to "pressing business," and Bob Sparks' response, when it arrived a day before the meeting, was a classic blow-off. He apologized. He was truly very sorry. He just didn't have the time. He suggested that the J.P Banking & Mortgage Committee make an appointment with the bank's PR director.

Mary called the meeting to order and read the letter from Commissioner Gray, and then the one from Sparks. Behind her, high on the wall, the organizers had tacked up two painted sheets that read,

FULL DISCLOSURE

and

STOP REDLINING

in dripping red letters against the stark white wall.

The organizers had found several neighborhood people who had been turned down for home-equity loans by the Five and who agreed to be put on the agenda. After Sparks' response was read, Mary Reagan got up and repeated her story about her experiences with the local branch of the Boston Five. She was a petite white-haired lady in her mid-sixties, and the attention at meetings had caused her to blossom as a speaker. It brought out the Irish in her, her brogue became more pronounced, and her story more heart-rending. She was followed by a couple of people who had been asked to speak, and several more stood up and told similar tales.

The anecdotal evidence was more than convincing, and by the time Mary Kavanaugh finished explaining the effects of redlining on property values and compared the bank's lending history with its assets and neighborhood deposits, the hall was getting hot and smoky, and people were visibly angry.

Willie-Joe Patrizzi stood up and walked to the podium. He was clothed in his signature pin stripes, but he had removed his jacket, loosened his tie and rolled up the sleeves of his dress shirt. Patrizzi was becoming fairly comfortable in his leadership role, and it showed. He gazed around the hall for a few moments, then raised his hand and the hall slowly quieted down.

"Well, there's one thing we know for sure and that is neither the State Banking Commissioner nor the Boston Five Cents Savings Bank gives a plug nickel for the people or the property values in Jamaica Plain."

The hall erupted in laughter and applause.

Patrizzi raised his hand and waited for the applause to die down. Even in the harsh fluorescent lighting his broad face was red and his brow slick with sweat. His dark eyes shone. He took hold of the microphone. "Thank you! We know, my friends and neighbors, that they don't give a plug nickel," Willie Joe enunciated into the microphone. "How do we know? We know because they couldn't be bothered to come down to the neighborhood that they're destroying and meet with us here tonight!

"As for Mrs. Louise Winthrop Gray," Patrizzi said, drawing out the name and doing a fairly good imitation of Brahmin lockjaw, "our State Banking Commissioner, at our last meeting with her, she told us that there was no such thing as redlining. Do you believe that?"

"No!" the room shouted.

"Well, there is a gubernatorial election coming up in November, and the banking commissioner may be able to avoid us, but we have two candidates for governor who will be looking for our votes, and we are going to have more to say to them in due course. The Boston Five Cents Savings Bank has a branch right up on Centre Street and is taking in millions of dollars in deposits—our money. I think it is time that they stopped taking our money and sending it to Newton and Wellesley and started using our money to help improve our neighborhoods.

We are not asking for a handout. We are willing to pay our way. We are asking that the bank stop using our money to redline our neighborhoods. Am I right?"

"Yes!" the crowd roared.

"Damn right! So, ladies and gentlemen," he said, holding up a sheet of paper, "We have a list of demands. The committee drew them up, and you all have read them. Tomorrow at 1pm, Mary and I and the rest of the committee will be boarding the Orange Line at the Green Street Station and going down to School Street to meet with the president of the Boston Five and present our demands. Since Mr. Sparks refuses to come to us, we will go to him. It is important that he, the press and the politicians see that there are more than just a few of us. So we need your help. How many of you will come with us?"

Almost half of those present raised their hands.

"Excellent. You have all read the fact-sheet. So bring along a nickel, because while we are at the bank, we might as well open an account with that nickel and show Mr. Bob Sparks that we do give a plug nickel. I'll see you all tomorrow at one pm. Don't forget to bring that nickel. Meeting adjourned," he said, and slammed his fist down on the podium.

The next day a big crowd was milling about the Green Street MBTA Station when Flynt, Mary and Willie-Joe arrived with Jeb, Alex and the other organizers in tow. Flynt was anticipating an interesting action, and he wanted the whole staff to witness it. They boarded the Orange Line, changing to the Red Line, which let them off a couple of blocks from the corner of School and Washington Streets where the Boston Five was headquartered. About a dozen more people were waiting in front of the bank when the group arrived.

It was a thing of beauty. Flynt found himself wishing that Trapp had been there, but the NPA organizer was back in

Chicago. J. P. residents lined up ten deep in front of the six-teller windows. It was an old-fashioned bank building with an interior tricked out like a European cathedral with massive gray marble columns soaring skyward in a clear bid to project a god-like sense of strength and stability. The floors and counter were marble and topped with old-fashioned gilt ironwork framing the teller's cages.

With all the stone and the high ceiling, the inside of the building had the acoustics of an echo chamber. It took about three hours to process all the new five-cent savings accounts. The people stood happily in line chatting and laughing. Channels 5 and 7, which had been alerted early that morning, sent film crews. Their strobe lights played up and down the lines while the people smiled and mugged for the cameras. Both Mary Kavanaugh and Willie-Joe Patrizzi were interviewed. The Globe ran a photo of Mary, Willie-Joe and about sixty other people standing outside the bank holding up their new passbooks while Teddy and Steve held up a huge Stop Redlining banner behind them.

Eventually Bob Sparks descended from the upper floor, but his attempt to charm the leadership fell flat. His talk of fiduciary responsibility elicited a collective groan from the people who surrounded him. Mary handed him a list of demands and an invitation to the housing conference. He solemnly promised to read over the list and check his calendar and then fled.

People were feeling good, and a sense of accomplishment permeated the atmosphere on the train ride back to J.P. Flynt and Mary sat shoulder-to-shoulder on the narrow café-style bench-seat, and the aging MBTA car clattered and rocked riotously along the track passing homes and factories along its route.

"It was a great action. The press coverage was fabulous," Flynt said, "and you and Willie-Joe were brilliant."

"I think so, too," Mary Kavanaugh said, and then she laughed, her face reddening. "That it was a successful action, I mean. Bill certainly knows how to stir up a crowd. Did you write that speech?" she asked, with a glance at Flynt out of the corner of her eye.

Flynt laughed. "I helped him write a speech, but not that one. I think he just decided to wing it."

"I guess. Well, he's a lawyer, so he's used to speaking in public."

"Yes, he should be," Flynt put in, "but this issue would not be going anywhere without you, Mary."

"Really, do you mean that? Or is it just more organizer malarkey? Sometimes, Jed Flynt," Mary said, the hands in her lap balled up into fists "sometimes I think you will do or say anything to get things to go the way you want them to."

Flynt leaned his head back against the seat and closed his eyes for a moment then turned his head, opened them and met hers.

"Well, Mary, the fact is you are right. My job is to move the agenda ahead. So I do what I can to accomplish that goal. But my cards are on the table, and you and the committee can pull me up short anytime you think I am overstepping."

"Mmm, sometimes I wonder!"

"Hey, who came up with the greenlining idea?"

"Yes, well."

"Yes, well nothing. It was your idea, and it's a brilliant tactic. You heard what Trapp said. It has legitimized the whole struggle in the minds of the press and everybody else. Without it we would be nowhere near as far ahead as we are."

"Bah, more organizer malarkey!"

"You're kidding, right? The press loves greenlining. The banks have been trying their best to spin this whole issue as an attempt by a bunch of scruffy, left-wing, commie malcontents to subvert the free enterprise system, but they can't get any traction because greenlining reminds people that it is our—I mean your—money that the banks are really playing with."

"Do you think it will really work? I mean half a million dollars. Don says it's a drop in the bucket. The mortgage market in Jamaica Plain requires millions of dollars to function effectively."

"Depends on what you mean by work. It's important not to confuse strategy with tactics. As a tactic it's already working, Mary. Remember, greenlining isn't the goal. The goal is to stop redlining. Don doesn't get that greenlining isn't a strategy; it's a tactic we are using against the banks," Flynt said.

"You're saying it really doesn't matter if the investment plan is ever implemented."

Flynt smiled. "The first Globe article on redlining made page seven. We had what, maybe forty people at the meeting? The meeting with the commissioner drew less than a hundred. The greenlining pledge campaign drew almost five hundred, with the Globe, Phoenix, and two TV stations, and it made page one. As you said, Mary, we are about to enter a close political race for governor. We've made redlining a campaign issue.

"Ha! That makes me feel a whole lot better. I just wish some people would stop criticizing," she said.

"What is Willie-Joe saying?" Flynt asked.

"I think he believes that the investment plan will work," Mary said.

"Good! Look, Mary, you're no political green-horn. You've been down this road before. What do you bet the bank action makes page one tomorrow morning? You're never going to please everyone."

The airbrakes screeched as the train slid out of the bright sunlight to an abrupt halt inside the murky womb of Egleston Station. "Right, okay," Mary said, sounding unconvinced. She stood up. "I'll get off here."

"You want me to walk you up the hill?"

"No, I'll be fine," she said, and stood up. "It's just a short walk home."

Flynt looked up at her. "I know more than a few grown men who are afraid to walk through Egleston Square."

"Oh, it's not such a big deal. I live here remember. Have a nice weekend," she said. Then she pointed her finger at Jed. "I'm planning a nice peaceful weekend with my family, so don't call me. I don't want to hear from you until Monday."

"Yes, Madam Chairman," Flynt said, grinning at her retreating back.

Mary glanced back and smiled before she could stop herself. "I mean it, now," she said, and exited out of the train door.

Chapter 23

Foreign Affairs

Jean-Luc Farge adjusted the hood of his balaclava. Wool made his forehead itch, and his knees ached from squatting. He checked the glowing dial of his watch: 3:00am. It was quiet, and there was no traffic on the Egertastrasse.

Farge crouched in the shadows of an arched portico directly across the street from the building where the law firm maintained its offices. He was a big man, standing two inches over six feet with dark curly hair. His rectangular face was fitted with a long Gallic nose and a cleft chin, and he sported a dark, exuberantly styled moustache, which had begun to show flecks of gray. The Frenchman was sure there would be no one in the offices at this early hour, but his training taught him never to take anything for granted. He had spent the last hour watching the windows of the office he sought. The night was clear, and there was no moon in the frosty night sky. He could just make out the outline of the grand duke's castle topping the ridge, a dark shadow looming over the town. Jean-Luc shifted his weight and rubbed his gloved hands together briskly.

He was not sure—well, actually, he was quite sure—why he had let Alexis Jordan talk him into this early-morning excursion. He had grown quite fond of her during their time together in Paris two summers previously. They had become lovers soon after they began working together.

It was all very straightforward, and he liked that she did not play the coquettish little games French women insist upon. When it was time for her to return to the United States, she did so with a minimum of tears. If this is what American feminism was about, he was all for it. Jean-Luc was a man's man. He'd had many liaisons, but he found himself thinking of Alex quite often. She was still young, of course, but that simply added a bit of spice, and he looked forward to renewing their acquaintance.

Farge had been recruited by the SDSE, the French CIA, during his mandatory two-year tour in the French Army. He had quit the agency at thirty-five and gone into private practice, and at thirty-nine he considered himself too old for that sort of life. Still, he found lawyer's work boring, and he missed the adrenalin-rush of playing the spy game.

Aside from the fact that it is the capital of the Duchy of Lichtenstein, the city of Vaduz looked exactly like what it was, a provincial European town. The building he watched had been built in the late eighteenth century in the French baroque style. Like its neighbors, it was three stories with long, narrow windows and a gabled roof.

Time to go! Farge stood, edged along the portico keeping well into the shadows, listened for a moment, then dashed down the wide stone steps, across the empty street and down a narrow alley between his objective and the adjacent building. He stopped at the heavy wooden door and extracted a slender penlight from a side pocket in his camouflage trousers. With the light clamped firmly between his teeth, he extracted a flat L-shaped, steel tool from a front pocket, slid it between the lock and door frame, pressing it back until he heard a distinct click. Then he pushed the door inward and slipped inside. With his flashlight playing along the corridor in front of him, he leaned back against the door and pressed it closed.

Once his breathing slowed, he could just hear the measured ticking of a clock. He compared it to the loud heartbeat hammering in his ears—his heart rate was elevated— It had been a long time since he had done anything like this. The previous day, dressed as the successful lawyer and carrying an expensive briefcase, he had reconnoitered the building by daylight. No one had given him a second look. He knew the exact location of his target, the third-floor offices of Attorney Dr. Dr. Herbert Altmann. He smiled at the twin titles, only a German, he thought, would insist on using the two degrees in tandem.

Two stairways led to his objective, a wide, main one in the front and a dark, narrow servant's staircase in the center rear. He mounted the latter and made his way to the third-floor hallway. The office door was half-glassed and proved no more difficult to open than the first, though Jean-Luc took extravagant care to see that he left no telltale marks of his entry. He pushed the door closed and locked it.

Using the penlight for illumination he systematically explored the interior of the offices. The first room was obviously a reception area. It was wood paneled, had a single desk, a very good oriental rug and several comfortable looking upholstered chairs. There were several doors leading into the inner offices. Beginning clockwise from the left he reconnoitered each in turn. Behind the third he found what he was looking for, a wall of standard four drawer, steel file cabinets. The drawers had been helpfully labeled alphabetically from left to right. In the second cabinet in the third drawer labeled Pa-Pq he found a file with "Paladin Properties" typed neatly across the tab.

"Qu'est-ce que...?" He froze! It sounded very much like footsteps approaching. Farge exited the file room, pulled the door closed, crossed the room and pressed himself into the wall so that he would be hidden behind the opening door.

Herr Professor, Dr. Dr. Herbert Altmann took the stairs two at a time. Altmann had overslept at his mistress's apartment, and he was in a tearing hurry to get home. Why had the silly bitch not awakened him? His wife would never believe that he had fallen asleep on the couch in his office, but he knew he must make a show of outrage at her charges and hope that she would allow herself to be mollified with an expensive gift. She had known about Julie for months; he was sure of it. The leather jeweler's box was in the bottom drawer of his desk. He had planned it as a surprise for his mistress, but now he supposed his wife, Anna, must have it.

The lawyer was puffing hard when he reached the top of the stairs. He reflected briefly on the five kilos he had added since he had stopped his morning runs. He paused for a few moments to catch his breath, flipped on the wall switch and a row of overhead tubes illuminated the corridor. He hurried down the hallway, reaching into his pocket for the office key. He unlocked the door, flung it open, and not bothering with the inside light switch, turned right and moved toward his office door.

As he groped forward, something grabbed his shoulder. He yelped and flinched, but before he could react further, he was spun around. A quick punch to the midsection drove the air from his lungs and doubled him over, and a rabbit punch dropped him face down onto the floor. Altmann twisted his head, attempting to catch a glimpse of his attacker. What he saw was a dark hulking shadow, then he felt a pain like a bright light, followed by an explosion along the side of his head, and he lost consciousness.

Jean-Luc stood over the lawyer's body sprawled across the rug. His heart was pounding, and his chest heaved like a steam engine. He examined the man's face in the beam of the penlight. "Merde!," he said out loud. He recognized the figure curled up on the floor. Whatever possessed the man to come back here at this time of night? He must work quickly. There was no telling how long the lawyer would remain unconscious. He placed his index finger just beneath Altmann's left ear. The pulse was strong, and the man was breathing evenly. Good! He didn't want to chance hitting him again, but when the lawyer came to, he would know that someone had broken into his office—exactly what Farge had hoped to avoid.

Jean-Luc returned to the file room, opened the drawer and removed the file. He brought it into the office, placed the lawyer's desk lamp in the middle of his blotter and turned on the lamp. He extracted an 8mm Minox miniature camera and a small tripod from a pocket. He spread the legs of the tripod and screwed the tiny camera at its apex.

Working methodically, he placed the contents, including some official-looking documents stamped with the seal of the duchy and several pages of accounting sheets with typed columns of figures one by one beneath the pool of light; He photographed them, then returned each to its proper place in the folder. He checked his victim from time to time, but Altmann seemed to be sleeping peacefully. When he had finished, he returned to the wall of cabinets and nestled the folder back into the file drawer between a folder marked Pam and another beginning Pap and slid the drawer closed. Then he checked his watch, 3:45am.

"Putain, what now? Create a diversion and allez!" He went back to the lawyer's office, swept everything off the top of the desk, pulled out drawers and scattered their contents around the room. He looked around at his handiwork. It looked as if someone had searched the desk for valuables. That should get them off the scent. He walked out of the office, kneeled and played his flashlight briefly over the crumpled unmoving figure on the floor of the reception area, then let himself out of the office. Merde! The hall lights were still burning. He ran down the hall, turned the switch to off, then disappeared down the back stairway.

Three hours later, Attorney Dr. Dr. Herbert Altmann groaned and rolled over onto his back. He blinked several times, then covered his eyes against the morning sun streaming 'though the office windows. "Where am I?" He winced. The sound of his voice sent a spike of pain across his temples. He lay still for several minutes as his memory began to return. He had come into the office to get what? He recalled the shape of the man astride him. Who was he? What did he want?

Altmann was not a naïve man. He knew that many of the two hundred or so companies he fronted were engaged in illegal activities and that the men who controlled the trusts he represented were criminals, some of them very dangerous men. But, he reminded himself, every man, no matter how bent or depraved, was entitled to equal protection under the law, and it was his job to see that they got it.

He groaned and put his hand to his face. There was a lot of swelling around his jaw. Had he lost any teeth? He ran his tongue gingerly around the inside of his mouth. No, everything seemed intact. With difficulty he forced himself onto his knees. Well, he thought, now I have a real alibi. Mugged in his own office. No need to give Anna that bracelet after all.

His head was pounding like a drum. He stood, tottered over to the couch and sat down heavily.

Someone had broken in to his office. This was not acceptable. His clients demanded security and confidentiality above all things. If word of this should get out, he could lose a great deal of business. He started to sweat. The money was good, good enough for him to afford what amounted to a small villa on several hectares in the hill country outside of Vaduz. It allowed him expensive vacations to French Polynesia, a wife, and a mistress.

He looked around the room and noticed that the file room door was ajar. He stood up with a groan and entered the room. Everything appeared to be as it should. One at a time, he pulled the drawers. Nothing seemed amiss, but he would check more carefully later. His head throbbed, and he was suddenly very thirsty. He turned and walked through the reception area into his private office.

"What a mess! What could anyone have wanted in here?" he asked himself. Money? He kept no money in the office—but then a robber would not know that. Remembering his thirst, he stepped over an overturned desk drawer, being careful to avoid the papers scattered around the floor and opened the door to his private washroom. He twisted the cold water tap, filled a glass, then opened the medicine cabinet, picked up a bottle, opened it and shook out two aspirins. He thought for a moment and shook out a third. He popped them into his mouth, swallowed and greedily emptied the glass. Ah, that's better! He studied his reflection in the mirror over the sink. His eyes were bloodshot, and the side of his face was beginning to turn purple. "Well, that should convince my wife," he thought.

Altmann loosened his tie and unbuttoned the top button of his shirt. It was Saturday. His staff would not be in until

Monday. Staring into the mirror he made a decision. Publicity must be avoided at all costs. He would straighten out the office and go home as if nothing had happened. What about the intruder? What did he want? He would figure that out later. Whoever it was certainly was not going to advertise his work. So he was safe. First, a call to his wife and then he would tidy up.

Chapter 24

Completing The Puzzle

Alexis Jordan felt her hand shake as she lowered the phone into its cradle. Her conversation with Jean-Luc had been short and horrifying. The documents were on their way, airmail. But he had given her the gist of the contents.

"I checked out these guys with an old friend who is still in intelligence, Alexis. Just as you thought, Paladin Properties is a holding company. The names of the principals are Andrew Tate and Herbert Yang.

"There are a couple of other companies named, but I had a problem and didn't have a chance to access those files. Tate is an Anglo-American developer, British father, American mother, so he holds dual citizenship. Educated at a toney prep school in Switzerland. His father started a construction company in Hong Kong just after the Great War. The company fell on hard times after the colony was turned over to the communists. Tate took it over and has been involved in several major construction projects in Hong Kong and Macao. He has done business with a couple of dicey organizations but has no criminal record so far as my friend could determine. I've typed a summary of all that, and I'll include it in the package.

"Here is the real dynamite. The financing appears to be coming from the White Dragon Group. Herbert Yang is, how do you say in English, the head dragon, or whatever they call le patron, the big boss. Alexis, Yang is a seriously bad actor. My sources tell me that the White Dragon Group is the public face of the Ghost Dragon Triad, one of Hong Kong's oldest and most successful criminal organizations. Their people are, how do you say, up to their necks in murder, kidnapping for profit, loan-sharking, the heroin trade, prostitution, you name it. The White Dragon Group owns a string of casinos in Asia and East Africa. The casinos provide a perfect conduit to clean the Triad's dirty laundry."

"From what I hear, Yang is a very smooth, well-spoken individual, and, would you believe, a graduate of your Harvard Business School. But, please, Alex, don't let his resume fool you. This man is a gangster, as ruthless as they come. SDCE has a thick file on him.

"So, he is not exactly an unknown quantity," Alexis ventured.

"Far from it, if you know how and where to look, "Farge said, smiling into the phone. "The word is, a few years ago, discipline in the Triad organization was breaking down—the younger gang members were in revolt against the old ways of doing things. When Yang became the patron, the rebels thought they had won a victory.

"Yang invited two of the biggest troublemakers, two brothers, to a meeting, to reconcile their differences. When the two young Turks showed up, Yang's men overpowered them and strapped them down to tables facing each other. The rumor is that Yang made the younger one watch while he personally skinned his older brother alive. It took the guy, howling in agony, almost two days to die. Then Yang released the younger brother, told him to go back and tell his friends what they could expect if they didn't toe the line. These people, Alex, are pure poison! I don't know exactly what is going on, but my advice to you is to keep away from them. Really—I am worried about you. "

"Jean-Luc, do the documents you copied shed any light on why a group of Asian gangsters might be buying worthless property in Boston?"

"No, Alexis. I copied the list of the properties they have acquired. That is in the packet I sent. These properties are the only assets listed besides cash. There is nothing more. I'll send it Express Mail. You should have it in a few days."

"How about their financing?" Alexis asked.

"They have established a numbered account in a bank in Zurich. It is in the packet," Jean-Luc said.

"How much money?"

"One hundred-seventy-five million Swiss Francs, just under forty million U. S. dollars."

"My God, Jean-Luc, that's a fortune. What could they be up to that requires that kind of money?"

"Who can tell, Alexis? There is nothing in the file. Perhaps, ma petite, they plan to ransom Patty Hearst?" Farge said with a droll smile into the phone.

"Very funny, Jean-Luc," Alex said suppressing a smile of her own.

"Seriously, as I said, gambling is their main business, building and running casinos. They are all over Asia and East Africa. I've been in the casino in Mauritius. Très beau, it must have cost millions to build. Perhaps they are planning to build a casino in Boston. Is that possible?" he asked.

Alexis thought for a moment. "Impossible, Jean-Luc. Gambling is illegal in Massachusetts. In fact, it is illegal in forty-nine out of the fifty states, except Nevada, I think. Massachusetts has a lottery, but they would have to pass a law to permit casino gambling and license it. No way that's going to happen."

"If you say so, but there is certainly something big going on. And if these people are involved, there is a great deal of money to be made. I will leave it to you, but do be careful, very careful."

"I'm worried about you, Jean-Luc. You took a big risk, and I am grateful. Was there any problem? Are you all right?"

"Yes, Alexis, no problem at all," Farge lied. "I mean to say, I think—yes, I am all right, and no, there was no problem, comprends-tu? You know that I am completely a professional in such matters."

"Yes, of course, Jean-Luc," she responded quickly. She knew Farge well enough to be sensitive to the Frenchman's ego.

"The operation went very smoothly. There is a proper way to do such things, you understand, Alexis."

"I am so impressed, and grateful, Jean-Luc. I am sure that you accomplished the whole thing flawlessly."

"Yes, well, merci ma souris. There is a small chance, you know, a very small chance that the lawyer in Lichtenstein will figure out what happened, so you must be careful with the photostats. Make sure to destroy the envelope immediately— that is evidence which could be used to trace the documents back to me."

"Yes Jean-Luc, I will do that right away. Don't worry," Alex said. "I am very grateful. What you have done will help a lot of people."

"It was my pleasure. But Alexis, I am very serious when I speak about these people. I am worried for you. Perhaps you should take some time, come to Paris. I would love to see you. we could, you know, visit some of the places we used to go . . ."

She smiled into the phone. Alexis Jordan knew exactly what Jean-Luc Farge was suggesting, and she was tempted. It's not as if she'd had much of a love life around here. But the information the Frenchman had provided was, as he had himself rightly said, pure dynamite. At the moment she was uncertain. Not all of the puzzle seemed to have pieces that fit. She knew that somewhere in the documents was the clue, the key they were looking for. She also knew that the greenlining project would need her—and that Jedediah Flynt, whether he chose to admit it or not, would need her, too.

"Oh, that would be lovely, but I can't possibly get away right now. The information you are sending is really important, Jean-Luc, and we must act on it immediately. Perhaps in a few months, when this is all over, we can talk."

"Well, okay, adieu, chérie, au revoir. I shall look forward to hearing from you," said Jean-Luc Farge. "And Alexis—please be careful."

Chapter 25

Forbidden Fruit

Jimmy Finnerty looked around, then knocked on the door a second time. He knocked so hard that he skinned his knuckles, but no one answered the rectory door. It was a gray afternoon, the sky a catacomb of low brooding clouds. Standing on tip-toe on the top of the stoop, he could just peer through the bottom windowpane into the empty hallway. He knocked again and waited. Finally working up his courage, he took hold of the knob. It turned easily. Jimmy took a deep breath, pushed the door open, then froze. Cowering like a game bird under a bush, he listened. The waxed floor tiles gleamed faintly in the murky, gray twilight of the winter afternoon. He stepped into the hallway and gently pushed the door closed behind him.

He half expected to hear Mrs. O'Riley, the hatchet-faced housekeeper, her grating voice like the sound of crumpling construction paper. "What are ya, a cripple? Pick up yer feet, ya young hoodlum, and don't be scuffing me floors, or I'll tell Father on ya!"

Jimmy's mother was a devout Catholic. She raised both her boys as she had been raised, strictly, so that each had an inkling of the rewards of Heaven but understood in graphic detail the snares of the Devil and the pain and suffering that awaited the sinner in Hell. She was pleased that Father Bob had taken an interest in her youngest. "He is a special little boy," Father Bob had told her, and she was fair to bursting with pride that the handsome young priest had picked her Jimmy to be an altar boy.

Suddenly Father Johnson's deep basso voice echoed down the passage. The pastor stepped through a door, accompanied by another priest. The second man was taller and wore a purple sash. That must be the door, Jimmy decided, that the priests use to enter the church. Father Johnson and his companion were talking together, and at first, they didn't notice the little boy cowering at the other end of the hallway.

Jimmy was curious about what lay behind closed doors. He was particularly curious about the sacristy. His brothers told stories about the holy room behind the altar that only the priests and altar boys were allowed to enter. That was where they kept the robes and the red cassock and white surplice that he would wear for the first time this coming Sunday at eight o'clock mass. Jimmy pictured himself wearing the pure, white garment. He could almost see his mother's shining eyes as she watched him from the third pew from the right, near the front of the church where he and his family always sat.

Jimmy's brother Kevin, a former altar boy, had warned the boy that he was never to enter the sacristy when Father Johnson was alone and to always make sure one of the other boys was with him. When Jimmy had asked why, his brother had just shrugged and when he had pressed, Kevin flew into a rage and ordered him to shut his fucking face and do what he was told. At such times Jimmy would bolt and hide from Kevin's angry fists.

"Aha, who's this now?" Father Johnson squinted at the boy and motioned him forward. "Come closer, lad," he said, beckoning. "Remind me now, my boy, I've forgotten your name?"

"Jimmy, Jimmy Finnerty, Father," he squeaked out his last name as his young voice broke from nervousness. He looked up at Father Johnson with large hazel eyes. "I'm sorry, Father. I knocked. Honest Father, but nobody answered the door, and it was open. I've come to see Father Bob," he said, straightening up. "I'm to be one of the new altar boys," he said, a touch of pride in his voice.

Johnson gazed at the boy. Jimmy was short for an eight-year-old, slightly plump with a pair of dimples set in a roundish face, fine skin and soft blond hair parted on the right side so that, combed over, it spilled down over his forehead like a waterfall covering his left eyebrow.

Father Johnson stooped down, looked the boy in the face and smiled. "You're a fine-looking lad," the priest said, smoothing back the boy's hair that slipped, soft as silk, through his fingers. The boy winced and shied like a young colt. The priest reached forward and cupped his chin.

"There now," the priest said, holding the boy firmly, "Father won't hurt you." His mouth smiled. Dark eyes like polished obsidian pinned the boy in place.

Father Johnson had a long angular face that was softening and beginning to jowl. "Finnerty, is it? Would you have a brother named Kevin at all?"

Like a small, trapped animal, the boy ceased his struggles and went limp.

"Yes, Father. Kevin is my brother. Could you tell me, Father, where I can find Father Bob, Father?" his eyes nervously darting from side to side, refusing to meet the priest's. "He said I was to report to him as soon as school let out. He said I was to come right along and not be late."

The priest's smiled broadened. "Aye, I thought so. A fine young man, your brother served as my altar boy when he was just about your age. Did you know that?"

Father Johnson let go of Jimmy's chin, placed his hands on his knees and struggled to his feet. "Do you know who this is, Jimmy?" he asked, looking down at the boy and indicating the other man.

"No, Father," the boy said, with a quick glance up at the elegant figure who smiled benevolently down at him from a great height.

"Well, young Jimmy, this is Monsignor Benedetti, come for a visit from the archdiocese. Say 'how do you do' to the monsignor, Jimmy. The priest's is a very important man. He stands at the right hand of the archbishop himself."

"Good afternoon, Jimmy," the man said.

Jimmy was awed. Hadn't his mother told him that priests like Father Johnson and Father Bob stood next to the Almighty himself and that he must always obey them? This man stood even above a priest.

"How do you do, monsignor," the boy said, staring resolutely down at the floor, afraid to look up lest he be blinded by the monsignor's magnificence.

"I do very well, thank you, and it is always a pleasure to meet a young man who is about to become an altar boy. It is a mark of special favor. I was an altar boy, too, when I was your age, and I remember serving my first mass. I was very nervous. Are you nervous, Jimmy?"

"You see there, Jimmy," said Father Johnson, "even a man as important as the monsignor—well, never mind. Father Robert will be expecting you, and I expect that you will find him in the church. Be off with you now, and remember, I will be keeping an eye on you, so be sure to do everything that

Father Robert tells you," Father Johnson said, patting the boy's head.

"A fine looking boy," the monsignor said as he watched Jimmy scamper down the hall and burst like a cannonball though the door, out into the darkening afternoon.

The two priests watched the boy go.

Johnson pushed open a door across the hall and stepped back, gesturing to the monsignor to precede him into a small parlor. The room was sparely furnished with a rag-rug covering the polished oak floor. He directed the monsignor to a well-stuffed armchair and sat down in another so that they faced each other across a low, dark wood table. Both chairs had lacy, hand-crocheted antimacassars which matched the window curtains.

"There now, we may as well be comfortable. May I offer you tea, coffee? The coffee is a bit old, I'm afraid. The housekeeper has the afternoon—"

Benedetti shook his head. "No, thank you," he said.

"Something stronger?"

"Thank you, no, Harold," the monsignor said with a tired smile. "This is to be a very brief visit, I'm afraid. I've come to ask a favor."

"Of course, Monsignor. It will be my pleasure to help however I can," the priest said. Father Harold Johnson was sixty-two, more than twenty years older than the monsignor. Johnson had met Benedetti just twice and knew of him mostly by his fearsome reputation. Father Johnson folded his hands, regarded the monsignor with what he hoped looked like humble deference and listened carefully to his instructions.

"So, I am to inform Mr. Flynt that, due to unforeseen circumstances, I must withdraw permission to use the parish hall for their housing conference?" Johnson replied.

"Exactly!"

"After which you will pretend to intervene, and I will reluctantly reverse that decision and allow the conference to go forward?"

"Yes!"

"Is it permitted to ask, Monsignor, the purpose this elaborate charade?"

"You have met Mr. Flynt"?

"I have. He introduced himself and came over to the rectory for a little talk when he was first hired," Johnson said.

"What do you think of him. Your honest opinion?"

"Well, the campaign is providing the funding, so I assume that he—"

Benedetti raised his hand and smiled. "I asked for your honest opinion, Father."

Johnson eyed Benedetti for a moment. "Well, Monsignor, since you ask, I think that the man is a dangerous radical. I must confess, I find it difficult to understand the direction the campaign has taken in recent years."

"Very astute!" Benedetti leaned forward and lowered his voice. "Between us, Harold, Mr. Flynt is, as you say, a dangerous radical, but as it happens, it is important to the archdiocese that I win his confidence, that he sees me as someone he can confide in." The intensity of Benedetti's look penetrated Johnson with an alarming unease. "It is important that we know his plans."

Johnson dropped his eyes, nodded. "I see. Well, you may rely on me to play my part, Monsignor."

Benedetti rose and held out his hand. "I depend upon that Harold," he said.

The two men shook hands.

"And I thank you. You may rest assured that I shall mention our conversation to the archbishop. I think the little problem last year about that young boy."

"It was a terrible misunderstanding, Monsignor. He is a very troubled young man."

"Yes, of course, Father, I quite understand." The Monsignor gripped the priest's shoulder firmly with his left hand. "These misunderstandings happen. Mother Church understands. Think no more about it. You have served the archdiocese well, and you can be sure that any mention of the... ah... incident will be removed from your file."

Chapter 26

Tip-Off

"Yes Linda, I know."

Flynt was pacing the floor with the phone body in one hand and the receiver held to his ear with the other when Alex arrived at the office. He acknowledged her with raised eyebrows as he spoke. "Look, Linda, I am really busy here. I'll come by next week," he said, pleading with the receiver.

He stopped abruptly in place. "Okay, okay. I get the point. I'm an awful dad, but I'm working on it, okay?"

Alexis looked around for something to do. She spotted Steve sitting at his desk and started off in his direction. But Flynt caught her eye and gestured for her to wait.

"Yes, okay, I sent the check yesterday. You should have it tomorrow. Listen Linda, I can't talk now, so I'll see you. Bye."

Flynt placed the receiver none too gently into its cradle and dropped the phone onto the desk.

"Sorry about that, Alex," Flynt said. "What have you got?"

He ran his hand though his hair as he looked around. Swift was on a call, and Sigel had just picked up the phone.

"Wait, better not talk here," he said and opened the door to the conference room.

They sat down, and Alexis laid out the photostats and outlined what Farge had told her.

Flynt got up and started pacing.

"Forty million dollars is one hell of a lot of money," he said. "It's ballsy as hell but a casino? It's the only thing that really does make sense. Look Alex, you were the one who made me see it. What is the Southwest Corridor? Fifty empty acres smack in the middle of Boston with dedicated six-lane access to a major highway."

Her eyes followed him. "But legalized gambling? Isn't that something of a reach? Surely no amount of money can buy a whole state legislature."

Flynt pulled out a chair, sat down facing her across the table, rubbed his chin and smiled.

"You don't think so? You should spend a little time over on Beacon Hill. With that kind of money those guys would sell you the deed to the statehouse. You know, I still can't believe you got this Jean-Luc guy to burglarize a lawyer's office to get this stuff," he said, waving his hand at the photostats laid out on the conference room table. "You're sure there's no chance he'll be caught?"

"Listen Jed, I didn't ask him to do it," Alex protested. "I had no idea until he told me. He said it was the only way he could get the information."

"You sure?" Flynt asked, looking down at her balefully.

Yes, Jed, and don't act so innocent. You knew he might have to bend a few laws."

"Well."

"Jean-Luc assured me that the whole thing went off very smoothly. He is a professional. The lawyer won't even know that the break-in ever happened, and that was the only way we were ever going to get the information. I mean, who was it that said: "If the ends don't justify the means, I don't know what does," she said.

Flynt sat down heavily. "Yeah, ok, you're right. You did a great job. If you hadn't uncovered the plot, these Chinese wise-guys might have turned the neighborhood into chop suey before anyone had a chance to object. But breaking and entering! This could have serious fallout if the archdiocese ever gets wind of it. Our funding would be out the window. Okay, so here's the story: this stuff was mailed to me anonymously, right? I have no idea of the source. Your name won't even be mentioned, understand?"

"Okay, that makes sense," she said.

He got up and resumed pacing. "Now we have to figure out if what we think might be happening actually is. In the meantime, I have another problem—seems like Father Johnson has had second thoughts about us using the Our Lady of Lourdes hall for the housing conference."

"But Jed, the conference is less than three weeks away. All the flyers and invitations have been sent out, haven't they?"

"Yeah, but that doesn't seem to concern the good father."

"I thought Lourdes was supporting the project."

"So did I. Bob Gale was a big help when the block club went to that slumlord's bank and demanded that the bank force the pig to clean up. He even gave the benediction at the pledge rally. I thought he was really hot-to-trot after that—excuse the expression— but all of a sudden I can't get him to even return my calls."

"So what happened?"

"Who knows? Maybe the slumlord was a big donor to the parish or some of this commie nonsense got to Johnson. This kind of shit happens all the time! Johnson has always been lukewarm about the project. He's a pal of Craven's, the local state rep, and that guy hates us. Thing is, Alex, organizing churns up a lot of enemies. People think that the status quo exists due to inertia, but the fact is, things are as they are usually because it's in someone's self-interest for them to be that way."

"So what now?"

"Not sure. I've got a call into Monsignor Benedetti over at the diocese. I'm hoping that he will intercede. Otherwise, we work all weekend getting out a new flyer and press release."

"And what do we do about our suspicions?" Alex asked.

"Move carefully, drop a few hints here and there and see what turns up. I'll have to let the committee in on this, but we'll wait until a few days before the conference. We don't want any leaks."

"Will they believe you?"

"With all the stuff you've turned up, you bet! First, I'll sound out Mary and Willie-Joe separately, see what they think. If these guys pull this thing off, it means the end of the neighborhood. With the election coming up in November, they're going to have to act soon. They can't afford to wait. Sargent and Dukakis are both strong candidates, and there's no telling who will win the governorship. If Dukakis wins they are sunk. The man is a monk. He'll never go for legalized gambling."

"What about Sargent?" she asked.

"Doesn't matter. The Democrats own the legislature. If Sargent doesn't go along, they'll simply override his veto," Flynt said.

"I've got a question about strategy. Slightly off the subject," Alex said.

"Ok, shoot."

"The investment plan, you know, greenlining? We've invested a lot of time and energy on it. I really don't understand why. Even if we raise a million dollars, is it really worth the effort? I've done some research, and it looks like Jamaica Plain requires about twelve million a year to finance the housing market. So how does greenlining work as a strategy?"

Flynt grinned. "Greenlining doesn't work as a strategy because it's not a strategy; it's a tactic. Look, what's our objective?"

"That's easy, stop redlining," she said.

"And, who has the power to do that?"

"Well, the banks could stop it, but they won't, so the state of Massachusetts or the state banking commissioner, I guess," she replied.

"Bingo!" he said aiming his finger at her.

"So it doesn't matter how much money we raise?"

"Sure, it matters. It's newsworthy, and it creates a rallying point. You can't build an organization on failure. This could be a long hard fight. We need victories to keep our momentum, and people perceive the investment plan as a victory. All good things, right?"

"But, it doesn't really matter how much we raise or even if the plan is never implemented," she said.

"There it is," Flynt said spreading his arms.

"Ok, I get it! Dumb question!" Alex said. She flipped open her notebook and clicked her ballpoint. "So what should I be doing now?"

"Well, focus on the evils of gambling. Start researching statements made by prominent Catholics, you know, priests, bishops. We need to prepare to build a wave of opposition. This casino promoter Tate has to be spreading some serious money around Beacon Hill. They can't keep a move this big under wraps for much longer, and when they move, we'd better be ready."

"What about the archdiocese. Wouldn't any legislative attempt to legalize gambling need the archbishop's support?" she asked.

"Well,.." Flynt halted in mid-thought and stared at Alex is if stunned. "Ye-s-s, absolutely. The church has always been opposed to gambling, at least I think it has," he said. "Look Alex, we need to know the Church's historical position on gambling. I'd better sound out Benedetti. He's Archbishop Doherty's right-hand man. If there has been any sort of approach to the archdiocese, Benedetti would have to know about it." Flynt rubbed his chin thoughtfully. Mmm, I've got to call Benedetti about the conference anyway. Let's see what he has to say."

Chapter 27

Buying Access

The Massachusetts General Court, the official name of the Massachusetts State Legislature, originated in 1631 when John Winthrop, the governor of the Massachusetts Bay Colony, imposed a public works tax on the citizens of Watertown. The citizens of the colony then fired the governor, and each town asserted its right to send two delegates to convene a general court to pass laws affecting the colony. This assembly became the second representative body to establish itself in the New World.

The 1974 legislature bore little resemblance to that first legislative body. In the late 19th century, the old Brahmin city by the Bay annexed the rowdy working-class Catholic enclaves of Dorchester, Brighton, Roxbury and Jamaica Plain. By the 1880s, the large Catholic families of immigrant Irish had replaced the descendants of the pilgrims in the majority and seized the reins of government in Boston. If the influx of Italian and black and later Hispanic immigrants, and the migration of second and third generation Irish to the suburbs in the 1960s had begun to loosen those reins, that was not yet in evidence.

The Massachusetts State House was designed by Charles Bullfinch and embodied both the confidence of a people who had just defeated the most powerful empire on earth and the poverty of a young nation exhausted by the struggle. Seventy years later an emergent world power gilded the copper-sheathed dome in twenty-three carat gold. In 1895, the last renovation, a Neo-Renaissance confection designed by Charles Brigham, was added.

None of this stirring history intruded on Andrew Tate's sour mood. He had sat in the hallway for the past half-hour, drumming his fingers on his knee awaiting a scheduled audience with John T. McCarthy, Democrat of Somerville and Chairman of the Massachusetts House Ways and Means Committee. The hall was drafty and the footsteps and voices of each passerby—pages hurrying from one office to another, legislators back-slapping, lobbyists button-holing —echoed off the vaulted ceiling and marble-clad walls.

Clapped between Tate's knees was a briefcase which contained ten bound packets of one hundred crisp hundred-dollar bills, a hundred thousand dollars in all. This was to be his fourth and last appointment, the first had been with the Senate President, the second with the Chairman of the state Senate Ways and Means Committee and the third with the Speaker of the House. To each Tate had conveyed similar packages. He was annoyed because at the end of each of these meetings, he left with hearty assurances of support, an empty briefcase, and a growing list of "a few lads whose support might prove useful."

A bill can be introduced in either the House or Senate by any legislator at any time during the legislative session. The Senate President or the House Speaker refers legislation with financial implications to the Standing Committees on Ways and Means of each chamber. If, say, the House Speaker is antagonistic, he might hold the bill for some time before referring it to committee, and the committee chairman himself may bury it once it arrives. Thus, the chairman of Ways and Means is the gatekeeper. If Tate were to achieve his objective, he would have to have the senate and house chairmen on his side, as the Senate President and the House Speaker. This would be, he fervently hoped, his last meeting.

"Mr. Tate, is it?" Representative McCarthy said, smiling as he emerged from behind his office door. He was short and rotund. Unlike most legislators who favored blue pinstripes, McCarthy expressed his independent streak in a baggy, tweed three-piece suit. The chairman had a moon-shaped face, a shock of white hair, a wide brow, a florid complexion, full cheeks and a doughy, red, finely-veined drinker's nose. Tate's eye noted the poor quality of the suit, and he sighed inwardly. Another ethnic politician with a sense of style inherited from an Irish undertaker.

"An honor, sir," McCarthy said, with one beefy paw extended. Tate took his hand. McCarthy swung his arm up and around Tate's shoulder and guided Tate through the reception area, down a short corridor and through the open door of his office. He gestured to an upholstered chair in front of the desk, then walked around to the back of his desk and sat down heavily. "My good friend, Monsignor Benedetti, speaks very highly of you, Mr. Tate. A grand man, the monsignor. A scholar, speaks three languages—or is it four?" He shook his white mane slowly back and forth. "I do so admire an educated man. Don't have much of an education myself, other than what the good sisters knocked into me thick head at St. Brendan's," he said, gazing through watery blue eyes across the desk.

"Well, never mind," he continued, "I am sure that an important man such as yourself has better things to do than listen to me blather. What can I do for you?" McCarthy rocked back in his high-backed leather chair, crossed his legs, folded his hands in his lap and gazed at Tate expectantly, as might a young boy on Christmas morning anticipating a gaily-wrapped present.

His eyes remained on Tate's face as the developer carefully laid out his proposal. He patiently waited for Tate to finish, then leaned back and regarded him with a bright twinkle in his eyes. "By Saints Peter and Paul, it's a grand plan you've got there, Mr. Tate. A grand, grand plan. Tell me, Mr. Tate, from you're accent I'd guess you'd be from England. Is that right?"

"I hold dual citizenship, Mr. Chairman. My father is British, but my late mother was a native Bostonian. Her family name was Scanlon. She grew up on Pond Street in Jamaica Plain."

The chairman beamed across the desk. "Scanlon you say. I know several Scanlons from Dorchester. Fine family, fine."

Tate paused, took a breath and forged on. "Mr. Chairman, this casino will be very good for Boston and the Commonwealth as well. It will mean jobs, thousands of jobs, and millions of dollars in tax revenues. I am here today to solicit your support in making this project a reality."

"Oh, yes, I am sure that you are, and, as I said, it is a grand plan, but I can see a number of political hurdles that must be jumped if this grand plan of yours is to succeed, Mr. Tate. You do seem to have the Church well in hand, and you must have a shrewd tongue indeed to have brought that off. Though Monsignor Benedetti is not the archbishop. I was honored to receive a call, just yesterday, from His Excellency. The Church's support is essential." McCarthy raised his arms and spread his hands in a gesture of helplessness. "But as I understand it, an official endorsement will be made, if needed, at the proper moment. My hat's off to you, Mr. Tate. Indeed it is."

Tate returned the smile as if he had some secret knowledge to impart but did not wish to say what they both knew.

"Mr. Chairman, I hoped you might accept a token of my regard for your help in this matter."

Tate rose. He picked up the briefcase and placed it on the desk's blotter, turning it so it faced the Ways and Means Chairman.

"Well, now, that is very kind!"

McCarthy snapped open the locks and raised the lid. First his eyes and then his smile widened in appreciation as he regarded the neatly wrapped, crisp packets of cash, each headed with a portrait of Benjamin Franklin.

"One hundred thousand dollars cash, Mr. Chairman, and another one hundred thousand on passage of our legislation legalizing casino gambling," Tate said.

"Well now, Mr. Tate, that is most generous. I can see that you are a serious man. I believe that we can do business. You realize, of course, that for a bill to legalize casino gambling to become law, it requires passage in both houses and the governor's signature."

"Yes sir, I am aware of that and I have taken the steps to secure help in the senate and the governor's office and with the speaker as well. I believe the senate president himself will introduce the bill into that chamber."

McCarthy nodded, slowly leaned forward and brought his chair upright. "For a measure as important as this to have a chance at passage, other palms may need to be greased as well."

"I am sure you are right, Mr. Chairman, and I have anticipated that," Tate said with a level stare. "However, I trust that the very generous commission I am offering will be sufficient to deliver a majority of the votes of your committee."

"To be sure, Mr. Tate. To be sure. Would you be having a draft of the bill, at all?"

"Just under the package. You see a manila folder?" Tate said.

McCarthy slid the folder out from beneath the neat packages of bills, opened it and scanned the pages.

"Very good, very good indeed! If I may take a little time to review this, Mr. Tate, I would consider it a privilege to personally introduce the bill into the House. Speed is of the essence, Mr. Tate. We are about to enter an election year. If your bill is to become law, it must pass this session before the governor's race begins in earnest."

"I would be honored if you would introduce it, Mr. Chairman. I have also taken the liberty of providing you with a list of other likely members of the House, including Representative James Craven of Jamaica Plain, who has pledged his support. Inside the envelope is a press release. You will see that we have drawn up a summary of the economic benefits that will accrue to the Commonwealth. We project that the building phase will generate twenty-five hundred construction jobs, and once completed, the casino will hire one hundred seventy-eight, permanent, full-time employees."

"I see. Tell me, Mr. Tate, will these permanent employees come from the Commonwealth or be brought in from outside?"

"Mr. Chairman, our plan is to hire right here in Boston. We will set up programs to train dealers and hostesses and junior management. Only a few senior people will be needed from beyond the state's borders."

"Of course, of course. But the majority of the employees will be recruited right here. Grand! Grand! With economic conditions as they stand in the Commonwealth, this will make it very difficult for the governor to veto. Good-paying jobs are a real benefit to our people, particularly in these hard economic times, and Jimmy Craven is a good man to have in your corner." McCarthy paused for a moment.

"I wonder, Mr. Tate. Please forgive me for changing the subject, but my brother-in-law, Billy Doyle, is a good man, but unlucky. A Boston College graduate and the apple of his sister's eye. Well, the lad has had some bad luck recently and is in need of a job. He has experience in the construction industry. I was wondering if you might know of anything you might be able to put in his way, anything at all?"

Tate's smile turned saccharin. He should have known to expect something of the sort. "Ah, well!"

"As it happens, Mr. Chairman, I might have just the thing. I'll be expanding my staff in Boston, and I have need of a man to act as a liaison with the legislature. The position pays well—twenty thousand to start. Send him to see me by next week. Let me see what I can do."

"Grand, grand! That will mean a lot to my wife. She does so dote on the boy, you know." McCarthy rose with a broad smile. "He's just the man for the job. He is well-liked here on Beacon Hill, and he knows how things work around the statehouse. I'll be sure to send Billy by, and if I can be of any help to you at all at any time, please call me," he said, extending his hand.

Chapter 28

The Gambit

"Jed Flynt, what a pleasant surprise. I have been avidly following your exploits in the Globe. My congratulations, wonderful stuff! What can I do for you?" Monsignor Benedetti spoke into the phone receiver, forcing a smile into the mouthpiece.

"Thank you for taking my call, Monsignor. Things are going well, but we have a problem I was hoping you might be able to help us with."

"But of course. As I said when we met, you must consider me a friend. What can I do to help?"

"Well, you may have read that we have a housing conference coming up in two weeks."

"Yes, it's being held at Our Lady of Lourdes. I was planning to attend," Benedetti said.

"Wonderful, Monsignor, I will pass that along to the committee. I know that they will be very pleased. But the problem is that Father Johnson has just cancelled our use of the hall," Flynt said.

"Really," Benedetti said, filling his voice with concern. "Did he give a reason?"

"Not really, Monsignor. He called and left a message. I have telephoned the rectory repeatedly, but he has not returned my calls. We have been trying to find another hall, but with so little notice we haven't been able to turn up anything large enough, and we can't really hope to get out the kind of publicity we need. This could spell disaster for the conference."

"Yes, I understand completely, Jed. Let me get off the phone. I'll call Father Johnson immediately and call you right back," Benedetti said, and he hung up.

Benedetti drummed his fingers on the desktop and smiled contentedly. He pressed the intercom. "Audrey, I'll be out for two hours. If Mr. Flynt calls back, you are not sure where I have gone and can't reach me. Understood?"

"Yes, Monsignor."

He hung up. "Good, the plan is working," he thought. "It will do our friend Flynt good to sweat it out for a while. I'll call Johnson later."

He stood, claimed his long black overcoat off the rack and went out for a leisurely lunch.

"Jed, Monsignor Benedetti on two," Sigel called out.

Flynt glanced up at the clock—3pm. He rubbed his sweaty palm against his pants and picked up the phone.

"Good news, Jed. You have the hall," Benedetti said.

"Great," Flynt said. As time ticked by, he had become increasingly sure that Benedetti would be the bearer of bad news.

"Thank you, Monsignor," Flynt said into the phone, feeling a wave of gratitude. "You have saved the conference! "May I ask why Father Johnson withdrew permission?"

"Well, it took some persuasion, I will tell you that. Father Gale is on your side, but Father Johnson is very conservative. He is very much influenced by the local politicians. James Craven is a prominent contributor to the parish, a member of the Knights of Columbus, and a long-time friend," Benedetti said.

Flynt nodded, "Craven, huh? I figured he had his hand in it. He doesn't like the block organizing, Monsignor, sees it as a threat to his precinct organizations. Problem is the precinct captains can't do anything about the real issues. Craven's doing his best to hang the commie label on me. Between our efforts and Mayor White bypassing him and building his own patronage arm through the Little City Hall program, I think he's nervous about his chances for reelection," Flynt said.

"The Democratic machine has been around a long time, Jed. Jimmy Craven is a powerful man. He's been in the legislature forever, and he has done a number of favors for men like Johnson. That is why they call him the Silver Fox. You understand, Jed, that much of my conversation with Father Johnson must remain in-house, but I can say you have some image problems over at Lourdes. In the end, I was able to make Father Johnson understand that the archdiocese supports the conference."

Flynt had been half-listening. The commie label really burned him. He had been sent to Asia to fight—who?—commies?—to save the asses of people like Craven, who wouldn't know a real communist if he tripped over one.

"I really have to thank you, Monsignor," Flynt repeated, meaning it. "Is there any way we can get the archbishop himself to open the conference? Perhaps provide the benediction?"

Benedetti eyed the receiver and chuckled. "I'll work on that, Jed. I can't promise anything. His Excellency usually leaves such things to me. But I think that, at this time, the archbishop would welcome an update on the progress of the project he's funding. Perhaps if you have a few spare minutes, you could fill me in."

Benedetti was a sympathetic listener and a skillful questioner, and he had just saved the conference. Flynt revealed much more than he had planned.

Benedetti's hand tightened on the receiver as Flynt laid out his suspicions. Flynt had it all figured out, and in his mind's eye Benedetti peered out at a landscape of ruin. "Excuse me, Jed, but Chinese gangsters? A gambling casino in Boston? I don't mean to question your veracity, but some of this seems rather far-fetched. I should be careful, Jed, with whom I shared these suspicions of yours. Many people might view them as paranoid or worse," Benedetti said, keeping his voice soft, reasonable.

"Look, Monsignor, this stuff sounded crazy to me too at first, but how do you explain the fact that an off-shore trust is buying up properties along the edge of the Southwest Corridor?"

"I really have no idea, Jed, but if true, it is very suspicious. And as you just pointed out, the corridor is a potentially valuable piece of real estate. Any number of business interests might recognize the value of a location with direct access to Route 128."

"Have you heard of anything?" Flynt asked.

"No, nothing. How sure are you of the quality of your information?"

"Very sure! Would you know if the archbishop had been approached to support casino gambling?"

"Jed, I am the archbishop's deputy. Any such proposal would come through my office. You know, Jed, I am thinking—that of all places—Massachusetts is the last state in the union that would ever countenance casino gambling! And as for the Church, Jed, we run the occasional bingo night, but…"

Flynt cut in. "We have proof, Monsignor," he said.

"Really." Benedetti paused. "Proof! What sort of proof exactly?"

"Documents, property lists, names, off-shore bank accounts, the works," Flynt said.

Sweat glistened on Benedetti's forehead. As he listened his palms became so slick with sweat that he could barely maintain his grip on the receiver.

"Jed, look sorry to interrupt," Benedetti said, barely able to control his voice, "but I have another call. Can I just put you on hold a moment? I'll be right back" he said, and without waiting for Flynt's reply, he punched the hold button and rocked back violently in his chair.

"My God, what a disaster—names, documents! Benedetti thought, his pulse hammering in both temples. "What a fool I was to believe anything Andrew Tate ever said!" He took several deep breaths, ordering himself to calm down. Finally, having regained some sense of control, he pushed the line button.

"Sorry, Jed, had to take the call. You are making some very serious charges. I believe you, of course, but it sounds so far-fetched. May I ask, where you obtained these documents?"

"That I can't tell you, Monsignor, but they are absolutely genuine. They tie the casino deal directly to an Asian gambling syndicate called the White Dragon Group, which is apparently a front for a Chinese criminal gang, the Ghost Dragon Triad.

"Who have you told about this?"

"No one. You are the first. This is a real hot potato. I would really appreciate your advice. And, please keep this conversation confidential."

"Of course, Jed. This is all so incredibly hard to believe. I hope that your proof is as indisputable, as you seem to believe it is. Perhaps, you might consider showing me these documents? You could bring them to the chancery, say this afternoon?" Benedetti said, keeping his voice calm and deliberate.

"No, sorry, Monsignor, no can do. The documents are well hidden. No offence, but they are not going anywhere until I get them copied. The originals are prints taken by an 8mm miniature camera. They are legible, but too dark to reproduce by ordinary xerox," he said. He had already rehearsed the lie. "Looks like we'll have to find an expert to lighten them and that's going to take some time. They'll be out soon enough. I should have legible copies a day or two before the conference. We will make them public then," he said.

Benedetti hung up, shaken. My God, documents, the housing conference! Every media outlet in the state will be there.

He had seriously underestimated Jed Flynt. He saw that now. Flynt had somehow stumbled on proof, and if that proof became public before the casino bill passed, it would cause a huge local outcry, and Andrew Tate's Chinese connection would doom any chance of passage.

For Flynt and his organizing project, this was a heaven-sent opportunity. Benedetti could see it all now. Headlines splashed, television crews camped out on the archdiocese steps. Andrew Tate was a fool; obviously he had not covered his tracks as well as he thought.

Benedetti seethed with anger. Tate had always been reckless and too sure of himself! Flynt's information would mobilize and energize Jamaica Plain—the whole city. The news outlets would plaster Boston with outrage. All that money would disappear and with it his position with the archbishop and any hope for advancement within the church.

And that, Monsignor Michael Benedetti decided, could not be allowed to happen.

There was still time. Something drastic must be done and done immediately before those documents reached the wrong hands! Was Flynt telling the truth about the difficulties of reproducing the documents? Sounds plausible! The man would not seek out my advice then lie to me. It didn't make sense. He drew a small card from his wallet, picked up the phone and carefully dialed a complicated number, his mind working furiously as he listened and waited for the phone to ring.

Perhaps Flynt could be bribed, a hundred thousand dollars? Benedetti's mind flirted with the possibility.

No, Flynt was a fanatic, a true believer.

The phone began to ring.

There was little choice. He and this researcher of his must be checked and checked hard, and those documents retrieved before they could be put to use. Benedetti harbored no illusions as to the means required. It was a harsh but necessary step. There was too much at risk.

While he waited, his mind began to sketch the outline of a plan. Well, he decided, Mr. Flynt has brought this on himself.

For some reason a passage from Shakespeare's Julius Caesar came to mind. He smiled sadly. "Cry havoc," he whispered softly, "and let slip the dogs of war."

He heard a click and a voice at the other end of the line.

Chapter 29

The Dragon's Claws

"Mr. Yang, This Is An Unexpected Pleasure," Andrew Tate Said, Catching His Breath. "I Got your message less than an hour ago. I had no idea that you were in Boston. You should have sent word sooner."

The restaurant was located on the second floor of a late 18th century building off Beach Street in Boston's Chinatown. It was mid-afternoon, and the traffic was particularly bad. Tate had had a difficult time locating it, finally finding the street number, just barely visible above the gaudily red-painted paifang gate with gilded Chinese characters which formed a facade around the entrance to the venerable brick structure.

The white jacketed waiter picked up a phone, punched a button and spoke a few words in Chinese, then signed to Tate to follow. He was led through the darkened dining room to the rear of the restaurant and down a short corridor to a single doorway. The waiter motioned Tate to stop. He knocked softly, then bowed gravely and disappeared.

"Ah, Mr. Tate, thank you for being so prompt," Herbert Yang said rising from behind a modern executive's desk and bowing slightly. He offered his hand. "Please sit down," he said, pointing to a leather, upholstered chair just in front of the desk.

There was a soft knock. Yang spoke a single word, and another waiter in white came in and placed a tray with a teapot and cups on the desk. He poured tea into two tiny cups, bowed and exited as silently as he had come.

"Please, you will take tea," he said.

"Wonderful idea. Thank you, but your message spoke of an emergency, what…"

Yang raised his hand. "You look like you could use some refreshment. First tea, then business," he said.

Tate nodded. He had been doing business in Asia for most of his life, and he knew better than to lose face by seeming impatient. "Lovely teapot," he said casting about for something to say. "I didn't realize your tastes ran to European moderne."

Yang beamed. "Yes, beautiful, isn't it? Faultless form and marvelous patina. Quite distinctive. It does have an almost modern sensibility. The design could pass for Wiener Werkstätte or perhaps Bauhaus, but then Chinese antecedents have influenced much of what is called 'Western' art.' The pot is Song Dynasty, made sometime after 960 and before 1279 A.D. This one is definitely 10th century. The style is known as Zi Sha Hu, or purple sand. The secret is in the sand. Iron, and also silica, produces the color and the blackened look. They are named for an ancient city located in Jiangsu Province. It is part of my collection. Many Chinese collect porcelains, but I prefer the simplicity of earthenware. I keep it here and reserve it for special occasions," Yang said.

"Bloody hell, better not drop the damned thing," Tate thought, as Yang refilled the delicate cups. "Beautiful, Mr. Yang.

I am deeply honored," he said. "Where's the bloody handle," he thought, gripping the tiny bowl between both hands, one little finger raised. Yang nodded and raised his bowl, sipping noisily at the steaming liquid. He looked at Tate across the lip of his cup and smiled. "A thousand apologies, Mr. Tate. I had forgotten how sensitive you British are to the sounds of the body's natural functions."

Tate sipped the steaming liquid and smiled, ignoring Yang's attempts to bait him as he thought, "Didn't help you buggers much a couple of centuries back when the European powers carved up your doddering empire like a Christmas goose." The tea was everything he hated, green and bitter. He longed for a jug of warm milk, but he finished it and placed the cup gingerly on the ornate lacquered tray.

Yang placed his cup on the desk in front of him. "Excellent, most refreshing, and now to business!" He stood up.

"Mr. Tate, if you will please accompany me, there is something that I wish you to see."

"Lead on and, please, call me Andrew," Tate said, rising.

Yang stood aside and gestured that Tate was to precede him down a narrow corridor that turned right just outside the office door. "Tell me, Andrew, did you notice the building on your way in? Not old, by Chinese standards. It was built around 1806, but in the 18th century style. The building was originally a stop on the famous underground railway, part of the route that Negro slaves took escaping from the South."

"Really!" Tate said.

"Yes, our organization acquired it some years ago, together with several other properties in Chinatown. It was expensive to renovate, but it has features very well suited to our purposes. This way. Yes—stop just here."

Yang put a key in the door of a rosewood wall cabinet then pressed a small section of the ornate marquetry. Tate stepped back in surprise as an entire section of wall slid back exposing the wrought-iron gate of an old-fashioned elevator.

Yang pulled open the gate, stood aside, gestured to Tate, then followed him into a vintage elevator car decorated with black iron filigree that reminded Tate of an oversized birdcage.

"The car is original," Yang said. "The elevator was part of the building. We have modernized the workings, of course."

Yang pulled the gate closed and the outer panel slid silently back into place. He grasped and pulled back on a black lever. The car jerked and began to descend with an audible grinding of gears.

Neither man spoke, and after perhaps forty-five seconds the car came to a halt with a slight bump.

"Ah, here we are."

Yang pulled the gate back. "After you, Andrew."

Tate stepped out into a narrow passage and looked about. They were in a corridor, flanked on either side by fieldstone walls of gray, New England granite.

"Marvelous joinery," he said, admiring how the stones had been meticulously fitted together without mortar. "Is this what I think it is?"

"Yes, a secret basement. I knew a builder would appreciate it," Yang said.

"Amazing. How far down are we?"

"About forty feet below street level. There are two corridors and several chambers. I am told that the abolitionists hid as many as fifty slaves at a time down here. The laws were very strict on the subject of those who aided runaway slaves. They also stored arms down here. The abolitionists took great pains to assure that they were not discovered."

Yang sighed. "Such romantic nonsense. Slavery has existed in every civilized society. It is part of the human condition. Some men are born to be masters, others to serve. The British

Raj was based on exactly the same principles, only your people enslaved whole societies and called it Christian enlightenment."

The air was cool and slightly damp with a distinct earthy smell. Tate began to feel a sense of unease. It was completely silent. The familiar, comforting murmur of human activity was totally absent. The sudden loss of audible touchstones can be profoundly disconcerting. Both men had reduced their utterances to a whisper, so as not to disturb the silence that seemed to surround them like a separate brooding presence.

In either direction, the passage was sheathed in stone, and the ceiling slightly vaulted. It had been recently wired. A series of white porcelain fixtures, each with a single bare light bulb was set into the thick, squarish hand-hewed beams which crossed and supported the ceiling every twenty feet. Each bulb cast a narrow pool of yellow light onto the stone floor. Tate heard an echo of something like water dripping in the far distance. Otherwise, all was still.

Yang led the way. Each footfall echoed off the stone floor and was then absorbed by the silence. They walked about fifty paces down the passageway, then turned right, and came to a roughly-arched, thick wooden door. The marks of a hand adz were visible along the edges of the vertical planks which,, like the door frame, were black with age.

"My God, Mr. Yang, this place is like something out of H. P. Lovecraft. What have you got behind this door, a torture chamber?" Tate asked, with a short laugh that echoed hollowly in his ear.

Yang smiled and reached for the latch.

"Not a bad guess, my friend. I am sorry, but I am not acquainted with the work of Mr. Lovecraft. But, then, I rarely read fiction. The door is original, however," he said, pulling the latch handle with both hands. "Please Andrew, after you," he said opening the door wide.

It was a broad chamber with high vaulted ceilings. There were bare bulbs set high in the ceiling and oil lamps set in niches at intervals all along the inner walls the chamber added to the chamber, a dim, flickering light. The walls had originally been plastered and white-washed, but the plaster had long since turned gray. Thick scabby patches of black mold bloomed along the walls and upwards toward the high ceiling. The room had the feel of a workshop. Several odd-looking pieces of apparatus that Tate could not identify filled much of the space.

Three men inhabited the chamber. Two were short, stocky Chinese with shaven heads.

They were stripped to the waist and identically dressed in black, coolie pants. They turned and stared at Tate with dark, incurious eyes, opaque as glazed stoneware. The two were alike as bookends, magnificent physical specimens with massive slab-like chests jutting out over rippling, abdominal muscles. Heavily tattooed and muscled arms and massive shoulders gleamed in the dim light.

The two bowed to Yang respectfully, but Tate hardly noticed. His attention was fixed on the chamber's third occupant. He was a young, thin Chinese man. He lay on his side on the rough, wooden floor between the two strongmen.

Spittle dripped from his lips. He moaned softly, making sounds like a wounded animal. He too was bare-chested and wore black pajama pants. His slender arms were pinned behind his back by a pair of iron shackles. Tate noticed a red dragon tattoo ran from his neck down along his right shoulder. Stringy, black hair was plastered to his face. He gazed up and his pain-filled eyes met Tate's in mute appeal.

The men stood on a low, wooden platform with four posts, one set at each corner, about eight feet apart. At the top of the posts, similar bars made an X-shaped bridge about twelve feet above the floor. At the junction of the X, a rope passed through a heavy block and tackle and between the prisoner's shackles, snaked across the floor where it was loosely held in one of the paired twins' massive paws.

Yang squatted over the man, grabbed a fistful of his hair and lifted his face toward Tate.

"Andrew Tate, meet Johnny Lowboy."

"Johnny Lowboy? Who the hell is Johnny Lowboy?" Tate demanded.

At the sound of his name, the prisoner raised his eyes and blinked. His face dripped sweat.

Yang dropped Johnny's head, stood and drew a handkerchief from the breast pocket of his suit and wiped his hands. "This is the man whom we sent, at your request, Andrew, to investigate the Jamaica Plain organizing project."

Tate glared. "If he is your man, Yang, why are you torturing him?"

"Come, come, Andrew. The problem, you see," Yang said pointing toward Lowboy's prone figure, "is that this miserable fool failed in his mission, and as I pointed out to you at our meeting in Hong Kong, our organization takes a dim view of failure."

Tate swallowed, his throat suddenly dry.

"I thought that it would amuse you to see how we deal with those who fail us," Yang said.

Tate noticed that Yang's forehead glowed with a thin sheen of sweat. His eyes seemed slightly out of focus.

"So he failed. This, this is barbaric," Tate said.

"Barbaric did you say? Interesting choice of words. In an organization such as ours, it is necessary to enforce discipline in the ranks, yes? You see, Andrew, Mr. Flynt caught this piece of shit. Caught, interrogated and then released him. Why is that, do you think?" he asked, looking down at Johnny, "Why is this creature not, at this moment, sitting in a Boston jail cell?"

"Flynt probably did not want to draw attention to himself," Tate said.

"Perhaps!" Yang barked a command in Chinese and stepped back. His two henchmen grabbed Johnny from either side, dragged him upright and propped his body, like a wet mop, sagging between them. Yang stepped over to the man and lifted his chin and stared straight into his eyes. Johnny began babbling in a mixture of Chinese and English, bawling and begging for mercy.

"You see," Yang said, "this miserable cur has no pride. He cries and begs like a woman." He slapped the prisoner hard across the face. "Raise him up," he ordered and stepped back.

Johnny began to gibber and beg. One twin took hold of the rope and began to haul. Johnny's arms were pulled up behind his back almost to the height of his shoulders, his body tilted forward as he was raised screaming several feet into the air. Tate clapped his hands to his ears to try to block the terrible screams that echoed off the chamber walls.

"My God, stop! You'll pull his arms right out of their sockets!"

Yang stepped closer and placed his hand on Tate's shoulder and spoke softly into his ear.

"Tell me, Andrew," he said, his eyes bright. "Do you recognize the particular method of persuasion we are using?"

"No!" Tate said. He was near panic. He wanted to run, but the gentle pressure of Yang's hand around his upper arm seemed to have frozen him in place. He was deep underground and completely at this man's mercy. What if Yang decided to torture or even kill him, who would ever know? No one would even hear his screams. "No!" Tate repeated, "but surely there is no need for this!"

"It is called the strappado, also known also as the queen of torments," Yang said, his mouth so close that Tate could feel his warm breath tickling his ear. "Quite ingenious! It was invented by the Black Friars, the Dominicans, in the 15th century and used by the Holy Office, on those it suspected of heresy. The procedure is really quite simple. It works with the dynamics of the human body. First, the hands are tied behind the back. The genius of it, you see, is that the strappado can be used almost anywhere. All that is required is a length of rope and a structure strong enough to support a man's weight."

"If the heretic was stubborn, he—or she—it was used on both sexes—was slowly raised off the floor. The feet were sometimes weighted, but as you can see, that is hardly necessary. The subject's own weight places great pressure on the elbow and shoulder joints."

Johnny Lowboy had stopped screaming. His face had turned impossibly red, and he was panting, fighting for each breath.

Yang took his hand from Tate's shoulder, stepped on to the platform, lifted Lowboy's chin and gazed into his eyes. The man's mouth opened and closed like a fish held out of the water.

"There, you see, Andrew, the screaming has stopped."

Tate stared aghast.

"You see, Andrew," Yang continued, "the angle of the arms levers the body forward, constricting the chest muscles, and all the subject's energy must be devoted to drawing breath. If the subject remains stubborn, he may be hoisted higher and the rope slacked off abruptly causing him to drop like a dead-weight part way to the floor."

Johnny began shaking his head and making mewing sounds like a kitten pleading for its mother.

"This stage requires great delicacy," Yang continued, his mouth turned down in disgust. "If the subject is allowed to drop too far, the momentum may break the shoulder joint or tear both arms from their sockets. Very much like twisting the leg off a partly roasted chicken," Yang said and stroked Johnny's head. "It was believed, you see, if a person was a true Christian, then God would give the strength to endure the pain. Lacking God's grace, the heretic, when put to the question, would quickly confess his errors and so damn himself."

He turned back to Tate. "Quite ingenious, don't you agree?"

"It's bloody inhuman," Tate said, staring back at the Tong chief.

"Oh, it is quite human, I assure you. You see, I have made a study of the various methods of torture, Mr. Tate—I mean Andrew. The quaint-looking devices that you see scattered about this chamber are a part of my collection."

"That heavy wooden table in the corner with the pulleys attached?" Yang said, pointing, "That is a rack. Another device favored by your Catholic priests. I acquired it in Goa. The good Portuguese fathers used it for three hundred years. The Goa Inquisition was very active and more brutal even than the Spanish. Did you know that it continued until the British put a stop to it in 1810? You see the ropes? They are original. One limb was bound to each and stretched using those wooden spools at either end until the body's sinews reached the breaking point and beyond. You have heard the term 'broken on the rack'? It was meant quite literally."

Yang gestured and one of the torturers stepped over to the bar and let go of the rope. Johnny Lowboy's body collapsed to the floor like a marionette deprived of his strings. He lay crumpled and moaning on the platform's wooden floor.

"What do you expect to gain, Yang?" Tate asked. "Will you tear his arms from his shoulders? This poor man will confess to anything you like. What will that prove?"

"What will it prove? You will see. Fong—that is his real name, by the way—insists that he told your organizer friend nothing. The fool expects us to believe that? He gave no information, and this Mr. Flynt simply let him go out of the goodness of his heart! Haul him to his feet," Yang barked.

The two torturers wrestled the man to his feet. Yang took hold of his hair, yanked his head upright and stared into his eyes.

"Speak," he commanded.

"Water," Lowboy croaked.

Yang stared into the prisoner's eyes for a moment, then smiled, reached down and took hold of a ladle that stood in a wooden bucket lying just to the side of the platform. He scooped a dipper of water and put the dipper to the prisoner's lips. The young Chinese swallowed, coughed, then swallowed greedily. Water cascaded down his chin.

"More, please, more," he begged.

Yang refilled the dipper, brought it almost to the prisoner's lips, then hesitated for a moment before he flung the water in Lowboy's face. "Enough!" he bellowed. "Tell me the truth, and I promise the torture will end. You will die quickly and without pain," he said, bringing his face close and searching the man's eyes.

"I told him the name of the Triad, lord, only the name," Lowboy said in a thick raspy voice. "No one warned me that he was a great martial artist. I attacked him in the dark. I used my strongest techniques, but he defeated me. He threatened to kill me. It is not my fault. I was afraid, and I told him. That is all, I swear. Please, lord, please spare me," he begged.

Yang turned to Tate. "There, you see?" he said with a look of triumph. "This stinking piece of shit has betrayed us

He turned back to the prisoner. "What else did you tell him? Speak!"

"Nothing, lord, I swear! I was ordered to break into the old church, steal the papers and set the place on fire. He asked me about another fire, but I didn't know what he was talking about. Please, lord, please. I will do anything you say!"

"We shall see," Yang stepped back. "Hoist him up high this time," he ordered his henchmen.

"No!" Johnny screamed. "Please, please! I will tell you! I told him the name of my dragon and the address of the dojo. I told him all I knew, and that is all," he said, sobbing. "Please, no more, please, I can't stand it."

"You see? It is as I thought," Yang said, addressing Tate, "The stinking turd spilled his guts. Luckily he knew very little, but now this fellow Flynt knows who we are. And now I am told he has obtained proof of our association and details of the entire project."

"Proof, what proof? That isn't possible! The papers are locked in our lawyer's office in Lichtenstein.

"Correction—were locked in your lawyer's office. They, or copies of them, are now in the position of Mr. Jedediah Flynt, who plans to make them public at a housing conference to be held next week.

"How do you know this?"

"All in due time, Andrew. We have many sources of information. I think you have seen enough. Shall we go?" he asked gently.

"Yes, yes! Please," Tate said. He was pale, and his lips trembled.

Yang barked a series of orders in rapid Cantonese. His two men bowed respectfully.

"You asked why I came to Boston, Andrew." They had retraced their steps, entered the elevator car and returned to Yang's office.

"We have put up a great deal of money, and we are concerned, Andrew, my colleagues and I, about the success of our joint venture. I sponsored you, and you have failed, and I have lost face. So, I have come to Boston to deal with this crisis personally. It appears that we must put an end to the activities of this Mr. Flynt. He has become a nuisance; he has embarrassed our organization, and now, it seems, he threatens the success of our project. This should not have been allowed to happen, Andrew."

"What! But how? That's not possible," Tate said, his face reddening. The developer was sweating profusely. His suit hung off him like a rag.

"Nonetheless…," Yang said staring fixedly at the developer.

"What sort of documents? You certainly don't think he got them from me," Tate said.

"No, Mr. Tate, I don't. You would not be so stupid. I had representatives of our organization call on our agent in Lichtenstein. Upon questioning, Dr. Altmann admitted that there had been a break in. He had found nothing missing, so he believed it to be a simple robbery and kept it to himself. But, upon examination, we found that our file had been tampered with. One or two documents were out of place."

"You mean that Flynt sent someone to break into Altman's office? Tate gazed at Yang incredulously. My God, if that information, if your organization's involvement in the project gets out, it will ruin us."

Yang leaned forward and placed his elbows on the desk. "Precisely, Mr. Tate. It would appear that Mr. Flynt is far more resourceful and tenacious than you thought. My sources say that he has sworn to avenge the death of the woman who was killed through your carelessness. His plan, apparently, is to release these documents to the press at his upcoming housing conference."

"How do you know all this?"

"As I said, we have many sources of information, Mr. Tate."

"We must stop him!"

"Obviously, strong measures will be taken and taken immediately. Mr. Flynt cannot be allowed to carry out his plan, and I am here to ensure that he does not."

"Well, the failure, if there was one, was not mine," Tate said.

"How, then, did this organizer trace your land acquisition company to Lichtenstein? You assured me that it was untraceable."

"How should I know? The attorney should have provided better security."

Yang stared across the table. "As you know, Andrew, under my leadership, the White Dragon Group has built a gambling empire spanning the Pan Pacific region. In twenty years, our organization will be completely legitimate. Added to our holdings in Hong Kong, Macao and Mauritius, this casino was—is—to be the crowning jewel of all my efforts. There was much opposition to your proposal among the leaders of the tong. Despite my achievements I have enemies. Many consider me too young and reckless and thought the plan too bold. I cast the deciding vote. If we fail, I fail, the loss of face will be irredeemable, you understand. That will be most unfortunate for me and for you. Someone must pay. So, you see it is imperative that we get those documents back and silence Mr. Flynt and anyone else with knowledge of those documents."

"My God!" Tate croaked, sweat breaking out on his forehead, "We are talking about murder."

Yang's lips formed a thin smile. "I have made enquires, and I understand that Flynt has a young woman doing research for his project," Yang said.

"Yes, some girl was nosing about. She was the one who contacted our local attorney enquiring about the properties."

"There is an old Chinese proverb: do not twist the dragon's tail. These people have, and now they shall feel his wrath."

Tate cleared his throat noisily. "Mr. Yang, this is Boston, Massachusetts, not some Shanghai back alley. People don't simply disappear, particularly prominent people. It will be noticed. The press—there will be an investigation."

"And, if we do not act decisively? We stand to lose a great deal of money and someone, Mr. Tate, will bear the blame for that," he said, staring across the desk. As for Mr. Flynt and the young lady, two young people—lovers perhaps—disappear. Have they have run off together? Young people are so irresponsible these days. But we understand, and we forgive them because we were all young once. They are sure to turn up eventually, and in the meantime, life goes on."

"What do you want me to do?" Tate asked.

"You will do exactly as you are told," Yang said, smiling serenely. "How are you progressing with the political side?"

"On that front, all is well," Mr. Yang. Tate said, sitting up in his chair. "It's been bloody expensive, but the seeds have been sown. I have one final meeting with a key legislator. Once he is lined up, we will have all the political support we need. The bill will be introduced in both houses as soon as I give the word."

"Very good, but let us hold off for the moment. We do not want—what is the word—to spook our friend, Mr. Flynt, into acting prematurely," Yang said.

"I have been warned that we must act quickly before the election season begins," Tate said.

"Not to worry, Andrew, I have a plan," Yang said, his eyes glittering. "I expect we will have solved our little problem in a matter of days."

Chapter 30

When It Rains

State Representative James J. Craven, Jr. had just sat down to his dinner when he heard his private phone ringing in the den.

He looked down at his plate. "Damn and blast!" he said, tossing his napkin onto the white tablecloth. Corn beef and cabbage was his favorite. His wife made it once a week, on Wednesday, and he preferred it piping hot.

He had been out much of the day on district business, but except when the legislature was in session, he was home for dinner most nights, and he took pride in never missing Sunday mass.

Craven closed the door to the den, picked up the phone and grimaced at the sound of a familiar voice. "Billy," he said addressing his legislative assistant, William Derry, "how many times must I tell you not to be calling during the dinner hour."

"Oh, gee, sorry, Jim," his assistant said. "I tried earlier, but I figured you would want to know right away that Father Johnson called. He said to apologize, but that he was going to have to allow the use of Lourdes parish hall for that housing conference after all. He said he got a call from the archbishop's deputy."

Jim Craven's bushy gray eyebrows lifted, and he scowled into the receiver. "Did he now? How do you suppose that son-of-a-bitch Flynt managed that?"

Flynt and his staff had been stirring up the residents and organizing block meetings throughout Ward Eleven, the heart of Craven's district, and he wasn't happy about it.

Craven's precinct captains were often low-level city employees, or "trainees" under locally-controlled, federal job and rehabilitation programs such as the Comprehensive Employment and Training Act (CETA). Some of these "trainees" had been rehabilitated a half dozen times—yet still lacked the ability to stop the organizing, or discourage the endless stream of complaints which funneled from these obnoxious little block-clubs into Craven's district office and Kevin White's Little City Hall. The complaints to White's people particularly aggravated Craven. He was known as a man who knew how to control his district. These complaints were an embarrassment.

Jimmy Craven served on the Massachusetts House Banking Committee. He had a good relationship with the banks and had received numerous campaign contributions from their executives. He had gotten a call from an old friend at the Boston Five. The banks were worried— "not that there is a grain of truth in any of this redlining nonsense, you understand, Jim"—but with all the trouble coming from groups in Craven's district, the bankers expected Representative Craven to do something about it.

"I don't know how he did it, Jimmy, but the housing conference is definitely on at Lourdes," his assistant said.

Craven sat down at his desk, took out his reading glasses and perched them on the end of his nose. He picked up a pen and scribbled a note on the legal pad in the center of his desk blotter.

He had met with Andrew Tate and thought the developer's plan to be sound. It would settle the brouhaha over that dammed Southwest Corridor and bring jobs, well-paying jobs, into the district, and Jim Craven would have the say-so over two dozen or more. He snorted, then a smile creased his lips as he remembered how the daft limey had offered him ten thousand. The man apparently didn't realize he was dealing with the Silver Fox. Jimmy lovingly smoothed back his mane of silver-gray hair. It was his signature, and he combed it straight back like a 1930s matinee idol. He had played the limey like a fish, and in the end, the daft bugger had forked over fifteen thousand in cash, with a promise of another fifteen once the casino legislation passed the House.

"Jimmy?"

Craven snapped out of his reverie. "Okay, Billy, now here's what you do. First, call all the precinct captains, every mother's son of them. I want to know any time Flynt or any of his people organize one of those damn block-meetings of his. I want no excuses. You tell those dumb sons-a-bitches to make sure they know and report to you when and where these block-meetings take place. They are to make sure they attend any meetings in their precinct, and I want a written report of what went on and a list of the leaders. Otherwise they'll find themselves out of a job come November. Is that clear?"

"Yes sir. The boys will be happy to do it. Flynt's people have been coming in and causing trouble in the precincts without so much as a by-your-leave," Billy said.

"Right. You make sure that the boys understand I'm serious, Billy. This Flynt boyo may have fooled the Church, but he doesn't fool me. He's hiding behind this monsignor's skirts now, but I'll flush him out, make no mistake. I'll be making it my personal business to see he is put down and put down hard. The man is nothing but a communist agitator, and that's the word I want put out on the street!"

"You want I should talk to some of the boys down at the Knights of Columbus hall about maybe givin' this guy a haircut?"

"We'll hold off on that for now, Billy. The man's the devil himself at generating press, and we don't want to be making him into a martyr. What I want you to do is to find out everything you can about the man. I want to know where he was born and who baptized him. And this Mary Kavanaugh—she's no better than Flynt. Some of those lace-curtain do-gooders up in the Parkside have been talking about running her against me in the next primary. I want to know all the dirt on her and her good-for-nothing husband as well."

"You got it, Jim."

"Good, and, Billy, get to work on this right away. Start tonight."

"Yes, sir!"

Craven dropped the receiver into its cradle, sat back in his chair and considered the options.

Jim Craven was a proud man, and Jedediah Flynt had injured that pride. He had survived almost twenty years in the rough-and-tumble of Boston politics, too long to allow some carpetbagger, commie agitator to get the better of him.

Jimmy had learned the art of dirty politics at the feet of the master as an aid to none other than James Michael Curley himself. "Jimmy, old son, you're getting soft," he thought, rocking back in his chair. Time to show this fellow Flynt how the game is played.

Craven sat forward, slapped his hand on his desk, rose from his chair, switched off the light, closed the door and returned to his corned beef and cabbage.

Chapter 31

Kidnapped

She refused Flynt's offer of a ride home and took the subway to Green Street Station. There was a waning moon, and the lights were mostly out in the factories and small workshops that lined Washington Street. She looked both ways, held her breath and sprinted beneath the darkened cavern of the El. The faint rustling of tiny feet caused the hair on the back of her neck to prickle. "Rats!" she thought with a shiver. "Come on, scaredy-cat, you're almost home," she whispered and mounted the curb in front of her apartment house. Her voice echoed hollowly and sounded overloud against the stillness of the night.

The porch light was out.

It all happened so fast, she had no time to react. The dark shape of a man detached itself from the shadows beneath the portico and jumped onto the sidewalk. She could not make out a face in the dark penumbra of the El. Fear surged though her, but before she could turn and flee, her arms were grabbed and pinned behind her and a rough hand clapped over her mouth. She struggled, but now the shadow from the porch was on her. He crouched down and hoisted her up by her feet. Alex tried to wriggle free, but the two specters held her, like a sack of potatoes, helpless between them.

A car screeched to the curb. A male voice spat out a few words in a language she did not understand. The click of a door opening, the sensation of falling, she hit hard, face down. She bit her lip. The salty taste of blood filled her mouth.

"My God, this is it," she thought. "These people are going to rape and kill me." She clamped her legs together, determined to resist. Strong hands yanked her arms up tightly behind her, she heard a tearing sound, and her wrists were lashed together. Her mind conjured up an image of steers, trussed and hung up by their feet on an assembly line of hooks moving inexorably toward the slaughter's knife. She tried to scream but her mouth was taped shut. She was flipped over like a freshly caught fish onto her back, and her legs were trussed. The bindings bit into her wrists and ankles. She felt pressure against her ears, and the plunge into blackness as the trunk slammed shut. Doors slammed, tires screeched. She felt a surge of acceleration.

Her chest heaved, and she fought for breath. She could not breathe through her mouth, and she felt panic. "Stop it, concentrate!" she ordered herself. She took a long breath through her nose and focused on taking long, deep inhalations. The keen edge of panic began to dull.

Who were these people? Where were they taking her? Voices were coming from the front of the car, but the words were completely foreign.

"My God!" She had never heard the language spoken except at the counter of the Chinese takeout, but it sounded so foreign she knew it had to be Chinese. They hadn't hurt her— not yet—they were taking her somewhere. Oh my God, they must be those Chinese gangsters. Suddenly it all made sense.

Somehow they had found out about her, found out where she lived.

They must be after Jed Flynt, too. They won't have such an easy time with him.

The car had slowed and was braking and accelerating smoothly. She tried to concentrate on the turns, but there were too many, and by the time she thought of it, several minutes had already passed.

After a while the turns stopped. The car seemed to be moving along at a constant rate She could hear the hum of the tires and felt a slight vibration through her body. No potholes. They must be on a highway, she realized

And what if they already have Jed Flynt? "How can he—or anyone—rescue me then?" she asked herself and felt a sense of deep despair.

Chapter 32

Captive

The car's motion stopped abruptly. Alex felt the chassis shift on its springs, and car doors close. She was instantly alert. The trunk lid opened, and rough hands took hold of her, cut the tape that bound her legs and hoisted her from the trunk. It was still dark. One set of hands pulled a cloth bag over her head. Another grabbed her arm.

"You go! Move it!" a voice next to her ear commanded.

She tried to stand, but she could hardly feel her legs, and she half collapsed. Hands grabbed her under both arms, a door opened, and she was half-carried, half-dragged inside a building into some sort of corridor. It was smooth underfoot, and the men's voices echoed. She heard something close by. She was in an elevator; she could feel the acceleration. It stopped. Another door opened. A rush of cool air hit her, and she was shoved roughly through the door and down another corridor. She heard an iron door slam.

The hood was pulled off her head, and the hands released her. Some of the circulation had returned. Still her balance was off. She stood teetering, trying to keep herself upright, blinking owlishly in the light.

"Good evening, Miss Jordan."

The voice came from a man standing in front of her. He was a thin man, tall for an oriental, with a narrow face, high cheekbones and carefully combed, thinning dark hair. He was dressed in a dark green, sharkskin suit. She shook her head to clear her vision and looked around. The room was damp and dank and smelled of mold. It looked like a basement or a workshop of some sort. There were machines. The only light emanated from oil lamps set in niches along the wall.

"Who, who are you?"

"My name is Yang. I must apologize for the necessity of bringing you here against your will, but it couldn't be helped. You can appreciate that, I hope."

"Where am I? Why have you brought me here?" Alexis demanded.

"Come, come, Miss Jordan. You are an intelligent young lady, a Harvard graduate I understand. I represent an organization, the White Dragon Group. You have heard of us, I believe," Yang said evenly. He was smiling. His slitted black eyes glittered in the like a serpent's in the dim flickering light.

Alexis stumbled backwards. An arm caught her. She shook it off and lurched forward to regain her balance.

"I have no idea what you are talking about," she said.

Yang spread his arms as if to encompass the world.

"Please, Miss Jordan, I had hoped that we could approach our problem like civilized people. But that will not be possible if you persist in playing undergraduate games with me. You are in the real world now. Please do not insult my intelligence. Let us begin again by establishing a few basic facts upon which we can agree. You work as a researcher for a community organizing project run by Mr. Jedediah Flynt. Correct so far?" Yang asked, his voice like silk, like ice.

"You will never get away with this." Alex spat out the words.

Yang smiled.

"Really, Miss Jordan, look around you. I believe that I have already have gotten away with it. Scream if you like. No one will hear you, and very soon I shall call your Mr. Flynt. We found his home phone number in your address book. That was useful. Thank you. You see that you have already helped us. You have provided us with important information, information that may well shorten your stay here with us. We will be calling him shortly to apprise him of our terms for your safe return."

Abruptly his voice and manner changed.

"Where are the documents, Miss Jordan? We searched your apartment and your briefcase and did not find them. Where are they?"

"I don't know what you are talking about," Alex said.

"Miss Jordan, please. Please! I asked you not to insult my intelligence! I warn you, I am not a patient man. I am talking about the documents you somehow managed to pilfer from our attorney's office. That was very clever, very clever indeed, Miss Jordan, and I am looking forward to your explaining just exactly how you managed that," Yang said, fitting the smile back into place.

"I won't tell you anything!"

"Oh, but you will, Miss Jordan. Let me explain. We are a large diversified organization, and one of our divisions owns brothels in many of Asia's largest cities. These enterprises require a large number of women to service our clients. When we run short, we must sometimes resort to extreme measures to recruit workers."

"You kidnap them, you mean."

"Exactly so, Miss Jordan. I expected an intelligent girl, and you have not disappointed me. Some of these girls are reluctant, so they must be persuaded to work for us. You see the two muscular gentlemen standing behind you? They are specialists, we call them the Gentlers. You see, Miss—or is it Ms. Jordan?"

"It's Ms. and I…"

"Yes, of course. You see, Ms. Jordan, a reluctant girl is much like a wild horse. She must be taught to take the bit. The Gentlers, or perhaps Breakers, would be more accurate, but we Chinese prefer the subtle irony of the former," he said. "At any rate, they take turns mounting and riding the young lady, applying the whip and spurs as necessary until she is, as the cowboys say in your quaint American Westerns, broken to the saddle," Yang said. He smiled at his own little joke.

"We then relocate the girl to a new city where she does not know the local language and cannot communicate, and she is put to work. You would be amazed the profits a healthy young whore can generate working six days a week, servicing, say, ten to twenty clients a night. Now let us have a good look at you. Strip off your clothes!" Yang ordered, his eyes bright and smoldering.

Alexis Jordan stared open-mouthed at Yang. "Are you mad? I will not."

"Oh, but you will—and these two gentlemen will assist you," Yang said.

He gestured toward the two men. They were dressed identically in loose, black cotton pants and bulging muscle shirts.

Alex twisted her head like a trapped bird, but before she could move, one of the men stepped behind her, immobilized her arms, his fingers like iron talons digging into her flesh.

The other twin stepped nonchalantly in front of her, took hold of her white cotton blouse with both hands and ripped it open sending buttons flying in all directions. He grinned at her, showing several gold teeth, then slowly and deliberately drew an object from his pants pocket and, smiling, held it within inches of her face and pressed the button. A thin, steel blade flashed in the light.

Alex flinched and bucked, but it was no use. Her arms were locked firmly behind her back. She tried to kick the man in the groin, but a block by a thick, tattooed forearm sent a sharp pain shooting down her shinbone.

"Ow!" she sobbed. "That hurt."

The Gentler regarded her with a slight smile. His eyes were dead as stones.

She knew then that she was quite capable of becoming completely hysterical.

The thug licked his lips and pressed the knife's cold tip against her chest. He looked down at the blade, then smilingly back at Alex.

She twisted violently. The cold steel slid upward like a snake and sliced through her bra. The cups sprang apart, exposing her breasts. Then with a quick movement and a flick of his wrist he slashed through the waistband of her wool skirt. It slithered down her legs and puddled around her feet, leaving her clothed in only a pair of skimpy, red, silk panties.

Her face burned red with embarrassment.

The thug stepped aside to allow Yang to consider his handiwork.

"Very good, Ms. Jordan. Now we are getting somewhere," Yang observed.

Yang was so close Alex could smell the pomade on his slicked combover.

Yang nodded to the knife-wielding thug. He grabbed hold of the thin material of her panties, sliced them off and stepped back.

Alex's chest heaved and tears streamed down her face. She glanced about for some way to cover herself. It was useless. The thug behind her held her immobile.

All the things she had been taught, all she had come to expect from a civilized society, of which she was a privileged member, was lying, in a pile of rags, scattered about her feet. It was as if she had been stripped of some part of her person, like a little bird without her protective plumage. She was completely at the mercy of these monsters. Jed Flynt did not know where she was. No one knew where she was. She was all alone. There would be no rescue, no knight in shining armor.

She was scared and cold, but she was also becoming angry, coldly, murderously angry. She felt that anger swell like a wave, crest and rush forward, overcoming the fear. Her hands balled into fists. She squeezed her eyes shut, determined to hold back the tears.

She stopped struggling, squared her shoulders, raised her chin and stared straight at her tormentor with as much disgust, revulsion and defiance as she could muster.

Yang smiled, clapped his hands together several times, slowly, in measured applause. "Very good, Miss Jordan. Very good," he said.

He circled slowly around her. Cocking his head, viewing her at different angles. Observing her as an art connoisseur might contemplate a sculpture he was considering adding to his collection.

"Mmm," he said, looking her up and down. His lips twisted with distaste. "Somewhat bovine for civilized taste. I will never understand the Western preoccupation with large breasts. I am thinking of one of our very best clients, a rich industrialist from Shanghai. He is interested only in white girls, you understand. Before the war, his mother was a maid in the home of an English taipan. He grew up in the home and became obsessed with one of the man's daughters. They had been playmates as children. But, as they grew older, the girl became aware of the social distinctions. She disdained and humiliated him. You are perfect. He will pay a high price for you to stand over him naked, with only that look of waspish disdain, and then piss in his face. It is the only thing that gets him hard. Unfortunately, once he gets an erection and has his fun, he tends to abuse the girl rather badly."

Alexis stared at him. Not in ten million years could she have imagined this—and she had to force herself to acknowledge that it was really happening.

"However, for the present, we must keep you intact and unblemished," Yang continued, "at least until we obtain what we require from Mr. Flynt. And, perhaps, if you are a good little girl and cooperate, once we have what we want, we will release you. That is something you must earn. You may begin by telling me about the documents."

Alex studied her tormentor—saw the moist eyes and dry lips, the cruel smile, the suit shining like a snake's skin. This was a man who delighted in creating fear and inflicting pain, and she understood with absolute clarity that regardless of what he might say, he was never going to let her go. She knew too much. He really had no choice; he would kill her, and Jed, too, if he could.

She had entered a nightmare, and she was completely on her own. She must bend all her thoughts, all her energies toward one goal—survival.

She saw no reason not to tell him something he already knew.

"Jed Flynt has the photostats," she said. "He told me that he would put them somewhere safe, and he did not tell me where."

Yang stepped forward and grasped her chin roughly in his hand, pulled it down and stared up into her eyes.

She caught a faint glint of annoyance that he had to look up at her, and that tiny victory soothed her pride and strengthened her resolve. She did not look away.

"As it happens, Ms. Jordan, I believe you, but he will hand them over, never fear. You are a beautiful woman, and American men are such fools about beautiful women. He has already lost one woman, and I suspect that Mr. Flynt will do just about anything to get you back unharmed," he said.

He squeezed her chin until the pain forced her to cry out then he abruptly let his hand drop.

"Enough!" Yang said and snapped his fingers. "Take her to her cell and give her something to cover herself. You are a very valuable piece of merchandise. We can't have you catching a cold, can we?"

Alex was hustled down a narrow, stone-lined passage and found herself in a tiny, dark room which had obviously been built as a prison cell. She had been tossed a gaudy, blue cheongsam, the sort of cheap silk dress with the buttons down the front that she had seen Chinese waitresses wear.

She slipped it over her head, pulled it down to cover herself, and sat down on the thin, filthy straw mattress laid out on the thick wooden slab that jutted out from the stone wall of the dank cell. The dress was a large size and covered her like a flour sack, but she was past caring.

There was nothing else. The only illumination, a bare light bulb in the corridor ceiling cast a grid of long, vertical shadows of the bars against the wall behind her. She looked around.

"My God! I've been so stupid!" She thought about her father. He had been right all along. She covered her face with her hands. "I'm sorry daddy!" she cried, then sunk her head into her hands and very silently began to sob.

Chapter 33

Guts & Glory

Flynt lifted the receiver.

It was 8am. Flynt had just rolled out of bed, and put a saucepan of water on for instant coffee. He was still in his underwear.

The voice on the other end of the phone was calm and deliberate. It was a man's voice:

"We have your associate, Miss Jordan, Mr. Flynt."

"What? Who is this?" Flynt replied.

"Let's not play games, shall we? I think you know who we are, Mr. Flynt. You have some documents that belong to us, which you are going to return," the voice said. "That is, if you ever expect to see your Miss Jordan alive again."

"I don't believe you, whoever you are," Flynt replied.

"Yes, of course. I understand. You desire proof," the voice said, soothingly. "One moment please."

Flynt heard a muffled sound like a hand clapped over the receiver and then Alex's voice.

"Jed, it's Alex. Please help me!"

"Alex, are you all right?"

"Yes, I'm okay. They haven't hurt me, but…"

Flynt heard a muffled noise, and the man's voice returned.

"Satisfied, Mr. Flynt?"

"You bastard, if you hurt her, I'll find you. I'll hunt you down!"

Flynt's hand held the receiver in a chokehold. He spat the words into the mouthpiece.

"Threats? Come, come, Mr. Flynt," the voice purred. "Consider for a moment. Surely you understand that you are in no position to make threats."

"All right, all right! Just please don't hurt her," Flynt said, trying to calm himself, trying to think.

"That's better. Now listen carefully. What we propose is a simple exchange. You will bring us the photostats, all copies, and we will give you back the girl," the voice said.

"Yes, all right, anything you say."

"Ah, much better, Mr. Flynt. Now, you see, we are getting somewhere. Have you made copies?"

"We tried—the photostats are too dark. The copies come out black."

"I hope that is the truth, Mr. Flynt. Miss Jordan's life depends on it."

"I am not lying," said Flynt. "You will be able to tell that for yourself once you see them."

"Very well, Mr. Flynt. Now, please listen carefully, very carefully, and do exactly as I tell you."

"I'm listening."

"Good! You will place the photostats in a plain, manila envelope and at precisely 11pm tonight you will enter the Southwest Corridor, and…"

The instructions were simply and straightforward. Flynt heard a click and slammed the receiver down, stood and began pacing. He had no idea what to do. His brain was in over-drive. The sour odor of panic filled his nostrils. The smell was familiar. It was his own sweat. He had been a fool. His mind raced. "Why didn't I make her quit? Because you needed her, couldn't have gotten the information any other way. I'd still be floundering in the dark, trying to figure it all out."

Sandy dead. Now Alex!

The guy on the phone said they would let her go tonight if I deliver the documents. He was talking to himself. "Yeah, right! They will just let her go. You had to keep pushing. Right, asshole? If anything happens to Alex, you're the one to blame, nobody else! So what now, smartass? The guy's probably got an army backing him up. Right. I need some heavy duty help, but who?" An idea struck him. Really, it was his only choice.

The gang who had taken Alex probably—hell, certainly—knew where he lived and might be watching. He dressed, kneeled down and peered through a street-side window. Empty! He slipped on his foul weather jacket and lowered himself out of a back window of the apartment. He paused, crouched be-hind a low bush, looked right and left and listened. He heard the sound of a car passing by. The sky was overcast. A light breeze brushed his cheek. He stood, scurried across the yard in a half crouch and vaulted the chain link fence into a neighbor's backyard. He ran along the side of the house and emerged onto the next street over. He made a right, jogged two blocks, made another, legged it three blocks up along the Jamaicaway and took the six remaining blocks to Lenny's place at a canter.

Flynt arrived, out of breath, in the alley behind the diner. It was a cramped space. Just enough room for a row of trash cans and a delivery truck. A couple of Navy issue mops stood drying in a rack outside the back door. The lights were out. Lenny's Diner was closed on Wednesdays. "Shit!"

He cupped his hands against the back window and peered in. The front of the diner was dark, but he could see a light illuminating the tiny window of Lenny's office just a few steps from where he stood. Flynt knew the retired Marine sometimes worked on his books on his day off. He pulled a couple of coins from his pocket and rapped sharply on the glass. Lenny was dressed in a red flannel shirt and jeans. He looked a lot different out of his whites, Jed thought, as the big man emerged and lumbered toward the door. Lenny's eyes lit up with pleasure and his expectant look morphed into a smile when he recognized his caller.

"What's up, Troop? Can't make it through a day without a cup of Lenny's coffee?" Lenny pulled the door inward, then stepped aside. Flynt looked warily left and right and stepped into a narrow corridor flanked with boxes of foodstuffs stacked in cardboard cartons against the wall.

"I've got a problem, Lenny, a big one, and I need your help!"

"Jed, whatever you need. You know that. You look all done in. Lenny Klausmeyer put his arm around Flynt's shoulder and urged him across the cracked checkerboard floor and into the tiny office. Sit down and tell Uncle Lenny all about it."

The place smelled of bacon. Despite himself, Flynt felt his stomach rumble.

"Hold on! I'll get you a coffee? Won't take a second, just put it on."

"Yeah, I could use one. Flynt sat drumming his fingers on Lenny's desk while the big man poured a cup. Lenny sat down, and Flynt laid it all out.

"So let me see if I got this straight," Lenny said, scratching his head. "These Triad fuckers are the ones who've been burning down abandoned buildings in J.P., and now they've kidnapped your girlfriend—right so far?"

"She's not my girlfriend."

"Sorry, they have kidnapped this researcher—she works for you—and they are going to kill her if you don't bring them these documents. But if you do hand over the photostats like a good boy, they are just going to let you and her waltz outa there, right?"

Flynt glanced up at Lenny then dropped his eyes to the white mug cupped between his hands. "There it is," he said.

"Wrong," said Lenny Klausmeyer. "We both know that ain't gonna happen. By the way, are you sleeping with this sweet young thing?"

"How many times do I have to say it? We're not together. She works for me, that's all

"Yeah, right. Well, that's one hell of a shame, Troop, 'cuz if you were it could be one of those Greek tragedy things. Ya know like Romeo and Juliet because she's gonna flat out get you killed. You understand that, right?"

"It's not her fault, Lenny."

"Right. And this exchange is going to take place where?"

"Well, like I said, at precisely 11pm. I am supposed to enter the Southwest Corridor construction site through the hole in the fence on Amory Street, just across from the office and walk south, find this post they setup, and they will contact me."

"You've got yourself into some serious shit here, Troop."

"Yeah, tell me something I don't already know."

Lenny rubbed his chin. "They're probably holding her in some cellar-hole. There's only a couple of possibilities—half-demolished buildings in that part of the corridor where they could keep out of sight. Lucky for you, Jed, me and my buddies know that whole section of the corridor like the back of our hands. Like I said, there are only a few spots, and we have scouted out all of them more than once," Lenny said.

"How is it you know your way around in there?"

"Because we're in there all the time. Listen, I understand you're one of them bleeding-heart, liberal, fucking pinko types, so I never told you about this. But me, I like to keep my options open and my powder dry. Don't get me wrong, I love this country, but like a lot of older vets I know, I don't like what's been goin' down. You know, Cambodia, Kent State, Judge Garrity and this bussing shit. I mean, what the fuck? Politicians lie, and I just don't trust the government. I mean this goes back a long time before I got involved in this redlining shit. Plus, I guess I just like playing cowboys and Indians," he said, grinning. "Me and a few of my buddies who feel the same way, spend Sundays practicin' you know, war-games," Lenny said with a sheepish grin. The corridor is a perfect place to simulate urban guerilla warfare, and if there's gonna be a war in this country, Troop, the cities is where it's gonna start."

"We've been using the corridor for a couple a years. Listen, there used to be a lot of serious bad guys using the corridor, a couple of Roxbury street gangs, one guy even set up a chop shop, you know, boosting cars and repainting and then selling them. The cops are scared shitless to go in there, so a lot of nasty shit goes down. Leastwise, it used to. Then we showed up. We sort of discouraged a lot of it, you know, as a public service like," Lenny said with a sly smile.

"This isn't a combat exercise, Gunny."

"Yeah, don't I know it, but you go in there alone, those slicky-boys are gonna just flat-out kill you both."

Flynt shrugged, "There it is!" he said meeting his friend's eyes.

"Yeah. Well. What we need is a plan. From what you said these are hard boys, but they lack discipline, right? And there are only one or two spots where they're likely to set up shop. Locating the enemy is half the battle, right?"

Flynt emptied his coffee cup. He was beginning to feel a flicker of hope.

"Thanks, Lenny. I'm sorry to drag you into this shit. I had no other place to turn."

Lenny smiled. "What the hell. Semper Fi, right?"

"Right!" Flynt stood up. "Mind if I get a refill?" he asked.

Lenny waved a hand in dismissal. "Sure, knock yourself out. There's some day-old donuts over there, case you're hungry."

Flynt filled his cup, picked up a donut and sat down on the other side of the narrow desk and focused his full attention on Lenny's plan.

"Okay, Troop, you remember the drill. First recon. They probably have your girl stashed in there already. So we scout out the area and find out where," Lenny said.

"Yeah, who handles that?"

"One of my guys. Jerry is his name. You might have seen him in here or down at the V.F.W. Tall, about thirty-five, sandy hair, not an ounce of fat on him?"

Flynt shook his head. "Doesn't ring a bell."

"Yeah, well he don't eat breakfast. Usually comes by for lunch. Ex-Green Beret sniper. Never know it to look at him. He was a wet-work specialist in Nam. He's operated solo up North for sometimes a month at a time. 100% kill ratio. He never missed, won a Silver Star. These Triad boys will never even get a whiff of him until it's too late."

"Sounds like an evil dude," Flynt said.

"Oh yeah, you'll like him." Lenny laughed. "Uses a Dragunov semi-automatic sniper rifle that he took off of a dead VC. It's lighter than the M14 and nowhere near as cranky. Russians built 'em for the Spetsnaz. Gas-operated, rotating bolt, fires a 6.62x54 millimeter, muzzle velocity 830 meters per second. At 800 meters it hits the target like a freight train at twice the speed of sound. Magazine only holds ten rounds, but it don't matter. He don't ever need more than one shot.

"Once he locates the target and radios the position, we move in, and hem 'em in from three sides. Got another buddy who will help. Jimmy Canavan, another Jarhead. You'll meet him later. Excellent marksman. Not the sociable type, keeps to himself. Likes the Armalite AR-15 modified with an M-16 BCG. He uses the civilian version. Got a variety of scopes, including infrared, which we're gonna need for this operation."

"You mean like the old Starlight?" Flynt asked.

"Negatory! You are seriously behind the times, my man," Lenny said. "Starlight was based on near infrared. The newest stuff is called FLIR, forward-looking infrared. One of these babies will silhouette a target even in a fog."

Flynt held up both hands. "Okay, Gunny, I surrender. I haven't paid much attention to military technology since I reentered the world."

"Well, that ain't the world's loss."

"You think these guys will help?"

"Shit, no problem, Marine! I told them about the work you're doing here, and besides both these guys are action junkies just like me."

"How do we flush the hostiles?"

"I've gotta think about that. Rushing their hideout is too risky. You're gonna have to play this thing out, Jed. You make contact but keep as far back as you can. Stay outside where we can cover you and make them come to you. Demand that they bring the girl out where you can see her," Lenny said, looking intently at Flynt.

"What if they refuse? I'm not exactly in a strong negotiating position here."

"No, but you understand that once inside their hideout, me and the boys will be operating blind, and neither one of you are likely to come out of this shit alive. Look, they won't do anything until they get the documents. That's number one. Then they have to kill you both to make sure you don't talk. They won't want to use guns, too much noise. So that'll mean one of them's gotta get in close and take you out.

"So, you bring along a big manila envelope, stuff it with something that looks like photos. They will probably have a man watching the entry point to make sure you don't bring backup. Just lose it along the way, tell the head honcho, who-ever the fuck he is, that you hid the photos, and you won't pro-duce them until he produces the girl. They'll probably bring her out and bunch up all around her.

"Then what?'"

"Three rifles. We take all the fuckers out at once,"

"Christ!"

"Well, you didn't expect that this would be a walk in the park," Lenny said, staring directly into his buddy's eyes.

Flynt's eyes were steel-hard. "No," Flynt said, "some people are gonna die. I don't care if it's me. I just don't want to see Alex hurt. It's my fault that she's involved."

"Right, I hear that. Look, if it works out right, it will be real clean. The bad guys will be dead before they hear a sound. We can take out four, maybe five. You get the drop on whoever's left. I'll be right behind you. I've got a Beretta 92FS millimeter, slim-line with a fifteen-round clip. You can tuck it into your waist-band without making a bulge. You ever shoot a 9 millimeter?"

"Sure, played with the Beretta a bit during my tour. A lot of the guys had them. I like it, less kick, better accuracy than the .45 auto. But I'm pretty rusty. Haven't had much time lately."

"No problem! I've got a range set up in my cellar. You can spend a couple of hours re-familiarizing yourself with the weapon."

"Practice? What the fuck, Lenny."

"Look, it will keep your mind occupied. There's nothing more you can do anyhow. I'll make some calls. By the way have you seen this morning's Globe?" Lenny slapped the paper down in front of Flynt. "Check out the headline! 'Senate Democrats to Back Casino Gambling Bill'."

"Holy shit!"

"Yeah, how about that? Looks like your Triad pals are moving fast. I got a lot of friends among the local pols, and I never caught even a whisper about this casino shit. Course I don't know Craven. He never comes in."

"Damn!"

"You say you were careful. You got any idea how they figured out what you and what's her name, Alexis, were up to? They hit you just a few days before your housing conference? You got a leak there somewheres, Troop!" Lenny said.

Flynt's eyes busily scanned the article. He looked up. "I've been thinking about that. There's really only one guy who knew about the documents, a priest down at the diocese. He helped me out, so I figured he was okay. You know, I had a feeling there was something not quite right about that guy. It looks like I fucked up big time, Lenny."

"Well, you sure stirred up a shit storm, that's for sure. But like the man said, Troop, it ain't over till it's over.

"Thanks Lenny."

Lenny stood up, began pacing then dropped back into his chair and slammed his fist down on the table. "Who do these Triad fuckers think they are? This ain't no third world fucking cesspool. This is the U. S. of A. We fought these bastards over there, and now they think they can come over here onto my turf, into my neighborhood, hurt our people, fuck with ex-Marines. Triads, my ass!"

"These are hard men, Lenny."

"Yeah, well if they're so tough how come they kidnapped a little girl? Why didn't they just come after you?"

Flynt shrugged.

"All I got to say is forgive the motherfuckers 'cause they know not what they do. They figure you're gonna be out there all alone. That's our one advantage. They won't expect what's about to go down. These fuckers are seriously in need of being taught a lesson, and me and my boys are just the lads to teach em." He raised one finger and eyed Jed fiercely. "These boy-sans don't know it, but they have made one serious, fucking mistake, Troop. I don't know how they got here, but I know how they're going home. We're gonna ship 'em back to where they came from, postpaid, in fucking body bags!"

Chapter 34

End Game

9:15pm

Jerry Holmes closed his eyes and sniffed the wind. Ah, there it was again. The faint, sweetish odor was unmistakable—cigarette smoke! His lips twisted. Lenny called it right–no discipline! Silly bugger might just as well send up a flare. The ex-Green-Beret was dressed in full camouflage, looking like a cinematic night-mare with his face and neck painted in alternating green and black. He had pushed back the hood of his balaclava so as not to restrict his hearing. The Russian-made sniper rifle strapped to his back was 44.7 inches long, weighed 9.48 pounds and was equipped with a PSO-1 passive infrared telescopic sight.

Jerry had set up a grid and had been working his way meticulously through it for about an hour and a half. He loved recon. There was nothing more satisfying than being out on his own, alone in the quiet night stalking his prey.

The psychology of the sniper is not well understood, even by other elite warriors. Snipers are seen as loners. Regular army guys think of them as nut-jobs who just get a kick out of killing people. But guys who exhibit that sort of pathology are almost always spotted and washed out early in the rigorous sniper training course.

Man is an animal who draws his legitimacy from the group. Only very stable individuals can endure the long hours of lonely vigil, the inner discipline to remain still for extended periods, ignoring physical discomfort. And few possess the cold-blooded self-confidence necessary to carry out executions of men and women who are no immediate threat to one's own survival—and still sleep untroubled at night.

For most of the hundred thousand years since human kind emerged out of the broad African savannah, necessity has selected and promoted those individuals with traits useful for tracking, trapping and killing. With the rise of complex civilization, other, less-lethal talents have surpassed, in usefulness and in value, man's propensity to slaughter other sentient beings. But some men in whom the breeding has run true, still possess the atavistic urge to pit themselves, in a life or death struggle, against a dangerous enemy—be it man or beast.

Jerry Holmes had felt that urge even before he had begged his father to take him on his first hunt. As he listened to Lenny explain the mission, Jerry had felt the beginnings of that heady buzz he first experienced as a sniper in Vietnam and nowhere since. Win or lose, man-hunting is the ultimate test. There is no game so difficult or so dangerous.

Jerry crept forward, keeping to the shadows. He circled around a mound of concrete refuse. The clear night sky cast inky shadows across a wasteland of broken and discarded refuse. As he closed in on the objective, he went prone and slithered like a snake along the knife-edged shadow cast by a crumbling foundation wall.

A twig snapped, and Jerry froze. His eyes swept the land-scape. Directly in front of him. About two hundred yards out, he saw the building. The place was familiar. Double wooden doors with peeling green paint set in a concrete wall. The structure had been built into a scooped out hillside. Jerry did not know its original purpose. But it looked to him like it might have been the underground garage of a small factory.

Off to his right a match flared, the man's cupped hands, framing his face. The perfect target. He was Asian and a chain smoker. Jerry could tell that he was definitely not Vietnamese. He had made a study of Asian faces. But Jerry was not close enough to make a definite ID. A good sniper trained himself to carefully observe every detail of the kill zone. It is important to retain a wide perspective and not focus overmuch on the target or become too confident. The depth of an enemy's cunning cannot be properly assessed until after he is dead. In combat, tunnel vision can get you killed.

The building, he knew, was empty except for some odds and ends of machinery, an old couch and some scattered junk. The roof had remained sound. It would be fairly dry inside. Jerry figured that if these tong guys were holed up anywhere in this section of the corridor, that's where they'd be. He could see no signs of activity, but his hunter's logic told him he had located his quarry.

His fingers slid into a side pocket and grasped his in-frared NVD spotter scope. He put it to his eye, and the world turned an eerie bright green. "Gotcha," he whispered. The scope showed him a thin halo of light framing the edges of the doors. There were two sets of double doors which could be swung outward to allow vehicles to enter. Both sets, Jerry knew from previous visits, were badly sprung and would be almost impossible to drag open. Anyone wanting to go in and out would likely use the side door to his left as he faced the building. He studied the area directly in front of the entrance. A driveway pitched upward from the doors and fanned out into a broad killing field flanked by a pair of concrete retaining walls that jutted out from either side of the building's façade.

The walls could be an effective shield. It is difficult to flank an alert defender. But, like a pair of blinders, it would shield an attacker crouching just behind the building. He would be beyond the peripheral view of a target, standing just outside the doors—if that target was focused on a threat directly in his face.

"Okay, how many more pickets? And where?" he wondered. He pulled up his sleeve and checked the time. Still more than an hour's leeway. Best do a three-sixty. The smoker might be a decoy. He would have to reconnoiter in a wide circle to find cover.

Jerry pictured the garage in his memory. He recalled a couple of narrow cellar windows set in the wall on the backside of the structure just beneath the roof. The flaring match had temporarily compromised the guard's night vision. It was the time to move.

Jerry stuffed the NVD back into his side pocket, rose into a crouch and began circling left, away from the guard. He worked his way around the structure until he could make out a faint rectangular glow on either side of center, just above ground level. Edging forward with his knees deeply flexed and weight on his back foot, his forefoot quested forward as delicately as a long-legged water bird. He crouched down in front of one of the windows, peered in, then moved to the other.

The windows were too narrow for a grown man to squeeze through, and the glass in both was covered with wire mesh—and decades of filth. He lay down, and closing one eye to preserve his night vision, ran the other over the glass, looking for a clean spot. The room was fairly well-lit, and he could see just well enough to make out several blurred man-shapes moving around inside. He heard muffled voices, but the cement foundation was too thick to make out any words. He counted the shapes. He saw nothing that looked like it might be the girl.

Lenny Klausmeyer and Jed Flynt sat side by side in the front seat of Lenny's old Chevrolet sedan. They were parked along the edge of the corridor. His radiotelephone crackled into life.

"Six. This is One. Contact made. Over." Jerry's voice came through loud and clear.

Lenny's eyes met Flynt's. He picked up the microphone and pressed Send.

"One. This is Six. Over?"

The radio code was the same as used between units in Vietnam. The command CP was always designated Six.

"Six, One. The hostiles are holed up on the Washington Street side about two clicks south of my entry point in that underground garage that's built like a bunker. Over."

There were two distinct breaks in the static. Someone had depressed a transmit button twice.

"That's Jimmy. He's listening," Lenny said. "Roger that, One. Know just where you mean. How many hostiles? Over."

"This is One. They've got the door closed. I circled around back, but not much help. One guard posted in a clump of bushes about fifty yards out in front and to the right as you face the building. Maybe three to four inside. I figure maximum five. Over."

"Roger that. Good work. Any sign of the girl?"

"Negative, Six, but the view through the window is obscured. I got barely a glimpse inside."

Flynt turned in his seat and put his hand on Lenny's shoulder, his eyebrows raised in a question mark.

"Wait, One," Lenny whispered, and released the transmit button.

"Two, Six. You copy that. Over?"

Jimmy's lazy drawl flowed out of the speaker. "Six, Two. That's affirmative. Over."

"Two, Six. Anything happening in your sector?" Lenny asked.

"Negative, Six. No hostiles so far."

"Okay, Jimmy. Keep your head down and rendezvous with Jerry and set up flanking positions as discussed. I'll be along soon as I can. Out."

"Where the hell is Alex?" Flynt asked.

Lenny put down the mike.

"She's probably in there. Jerry couldn't see much. Most likely they've got her tied up in a corner."

"What if she isn't? What if they've already killed her?"

"Listen, Troop, it's you they're after. You've got what they want, the documents. They'll keep her alive as bait."

"Yeah, but what if you're wrong?"

Lenny gazed back at his friend. "There it is," he said.

9:45pm

Jimmy Canavan double-clicked the transmit button in acknowledgement, removed the ear-bud and stowed the walkie-talkie in his vest. Like Jerry Holmes, he had hidden his freckled Irish complexion behind alternating colored layers of camouflage paste. He crouched behind a low bush and checked his gear.

The Tac-16 noise-suppressor added a full five inches to the AR's twenty-four inch barrel. The silencer, as it is commonly known, functions much like a car's muffler. A series of baffles choke off gas emissions caused by the gun powder explosion that propels the bullet and substantially reduces the sharp report of a round leaving the muzzle. However, what most people don't understand is that a shot from a high-powered rifle cannot be made silent. A bullet traveling at thirty-five hundred feet per second makes an audible crack as it tears a hole through the sound barrier.

Jimmy drew his seven-inch KA-BAR from his thigh-sheath. The straight blade was black, but a cold, thin line of newly honed steel edge gleamed wickedly in the starlight. He did not carry a handgun. Lenny had made the point that gunplay had to be kept to a minimum. Jimmy had brought along a Beta C -100 round magazine for the AR in his pack, just in case, but he knew he could only use it as a last resort. The noise of a few rounds might be shrugged off as a car backfiring, but a sustained firefight would bring the cops into the corridor in force. Jimmy Canavan didn't mind. He preferred the knife for close-in work.

He found a sheltered spot hidden between two low-lying bushes with a good view of the target area and settled in. He wrapped the Armalite's leather sling around his upper arm at precisely the sweet spot, with a half-twist around his forearm. Testing his position, he leaned onto his left shoulder, worked the rifle butt tight into the crux of his right shoulder and felt the sling tighten. The strap bit into his upper arm as he slid his gloved hand along the guard and wrapped his finger around the trigger. Perfect. He backed off, relaxed, took a few deep breaths and settled down to wait.

11:00pm

Flynt crossed Amory Street and slipped through the opening where the chain link mesh had been peeled back from the steel pole.

The sky was crisp, the stars bright. The night was cold, but by day scabby tufts of green grass had begun to show up against the brown. The few scraggly trees were budding out, the first whisper of spring.

There was no moon, but the night was clear, and the stars provided just enough light so that the landscape appeared ghostly and indistinct. Flynt carried a small flashlight with a coated red lens to preserve his night vision. He wore his old gray-green, Navy-issue, foul weather jacket and knitted black watch cap. He left the coat unbuttoned so he could quickly reach the Beretta. He had tucked it into his waistband flat against his spine.

Flynt knew about the watcher from Lenny's last radio transmission. He had no walkie-talkie. They were too bulky and would give away the fact that he was not alone. He was now running blind, but he had a good idea where Lenny had gone to ground.

He turned right and left, pretending to scan the terrain. He wanted to be sure that any watcher got a good look at the manila envelope he carried tucked under one arm. There was a light wind out of the north. He stopped to listen but heard nothing beyond the occasional buzz of cars moving along Washington Street.

Flynt's nerves were poised on a dagger's edge. The whole rescue plan depended upon his being able to get close to Alex. But where was she? Was she really inside the garage? He and Lenny had argued and he had almost called the operation off.

Out of long habit, Flynt looked up and took a visual fix on the north star, loosened his jacket, shoved his hands into his pockets and began to make his way southwest, paralleling the waist-high, chain link fence which bordered the corridor.

Behind him, a man-shape rose from the shadows and followed.

Lenny was well situated. He had dropped Flynt off, driven up Columbus Avenue, parked and jumped the corridor fence just after 10pm. Far enough north, he figured, to avoid any hostiles. He began working his way southward. His face was made up in camo He carried his personal weapon—a Remington Model 700P bolt-action rifle slung over his shoulder and a KA-BAR strapped to his thigh for close-in work. Lenny was no sniper, but he knew recon. He had done plenty of it in Korea and in Vietnam. He found the perfect "hide," a shallow trench with a section of broken thirty-inch concrete pipe and a convenient view of Flynt's Amory Street office. The fit was a little tight, but he burrowed in like a burly woodchuck, made himself at home, and waited.

About a half-hour passed when he heard someone coming from the general direction of the garage.

The man was obviously not expecting trouble. He sauntered along, smoking a cigarette, making no attempt to hide his presence. He passed within twenty feet of Lenny's hiding place. He was slender, in his twenties, dressed in black street shoes, dark slacks and a black overcoat. A long thin object dangled from his right hand. Lenny watched as he picked out a clump of thick bushes, crouched behind them and stuck the object into the ground. Lenny waited until the man had settled himself, then extracted his night scope and put it to his eye. He smiled and shook his head slowly side to side, "Well, I'll be damned, a fucking sword." This shit was beginning to get interesting.

Lenny had watched Flynt slip though the fence and enter the corridor. He waited quietly, giving Flynt and his shadow time to draw well ahead before he slipped out of his hiding place and worked his way quietly along the narrow path behind them. He was about thirty feet back when the young Chinese thug, his sword propped up on his shoulder like he was a soldier on parade, sauntered up behind Flynt and cleared his throat. "Okay, hold it right there," he called out. "That's far enough." Flynt had precise instructions, but Yang was obviously taking no chances. He had ordered his man to disarm the organizer before he got near the garage.

It had been some years since Flynt had scouted a trail, but he had led his squad on many a patrol in the thick jungles of southeast Asia, his eyes and ears hyper-alert to every moving branch, fluttering wing and scratching claw. Flynt knew the man was there. His clumsy movements had betrayed him long before he spoke. Flynt's uncertainty about Alex's fate had been gnawing at his guts all day, and guilt and rage had been building like the pressure inside a covered pot slowly approaching a boil. The entire strategy depended upon retaining flexibility of movement. He could not allow himself to be taken. Like an erupting volcano, Flynt turned on his heel and attacked.

Startled, the young Chinese managed to raise his sword, intending to slash downward, but Flynt was too quick. He pierced his guard, caught the man's arm just below the elbow, and blocked the downward thrust with a rising left forearm. He levered the man's weapon up just above his head and as he did so, twisted his open hand outward, clamped his fingers down on the man's bicep, pulling him forward and off-balance.

As he performed the block with his left, Flynt retracted his right hand to the side of his ribcage just below his nipple, took another quick step forward, and thrust his open right palm upward between the Chinese thug's flailing arms and hard against his chin. The head of an adult male weighs approximately twelve pounds, and the point of attachment to the neck is at that precise nexus where the spinal cord meets the brain-stem. The power of the palm-heel thrust the thug's chin up and levered his head back like a shutter tossed back against its hinges. The trauma resulting from the power of the thrust short-circuited the complex of nerves within the neural pathway leading to the brain's command center.

It happened so fast that Lenny was taken completely by surprise. He was aware of his friend's skills but had never seen him in action. By the time he covered the distance between them, Flynt was gazing down at the thug's body splayed across the path, his sword by his side.

"I'll be God-dammed, Troop," he said, staring. "I think you killed the fucker!"

Flynt regarded the man's prone body for a moment, then gazed at Lenny.

"I don't know," he said in an even tone. He was calm and breathing normally.

Lenny noted Flynt's eerie calm in the wake of the savagery of his act. He had seen it before in men pushed to the edge during extreme combat. Flynt was like a tightly coiled spring with a hair trigger. Lenny kneeled down and placed two fingers beneath the man's ear. "Nope, still got a pulse," he said.

Flynt just gazed down at the prone body in silence.

"Well, one thing's sure," Lenny said. "We can't leave the fucker here in the middle of the trail. Look, you go ahead, keep to the plan and I'll clean up."

He reached down grabbed the man beneath the arms and started dragging his unconscious body toward a dense growth of bushes just to the side of the path.

Flynt worked his way slowly southwestward along the trail. He felt better. Like a boil, a portion of the poisonous mix of guilt and rage had been lanced and temporarily drained, leaving behind a clear and steely focus.

The instructions were to look for a wooden post stuck in the ground with a flashlight taped to it, its light pointing downward. Five minutes later he found it. As he had been instructed, he found a folded sheet of paper stuck to a nail at the top of the post. The paper instructed him to turn left and follow a narrow path between two mounds of debris. He crumpled the paper in his fist, then thinking better of it, unfolded it and stuck it back onto the post to guide Lenny. He turned left and moved out, emerging in an open area. The dark shape of the garage loomed up before him out of the darkness about sixty feet away.

The sound of Flynt's footsteps alerted the lookout Jerry had spotted earlier that evening.

"About fucking time," the man groused silently as he stood up. His name was Chang. He had been crouched down behind some thick bushes off to Flynt's right as the organizer halted just parallel to his hiding place. He was a local Triad, and he had been on lookout for over two hours. His hands were frozen, and his feet were numb. He flexed his fingers and stood up slowly—carefully, so as not to make any noise. He slipped a gloved hand inside his jacket and extracted a short wooden club. The thick tapered oak cylinder was lead-lined.

Chang had been warned. This guy Flynt had messed up Johnny Lowboy. Johnny was a tough kid, and Chang wasn't about to take any chances. He tapped the club against his open palm and squinted into the darkness. The organizer came into view. Something was wrong. "Where the fuck is Fong? He shoulda' already taken charge of this guy."

Huh? A faint rustle of sound just behind his head. Chang felt his breath choked off, his body hoisted off its feet like a sack of rice. The club dropped. Desperate fingers clawed at the arm, like an iron bar, wrapped around his throat. His body wriggled and thrashed like a hooked fish as it fought for air.

Jerry Holmes counted slowly to ten. The thug's body went limp as a wet dishrag. Coming from behind, Jerry had snaked his arm around Chang's neck, cocking his hip, he levered the man up and off his feet. The move cut off the blood flow through the carotids, the twin arteries on either side of the neck that control blood flow to the brain.

Timing is important. Once the lights go out, death follows close behind.

Jerry loosened his grip and let the unconscious thug slide into an untidy heap on the ground. He would be out for at least half an hour. By that time, Jerry figured, this little party would be over.

Flynt had heard the commotion and dropped to the ground. A few seconds later, a low whistle told him that the danger had been neutralized.

Flynt stood up, walked ten paces forward, and cupped his hands around his mouth.

"Hey!" he called out. "You there, in the garage. It's Jedediah Flynt. Here I am. Show yourselves."

Inside the building, Yang had been pacing back and forth, checking his watch. Flynt's shout took the Triad boss by surprise.

"What? Where are Fong and Chang?" Yang demanded, staring at his twin henchmen. Both men stared back at him uncomprehendingly.

The script-change unnerved the Triad boss. Something had obviously gone wrong. His quarry was standing outside bellowing at him. "Could this be a trap? Damned incompetents!" Yang thought. He had little respect for the Americanized

Chinese in his Boston organization. They were overweight and soft, but he had no choice but to use them or the local boss would lose face. Yang needed cooperation, not petulance. Perhaps if he had let them keep their guns?

"Well," he thought, "I still have the girl." The cards had been dealt, and he held trump. Like many Asians, Yang held a casual belief that some sort of joss controlled much of a man's fate. There was good joss and bad joss. A man could affect but could not control his joss.

He decided to play for time.

Three Coleman lanterns illuminated the interior of the garage. Yang lifted the one hanging from a wooden post just inside the door.

Outside Flynt watched as Yang emerged from the side door. He held the lantern above his head squinting at the dim presence, barely visible beyond the sweep of the lantern's glow.

"All right, you son of a bitch, here I am. Where is Alexis Jordan?" Flynt yelled.

"Ah, Mr. Flynt," Yang said, improvising smoothly. He hung the lantern on a nail which protruded from the doorframe and shaded his eyes with one hand.

"I am pleased to see that you have arrived on time. I take it you have brought the photostats?"

"Yeah, right, I brought them. I've got them hidden nearby where you'll never find them. You produce my researcher, and I hand them over. That was our deal."

"Indeed, it was. Your young lady is quite well and just inside," he said, gesturing toward the door.

Flynt stood—stationary and silent.

"It is cold out here," said Yang. He gestured toward Flynt. "Come inside. We can take care of our business like civilized men."

Flynt shifted from one foot to the other and snorted a laugh. "You must take me for a fool, Yang, or whatever your name is. I am standing right here. We had a deal! You produce the girl. Then, I produce the documents."

Yang was surprised at the use of his name. The documents had been more revealing than he thought. He made a mental note to send a couple of his men to Lichtenstein to deal with that fool of a lawyer. Yang hated incompetence, and such stupidity could not be allowed to go unpunished.

As for the fool who stood before him, a bit more patience would be required. His death warrant has already been signed, and Yang relished the thought of personally looking into his eyes when his fate finally became clear to him. Yang pointed his finger directly at Flynt. "You are in no position to make demands," he said.

Flynt folded his arms across his chest and said nothing.

Yang peered about suspiciously. Flynt's confidence unnerved him. He thought about the pistol tucked in his breast pocket. He didn't dare risk a shot, and he knew that Flynt knew it, too. Everything beyond the glow of the lantern was dim and shadowed. "Where are those two fools?"

"Looking for something?" Flynt asked.

"Where are my men?" Yang demanded.

"What men?" Flynt asked. He made a show of looking left and right. "What are you playing at, Yang?"

The man seemed genuinely surprised at the question, but Yang couldn't shake his bad feeling. He was assailed by doubt. The man detailed to shadow Flynt's movements might have been delayed, but Fong had been stationed less than thirty feet from where the organizer now stood, and Yang had made his instructions excruciatingly clear. Had Flynt somehow managed to neutralize both of his men? Did he have help? How was that possible? Had the scum simply run away? They would pay for their cowardice.

"I don't know what you think you are playing at, Mr. Flynt, but I warn you, Ms. Jordan's life hangs in the balance. You were instructed to come alone."

"I am alone, Yang," Flynt said extending his arms. "Who did you expect, the Marines?" he sneered.

"Look around," Flynt continued, gesturing with open hands. "I followed your instructions exactly. I saw no one along the way."

Yang hesitated. Flynt might have surprised one of his men, but he could not have eliminated both. Did he have help? Where could this man have found people willing to risk their lives against armed men in the middle of the night?

It seemed unlikely to Yang, and he had to have those documents. Millions of dollars rested on it. He made a choice. He would play out the hand.

"Very well, Mr. Flynt. A moment, please."

Yang ducked back inside the building.

"Chiang, Liang," he ordered the twins, in Chinese, "bring the girl, keep her close, and Chiang—" Yang raised his voice, switched to English, "have your knife where this stinking 'gweilo' can see it. If he tries anything, anything at all, cut the girl's throat."

Alexis Jordan had heard her name pronounced by Yang. She had recognized Flynt's voice. Hope coursed through her like an electrical current.

After several hours in the filthy, damp cell, with nothing to drink, and not even a chamber pot, she had been awakened, jerked roughly to her feet, gagged, blindfolded, and shoved into an elevator. She was not sure how much time had passed. She remembered hearing Yang's voice barking orders. She was forced onto the floor, rolled up in a rug like a human crêpe, and roughly tossed onto the floor of what she quickly realized was a vehicle, with its motor running.

She could see daylight. "Was it morning? Where are they taking me?" The van made its way through the center of Boston, up Columbus Avenue, made a left turn onto Washington Street and a right onto Williams Street, just across from Doyle's Tavern. It came to a stop at the dead end next to the corridor fence. People were always going into the corridor. No one took much notice of a pair of men carrying a rolled carpet along a well-worn path through a break in the fence.

Once inside the garage, the men unrolled the rug. They removed the blindfold and deposited the frightened girl in a far corner on the damp, cold cement floor. One of the twins poked a thick finger in her face. "You stay. No move! No talk!" he ordered the frightened girl.

Men came in and out; Yang came, left, then returned. No one spoke to her. She had put up a brave front the previous night, but the stark reality of her situation had arrived with the dawn. She still hoped that Flynt would come, but if he did, what could he do against all these armed men? No, she could not depend on him. She must do her best to not draw attention to herself. Alex's thought processes reverted to those of an injured child. She sat quietly with her head down like a beaten dog. Against all logic, she grasped at the hope that if she was very good her captors might take pity and release her.

Alex sat with her knees drawn up to her chest and watched daylight turn slowly into night. She was fed once when Yang returned to the hideout late in the day and given water, which she drank greedily. Three times she was dragged to her feet and shoved outside into the cold to relieve herself. They made her squat and do it right in front of them while they watched, laughed and joked. Her futile attempts to preserve her modesty seem to provide them with no end of amusement.

Yang's orders pleased the twins. They grinned at each other in anticipation, turned and bowed simultaneously to Yang like a pair of cartoon cutouts. Chiang reached down, and Alexis Jordan was dragged to her feet.

"You two," Yang ordered in English, gesturing to the two remaining local thugs. They were taller. "You both go out first and screen the girl. My men will be right behind you. On my order, you move aside just enough so the 'gweilo' can see her. Understand?"

Chiang covered Alex's mouth with a piece of duct tape, then leaned close and grinned into her eyes. He snapped open his knife, grabbed the back of her neck, slid the cold blade up under her chin. "No move," he said and shoved her out into the frigid night.

"Here she is, Mr. Flynt," said Yang. "As you can see she is healthy and unhurt. Now, if you please, I will see those documents."

The lantern cast a circular pool of light which surrounded Alexis Jordan and her captors like a dim spotlight.

"The gag," Flynt demanded, "take it off. I want to see her face."

The temperature had dropped significantly. His breath came out in bursts of white vapor.

Alex shivered in the chill night air.

Yang sighed, started to speak, shrugged, and snapped his fingers.

Chiang ripped off Alex's gag, grabbed a handful of her hair and pushed her to the left more clearly into Flynt's visual field.

At that moment, Chiang's head slid right between the crosshairs of Jerry's telescopic sight. Jerry Holmes smiled, exhaled slowly and gently squeezed the trigger. A one hundred sixty grain bullet punched through the sound barrier and drilled a five-millimeter hole in the Chinese thug's right temple. Passing through his skull, it spread apart like an opening umbrella and blew a jagged chunk out of the left side of his cranium, spattering a couple of pounds of gray brain matter over Alexis Jordan and the door just to her right.

From his prone firing position approximately ninety degrees to Jerry's right, Jimmy held a second target framed in his crosshairs. His bullet entered through the left eye-hole of one of the two local thugs with so much force it lifted the man up off his feet and drove him backward. Jimmy preferred hollow point ammo. The copper jacketed slug mushroomed as it entered the thug's cranium and reduced his brain to jello. The force pushed Yang aside and threw the thug back against the building. His body sagged against the heavy garage door to Alex's left. The blood-soaked hair on the back of his head brushed a broad red trail behind him as his corpse slid like a bloody beanbag slowly to the ground.

One of the taller thugs eliminated, his field of fire clear, Jimmy shifted his aim left and down. Yang's pudgy face loomed in his scope. Just as his finger tightened on the butterfly shaped trigger, Yang flinched. That small movement saved his life. Jimmy's slug shaved Yang's left ear close enough for him to feel the breeze and buried itself in the wood behind his head. Yang froze and threw up his hands in surrender.

Of the men surrounding Alexis, two were dead and the boss was out of the action. The taller American thug and one of the twins remained standing. The local guy held the hysterical, blood spattered girl before him like a human shield. Flynt, standing twenty feet in front of the group, realized that the shock of the surprise assault had passed and Alex was still in lethal danger.

Jimmy Canavan held Yang's face steady between his cross-hairs, but Jerry Holmes had no clear shot at either of the remaining thugs without endangering the girl.

Flynt groped around his back for the Beretta and stopped. Two hours of practice in Lenny's basement had convinced him of one thing—his aim was far from reliable. He inhaled, bellowed a war cry and charged forward empty-handed.

The remaining American-Chinese pushed Alex aside and strode forward to meet Flynt's charge. He was tall for a Chinese and built like a barrel equipped with arms and legs. He held a flat-bladed Chinese sword clutched in one hand. He raised his sword arm. It was an obvious move. Flynt anticipated the scything overhand cut and sprung forward and left. The flashing blade sliced through the right sleeve of his foul weather jacket missing his shoulder by millimeters.

Believing that he had wounded Flynt, the thug grimaced, pointed his sword and lurched forward seeking to disembowel his quarry.

Flynt took one step back, spun like a ballet dancer. His right leg flanked the sword's point, skirted the thug's arm and slammed against the right side of his skull with the full force of a spinning back kick. The man grunted once and dropped heavily to the ground.

Yang and one twin remained alive.

With Flynt's body directly in front of him blocking the shooters, Yang saw his chance and scrambled to his feet.

One sleeve of his expensive suit was ripped at his right shoulder exposing a starched white shirt. He drew a short-barreled revolver from his waistband, grabbed Alexis Jordan, and pressed the muzzle against her right temple.

"Enough! Stop! Stop now!" Yang shouted. "Everybody backs off right now or the girl dies!"

"It's over Yang. Let her go!" Flynt responded. "Five of your men are dead, and two expert marksmen have your head framed in their fucking crosshairs. You can surrender, or you can die. Your choice!"

Surrender was impossible. No Supreme Leader of the Ghost Dragon Triad had been captured in one hundred fifty years. He would never survive the loss of face. Beside him, Liang, the last twin, stood, dumbstruck by the sight of his beloved brother's blood puddling at his feet.

What Yang needed was a diversion, a sacrifice. He barked an order in Chinese. From long habit Liang heard and instantly obeyed his master's command.

The Chinese thug raised his head, glared at Flynt and ripped open his shirt exposing his grotesquely muscled chest. His eyes blazed, his brain screamed. "You kill my brother. Now!", he bellowed in English and slapped his chest, "Come! You try, kill me!"

Flynt held up his hand to signal his friends. "Hold your fire, this guy is mine," Flynt said, flexed his knees and dropped his weight into a fighting stance. "Ok, tough guy," he said, beckoning the man forward. "Come on!"

The strongman eyed Flynt with a look of disdain. He hawked and spit on the ground, then strode forward, straight into Flynt's vicious, front snap-kick.

The technique, delivered with full power and aimed at a point just below the solar plexus, would have brought a normal man to his knees, but Flynt's foot bounced off Liang's heavily muscled torso like a basketball off a backboard.

The Chinese thug had spent years and countless hours hardening and shaping his body into a formidable weapon. Flynt tried again, but the brute blocked his kick with a sharp downward block from a hardened forearm, which sent a lance of pain down the length of Flynt's leg. He strode forward, grabbed the organizer by the front of his jacket and delivered a savage head-butt to the bridge of his nose.

Skyrockets exploded in Flynt's eyes. The force of the blow had broken his nose. The Gentler hoisted him off the ground and tossed him backwards like a used Kleenex.

Flynt landed face down in the dirt, his eyes sheeted in blood. Flynt was in deep trouble. He struggled to his knees. Blood gushed from his broken nose, down his chest and filled his mouth. He stood up, hawked and spit out a great glob of dirt and blood. He shook his head trying to clear his vision, but all he could make out was a ghostly shadow. Flynt's brain screamed, but his long hours of repetitive training took over. He retreated backward, dropped back into a defensive stance, raised his hands and prepared to sell his life at the highest possible price.

Coming from nowhere, Lenny Klausmeyer grabbed Flynt, pulled him aside and stepped out of the shadows into the circle of death. "Okay, fucker," he said, smiling at the Chinese strong man, "let's dance!"

Keeping to the shadows, Lenny had crept in close. He could see that his buddy was injured and stood no chance against the awesome power of the Chinese fighter. Lenny was a warrior. His bravery had been tested in battle on the frigid winter hills above Inchon and in the steaming heat of the A Shau Valley. Those who have never been at war believe that men fight for the big things, a cause or a flag, but those who have been there know that a man fights for the little things, for his friends, for the man who stands next to him in the battle line.

Lenny moved forward, both arms held out away from his body like a wrestler ready to grapple. The retired Marine had watched him deal with Flynt, and he had no illusions about his ability to overcome this man hand-to-hand. His heavy KA-BAR fighting knife sat lightly in the palm in a right underhand grip. The thug's pig-eyes glared at the new threat pointedly ignoring the blade.

"Come on, numb-nuts," Lenny said and beckoned him forward with a grin.

The Chinese thug also grinned, then charged forward like a freight train, his arms open to engulf his antagonist.

For a big man, he was incredibly fast on his feet. Lenny feinted right, then sidestepped left, and slashed the huge Chinese thug's questing forearm. The wound spurted blood. Lenny backed off. The thug looked down and examined the blood welling up just below his elbow and raised his arm. He grinned at Lenny and ran his tongue along the inside of his forearm, licking the blood. Then he dropped the arm and came on. He made an awkward grab for Lenny's right arm.

The ex-Marine dodged sideways then closed in again searching for an opening. Lenny was on dangerous ground and he knew it, the man was built like a tank. He had to find a soft target, the throat, an eye or the temple, something that would put the big man down. To do that he had to get in close. Lenny felt something catch in the corner of his eye. He blinked. It was all the opening his opponent needed. With lightning speed, the Chinese strongman stepped in and drilled Lenny's midsection with a straight kick.

The kick would have finished most fighters, but Lenny had been taught to keep tension in his abdominal muscles and to take short quick breaths to cushion his diaphragm and protect his internal organs. He grunted, jumped back and re-focused. The kick had been awesomely powerful. Lenny knew that his traumatized abdominals would not withstand another.

Lenny grinned, slapped his chest in a parody of his opponent, hunched his shoulders and growled a challenge. He raised his knife.

The thug, seizing the chance to immobilize Lenny's knife, rushed forward and grasped the ex-marine's right wrist. Lenny had anticipated the move and with a quick flick of the wrist, had already shifted the knife to his left hand. It was a subtly quick move and the Chinese thug missed it. As he dragged Lenny forward into the circle of his arms, the retired Marine struck.

His left arm rose in a shallow arc. The razor-sharp blade sliced through the soft tissue beneath the strongman's chin, punctured his palate and sliced upward piercing his brain. The strongman's eyes popped open like twin flashbulbs. His jaws separated. His mouth gaped open, then snapped shut as he teetered then crashed like a giant oak, hitting the ground dead at Lenny's feet.

Flynt, his vision beginning to clear, saw the man fall. He squinted toward the garage. Alexis Jordan was sitting sandwiched between two dead men, her legs splayed and her back against the garage door. Her face was buried in her hands. She was sobbing. Yang had vanished.

Flynt wiped his bloody face with the back of his sleeve, ran to Alexis, dropped to his knees and folded her into his arms. Her body was shaking uncontrollably.

Jedediah Flynt looked up at the gathering circle of his buddies and cursed. "Son-of-a-bitch! Spread out. The bastard must be nearby. He can't have gotten far!"

Rifles in hand, Jerry Holmes and Jimmy Canavan took off toward either side of the garage in an attempt to flank the fleeing tong boss.

Lenny stooped down to help his friend.

Yang watched and waited until all eyes were focused on the struggle between Lenny and the remaining twin, then shoved the pistol into his waistband, vaulted up over the concrete wall, rolled down the hill, ducked around the corner of the garage and ran down a barely discernible path behind the building, his casino plan in ruins.

This man Flynt had beat him, and the failure turned to bile in his mouth. His facile mind had already begun to formulate a plan to preserve himself as he fumbled his way through the bushes. The Ghost Dragon Triad did not countenance failure. Someone would pay and pay in blood, but Yang was determined that the blood would not be his.

Holmes and Canavan appeared almost simultaneously at either side of the building's rear. Yang could hear them thrashing blindly through the thick underbrush behind him as his hand reached down, found and gripped a pair of steel handlebars. Yang was a careful man. He would not have survived to reach his current position if he had not made sure to cover all contingencies.

He hauled the motorcycle upright. The 350cc Honda scrambler was perfect for the terrain. Yang was an experienced rider. He had checked the machine carefully the day prior, just before he had personally planted it after carefully reconnoitering his escape route.

Yang depressed the hand-clutch and stamped down on the kick-starter. Nothing! He felt a stab of fear.

The two hunters were close, very close. They had circled wide, and when they found no sign, began moving back toward the center of the search area.

Sweating profusely, Yang hauled the bike around facing the trail that lead through the tangled mass of underbrush, depressed the clutch and pushed the scrambler several yards down the trail. He mounted and pumped the kick-starter again. Nothing!

He could hear the two snipers' labored breathing. They were almost on him.

The choke. Yang gritted his teeth reached down, fumbled, his fingers searching frantically. Ah! He flipped the lever up to the halfway position and stamped down on the kick-starter. The engine caught. The staccato roar pierced the hollow darkness just as Jimmy Canavan burst into the tiny clearing in front of Yang, blocking his escape route.

"Hey, over here," he yelled at Jerry, as Yang lifted his right foot and felt the click of the scrambler's transmission shifting into first gear. He squeezed the hand brake and cranked back the throttle. The engine screamed. Jimmy was six feet in front of Yang when he slipped the clutch. The front wheel lifted. Yang popped the brake, and the bike leaped forward. The front wheel caught Jimmy Canavan square in the stomach, knocking the ex-GI backwards into the underbrush. Yang roared off down the trail just as Jerry crashed onto the path behind him. Jerry unslung his rifle, but by the time he had chambered a round, the bike's headlamp was no longer visible. He stamped his foot in frustration.

"Shit, shit, shit" Lenny exploded! He had jumped to his feet. "Damn! The slimy little fucker must have stashed a bike, and here we are on foot!"

The two ex-soldiers returned a few minutes later looking dejected. Canavan limped slightly but was otherwise unhurt.

Jerry shrugged. "How's the patient doing?" he asked, looking down at the young woman who sat with her back propped up against the garage doors.

The men were gathered around Alexis Jordan. She had begun to calm down. Fearing the effects of shock, Flynt had wrapped her in a blanket from Lenny's pack.

Alex looked up. "Thank you," she said.

"I think she'll be all right," Flynt said.

"I don't know how to thank you guys," he said and adjusted the blanket around Alexis Jordan's shoulders.

"Thank you, Lenny. Thank you all," Alex mumbled.

Lenny shrugged. "No biggie. Your boss would have done the same for me if the situation had been reversed. Listen," he said speaking quickly to hide his embarrassment, "what do you say we take Alex here over to my place and put her to bed. I got a spare bedroom."

"Okay, sounds good," Flynt said. "I don't think Alex wants to be alone just now, and my place isn't safe."

Alexis nodded as a shudder ran through her.

Lenny gently reached out, lifted Flynt's chin and examined his swelling nose.

"Thing's running like a bloody stream. Lean back and raise your head. I'll pack it with cotton, and we can ice it down when we get to Lenny's Emergency Room. Got a couch for you, too, Troop."

Lenny grimaced. His stomach muscles were still tender. He fumbled in a side pocket and extricated a roll of cotton wadding.

He gently packed his dripping nostrils. "That ought to do it," he said, sitting back on his heels.

"Thanks," Flynt said, his voice thick.

"Keep your head back."

"Right doc. What's the butcher's bill?"

"Four KIA and a pair of slant-eyed oven-stuffer's all trussed up, with one, at least, ready to sing," Lenny replied.

"They're willing to talk? Really. I expected they would be loyal to the Triad, out of fear if nothing else," Flynt said.

"Oh, they're scared, all right." Jimmy Canavan had sauntered over and squatted down next to Alex. "How you feeling, Miss Jordan?" he asked.

Alexis raised her head and looked directly at the young sniper. Jimmy's eyes seemed hugely bright, contrasted against his dark war paint.

"Thank you so much for everything you did," she said, trying to smile. Her lips quivered.

"My pleasure. Sorry that other guy got away."

He turned to Lenny.

"I talked to the prisoners. They're local boys, second generation, not so keen on the loyalty unto death shit," he said, keeping his voice low. He turned his head and spat on the ground. "The one Jed took care of along the trail is pretty fucked up. Dizzy, can't seem to stand, but the other one is practically begging for witness protection. Seems like this guy Yang has a big reputation. They think he's a ghost, some kind of chink superstition, I guess. Doesn't take well to failure and these guys failed big time, and they're scared shitless. Jerry is talking to him now."

"Well—listen," Lenny said, "sooner rather than later we are going to have to deal with the cops. I'll call Billy, you know the ex-jarhead down at the 13th. I checked. He'll be on duty this morning. Meanwhile, you think you can keep these guys on ice?"

"No problem, sarge," Jimmy said.

Flynt rubbed his chin, checked his watch and looked at Alexis.

"Okay, its 2:00am. We can't stay here. Better get moving. I've got a lot of work to do."

"You mean we've got a lot of work to do," Alexis Jordan said weakly.

Flynt winked at her. "Right! Don't try to talk now, Alex. Sleep first. Tomorrow, we'll talk about it," he said.

Chapter 35

The Wages Of Evil

Andrew Tate stood at the top of the statehouse steps and gazed down the long stairway and across the sloping lawn at the traffic moving along Beacon Street. He had just come from the Ways and Means Chairman's office, and he was seething. The chairman had made it short and to the point.

"Your bill is dead, Mr. Tate. Dead and cold as a mackerel."

All that money! Tate was still steaming as he paused on the top stair, pulled up the collar of his topcoat against the wind and lit a cigarette. It had been raining, the sky overcast, but the early spring air had been washed clean, and Tate had a view across the green expanse of the Boston Common. Looking down the long marble staircase toward the street, he saw an elegant, black, town car pull up at the curb.

The driver's door opened and a large broad-shouldered Chinese man dressed in full livery stepped out onto the curb and looked up in Tate's direction.

Tate froze like a rabbit under the eye of a hawk.

His eyes darted side-to-side seeking an escape route. "Bloody hell," he said, exhaling a lungful of smoke.

Tate was so focused that he failed to notice two men in three-button suits and matching, short-brimmed fedoras ascending the marble stairway. Neither was wearing an overcoat. They drew parallel to him, abruptly changed course like a pair of bird dogs and converged on the point where Tate was standing.

"Andrew Tate?"

Both sported crew cuts, one blond, the other gray. The gray one flipped open a black wallet and flashed a plasticized card bearing the distinctive black letters. "Leslie Sikes, Special Agent, Federal Bureau of Investigation, Mr. Tate. This is my colleague, Mr. Reed." The younger man stood tense and unsmiling, a slight bulge visible beneath the armpit of his slim fitting suit.

"Gentlemen," Tate said, a sense of relief flooding through him like a spring tide. "How may I be of service to the F.B.I.?"

"You're to come with us," the older official said. "The Bureau has a number of questions about your business dealings here in Boston and elsewhere."

"Gladly, gentlemen," Tate said, favoring both officials with a brilliant smile. "I am entirely at your service, but the man you really want to talk to, a Mr. Yang, is sitting, as we speak, in the back of that town car," he said, pointing toward the limo parked at the base of the stairs.

The two officials turned and followed Tate's finger. The Chinese driver jumped into the car and slammed the door.

"I am sorry sir, but we have no orders concerning anyone but you, Mr. Tate," Sikes said, as the driver gunned the big car out into the stream of traffic. "Now, if you will agree to come quietly, we can spare you the indignity of handcuffs," he said.

"Pity," Tate said, favoring the two agents with another brilliant smile. "As I said, Inspector, I am completely at your service."

The two officials flanked Tate, and each took an arm and escorted him down the stairs and across the street toward a black, four-door Chevrolet with U. S. Government plates.

Archbishop Doherty glared across his desk. "You have read this morning's Globe, Monsignor?"

"I have, Your Excellency, and I hardly know what to say."

"Come now, Michael. You will not be telling me that you were unaware of your friend's association with these people," the archbishop said, holding the front page up in front of him with both hands like a banner.

"No, I was totally unaware of it, Your Excellency. I promise you. I was as shocked as you were when I read the story. I knew that he had partners, financing, but I assumed they were investors, not gangsters. The man misled me. I had no idea that Andrew Tate could be so foolish," Benedetti said.

"Foolish!" The archbishop slammed the folded paper onto the desk. His face reddened. "They tried to murder two people. I don't call that foolish, Monsignor. I call it criminal!"

"Yes, of course, Your Excellency. You are absolutely right. Andrew Tate is a weak vessel, but I am at fault. I made the introductions. I only thank God that the Church is not involved."

"Not involved? My God, man. Thanks to you, we were practically in partnership with these hooligans. If any of this blows back on us, Monsignor Benedetti, there will be hell to pay—I promise you that. You understand what I am saying, Michael? I hold you personally responsible."

"Yes, Your Excellency, I understand you completely, and I assure you that there is absolutely no danger. There is nothing in writing, no evidence, nothing at all that could embarrass the archdiocese. You yourself wisely saw to that, Excellency."

"Yes, and a good thing, too! It was at your insistence that I involved myself in this idiotic plan in the first place!"

"No, Your Excellency, we did not commit ourselves, and thanks to Your Excellency's foresight, there is nothing that ties us to these people. Publicly we will say that we agreed to study the proposal. I have already spoken to several of our journalist friends and clarified our, that is, Your Excellency's, position. And if I may say so, the five million dollars that you, that is the Church received, is totally untraceable."

"What if your friend Tate goes public?"

"He will not, Excellency, and if he should be so foolish, again, there is absolutely no paper trail. I have spoken to him. He is hoping we might intervene with the Boston Police, unofficially of course. I made a call to a friend at the commissioner's office, and he assures me that there are no charges pending against Tate but advises that he leave town immediately. I have passed that along. I think we have seen the last of Andrew Tate."

The archbishop stared at his protégé. "I hope you are right. And what, may I ask, did you personally get out of all of this, Michael?" the prelate asked, his eyes studying Benedetti's face as if the truth would be written there.

Benedetti met his superior's eye. "Nothing, Your Excellency, other than the satisfaction of serving Mother Church. Surely, Your Excellency doesn't believe I profited personally in this matter?"

"I know you, Michael, better than you think I do—better, I think, than you know yourself. And that exact thought had crossed my mind," the archbishop said.

"I am sorry if I have done something to give you cause to judge me in that way, Excellency. I have tried to be a faithful son of the Church, and I hope that over the years I have provided proof of my loyalty to your person. I have made many mistakes. Please forgive my transgressions," he said, bowing his head.

"On your holy oath?"

Benedetti looked up and raised his right hand. "Before God, Your Excellency."

The archbishop sighed. "Very well, I suppose that what is done is done, my son. You are sure that none of this can be traced back to us?"

"Absolutely sure, Your Excellency," Benedetti said.

"Very well. And you may inform Mr. Tate," the prelate said, peering over his spectacles with one finger raised in admonition, "that the money will not be returned. The Church acted in good faith in this matter. We did our part. What with his consorting with criminals, he has only his own reckless behavior to blame for its failure."

Benedetti raised his head. "I completely agree, Excellency. In my conversation with him, he never even spoke of it."

"Mmm. Very well, then. Two things: first, I wish to close down that damnable organizing project. As I believe I warned you, Michael—imagine!—gunfights, dead bodies strewn across a Boston neighborhood by a man in our employ! It's time we saw the last of Mr. Flynt. The man is a positive menace."

"Yes, Your Excellency did warn me, and, as usual, you were right. Flynt can easily be dealt with. The organizing project is almost totally dependent on the campaign for its funding. In the highly unlikely event that the campaign renews his grant, Your Excellency can simply veto it. I think perhaps a discreet call to Washington detailing the circumstances will take care of that contingency. I doubt the pastors of the sponsoring churches will make any complaint. They certainly cannot be pleased with the publicity."

"I understand he has a contract?" the archbishop said.

"Yes, two years, but the project is a non-profit, and without funding, the contract is worthless. Flynt won't receive any salary, though there is a contingency, I believe, which calls for a certain amount of severance pay."

Archbishop Doherty nodded. "Fair enough! If he gets his money, perhaps he will go quietly. We want no more scandal. We will pay for it out of diocesan funds, if necessary. It will be well worth it to see the back of the man. The second thing is, and I am very sorry to have to say this, Michael, but I have decided it is best you be transferred out of the diocese. You put yourself out front with this project. You spoke to a number of our political friends. Out of sight, out of mind, if you understand me?"

Benedetti was expecting this. In fact, he was hoping for it. He lowered his eyes, not trusting himself. "I understand completely, Your Excellency. I have failed you."

The archbishop waved his hand dismissively and stood. "Now, now, my son, let's have none of that. I have arranged a posting to the Vatican. You will go with my blessing and shall remain in my prayers, and if circumstances work out as I expect, you may depend upon my patronage in the future. I believe that there are big changes coming, and the Church will need young men like you." Doherty stood, lifted his right hand and made the sign of the cross. "Go with God, my son."

Chapter 36

Intermezzo

The sun streamed through the venetian blinds casting a ribbed pattern of sunlight across the unmade bed. Alexis Jordan raised her arms over her head, arched her naked back and stretched, her breasts swelling out from her ribcage, which would have caused Flynt's breath to catch in his throat had he not been floating contentedly in a post-coital haze, synapses purring along like a milk-fed cat. She flipped over on her stomach, propped herself up on her elbows and regarded his supine form.

"I love a lazy Sunday afternoon."

His eyes were closed, hands folded across his chest. A low growl came from deep in his throat.

"Is there something wrong?" she asked.

"No," he said and opened one eye, "just dozing."

"Okay. Well now you've had your way with me, sir, don't you think it's time you fed me?"

"What, now? It's a little early, isn't it," he asked. He turned and reached for her.

She slapped his hand. "Food first!"

"Is that the latest feminist rallying cry?"

She stuck out her tongue at him as she reached over and poked him gently between the ribs.

"Come on, bozo, rise and shine. You're buying. I would offer to go Dutch, but I am presently unemployed."

"Okay, okay. Where do you want to go? The Galway House? Doyle's?"

"Oh, come on, Jed. Let's not be so provincial, okay? Live a little. There's this great German restaurant over in Harvard Square," she said.

"Yeah, right, the Wursthaus. I know it," he said, crawling off the King-size mattress onto the bare wooden floor. "I know I've got some clean skivvies around here somewhere."

"Didn't I see a pile of stuff in a basket in the hall?" she asked.

"Oh yeah, right. Thanks, I forgot," he said, padding toward the doorway into the hall.

"Um, nice butt," she said.

He turned, grinned and marched out of the room. "Ah, here we are." His disembodied voice drifted in from the hallway.

"Jed," she called, biting her lip. "I didn't mean anything with that crack about being unemployed. I mean, I know that's not your fault. I was—well, I just didn't think."

"What's that?" he asked, coming back into the room. "Hey, don't worry about it. No offense taken."

She was still in recovery, having daily moments-in-time—awful nightmares trying to sleep. He was worried about her.

"Okay, I know you don't want to talk about it," Alex said, "but it makes me so mad. You got the short end of the stick. I mean, you really did save this neighborhood. Look at what happened at the housing conference. Dukakis promised a disclosure regulation, and you've got three banks bidding for the greenlining money."

"Right, let the gentrification begin. Pretty soon we'll be seeing condominiums on Lamartine Street."

"Who said that?"

"Some banker."

"Oh, come on, Jed!"

"Look, Alex, one thing is clear, 'veni, vidi, vici.' Well, almost. Like Caesar, I came, I saw… only in my case, I fucked up. Don't know the Latin for that."

"Nonsense! You stopped those awful men who killed Sandy Morgan."

"Hey, not to change the subject but did I mention? I do have something in the works. Remember the round-the-world trip idea. Well, with the balance of the money they paid on my contract, I can prepay my child support and have enough left over for one of those cheapie round-the-world tickets and maybe eight to twelve months' expenses. Want to come along?"

She sat up straight. "You're inviting me?"

"I think I just did. Strictly Dutch though. I've got a whole itinerary. The Sistine, Angkor Wat, the Taj Mahal" he said, smiling down at her.

"Wow, you're serious. Can I have some time to think about it?"

"Take all the time you need. Now get yourself dressed, little lady. I've got my mouth all set for bratwurst."

She groaned. "Oh God, must we have another poor John Wayne imitation?"

They took the BU Bridge over the Charles River and made a left on Memorial Drive, skirting along the Cambridge side of the Charles.

The restaurant had been a Harvard hangout for over thirty years. They sat in a high-backed booth. The inside of the place was wood paneled. Over the years the wood had turned the color of the dark beer that overflowed the tall glass stein next to Flynt's elbow.

Alex looked across the table. "About your trip."

"Mmm?" he said, slathering mustard on a fat sausage.

"Jed, the trip sounds really great, and I would love to go with you, I really would, but I can't—at least, not right now."

"Okay," Flynt said.

"My parents want me to apply to law school this fall."

They ate in silence for a while.

"So," he said finally, "this is it then—used, abused and cast aside?"

"No," she said, "it's not like that."

"Okay," he said.

The waiter cleared away the plates. Neither spoke until he waddled off. Alex tried to make eye contact, but Flynt gazed past her into the distance.

"Jed, look, the truth is, I just need time to think," Alex began. "I mean here I was all set to apply to law school, and you come along. I know, I know, I applied to work for you. I'm not being fair, am I?"

He slid his hands across the table, picked up both her hands and gazed into her eyes. "Hey, Alex, you're young, beautiful and a Harvard graduate. The world...hey, it's all spread out, out there waiting for you. Law school is a good career choice. You'll make a great attorney."

She pulled back her hands and turned her head away. There were tears in her eyes. "But I really love you."

"You'll sort it out."

"I've got to sort myself out first," she said.

"Alex, it's okay! Sometimes I wish I had gone to law school myself," he said.

"Right," she said. "I'm going to lose you. I just know it."

"Well?"

She stared down at her hands folded primly on the table in front of her.

"Come on, Alex. You understand I'm talking about a trip—not the whole contract."

"Oh, yes, you've made that quite clear."

"Really, I mean, can you imagine someone doing what I do with a wife and kids? It's a prescription for failure."

She turned back and met his eyes. "Have you ever thought, you or Trapp or any of you of the future? This image you have of yourselves, you know, is just so much romantic bullshit?"

He winced. "I don't know. I haven't thought that far ahead."

She snatched up his hands and squeezed them. "Oh, Jed, I'm sorry, I didn't mean it that way."

He gently placed them flat onto the table and covered them with his. "Look Alex, I tried the marriage and kids thing. I wasn't any good at it."

"I know, but, you see, I want kids. Not right now, but sometime. Don't you want to lead a normal life, Jed?"

"Normal? —Define normal? Look, I understand, you want kids. Most women do—sometime—but right now we're talking about going on a trip, fun in the sun and all that."

"That's not the point."

"What is the point then?"

"What about having your own kids, you know, passing something of yourself along to the next generation?"

Flynt sighed. "You mean immortality. Yeah, I'd like to pass something along. I'd like to accomplish something, you know, do something important, something that people will remember. But passing along a few genes, the shape of a nose, I just don't see that as any sort of real legacy."

Alex lifted her eyes and gazed across the table. "Is that the real reason you became a community organizer?"

"There it is," he said spreading his hands.

"I figured somewhere in there was a great ambition. I guess I just have smaller dreams," she said.

"Not so small," he said.

"Yes, Jed, I had a lot of time to think, you know, back in the cage that awful man put me in and since. And I learned one thing—I'm not like you. I'm not a crusader. I used to think of myself as brave. You know, like one of those girls in the adventure stories I read when I was a little girl. One of the things this whole experience has taught me is that I'm not that girl. I was scared to death, and I don't want to feel that way ever again. I just want to feel safe. You know, lead a normal life."

"I understand," he said, "but I think you were plenty brave, Alex."

"Do you? Thanks, but you know, my roommate, Carol, was right. I don't really have anything in common with the people in these neighborhoods."

"Well, we're all part of the same species, but you know what the big difference is, Alex? The big difference is that you have options. In the back of your mind you have always known that. Most of the people here have no options. They're trapped. They have to make the best of it."

"So, what makes you so different? You're not trapped here. You have options, too."

"That's true."

"So why not get out? I mean look what happened. You saved a neighborhood. What did that get you?"

Flynt shrugged. "Ask me again in about a year," he said.

"Jed, maybe I could meet you somewhere, couldn't I, say in a couple of months? You know, in case I change my mind about law school," she asked.

"Absolutely! Look, I've got an old Marine buddy, lives in Singapore. Invited me to visit, says he's got a great apartment, a pool, the works. I don't know, does some kind of training for the army there. Anyway, I'll probably be camped-out there in early September. I'll be hanging out for a few weeks. Anyway, I've got your home number, and I'll leave you his address."

"Ok," she said, "that'll be great."

"Good," he said, and signaled the waiter for the check, both knowing that they had just said goodbye.

Epilogue

On May 14, 1975 Governor Michael Dukakis' Commissioner of Banks issued the country's first ever directive requiring Boston banks to report mortgage lending by census track. In June, a coalition of banks, including the Boston Five, sued the commissioner claiming that the regulation exceeded her authority. The suit was dismissed. Massachusetts' success in getting banks to reveal their mortgage lending patterns was followed by similar regulations in California, Illinois and New York.

In 1975 the Jamaica Plain Banking & Mortgage Committee signed an agreement with The Roxbury-Highland, a local bank, to implement The Community Investment Plan.

About the Author

Richard Wise is the author of three books. The author's first book, SECRETS OF THE GEM TRADE, THE CONNOIS-SEUR'S GUIDE TO PRECIOUS GEMSTONES, was originally published in 2003. Extensively revised and rewritten, the 2016 2nd edition has added 127 pages, 11 new chapters, 5 new introductory essays and 161 additional photographs. http://www.secretsofthegemtrade.com

Mr. Wise's second book, THE FRENCH BLUE, a historical novel published in 2010, was the winner of a 2011 International Book Award in Historical Fiction. The novel is set in the 17th century gem trade. Called "a fine piece of historical fiction" in a 5-star review by Midwest Book Review, The French Blue tells the back-story of the Hope Diamond and the true-life adventures of 17th century gem merchant Jean-Baptiste Tavernier. http://www.thefrenchblue.com

REDLINED, a mystery thriller, is the author's third book.

Mr. Wise has enjoyed a diverse career. He is a former professional community organizer who ran organizing projects in Massachusetts and Rhode Island in the 1970s. He became a goldsmith and Graduate Gemologist in the 1980s and began traveling internationally and writing about gemstones in 1986. His articles have appeared in Gems & Gemology and many other industry publications. He is a former Gemology Columnist for National Jeweler and a Contributing Editor to Gem Market News. He currently writes a book review column in Gemmology Today.

Made in the USA
Middletown, DE
19 April 2021